THE GALILEO PROJECT

Paddy Kelly

THE GALILEO PROJECT

FICTION4ALL

Paddy Kelly

**This work is
Dedicated to:**

Dr. Al Wilson

Chemistry Professor

**The man who taught me scientific thinking,
in particular how to base my opinions on facts
not what I 'felt' to be the truth.**

The Galileo Project

Paddy Kelly

It has become appalling obvious that our technology has exceeded our humanity. The human spirit must prevail over technology!

-Albert Einstein

The Galileo Project

Paddy Kelly

PROLOGUE

Tsim Sha Tsui District
Hong Kong
Friday, 31 December, 1999
22:15 Local

F ireworks had filled the black night sky over the vast expanse of Kowloon Bay since long before sundown. The continual bursts of gaily colored explosions formed a constant illuminating umbrella over the plethora of various sized boats carpeting the bay, each packed with party-goers.

Throughout the Sha Tsui district an enormous throng undulated though the avenues spilling over into every side street and back alley while the crammed piers of the bay area at the city's edge were peppered with scurrying children in traditional costume terrorizing locales, tourists and merchants alike lighting off harmless firecrackers

The largest human mass migration in the world had peaked. *The Spring Festival* was in full swing.

However, not all present were in party mode.

Down on Austin Street a dishevelled Westerner in a red knock-off Puma track suit continually glanced over his shoulder as he hurriedly made his way through the packed streets of downtown. The harried man went unnoticed by everyone, everyone save one man calmly but doggedly stalking him through the melee.

The track suit suddenly turned west onto Austin Road and crossed over onto Nathan where he skirted Kowloon Park apparently heading for the waterfront.

Though still a full city block away, the younger guy in the dark jacket, blue Polo shirt, khakis and dark blazer was gradually closing the distance, almost seeming to know where his prey was heading.

Increasingly desperate but maintaining his composure the track suit ducked into the low lighting and soft music of the *Pierside Bar & Restaurant*, a swank dockside place where people gathered to be seen, to impress each other or to use as a means of expensive foreplay.

Disregarding the dozen people already in line he slowed his pace to maintain a low profile.

"I'm sorry sir, we're fully book–" Ignoring the well-dressed, attractive Asian receptionist at the podium he darted around the tables, past the bar and headed into the stairwell leading down to the restrooms but the hostess signalled a member of the floor staff and he was suddenly cut off by a large waiter.

"Toilet for customer only!" The enormous Samoan waiter declared as he stepped in front of the man. The runner quickly grabbed his lower abdomen and assumed a look of agony.

"Yes, sorry. I want to have only a drinks in the bar. It is possible to have two Manhattans on the bar, yes please?" He offered the waiter a fifty pound Sterling note which only briefly saw the light of day. After showing the bank note to its new home in his hip pocket the big Polynesian looked him over then stepped aside.

Just as the track suit disappeared down the stair his pursuer stepped through the front door and quickly scanned the floor just in time to see the big waiter walking away shaking his head and, behind him, the flash of the red track suit off to the left descending the stairwell.

"The year of the rabbit! How appropriate!" The blue blazer whispered to himself.

As the receptionist was occupied escorting a party of four to their table the blazer leaned over and quickly scanned the open reservation book. She returned in time to see him but not in time catch him looking at the book.

"I'm going to grab a quick drink at the bar while I wait for the others to arrive." He casually informed her as he stepped away.

"I'm sorry sir, may I have the name of your party?"

"Yes of course. It should be under the name of Yakura, with the Hatsutashi Corporation. Reservation's for nine." Hands in pockets he smiled and shrugged. "I'm early."

Her delicate finger diligently shot to the reservation book and scanned down.

"Of course sir. Thank you. Please enjoy your drink and I'll send someone over as soon as the rest of your Party arrives."

"Chi chi!" With a slight koutou he thanked her. "You're very kind." He headed towards the bar.

Once at the bar he ordered a drink and veered off to the staircase.

At the base of the wrought iron stairs he was faced with a wall forcing him to choose left for the ladies or right for the men's' room. There was no way out except back up the stairs.

Additionally there were no doors on the entrances to the rest rooms proper. The required privacy was afforded by the two entrances being set back from the walled off area by a few feet.

With no one in sight he cautiously headed to the entrance of the Ladies' Room. Suddenly a toilet flushed and he retreated. As he stood back by the staircase, a well-dressed middle-aged woman emerged, smiled at him and headed upstairs.

Quickly but silently scurrying back into the ladies he dropped to floor and scanned underneath the two rows of stalls and spotted nothing.

Chancing there was no one balanced on a toilet he ducked back into the Men's simultaneously producing a 9mm Berretta sporting a silencer.

He quickly poked his head into the space just in time to see his prey peeking out the door of the center stall.

A sharp 'CRACK!' was immediately followed by a thud and the stall door slowly closed over but stopped when it hit the red track suit who had just lost the room temperature challenge. A slowly growing pool of blood seeped onto the floor.

As he holstered his pistol and moved to the body, the young man congratulated himself.

"Just like Quantico. One shot, one kill!"

With little effort he dragged the man back up into an empty stall, removed the man's jacket and placed it over the blood stain.

"Appreciate you wearing red, fella." He whispered to the corpse.

He propped the corpse up on the toilet and after being sure the stall door was locked he quickly rummaged through the dead man's pockets and relieved him of his belongings.

****

A half hour later, sitting in his 12th floor suite across town in the Hyatt Regency off Hanoi Road, a glass of scotch by his side, he inventoried the take by spreading it along the glass coffee table.

In a manila envelope there was over 1,200 Sterling, 1,700 U.S., 13,400 Yuan and an odd mixture of coins. In a large alligator skin billfold he found a three day old British Airways plane ticket, return, a boarding pass dated for the 3rd and Columbian and Venezuelan passports. Both passports contained photos of the man, the man he had just erased, but under two different names.

He double checked the envelope, wallet and passports for anything hidden.

"SHIT! It's not here!"

He separated and pocketed the cash, stashed the passports in the room safe and burned then flushed the travel documents before heading down to the bar for a night cap.

The first leg of his flight back to D.C. would be wheels up at 07:00 so he planned a light night.

Outside a soft drizzle had developed and a little further south, at the far end of the public rental docks in Kowloon Bay a small, open speed boat gently bobbed in the water. One of the two men sitting in it impatiently glanced at his wristwatch as the other hunched down against the cold, damp breeze.

It had just gone nine-thirty.

"¡Mierda! No, no vendrá!"

"Perhaps-"

"NO! No vendrá! Vámonos." The big guy grumbled as he fell back onto his middle seat in the boat.

"Pero señor –" The driver insisted.

"Dije vamos!"

The single engine skiff sped off into the night.

****

CHAPTER ONE

**Waxman's 24 Hour Pharmco
Harlesden, Brent
NW London
31 December; 21:18 Local**

Axel's mind drifted back to the Spanish bird he'd chatted up on the weekend in that kip over on Wardour Street. He easily lost himself in memories of how the lights of the Aquarius Lounge played off her soft brown skin and how her tight fitting red silk dress accented those black eyes glossed over with booze, hash and sexual arousal . . .

"Axel!"

FUCK! Not that wanker! The voice grated through his ears and saturated his brain as it echoed off the pale, lime green tiled walls of the toilet.

Waxman's All Night Chemist's was a local institution slowly shifting its inventory over the years from general household products to pharmaceuticals, compliments of Sir Clive Martin's recent support of the government's failing methadone program.

Snapped out of his fantasy, the coarse sound of the toilet brush suddenly came into focus as he scrubbed harder and faster to dissipate his anger.

"Axel!" A man, late middle age, impeccably dressed in a rumpled, 1970's olive green suit and blood orange tie, swung his right leg in a wide arc to facilitate his forward motion across the floor to where the youth slowly emerged from the last toilet stall on the right.

"Good evening officer Coleman." The nineteen year old stood up in an attempt to give the false impression of respect, his condescending tone well-rehearsed. Coleman stared at Axel's double nose ring.

"How're we keepin' lad?" The parole officer removed his small, sweat stained fedora to reveal a balding pate and wiped the inner head band with a discolored handkerchief. Axel idly ran the toilet brush back and forth under the rim of the crapper in sync with Coleman's hat strokes as he automatically responded in his not-so-bright Birmingham dialect.

"Brilliant officer Coleman! How are you and the missus this fine December eve?"

The acrid smells of urine and cleaning fluid combined to form an unidentifiable odor.

"Couldn't be better lad! Thanks fer askin'. I trust all's in order here?" He set the accoutrement back on his head.

"She still takin' it up the ass you old geezer?" The teen uttered under his breath as he bent to replace the tools of the trade on the small chrome trolley standing next to him.

"What's that you say?"

"I say, is she still givin' you a gas, you old sheik?!"

"Ohh! Absolutely old boy! Thanks fer askin!"

Are we in good form this evening?"

As if you give a fuck, you breathing antique! "Sterling, officer Coleman. Simply sterling!" Coleman was well past his sell-by-date, but was no dunce by a long shot. What he lacked in ambulatory capability he more than compensated for with astuteness.

"Life back on track, is it?" Coleman baited.

Coleman had been attending Axel's case since 1995 when the then fifteen year old was given a five year probationary sentence for being an accomplice in a carjacking. Now with less than a year to go, Coleman didn't want Axel to form the mis-impression he was out of the woods.

The mental gymnastics continued.

"I only thank our fine Members of Parliament for passing the Juvenile Offender's Work Release Bill. Otherwise where would I be? I'm sure it had your full support sir?" Axel baited.

"Most misguided, politically correct, sheit piece of bleedin' heart legislation to slip through the cracks in the last ten years. Thank you for askin'."

"Glad you feel that way, Officer Coleman."

"We didn't make our appointment at the parole office this afternoon now did we Axel old boy?"

*What's this **we** shit, geezer? You got worms?*

"Had to do a double shift, sir. Bills you know."

"Double shift is it? Very industrious. The Board will be impressed."

"Thank you sir." *Impress this fucker!*

"I suppose I should pop by and say hello to Mr.

Waxman. Be rude not to." Coleman tested.

Yeah, check out my story then get the hell outta my life!

"You'll excuse me if I don't show you out officer?" Axel raised both his hands to display his oversized, pink rubber gloves. "I'm up to me elbows here." Axel offered.

Coleman smirked to himself as he turned and limped out of the toilet.

"Shit!" Realizing he had no choice at this point in the scheme of things but to sit back and wait for the hammer to drop, Axel kicked the cleaning trolley in anger and sent it crashing into the far wall.

If it had been the first, second or third time he had lied to Coleman he might have skated out with a slap on the hand. But then . . . CRACK!

The first sound might not have been a shot at all. Maybe one of the dozens of piles of crap on wheels the Pakies used to get around this shit hole of a neighborhood.

The next two sharp reports were unmistakable.

Axel didn't know why he ripped off his apron and latex gloves, but he wasn't about to dwell on it as he quietly squeezed his head through the front door of the toilet into the small vestibule leading out to the main floor. The dull glare of the old fluorescent lights seeped in.

As he gingerly opened the outer door and peered up the cosmetics aisle, he could see officer Coleman, up near the front, sitting on floor near the end cap of aisle three, his hat upside down in a pile of deodorant cans.

The Lite Music orchestral rendition of Tom Jones" *"Sex Bomb"* crackling over the speaker system catapulted Axel into the surreal.

The old man, sitting propped up against the feminine hygiene products, looked bad. His breathing was sporadic and his blood covered left hand was clutching at his chest. Staring back he slowly tipped over, stopped breathing and stared up at the Colgate toothpaste across the aisle.

Approved by the American Dental Association.

"Bon voyage Officer Coleman!" Axel sympathetically mumbled.

A young black, his Jay-Z hat turned to the side, appeared from around the front end cap display up front while two others frantically mashed cash register buttons fruitlessly trying to open the two till cash boxes. The younger of the two peered down the aisle, saw the toilet door close over and yelled to the others.

"OY! IN THE BACK!" The crooked hat suddenly ran at a dead sprint towards the toilets. A second, the one with the gun, vaulted over the till counter and jogged behind him as the third one vanished from sight. Then, suddenly, the young one slowed to a walk as the one with the gun yelled after him.

"Oy, T. J.! Lemme at 'em firs!" The Jay-Z hat halted at the toilet door and slowly pushed it open for the armed, older assailant, as if he were a celebrity rock star about to take the stage and perform a show.

Unknowingly this wasn't far from the truth.

Axel wasn't the most street wise individual in Brent, but he knew the difference between the hunters and the hunted.

By now he had ducked back into the ladies' toilet and was moving as fast as his brain would tell his fingers to empty the liquid soap bottle all over the floor in front of the door. He grabbed an aerosol can of glass cleaner, adjusted the small yellow spray cap to wide open, hugged both the spray bottle and his cigarette lighter close to his chest and tried to press his body harder into the wall behind the door.

Carefully stepping through the lady's room door after his brother, young T.J. told his legs to move but there was no response. It was if someone had glued his feet to the floor. His brain wouldn't process what he his eyes were seeing.

He had never heard Gerard scream like a girl but now his high pitched, uncontrolled screams of agony filled the room as he clutched his flaming face.

That sick, mulatto boy was actually following his older brother around the floor with the improvised flame thrower until his entire head was engulfed in blue-white flames. Gerard struggled wildly to regain his footing on the slimy green, soap coated floor but without success. The crackling of his flame engulfed head was only briefly interrupted as his scull hit the concrete floor and echoed through the small toilet space.

Axel dropped the spray bottle and deftly retrieved the Glock 17 from the floor.

When the older teen's struggles slowed to an occasional, sporadic twitching, it was all T. J. could do to raise his hand straight out in front of him in the hope it would stop the oncoming bullets.

It didn't.

Stepping over his second victim Axel burst out of the toilets and onto the main floor, the pistol held stiff-armed in front of him. When he saw no one he paused. Backed against the rear wall he ejected then checked the load in the magazine. Three rounds left.

His brain raced. Three rounds left meant that Coleman was probably killed with this gun. Axel's prints now on the weapon.

Through barely controlled heavy breathing and with trembling fingers he gingerly slid the magazine back into place.

The rear of the shop looked to be clear. He prayed there were only three and the last of them had run off.

Making his way through the open office door in the rear corner, the weapon in front, his confidence now mustered, he watched the third youth continue to pommel the now unconscious Mr. Waxman with a short length of pipe.

"OY! STATISTIC!" As if choreographed, the black teen turned, stood motionless and held his breath. He dropped the pipe and, on seeing the pistol, shot his hands into the air. The two foot length of steel slowly rolled off to the side. Axel looked at Waxman's bloody face as the old man struggled to sit up.

Time froze.

Axle, now drenched in sweat, hands quivering just enough to expose his fear, slowly lowered the gun. The black youth drew a faint smile and gingerly lowered his hands.

As the police entered through the front door of Waxman's 24 Hour Pharmco and an andante, instrumental of Groove Armada's *Everybody Looked the Same* faded into its monotonous conclusion, three shots rang out from the rear office area.

The shallow end of Brent's gene pool had just been culled.

*** * ***

Holborn, Central London
21:30

A frigid northerly howled south rattling the Christmas lights strung across the main portico of the Soho Hospital for Women. A string of similar lights with several burnt out bulbs hung halfway down an adjoining window and, as if trying to draw attention to its dilemma, banged repeatedly against the glass panes.

A black, Vauxhall Cavalier drifted through the dark, driving over the thin wisps of snow swirling down Charlton Street, past the medical facility away from the wind and towards the school on the corner.

The St. Aloysius parish grounds, only seven short years ago, was twice the size it is now. However, with the receding economy, even the church was faced with downsizing.

The acre and a half of parish property was sold for a sacrificial price, just over fifty per cent of its appraised value, thanks to Monsignor Riley's good conscience, and was purchased in 1992 by Alex Goldman, a man with a vision.

That man has since taken up residence at the Sunhill Fields Burial Grounds, St. Luke's, but his vision lives on.

Hamlet Security Transport Ltd, the only unlisted, unmarked and one of only three secretly licensed security transport firms in the greater London area, had remained a thorn in the side of the big boys such as Securicor, Binks and United Armor since its inception. Goldman's brainchild was the smallest armored transport company in Europe, four vans and one 1988 black Cavalier, but was the one to turn to when money was no object.

In 1996 Hamlet were the only company to guarantee the safety of the crown jewels as they were transported across the country for the Queen Mother's 70th birthday celebration. The royals were more than pleased, if not a little suspicious, when their Secretary of Affairs opened the sealed bid and found Goldman had bid £1. At the bottom of the page was a hand written note, "For Queen and country."

The Galileo Project

The British subjects got their yearly dose of royal pomp and circumstance, the Queen got her much needed notoriety, and, now three years later, Hamlet's position in London's world of corporate security was well established.

With the church, convent and school grounds just off Phoenix Street, it was necessary for the unmarked vehicles to enter and exit the compact, high security compound through the well monitored Charlton Street security gate.

Traffic into and out of the compound was restricted to between the hours of six in the evening and the onset of the morning rush hour and the opening of the St. Aloysius school which was approximately six a.m. Regular business was handled at their off premises office in Broadgate Tower in central London.

Triggered by one of the pressure sensitive monitors buried in the road bed, four of the compound's CCTV mini-cams automatically rotated to intercept the Vauxhall as it slowed to enter the gate.

The center camera transmitted the vehicle's image to the main monitor in the security office for identification, the second scanned a fifteen meter radius around the car for any secondary activity while the third and fourth utilized their infra-red and Starlight night vision capabilities to reinforce the information being transferred to the night crew inside.

The mini-cam's servos had hardly ceased their

high pitched whine when all the required data had been transmitted, processed and referred back to the entrance's custom designed auto lock system. Following a brief delay the armor plated gate ponderously swung open.

A minute later as the large gate slowly closed over behind it, the Vauxhall drove past a small warehouse, one of only two structures on the grounds. Parking in front of the adjacent structure, known as 'the front office', Goldman's nephew Anakin, whose parents' first date was at a *Star Wars* film, climbed out of the car and approached the office door then punched in his seven digit code, placed his chin on a tray near the door, and peered with one eye into a red peep hole. The retinal scan complete, the door clicked open and he entered.

Uncle Alex had re-invested his profits wisely.

Once inside the spacious, overly elaborate office he went straight to his Louis XIV desk, pressed a button and spoke into the intercom.

"Evening George!"

Evening Mr. Banbury.

"Have a good Christmas did you?"

Very good sir, wife spent the entire bonus check!

"That's what they do I suppose. Anyone else around?"

Just the last two guards who'll be with van number 1989.

"Alright. Have a good night George. And Happy New Year!"

To you as well Mr. Banbury!

Banbury flicked to another channel and again spoke into the intercom.

"Hal, are we on schedule?" A static laced voice responded immediately.

Last one's out in twenty minutes sir.

"Well done Hal. Give me a bell when they're through the gate."

Will do sir. The dispatcher responded as he returned to his mini TV on the desk next to him.

CNN's Wolf Blitzer has the story, a CNN exclusive.

Sergei Khrushchev, son of Soviet leader Nikita, the Soviet Premier who once removed his shoe banging it on the podium while yelling 'we will bury you!' to President Kennedy, will take the oath of citizenship for the U.S. in Rhode Island in three days. Following a long arduous background investigation by the intelligence services, Sergei, along with wife Valentina will become a U.S. citizen later this week.

Believing himself, the two guards in the warehouse and the dispatcher the only ones in the compound Banbury was surprised when there was a knock at his office door.

"Who?"

"Me." He recognized the voice of his GM Peter Grahams.

"Yes?" A sixty-something, heavy set man in a cable knit Cardigan and khakis entered.

"Can I have a minute?"

"Of course you can Peter! Drink?"

"Love one!" Anakin moved to the walnut wall cabinet and fixed two scotch and rocks handing one to his colleague.

"Happy New Year Peter!"

"To another profitable four quarters." Peter offered.

"Why are you not making ready to have your annual New Year's shag with the missus?" Anakin teased.

"I'm. . . I'm having second thoughts."

"Well, you have been together some time now and comes a stage in a marriage when-"

"Very comical! Not about my marriage. About the company's plans to stash so much cash around the city. If we keep the trucks here –"

"A bit late for that mate! The last one leaves directly!"

"We could recall them. It'd be a lot safer to sit on them here until Monday. Besides the Peelers are just four blocks away. If something were to happen they could be here–"

"Peter old chum, I get your concerns, I really do. I tossed and turned for the better part of a fortnight before I decided to okay it. But if you look at it- "

"I'm still not convinced it's worth all the risk."

"You mean aside from the fact that the contract is worth nearly fourteen million Sterling in commission not to mention how far ahead of the game we'll be if this Y2K thing actually does rear its ugly head? Not to mention the projected rise in rate after the Continent institutes the change over to the Euro!" Anakin argued.

"Bank of England'll be happy enough I'd say." Peter reluctantly reaffirmed. Grahams smiled at that prospect. "Hard to believe that all those eggheads who spent half a century giving us computer technology could overlook something like missing the potential damage that could come from not using '00' just to save a bit of space." Grahms tried to relax and took a seat. "Anakin, please don't misunderstand, I'm completely behind you with the precaution of stowing over two billion quid in trucks around the city for a day so, and kudos for secretly selling it to the Big Four bankers, I'm just a bit nervous about not letting on to the Board that we're doing it."

"Peter . . . we tell the Board, who each have their little, pet stockholders, and sure as Tony Blair is lying about Afghanistan, the plan gets leaked to the public and there goes the plan. And if the Y2K does hit and we didn't go through with it, the whole company, stockholders and all, would be fucked into a cocked hat!"

"And if it doesn't hit?" Grahams pushed.

"If it doesn't, a couple of billion quid sat in a couple of armored vans for a night or so, all the dosh is back nice and snug in the vaults by Monday morning and nobody's the wiser." Grahams still wasn't convinced. "Besides, if it's good enough for the Yanks and the Canadians to do it, it can't be such a terrible idea for a little, off-the-map, independent set up like us to do it!"

"I just have a bad feeling, that's all I'm saying."

"Completely understandable. It'll be alright." He poured two more drinks. "Look if it'll make you feel any better, you have a key to my office."

Grahams nodded as Anakin went round behind his desk and produced a single sheet of paper. "This is a list of all the GPS locations by van numbers and drivers. These are ten digit grid coordinates, like they use in the military. Very precise! It's the only complete copy in existence! I took the precaution of not letting even the dispatcher have the locations. Only the drivers are privy to them and then each driver was made to memorize his location and his alone." He folded it into an envelope then locked it in the top drawer of his desk and brandished the desk key. "Now there are only two people on the planet who know of its location and existence."

"I suppose you're right." They shared their second drink. Grahams threw his back in one shot. "What could go wrong?" Peter's retort lacked conviction.

✲

Over in the warehouse a lone, armored van had been backed into the single loading bay, two uniformed security guards were loading it up.

"Who in bloody hell would think paper dosh could be so heavy!" The overweight guard grumbled

Save for the company number, #1989 on the right front fender, the metallic blue van was unmarked.

Via a four wheeled convertible cart, they were loading pallets of bagged and sealed cash into the armored vehicle.

With the space being too small to operate a standard forklift and the rest of the crew off for the holiday the two had been compelled to load each of the one hundred racks onto the six pallets manually then wrestle them into the truck via a pneumatically operated pallet truck.

A third man, his pastel, satin shirt, pressed chinos and highly polished Italian shoes indicating he was primed for a big night out, stood by counting as they wrestled the last of the pallets into the vehicle.

"How is it we ain't using the steel security boxes? This cello wrap can be cut open with a pocket knife!" The big guard asked, his Yorkshire accent punctuated by his labored breathing as he reached for the large cooler by the office.

The satin shirt, clipboard in hand, stepped over to the opened rear of the van.

"Less weight, more room. That's why no steel boxes." The short, bespecled satin shirt shot back as he continued to check the seals on the outer most racks, transfer the label numbers to his clipboard and quickly scribble his initials in the margin of the page.

After the last of the pallets was recorded and neatly loaded into the now full vehicle the larger of the two guards rolled the empty hydraulic hand truck to the far side of the loading bay and loaded three large, plastic Coleman coolers onto the dolly. He then gently rolled the cargo back over to the van and carefully wedged the three red and white containers onto what little space remained in the back of the armored van.

When the large man had finished and was stowing the hand truck back over in the corner of the bay, the Asian guard stepped forward and placed his single, hand-held container in an unoccupied corner of the vehicle along with several novels and a pair of university texts.

The soft skinned inspector, who appeared as if he had bathed in Nivea cream his whole life, didn't bother to hide his anxiety to finish his task and leave. He spoke hurriedly as he delivered his well memorized speech.

"Right then! Ten bundles at £100,000 per bundle equals one million, 100 racks per pallet and six pallets for nearly £600,000,000 Pounds Sterling!"

"Over half a billion!" The smaller of the two, the slender, well groomed Asian, adjusted his cap, folded his arms and shook his head in disbelief.

"All seals intact. All merchandise on board. Sign here, please." Both guards signed and were given a copy of the manifest.

"Five hundred, sixty-two million Pounds Sterling to be exact!" The dispatcher corrected. "Weapons?"

Each man unholstered his Glock 9mm, did a cursory functions check and replaced the weapons.

"Two magazines?" They turned so that he could visualize the two magazine cartouches on their Sam Brown belts and all the armament was so recorded.

"Good night and happy millennium Gentlemen! See ya Tuesday. I've got a set of lovely blond twins on hold at my flat."

"Hot game of Crazy Eights lined up for the night have we then?"

"Fuck you John!"

The Asian guard began to close up the back of the van as the portly guard stood by, hands on hips watching the dispatcher gather up his black leather coat and scurry out the door.

"Nigel, two weeks ago he had twins. Now another set of twins. They say in London there's two women for every man. I think I finally found the bastard what's got my ration!" The big man declared.

"John, trust me when I tell you wouldn't want . . . never mind."

Both men walked across the short dock to the dispatcher's cage to sign out.

"You know if some geezers are dead set on getting' at this stash, these pop guns will be worthless!"

"Not if we use them properly John Old Boy!" The small one argued.

"And how exactly do we do that?"

"Take them out of our holsters, gently lay them

on the ground, raise both hands, back away and tell them to take the money!"

"Fuckin' millennium!" John complained.

"Why do you always complain oh rotund one?" Nigel queried in a mock oriental dialect. Knocking a rise out of his partner was never a challenge.

"These fuckin' pallets have got some weight behind them, and if we had to . . ."

"We are being paid one hundred and fifty pounds per hour John. That's why. We will take home 5,760 Pounds Sterling, after taxes for forty-eight hours work. This I find very difficult to complain about. In addition I feel compelled to point out, my lumbering dirigible, that tonight is not actually the millennium!"

"Clocks are ready to count down all over the world, billions of people getting locked outta their minds, and Hodji here says it's not the millennium! Well ring the *Daily Mail*! I suppose you're gonna tell me the Arabs have the one true calendar!?"

"No, just older."

"So if older is better, how come me grand'da shiets the bed twice a day?"

"Probably genetic." John pondered Nigel's offering as the night dispatcher peered out through the mesh reinforced glass. The discussion continued as they went up to the window.

"And another thing. How come there's all these weird names of towns in Pakistan like Cattle pool, Candy bar and Omar Sheriff?"

"Those are cities, not towns, in Afghanistan. Not

33

Pakistan, my large one. Incidentally, I was born in Mayfair, same as the Queen Mother. Never actually been out of Britain in my life."

The dispatcher, no longer able to hold his tongue, smirked as he handed out their trip disc, incident log and ventured a prophecy.

"You two are gonna be locked up for forty-eight hours in that anchovy tin? I shudder to think what will be left when they open the door back here on Monday."

Once inside the vehicle, John took the driver's seat and Nigel activated the switch board in front of the passenger seat. The dispatcher's voice filled the compartment through the radio.

You two lovebirds ready for your electronic functions check? The dispatcher queried.

The rear radio, personal transponders and hand held radios all checked out. Then, proceeding down the check list, the dual alarms, silent and public broadcast, and the auto lock systems were tested. Last on the list was the navigational/ SATCOM location unit, the GPS/GAL.

"Last year these things were smaller. I thought technology was supposed to get less imposing as it developed?" Nigel queried as he threw the toggle switch on the dashboard.

"Budget cuts."

Once activated a yellow blip, centered in the middle of the eight inch screen, flashed once per second.

"We're clear dispatch." Nigel spoke into the

overhead transceiver.

Happy New Year Team 13. Good luck.

The squelch of the dispatcher's mike vanished and the heavy bay door lumbered open. Three minutes later John and Nigel were heading east on the A501.

"Does that mean it's the same in Mayfair?"

John felt compelled to re-ignite the banter.

"Does that mean it's the same in Mayfair as what?"

"In that there's nowhere to sit in church, everyone wears a tea towel for a hat and no one owns a razor?" John intentionally antagonized.

"No more than everyone is the same in Yorkshire."

"What's that supposed to mean?"

"I mean, is it necessary to strip everyone down and coat them with butter in order to get them through a conventional doorway?"

"You sayin' I'm fat? I'm not fat! Look!" He insisted holding his flabby belly away from the steering wheel. "I still got a good six to eight inches in between there!"

"If that's what you call six inches I feel bad for your wife!"

Nigel opened the glove box and removed the portable keyboard attached to the on-board computer by a heavy spring cable and punched in the command; 'Locate G-1989'

As he held it in his lap the blip reappeared on the small screen only this time superimposed over a map of Hagerstown.

"Take the A10 north. Right on Whiston Road and it's just the other side of the sports ground." Nigel directed.

"Check." After another ten minutes, with the headlamps off, the men were cruising down an unlit alley with rows of garage doors on either side. The narrow alley way as was the surrounding street, completely abandoned.

"Switch to security lights." Nigel instructed, carefully reading the numbers on the garage doors as they coasted down the narrow lane. John rotated a toggle switch on the overhead panel board and the headlamps came back on but this time with a narrow slit beam in dull yellow

"That's us. Number 13." Nigel called out.

"I don't like this!"

"Relax, it's bad luck to be superstitious." Nigel activated a hand held remote and the over-sized garage door began to rise. John drove just past the entrance, turned the wheel and backed the armored vehicle into the enclosure then switched off the headlamps and the engine as the door came down. The last of the late night, ambient city lights began to fade then eventually vanished.

Nigel switched on a small cabin light and spoke into a recording device housed in his overhead space.

"23:58 31.12.99. Team 13 in van #1989 on station at G-12. Activating electronic surveillance. See you next year. Out." Smiling at John he climbed into the back of the vehicle, returning a few seconds later with one of his novels.

"Why'd you bring books?" John asked with genuine curiosity.

"Maybe that is why you failed your leaving cert twice, Jaba."

"True. But I passed my security guard exam with flying colors, first shot outta the box." Nigel settled into his novel and John reached into one of the open dash compartments, his massive hand returning with a large cello wrapped baguette oozing meats, cheeses and dressings. After a couple of bites, something dawned on him.

"Hey, I just had a thought!" John exclaimed.

"Very good! That's twice this month!"

"Where do we shit?"

By way of an answer Nigel reached under his seat and produced a cardboard box approximately the size of a shoe box. Smiling, he presented it to John, who reached into it with his unoccupied hand and retrieved a zip lock plastic bag, approximately eight inches square. The big man's face was mired in consternation.

Nigel then held up some pink toilet roll.

"They've thought of everything."

*** ***

Brixton Gaol
Monday 10:30
3 January, 2000

There had been no late night New Year's celebration for one young man. Axel had been held for questioning and due to the holiday, was not afforded a hearing until this morning. Based on the responding police officers' statements regarding the Waxman's Pharmco shooting, Axel was released without charge and as he left Brixton Station he glanced at the *Daily Mail* stacked in the coin operated vending box which stood outside the corner McDonald's where he was met by a Hackney cab.

Fuckin' Monday! Three nights in that fucking hole! Now the payoff! Axel's inner voice enthusiastically announced.

Old man Waxman had sent a taxi to collect Axel after his release from Brixton Gaol and instructed the driver to bring the kid to the hospital where he was still recovering. Waxman intended to reward him for his heroics. It was common knowledge that the old man was worth a bundle and so Axel's mouth watered at the thought of an impending reward. He was escorted to the private suite and waited while the nurse opened the door to the only private room on the floor.

"Mr. Waxman, you have a visitor." She quietly announced.

38

"Axel! Come in, come in! We have so much to talk about!" Waxman trumpeted from his bed.

Fuck the talk! Where's the dosh?

"Good to see you're doin' awright Mr. Waxman!"

"That was quite a brave bit of business you pulled off the other night young man!"

"Thank you, sir." Axel took his seat besides the large bed as indicated.

"I spoke to the chairman of your parole board yesterday. And I have some good news! As of today, you are no longer required to report to your parole officer!"

Well fuck me! I'm sittin' here wif Albert fuckin' Einstein! My parole officer is fertilizer and my parole is up in two weeks anyway!

"That's great to hear sir." Axel smiled just enough as he nodded. Waxman spoke again as he reached into the bedside commode, opened the drawer and produced a folded over document.

"In addition I'm promoting you to probationary, assistant, night manager, effective immediately."

Lovely! £3.75 per hour to £4.20 per hour. Now I can buy that semi-detached in Kensington!

"And lastly . . ." The old man reached across and handed the envelope to Axel. The young man could discern there was a cheque inside but the envelope had been taped shut and so he decided to open it after the meeting.

"So young man, you ready to assume your new responsibilities as of tomorrow?"

"Absolutely sir." Waxman manned the remote and raised the head portion of his bed to sit more upright and offered his hand. Axel shook it once.

"Eight sharp?!"

"I'll be there at half seven sir!"

Once out of the office the criminal/hero was unable to contain himself. Tearing wildly at the envelope Axel stopped in front of the lift and stared in disbelief as he allowed the torn envelope to fall to the floor.

The payment amount on the draft was £50.

****

Present Day

CHAPTER TWO

St. John's Cemetery
Metropolitan Ave, Queens, NYC
Monday, June 10, 2019

A gentle breeze floated through the cemetery drifting over the endless rolling hills forested with marble and granite monuments.

As if to show pity for the mourners, the relentless heat wave which had held New York City hostage for the last three weeks had momentarily gone on sabbatical.

In the shadow of one of the lager white oaks on the grounds a small crowd gathered to the side of the burial pit as the NYPD Honor Guard stood off to the side at parade rest, the pipe band off to their immediate left.

Departmental banners gently flapped behind the portable, graveside podium which stood in front of a flag shrouded casket, floating prominently above its final resting place.

The band's Pipe Major, perspiration pouring from under his black, feathered bonnet, had strategically placed his men under one of the larger elms on the hillside, where they also stood at parade rest.

The number of police present far outnumbered the civilians, even taking into account the attending

42

officers' spouses.

". . . his law enforcement career of only nine short years officer Ciccione . . ." The Commissioner continued his all to-well memorized eulogy.

Frank Mahone, all six foot two of him stood ram rod straight and expressionless off to one side of the podium, eyes locked straight ahead as The Commissioner introduced the Police Chaplin.

"Let us bow our heads and pray." Frank saw no point in mumbling a meaningless collection of phrases to his shoes and so continued to stare out over the top of his former partner's casket.

Ex-partner. No, fuck that! He's still above ground! Partner. Frank argued with himself.

The police Chaplain concluded his remarks and another New Yorker was prepared to make the journey from the over crowded streets to the overcrowded burial grounds of Saint John's.

Mahone's eyes involuntarily darted towards a woman standing away from the rest of the small gathering of civilians just out of sight, leaning against a tree. The collar of her flower print dress stuck out over the top of her grey jacket when she bent to snub out her cigarette.

Can't believe the bitch showed up! Probably here to fucking gloat!

Unprompted, Mahone's inner dialogue popped on again.

The Chaplin and the Commissioner traded places as the Honor Guard removed the flag from the coffin and began the ceremony of folding it into the familiar triangle.

"Lieutenant Detective Frank Mahone will now say a few words about Detective Ciccione, with whom he served for the last four months. Following his comments Lieutenant Mahone will present the flag of valor to Detective Ciccioni's wife and son." The grey-haired senior officer announced before stepping away from the podium.

However, instead of taking the podium, Mahone slowly walked over, saluted the Honor Guard Captain, accepted the flag and solemnly approached Mrs. Ciccione and, sitting next to her, her twelve year old son. The black mesh of her veil hid her eyes as she sat motionless, and despite having remained composed throughout the ceremony, her obvious disheveled physical condition was testimony to her despondent emotional state.

Frank graciously bent and offered the flag with both hands, his weathered green eyes softened to meet her gaze. The pregnant widow began to stand on uneasy feet to accept the offering, but immediately fell back into her chair crying uncontrollably. Several friends and family members rushed to her aid. Frank patiently held his pose.

The Commissioner gestured towards the podium. Frank pretended not to see the gesture.

The young boy, who had not until now, reacted to his mother's inevitable breakdown, rose from his seat, approached Frank and held out his hands.

Mahone lowered the flag onto the boys small outstretched palms and as he turned to walk away, the boy rendered a salute. Frank faced him, stood at attention and returned the gesture.

The casket hoist was activated and the dark oak coffin began to gently lower into the ground.

"Honor Guard hand . . . salute!" The Color Sergeant ordered. In succession seven riflemen fired three rounds each and a long thirty seconds later the hoist fell silent and along with John Gotti, Carlo Gambino, Vito Genovese, Charlie "Lucky" Luciano and nearly two dozen other cops and gangsters, Detective Edward Joseph Ciccione was laid to rest.

"Honor Guard! Dismissed!"

Mahone loosened the tie on his uniform and waded through several well-wishers as he made his way towards the tree where the woman in the print dress had been standing. But there was no point, she had long since vanished.

He stood and watched from across the gathering as various colleagues and friends queued up to offer condolences to the bereaved.

Maybe the unsympathetic bitch has a point. He mused.

"You got a ride out to the Island?" Although the words didn't register while Frank was lost in his thoughts, the voice from behind was instantly recognized.

"What?" Frank asked.

"The reception. You were plannin' on going?" The myriad of medals draped across the big officer's uniform spoke for the stout man's years in service.

Frank accepted Chief Wachowski's ride out to the Long Island home of the Ciccione's and was relieved when they finally arrived without a word having passed between them.

Initially the house was distressingly quiet but as the women gravitated towards the kitchen to help with the food and the men drifted towards the back garden to help with the two kegs of lager begging to lose their virginity, things began to relax slightly.

Frank took his Seven-Up and headed for a seat on the steps of the front porch, away from the crowd. His solitude didn't last long.

"Jan a no show?" The Chief asked as he approached the steps of the front porch where Frank sat.

"You don't see her, do ya?" Mahone answered curtly. The Chief, his cravat undone and jacket open, laid a hand on Frank's shoulder, taking a seat one step up from him. An Hispanic colleague, nursing a long neck bottle of Bud, looked on from the bottom of the oversized wooden porch.

"It's not the heat, Mahone. It's the humility." The Chief consoled.

"That joke's near as old as you fer Christ's sake!" Frank replied without looking around. The young Hispanic officer wanted desperately to help relieve the gloom that haunted his friends but wasn't sure how.

"Hell! Chief's so old when he made Detective you had to buy your own magnifying glass! Ain't that right Chief?" The young cop smirked as he took a long drag of his beer.

"Enrique, you still after a change of assignment?"

"Shit yeah Chief! You serious?" Frank saw it coming and couldn't fight back a smirk.

"Report Monday morning to the old Staten Island Landfill."

Enrique got the hint and headed away from the porch, down the driveway and back towards the kegs.

"How come you don't drink?" Wachowski ventured.

The city Management Techniques courses which were now required to make rank said you should strike up a casual, non-subject related conversation when attempting to council a grieving officer.

"How come you always hoverin' over me like a mother hen?!" Mahone shot back. Such courses weren't meant to council the Frank Mahones of the world.

"I asked you a serious question, asshole!" Chief snapped.

So much for pop psychology.

"Father had some bad breaks. Turned to the sauce. Vowed it would never happen to me."

Sometimes the old ways worked best.

"There's worse shit than physical addictions ya know?" the Chief pushed. Mahone flinched as he saw what was coming again. "It doesn't have to come down to her or the force Frank."

"It's not about her or the force. It's about another

dress, another new pair of shoes. A new house for fuck's sake! How much shit does one person need?!"

"You sure it's not about the attention?"

Although the Department officially cautioned against it, to avoid unwanted lawsuits, Chief Wachowski's old school mindset had built him a reputation for taking a personal interest in the private lives of his people.

A well-adjusted homicide bureau is a happy homicide bureau is how he would explain it to the Commissioner whenever the subject came up.

"If she wanted a nine to five'er she should'a married a rich accountant! The money thing has taken the forefront this last couple'a months." Frank argued.

"Time and money take a back seat when you're young and in love." The Chief added.

A small group of late comers pulled up outside the house as Frank, waiting until they had piled out of the car, continued.

"There's more to it than that." Frank mumbled. Wachowski's face instantly registered the inference.

"You think she's . . ." The late comers piled up the stairs walking between the two men compelling The Chief to hold his question until they were out of earshot. However, from the expression on Frank's face Wachowski saw that he didn't have to finish the question.

"All I'm sayin' is this ain't the old days Frank. You don't have to John Wayne this shit out ya know."

"What's next Ski? A group hug?" Chief knew his limits and sensed it was time to go inside and circulate.

"Just so's you know, PBA's got marriage counseling programs, tough guy."

"I'd say I'm better off where I am."

"Oh yeah? Where's that?"

"I'm still on my first marriage. Most of those councilors are on their third or fourth."

"That's why they're qualified councilors. Experience." Frank looked away and smiled. The Chief stood to go. "I'm just sayin' don't throw in the towel."

"Let's change the subject."

"Okay. You goin' in to talk to Maria?"

"After a while."

"Frank look at me."

"What?" Mahone looked up at Wachowski.

"Look at me. Read my lips. It wasn't your fault! Eddie made the mistake. Not you."

"We finished?"

"Yeah!"

"One question."

"What?!"

"How come every time you're done cheerin' me up, I feel worse?"

"Alright tough guy. But as of right now you've got two week's convalescent leave. Don't even think about showin' up Monday morning or I'll have you arrested! Questions, comments snide

49

remarks?!"

"Yeah? Is this the part where you're supposed to give me a hug?"

"Asshole!"

Frank smirked as he heard the screen door slam shut behind him.

＊

CHAPTER THREE

Town Hall
Queen's Walk, London

Sadiq Khan had always considered one of the more interesting aspects of politics the fact that how, after a relatively short period in any public office, the job developed its own set of dynamics. Although you were supposed to be driving the train, at some point the train began to drive you.

This at least was his rationalization as he slowly began to realize he was losing control of crime in London.

The Lord Mayor came to realize the full potential of this theory of dynamic of inter-dependence when, in mid-July, the 2018 second quarter statistics for violent crime came across his desk.

Predicatively in a standard political P.R. move, The Yard reported overall crime down. The detailed breakdown on the spread sheets of the thirty boroughs of the greater London area however, painted a more realistically gruesome picture.

Although incidents such as tourism based crimes and the latest mobile phone snatching spree had been more or less successfully tackled, violent assault and car-jackings at knife and gun point peaked dramatically through the summer months. The one saving grace of these crimes was that, although they were far from being contained to an isolated area, they were taking place in more or less the same districts repeatedly, allowing special squads to tackle them more effectively.

There was however a very serious, new crime cancer threatening the public health. Homicide in conjunction with racially related crimes was up 43% from this time last year.

Some in the government argued it was predictable, even anticipated. What with the uncontrollable influx of asylum seekers flooding the shores, an economy already in recession being pummeled by the Euro and the spate of recent scandals cascading through the press, some increase in violent crime was predictable. But the velocity of the increase coupled with the diversity of the geographic it encompassed was real cause for alarm.

With the homicide rates threatening to once again rise above those of New York City the tabloids and even some of the broadsheets had already begun drawing comparisons again with America. Measures were needed. Measures which would yield results before the next election.

The Lord Mayor's solution to the homicide epidemic followed the usual pattern. Assign a special task force, see what they can do and as long as they produced results, stand behind them and take the credit. If things didn't go according to plan, help them fade quietly into the background, let the criticism in the popular press die down and switch to plan B that is for another 'special' task force to find out why things didn't go as predicted then organize another 'special' unit.

Never one to miss, or create, a political opportunity, the chief public servant of the city of London, Khan, deemed that his newly created Special Homicide Investigation Unit should be as P.C. as possible and ethnic diversity was the order of the day. Liberals not being big fans of meritocracy, technical qualifications were a secondary consideration. Besides, he argued, the nuts and bolts of homicide duties could easily be picked up along the way. After all, police work was police work. Find the body, gather the evidence arrest someone. Not exactly rocket science.

So Khan reasoned.

So, the New Scotland Yard Commissioner was informed there would be one black inspector, one Asian inspector, one Caucasian inspector and one female inspector. Preferably a woman of color for whom he drew up and submitted a list. When the Commissioner reported back that there were no Asian-African-Jewish females with Muslim backgrounds in the ranks, a compromise was reached.

They settled on a girl from Dublin.

*** *** ***

HQ Metropolitan Police Service
Curtis Green Building
Victoria Embankment, London

And so the special task force, consisting of four sergeants was formed and placed under the custodial care of a one Inspector Nigel Morrissey.

The reluctant Morrissey had been with New Scotland Yard since it had been old Scotland Yard. He, as with the rest of the Homicide Unit, were more than grateful for the increase in funding, improved access to the updated data bases and newly remolded premises when the long promised premises of the New New Scotland Yard finally materialized in November of 2016.

However Morrissey, along with the rest of his colleagues, did not overlook the political impetus for the revamping of the most well-known police force in the world.

Just as The Yard had spawned the myth of Sherlock Holmes, so too was it regarded as a myth that these "new and improved" premises would make them win the crime war and more importantly garner more public support which would, so the theory went, swell into kudos which would overflow into Khan's office.

The popular press and the criminal element both agreed it was a myth but the PR war was, as always, viewed by the higher ups as much more important than the actual war regardless of results.

Knowing the crooks were backed by barristers and solicitors whose only motivation was financial gain, the criminals would still not have to play by the rules.

There would remain too little resources to feed the less fortunate of the city in order to avoid having their young grow up to hate and despise their adopted country. And, in time honored fashion, those with political and or criminal aspirations, both immigrants and indigents, would continue to skirt the law.

With the deranged and misguided radical Islamic element now thrown into the mix, the game moved up a notch.

The financial pressures of the Brexit debacle, due to have happened last month, were still this late in the game, incalculable.

The honor of this two edged sword awarded Nigel Morrissey was not solely based on his expertise in his chosen profession. He was good at his job because he was dedicated. Dedicated but not stupid.

Morrissey had never in eighteen years in service allowed a crime to consume him to the point of obsession. In the minds of the higher ups this factor, combined with being so close to retirement, not only made him expendable but gave him a five star rating on the "subject to influence" or "team player" political scale.

Unbeknownst to the politicos, on this point Morrissey disagreed.

Traditionally any homicide unit had been located on the third floor, however Morrissey had not worked out of his assigned office there since early May. A unit briefing room was assigned his team and they were expected to bounce between their desks, presently spread all over the Yard's main building and this room so conveniently located near the Dacre Street exit on the far north end of the building.

Taking full advantage of his promised autonomy, the team members were told to abandon their desks and relocate to the briefing room on a temporarily-permanent basis.

A discarded, folding canteen table set off to the right side in the front of the lecture room served as a place Morrissey could call a desk.

A hand carved sign prominently displayed on the wall behind it read:

Morrissey's two rules for success;

Rule #1: Don't sweat the small shit.
Rule #2: It's all small shit!

Although not appreciated by the department Head of Specialist Crime, the inspector's underlings found this trace of reality in a sometimes unreal world, reassuring.

When he was told the plague was inappropriate and to take it down, Morrissey reminded the Chief Superintendent about the wrongful action suit filed against The Yard two years ago when a black female officer was directed to remove a poster of the African god Shango.

She argued, through the P.F.E.W., the Police Federation of England & Wales, that being ordered to remove the poster violated her right to religious freedom, a mandate reinforced by the Lord Mayor himself back in 2008.

Morrissey argued his words of wisdom were as well in accordance with his religion: Discordianism. The plaque was in praise of Eris the Greek goddess of chaos and discord.

"An appropriate metaphor for this place." He reasoned.

The matter was dropped.

******

The three males and one female officer of Morrissey's squad were at present loosely huddled together in intense argument in the hallway just outside the men's toilet on the first floor.

"I did it last time!" Rankor argued.

"I'm certainly not doin' it!" Dunn, the lone woman, affirmed.

"Looks like it's your shout Heath!" Enfield directed.

Resignedly the tall African pushed open the door and without stepping all the way in, called into the white tiled chamber.

"Chief we need to get on with this meeting!" His

booming voice echoed. "You're due to brief the Mayor on the London Bridge attack suspect at eleven."

The reply echoed out from behind the fourth stall down.

"Tell His Honor I'm about to wrap up the paperwork on a very big case I've been struggling with since this morning."

The toilet flushed and Heath withdrew in disgust.

It was early in the first week after settling in, that Morrissey's squad had been given an insignificant, cold case, a violent robbery gone wrong, which he promptly set aside reasoning that someone higher up the ladder didn't want to chance them screwing up a more high profile case and embarrassing the Mayor's office so early on. Either that or they didn't want Morrissey grabbing all the glory by closing any high profile cases too soon.

Taking on the nearly two decades old case was suggested by Khan then recommended to the Chief Inspector and finally ordered by the department head to be assigned to Morrissey et al. There was no real interest in solving the case but appearances had to be maintained.

So let it be said, so let it be written.

The old robbery case was assigned.

****

Early the next morning as the sun peeked over the horizon and now filtered through the forest of buildings to glare through the windows on the fourth floor of The Yard, the lift door opened and the mixed bag of detectives noisily piled out. The resulting ruckus caused several early morning workers gathered around the coffee station pretending to be getting a jump on the day, to peer out into the long hall and stare.

The pot-bellied, middle aged Morrissey at the head of the swiftly moving group spoke as he held a VCR tape in both hands out in front of him like a sacrificial offering to the gods of material evidence.

"Pay attention boys and girls, some of this material may appear on your leaving cert." Morrissey lectured as they gaggle piled down the hall like a rugby maul sans opponents.

"We know, the second robbery was executed by different perpetrators. Between the two incidents which were two weeks apart, our tally jumps to-"

"How do we know that Inspector?" Sgt Enfield, alias FNG asked.

"Because my dear FNG, the first set of raiders are dead."

"Sir how do we know the two incidents are connected?"

"We don't Sergeant Enfield however, multiple deaths in the same location in a little over two weeks . . ."

They turned right and headed for their commandeered command room.

"And in as much as there is no second tape we must glean what we can from what we have, namely this hopefully watchable gem. Rankor, did you manage to contact forensics on durability of VHS tapes?"

"Yes Chief they said they'd get back to me."

"Did they think you were down there to audition for a roll in an upcoming police drama?"

"Possibly sir which is why I took the liberty of ringing Mancuso's-"

"The Italian restaurant?"

"No sir, Mancuso's Discount Electronics on Oxford Street. They say the average deterioration rate of standard TDK VHS is between ten to twenty percent over a ten year period depending on storage, temperature humidity etc . . ."

Morrissey abruptly halted the small parade in the center of the hallway, turned to the diminutive Indian and smiled.

"THAT boys and girl is exactly why we are The SHITS! Well done sergeant!"

"Thank you sir." They moved on

The attractive thirty-something, Maureen Dunn, trailing behind carried a pair of manila folders for the morning's briefing as the group headed towards the Viewing Room at the end of the hall.

"Axel N.L.N., sir." Dunn prompted.

"Why no last name?"

"Would only give his Christian name. Said he was a 'prisoner of the proletariat regime'. We're running back through the prints records now. Since he wasn't charged with anything back in ninety-nine there's no record on him in recent files. If we get a hit I'll send it over to archives to see if they have anything on him."

"When we're finished here, send over anyway. All bases you now."

"Yes Inspector."

"Would only give his first name?" Morrissey pushed.

"Yes sir."

"No rank or serial number?" Morrissey quipped. No one laughed. "What? No sense of humor this morning?" He chided.

"Morning?! More like dead of night!" Rankor remarked.

"I haven't been up this early since we had our baby!" John Enfield was the only married member of the group.

"WE?! As if you had sweet F.A. to do with it after you rolled over and passed out in a drunken stupor!" Dunn was always available to force feed a woman's point of view.

"I don't get it?" Now it was Franklin Heath's turn at bat. "Why would you be up all hours of the night for your baby?" Born in Nigeria and brought to England illegally, Heath had since become a crown subject and was now ten years into a sterling police career in his adopted country.

"What's that supposed to mean?" Enfield realized that as the newcomer this only the onset of his baptism by fire.

"The artificial insemination labs don't open until half nine." Heath's jab elicited a laugh.

The three workers standing sentry over the coffee urn were the first to notice Morrissey's entourage approach and whiz past.

"Who the hell's that lot?" One of the clerks queried as the squad quick stepped down the main hall way of the Operational Support wing and vanished around the corner.

"The Sod Squad." Someone in the small cluster of office workers replied.

"Morrissey and his flippin' U.N." Someone else chimed in.

"Who in hell are they and why are they here at ten past six in the morning?"

"They're coming off a 72 hour shift. Why are you here at ten past six in the morning?!"

"More likely the pubs are shut." A short, bespecled man drifted over to the tiny assembly.

Noticing a shoulder holster as Morrissey's jacket flopped open they were surprised.

"They're authorized side arms?!"

"Apparently part of the deal Morrissey insisted on. The Chief Inspector ran it through the ACPO and they green lighted it. But they never use them." The cluster of pencil pushers continued their commentary.

The British Association of Chief Police Officers are the governing body which decides armament of its officers and detectives.

"Khan's brainchild. A politically correct, swift reaction team. They're to be assigned all the cases deemed too hot for the peons. Morrissey calls them his SHIT squad." The Communications Centre Head Clerk reported to his underlings.

"How does he get away with that?"

"After HSC picked him, Khan asked to have a chat with him. When Morrissey referred to himself as head of the Special Homicide Investigation Team The Lord Mayor completely missing the sarcasm commented, 'I like it! Change their title!'"

"How didn't he tick on?" A sideward glance conferred the answer.

"Probably too busy having a go at Trump!"

"Or getting ready to christen a new mosque!" Another commented.

"**Christen a** new **mosque**!? Are we allowed to say that?"

"More importantly are they worth a shit?" Another asked.

"They're three for three in four weeks." The oldest in the group threw out.

"Only because those cases were handed to 'em on a silver platter. Wait till they run up against a genuine homicide!"

"The worst kind of political tripe. I give them a month."

"Six weeks."

"Twenty pounds!"

"You're on!" The two shook and they, along with the rest of the peons drifted back to their desks.

As the pencil pushers returned to work the squad piled into the viewing room. Out in the hall the Communications Centre Head Clerk knitted his brow and, like a turtle ducking into his shell, vanished into his office only to re-emerge again seconds later carrying a thick log book and scurrying towards the Viewing Room.

Inside the multi-purpose room the air was electric with excitement.

The security VHS video from Waxman's Pharmco had been overlooked after the initial arrests and when it was ordered to be retrieved, some eight hours later, it was found to be missing. A subsequent bust at a small time junkie's house three hours ago yielded some low grade pot, two stolen ID's, a carry-all full of mobile phones and strangely the missing tape. The front label was smeared beyond legibility but 'Waxman's back office' scrawled across the outer edge was somewhat legible.

Axel had friends in low places.

"Heath, when we're done you ring the tabloids, I'll take the broadsheets." Rankor boasted.

"Special Homicide Unit Solves Double-Triple Murder!" Enfield enthusiastically announced as they entered the room and moved to their desks.

When Morrissey was first confronted by the fact that he was not going to be allowed to choose his own people for the unit he declined the assignment. However that night at the Wellington Gentlemen's Social Club the Commissioner reminded him of the relative autonomy he would be entitled to as well as the potential for increased resources. To say nothing of the impending promotion at the end of the assignment. Oh yes, there was the small matter of the embarrassment Morrissey would cause to The Yard in declining the assignment after his name had already been put forward. "But no pressure mind you." The Commission reassured.

Resolving to stretch the definition of "relative autonomy" like a twenty year old Dacron jumpsuit on the body of a forty- five stone, middle-aged man and being a true soldier, Morrissey changed his plea and accepted the assignment.

However he also resolved that whoever they gave him would swear a blood oath of undying loyalty, do things his way and be re-christened with nicknames to reinforce their new identities as well as to demonstrate his disdain for the cancerous new PC culture infecting the government. All of this of course after they were clandestinely given a bill of clean health by Morrissey's in-house-network of trusted spies.

"Double-triple would be six, ya yob! You're short one body!" Dunn, the token female offered.

"Enfield, fine product of the National School system that you are, I'm surprised at you! It's a quadruple murder we're about to solve!" Rankor sarcastically chided.

"I believe it's quintuplet you anthropoids are looking for." Dunn again interjected.

"Boys and girls!" The banter came to a sudden halt as Morrissey spoke from the front of the room without turning around. "Shouldn't we view the video recording before we go dislocating our arms patting ourselves on the back?"

Everyone took a seat in the classroom styled AV room.

"Now, as I was saying, four dead in the first incident and two weeks later, one more for a grand total of five dead in same location in fifteen days. Both incidents motivated by robbery."

"Details on the fifth homicide Chief?" Heath inquired.

"Second incident deceased was a Maxwell R. Waxman, sixty-two years old at time of death and sole owner of the premises. Cause of death GSW to the abdomen fired at close range suspected to have been inflicted in conjunction with the robbery with no chance it was carried out by the same perpetrators the second time. Ali, set it up please."

"Right Chief!"

The tall black man came forward and retrieved the video from the inspector and was heading for the back of the class as the door burst open. The diminutive communications clerk stood there, casting a short shadow, log book and pen in hand, projecting a cute form of anger.

"Inspector Morrissey, you know full well . . ."

"I know perfectly well all personnel are required to be signed in before utilization of any Operational Support Facility." Morrissey cut him off. "Apologies to the Headmaster for violation of school policy. Give it here." The clerk handed the log over. Morrissey opened it and called out.

"Token?"

"Present!"

"You're required Christian names as well as family names, Inspector!" The annoyed clerk corrected.

"Right, of course. Female, Token?"

"Still present." Dunn called back as she adjusted the window blinds to lessen the light in the room. Morrissey scribbled in the oversized book as he called roll.

"Ali, Mohammad?"

"Present Mr. Morrissey." Heath answered.

"New Guy, Fucking?"

"Present and accounted for." Enfield called back.

"Din, Gunga?"

"Most happy to be here, Sahib sir!" Rankor laughingly responded as he settled into his seat. Closing the book over on the pen after scribbling his own name in the appropriate space he handed it back to the clerk.

"Now, we have a classified briefing, so if you will excuse us?" Satisfied that he still maintained control of his tiny domicile, the clerk left.

"We're up Chief." Heath called up from the back of the room adjusting the VCR array.

"Lights, camera, action! I'm ready for my close-up Mr. DeMille!" Morrissey said by way of signaling Heath to roll the VHS tape.

Unsurprisingly no one got the reference.

An only child with a father from St. John's Wood and a mother from Hoboken New Jersey, Nigel Morrissey always considered himself to have grown up with the best of both worlds. An invaluable, if stringently enforced, classical education at a private boy's academy combined with the experience of a bankrupt culture whose sole redeeming value was its unending contribution to the entertainment industry via big budget films and the ability to muster ridiculous amounts of fire power to any theater of war it choose to invest in.

Oh yeah, and the deepest pockets on the planet.

But a comic resignation to the harsh realities of his career bolstered by the old stiff upper lip were hard to beat.

Now in his late forties and still single, he entered the police academy at nineteen, finished second in his class and made detective in record time five years later. All while still living with and supporting his aged mother.

Unbeknownst to Inspector Morrissey there were actually

two reasons he was handpicked to run the SHIT Squad.

With no personal life he had become dedicated to spending ungodly amounts of time on the job and so had also cultivated a reputation for being something of a slave driver.

The other was tenacity. Although having become somewhat cliché by most standards, Morrissey, in twenty-three plus years had never given up on a case, even when instructed to do so.

But he was, along with all else, a practical man. He fully accepted what few other law enforcement people dare not speak aloud: that is that the good guys don't always win, the bad guys don't always lose and so, in the harsh reality of the real world, not every case can be solved.

In the immortal words of one of Nigel's heroes, Clint Eastwood, "A man's got to know his limitations."

Morrissey certainly knew his.

Actually there was a third reason he was chosen. The higher ups determined him to be expendable.

Still bent over fidgeting with the remote control pointing it at the large video monitor on the front wall, Morrissey addressed his team.

"Why aren't our Aisling notebooks out, boys and girls?" Everyone scrambled to break out their note pads and writing implements. All except Dunn who was already poised, pen in hand.

FNG shook his head at her.

She flipped him off.

"Token, Ali and Din one bad guy each. FNG you've got the clerk, I'll take the parole officer and Axel N.L.N."

The grainy, black and white picture faded into focus on the 56 inch screen and Morrissey immediately noticed the digital read out on the upper left hand corner of the screen which read: 12:00.31.12.99.

"It's on auto rewind. Ali, fast forward to . . . Din! The Coroner has fixed time of death of first victim at?"

Din instantly referenced his pocket note book

and called back.

"Blood clotting factor cross referenced with the responding unit's time of arrival approximately 21:55, sir."

"Give yourself a gold star Din. Ali, fast forward to 20:50 please."

The rapidly rolling picture stopped on an overhead, skewed angled of a shot showing the front of the pharmacy where there was a tall, thin clerk, in his late teens, leaning on the till counter flipping through an auto magazine. The black and white video was without audio.

Except for the two minutes when a young girl came into the shop and was given several packs of Silk Cuts in exchange for a prolonged snog and a breast groping, the next twenty-two minutes of video were virtually uneventful. Then within ninety-seven seconds of taped footage, one young clerk was wounded and four people were dead.

The three youths, all wearing Man United jerseys, had come through the front door and immediately eliminated all doubt as to their intent.

Pulling his pistol from his belt, the elder of the three youths fired a shot at the female stock girl hitting the glass behind her as she disappeared off camera. The clerk ducked down behind his till but the gun wielding criminal casually walked up to the low counter and aimed the weapon against the clerk's thigh and fired a single round. The young man writhed on the floor in agony attempting to use his apron as a compress.

"Dunn, annotate the time on the tape. That clip'll go to the press." Morrissey ordered.

"A bit gruesome don't ya think?" Enfield commented.

"Not as gruesome as when some wanker of a barrister stands in court, musters a single tear in his eye and explains in a pathetic voice how the poor, young lad is not really responsible for the shooting by virtue of his deprived upbringing and the jury let him off with a slap on the wrist."

An instant after the helpless clerk crumpled to the floor Parole officer Coleman, brandishing his service revolver, came around the end of the aisle and was immediately shot twice in the chest.

"That one's Gerard Havershaw before the face melt." Heath announced. "Couldn't have happened to a nicer guy."

The detectives continued to watch as the three perpetrators were startled and two ran towards the rear of the pharmacy.

After a three second pause the monitor displayed a split screen with the view of the front till area remaining and the right side of the screen now showing a youth entering Waxman's office.

"Who did that?" Enfield inquired.

"Infrared initiator. Senses the presence of someone in another sector and automatically activates another camera. If it's already engaged in another sector, it flips to split screen. State-of-the-art at the time" The Inspector explained.

The next scene was of Axel leaving the loo,

checking the gun and then entering the office, gun at his side. From the office door he could be seen to raise the weapon at Waxman's assailant.

"This town ain't big enough for the both of us!" Morrissey's mumbled comment elicited a few giggles.

"Maybe there's hope for you yet Chief." Rankor remarked.

"Before P.R. releases what we've found to the press wolves, someone will get the privilege of informing the families what we found. Might as well be you Rankor."

"Shit!" Rankor swore at his punishment.

After they watched Axel shoot the third youth in the office and the Tactical Weapons Unit stormed the shop, arresting Axel the video ended.

"Questions comments snide remarks anyone?"

"Well it's clear Axel NLN has little compunction about killing, but is it realistic he would have killed Waxman?"

"Now who would ever want to kill their boss?"

"Careful sergeant Dunn, there's no regulatory requirement for me to have a **specific** female on this squad." Morrissey snapped.

"I was merely theorizing, Boss."

"Is it accurate that Old Man Waxman gave him a reward and a promotion?" Heath asked.

"A check for fifty quid and promotion to assistant night manager. Questions, comments snide remarks on chapter one? Morrissey again threw out to his crew.

Paddy Kelly

"Big spender was he?" Heath quipped.

"Waxman's solicitor also petitioned the court to release him from the remainder of his parole obligation."

"Why was he on parole?" Dunn asked.

"Two to three years for Grand Theft Auto, Grievous Bodily Harm and resisting arrest. Served nineteen months, remainder of time converted by petition."

"Was there any connection found between Axel and the fella's he iced?" Enfield asked.

"Iced?! You really must stop watching so many American crime films Enfield!" Heath challenged.

"Sergeant Heath let's don't knock American films after all where would we be without John McClane in the most beloved Christmas movie of all time?" Morrissey quipped. "FNG, good question! No, there was no connection found. The three thugs were actually not even from London. All from Manchester. Now that we're all caught up on chapter one we can explore the limited mental depths of some of the misguided individuals we are dealing with in this case." Morrissey continued while he rifled through a report on his desk. "The case lovingly dubbed, by the unbelievably prolific, pontificating pencil pushers of the paparazzi, the 'Brixton Blood-bath', actually goes back to late September of that year when Waxman, owner of a chain of chemists, agreed to hire Axel when no one else would. It would seem according to our 'inside' source-"

"Who would be?" Dunn pushed.

"James Franklin Axel's partner in crime or so we suspect." He pulled a glossy full color mug shot from the manila briefing folder and passed it around.

"This Franklin character, do we have him?" Heath asked.

"He's managed to evade us so far but we anticipate his arrest within the next twenty-four to forty-eight hours. Special Unit's on it."

"Wait a minute Chief!" It was Rankor. "Franklin or who ever had the-where-with-for to snatch the VHS security tape but didn't destroy it, one of the only things that could implicate him? **Why** in God's name would he do that?"

"Not the **only** thing that could implicate him. Besides, we don't know Franklin was the one who initially took it." Morrissey countered. "My guess is whoever took it probably wanted to hold it as evidence against his mates in case any of them turned snitch."

"Waxman was killed only two weeks later? Poor old bastard was only out of hospital a few days." Dunn observed.

"Obviously it wasn't his month." Morrissey remarked.

"Did the initial investigation consider that our boy, Axel No Last Name, as an assistant manager may or may not have known that Waxman would be there but took the op to express how he felt about his measly little fifty pound reward?"

"Apparently they did consider it, but due to his actions two weeks earlier, the fact that he didn't quit his job combined with character witness testimony and absence of any other evidence he was considered above suspicion."

"Chief, why is there no second tape?" FNG queried.

"It appears simply that January the 13th a Sunday evening, knowing that the weekly deposit was made on Monday after the weekend take, was likely to be substantial, the perpetrators decided to strike. Apparently, in the chaos following the thwarted robbery no one took it on themselves to replace the security tape with a new blank."

"Was this tape tampered with in any way?" FNG asked.

"Not that forensics could determine, no." Rankor informed.

"Heath, take a car, get over to the South End and tell Axel its check out time at the Brixton Arms." The Inspector ordered.

"You're letting him go?!" FNG challenged.

"No, we've nothing to hold him on, he was politely 'requested' to come in for some questions and he politely consented. Token, explain to our latest addition why this course of action is necessary." Dunn purposely exaggerated her Cork dialect.

"We're releasing him under his own recognizance subject to later questioning. If he legs it, he implicates himself, but until something points to his or his mates' involvement, he's simply one more of Her Majesty's humble subjects."

"And . . ." Morrissey coached.

"And, Pharmco Ltd, is one of the largest franchises of all night chemists in the U.K. and therefore not without political influence in what's left of the known kingdom."

"Now, now Missy, let's not let our Irishness get the better of us!" Heath said with half a grin.

"Any first year law student could argue that because Axel saved Waxman's life two weeks before, there's no real evidence he later murdered the old guy and, as the Inspector has pointed out, Axel had no demonstrable motivation, ergo there's no case." Dunn further explained.

"Have we given any weight to how the black community of Brixton's going to handle this? That last arsehole was unarmed when he was shot!" Enfield persisted.

"Firstly, it's none of our concern. Let the lawyers fight that out. However, by way of helping our good neighbors in Community Safety Branch we will be sure to leak a copy of the essential parts of this video to the BBC so the good people of Brixton can see two innocent bystanders were gunned down in cold blood for the one hundred thirty-one pounds, twenty-seven that was in the till."

Enfield began to understand, if not condone the methodology.

"Secondly, although those young men didn't necessarily deserve to die, if we get to trade three bad guys for one, that is known as victory by attrition." Heath explained.

"What?"

"Giap's Treatise on the American involvement in Viet Nam." Morrissey stood and switched off the monitor. Heath manned the lights.

"And, lastly, it's time to get some rest. Well done over the last few days boys and girls. Class dismissed! And let's don't forget, homework due on my desk NLT 0900 hours tomorrow!"

"Breakfast Chief?" Heath came up to the Inspector and returned the tape.

"Thanks no. Have to interview a witness."

"Witness to what?" Heath pushed.

"A witness." Morrissey shot back.

For the first time that morning the joviality of the atmosphere was punctuated with an awkward silence. Morrissey made no attempt to alter the mood but gathered his topcoat and headed straight for the door. As the door closed behind him everyone exchanged glances.

Token quietly walked over to the coffee urn and selected four plastic coffee stirrers. The other three watched in silence as she approached them and extended her arm, the four small green straws were clenched in her fist so only an inch of each peeked above her slender fingers.

FNG drew first. The other two hesitated. Din then Ali drew one after the other then, as if to signal to the rest of the group, "Let's get this over with." FNG held up his straw. It was half the size of the others. No words were needed, he had previously been briefed on the drill.

Enfield was compelled to run the length of the hall but on reaching the stairwell he could hear the unmistakable footsteps produced by the unique gait of his supervisor.

Exiting through the rear of the building, Morrissey, with Enfield following at a discreet distance, once downstairs, crossed Broadway and made for Caxton Street. Ten minutes later, at approximately six forty-five a.m., Enfield's, and thus the SHIT squad's worst fears were confirmed. Inspector Nigel Morrissey was standing at the back door of Cat's Cradle public house on Wilfred Street.

From the corner of Rine Place Enfield watched in dismay as someone unbolted the rear emergency exit, peered up and down the alley and signaled the inspector to enter.

Nigel Morrissey was going to have breakfast.

*

London Fields Estate
Hackney, London

The wooden door frame splintered as the Big Red Pass Key, or battering ram in the police lingua franca, hit for only the second time and the low budget front door swung open to hang by one hinge. The six heavily armored Specialist & Crime Operations, or SCO19, officers flooded into the ground floor flat and cleared all three rooms in less than 20 seconds. The heavy-set, half stoned Rastafarian slowly sat up on the front room couch and raised his hands. The lead officer yanked the nearly spent joint from his mouth and snuffed it out on the floor.

"Don't you read the papers Franklin? Smoking's bad for you son."

The iconic black cabs may be revered by the rest of the English speaking world but parts of the borough of Hackney in East London are listed as one of the most dangerous areas in the capital. One of the three most dangerous in the nation.

Two of the SU officers cuffed the suspect and escorted him out to the street where a standard police unit stood by to take him to jail. Inside the shambolic residence a routine search was on.

They found an inordinate amount of drugs paraphernalia, half a kilo of low grade weed, several hash pipes, one with what appeared to be residual traces of crack and a Bic lighter.

"What about this?" One of the coppers asked his boss as he held up a brown canvas bank bag.

"What's in it?" They opened it to find another collection of pills, some more weed, several cubes of hash and some more rolling papers. The front of the bag was labeled with a serial number: 09361-99. Property of Hamlet Security.

"Tag it and bag it." The team leader ordered.

****

CHAPTER FOUR

13th Precinct
230 E. 21st Street
Gramercy Park, Manhattan

Far from the glitz and glamor of Broadway or Fifth Avenue the chaos and clatter of the unassuming station house designated the 13th Precinct is tucked away in Lower Manhattan between 2nd and 3rd Avenues down on 21st Street.

Visitors and passers-by are greeted at the 1960's styled glass and aluminum front entrance with a large piece of twisted wreckage from the 911 bombings of the Twin Towers mounted on a low pedestal to the left of the door. The words "Never Forget" sit below the photos of the three officers from the 13th who, along with 409 other police and emergency workers sacrificed their lives in those attacks.

Upstairs the early morning clatter of the Robbery Division faded behind him as Mahone entered the Division Chief's office and closed the door.

Perusing the cluttered office, Frank was not pleased at the sight which greeted him.

"What the hell you doin' back here? What I gotta do ta make you give it a rest, shoot you?" Chief Wachowski offered by way of a morning greeting.

"Already been tried, didn't work." He shot back. "Right back in the saddle and all that shit. You sent for me?" Mahone's answer was saturated in sarcasm. He ignored the guy sitting on the couch aside of the door.

"You know god-damned well I didn't send for you! But as long as you're here, Officer Lewis McCray this is your new mentor, Lieutenant Detective Frank Mahone." Frank scanned the young, impeccably dressed plain clothed cop as he stood to greet Frank.

"Where the hell'd you find him? GQ Magazine?"

"Reel it in Frank!"

McCray extended his hand.

"Glad to meet . . ." McCray started but Mahone ignored him and turned back to the Chief to enter his plea.

"Christ Chief!" McCray, standing off to one side of the two senior officers suddenly remembered the time in eighth grade when he showed up at Imelda Jenkins' house for his first date and discovered she had invited the whole class to her party, not just him.

"Give us a minute McCray." The Chief nodded towards the door and the probationary detective quietly exited the small office.

"What's wrong with this one, Mahone?"

"What's wrong with him?! He was just at the Junior Prom last week fer Christ's sake! I realize the politicians have to drop all the height and physical requirement restrictions so all the fat, little females can get in and the Democrats can get re-elected, but doesn't the Academy even have an age limit any more?!"

"You gotta take this one Frank." Wachowski quietly informed. Mahone ticked on immediately.

"Who's kid is he?"

"That's not important. He . . ."

"Don't bullshit me Ski! Everyone in the god-damned precinct is gonna know by lunchtime, if they don't already and just like when a cop's wife's fuckin' around on him, I don't wanna be the last to know." Mahone flopped down on the over-stuffed couch and sat slumped over. "I'll find out eventually."

"I don't understand why your marriage is on the rocks Mahone, honest ta shit, I don't!"

"I'm a lousy lay. Common, give."

"They wanna make sure the kid stays in one piece for his six month probie period."

"SO THEY PUT HIM WITH DOCTOR DEATH?! My body count makes a Schwarzenegger movie look like a fuckin' Disney extravaganza! I'm responsible for twelve dead people in fifteen months! I been suspended and investigated three times by I.A. this year alone!"

"Nine of them were bad guys and you were cleared of any wrong doing every time!"

"The year ain't over, it's only June." Mahone stood, turned and walked away from the desk in frustration.

"Spare me the martyr crap. You ain't killing abused and confused out there Frank! Those were dyed in the wool bad guys!"

"And Sommers and Ciccione?" There was an uncomfortable pause.

"We been down that road. Everybody here signed on the dotted line. Under those circumstances they'd have bought the farm with or without you."

The Chief tossed the probie's file across his desk to Mahone picked it up and briefly perused it.

"WHO the HELL came up with this one?!" Mahone asked rhetorically as he read.

The Chief sat back in his chair and fiddled with a glass paper weight. When he looked back down at the open file Mahone realized the Wachowski's dilemma and why his boss was under strict orders not to tell anyone anything. Mahone suddenly looked up from the file.

"Isn't DeBlasio's wife's maiden name McCray?!" Frank spurted out. Wachowski responded by not responding.

Mahone didn't bother to close the door on the way out and Officer McCray watched in amazement as Frank stormed past him. McCray hesitated before re-entering the Chief's office. Not venturing past the doorway, he spoke in a tentative tone.

"Am I still assigned to him, Chief?"

"Don't let him fool ya kid. He's quite enthusiastic about it!"

"What's eating him anyways?" He stepped just inside the office.

"Lost his partner last week."

"So I've been told. They say he's a good officer,

given time he'll get over it."

"Frank's got other considerations."

"Lots'a guys lose partners."

"You're his third."

"Oh."

"So far this year."

"Oh." The probie quietly faded back out through the office door.

****

Although well past sunset the thermometer still hovered around 96 degrees Fahrenheit that evening. The buildings and asphalt streets radiated their stored heat as fast as the slightly cooler evening air attempted to carry it away.

Mahone and McCray cruised up Fourth Avenue through the Bowery.

On patrol for the better part of an hour now, neither man had uttered a word. McCray peeled first himself then his sports jacket and shirt off the vinyl seat as he adjusted his position on the passenger's side of the unmarked cruiser. The lack of conversation didn't necessarily bother McCray, he was fascinated with the seemingly endless stream of human disenfranchised debris which littered the streets.

"It really is the modern day Rome isn't it? Sinclair had it right." He mumbled to himself.

Mahone casually glanced at him and then up at the traffic light as it turned red. A hobo approached the car with a squeegee and a spray bottle.

"*The Asphalt Jungle*." McCray informed a mute Mahone. Before either man took notice, the vagrant had deftly sprayed the entire windshield and had begun pulling the worn red rubber squeegee across the glass.

"Get the hell outta here!" McCray yelled out his window.

"Give 'em a buck."

"What?!"

"Pay the man!"

"What the hell for?" The car behind blasted its horn as the light changed green. McCray held a dollar bill out the window and it was quickly snatched by the hobo as he scurried back to the haven of the pavement.

"Why the hell did I give him money?!" McCray grunted.

"So he wouldn't think we were cops. You might need that guy someday."

"Even in an unmarked unit and plain clothes these people can see we're cops!" McCray argued.

"In that case he made us as friendly cops and is more likely to work with us in the future."

McCray stared briefly stared at Frank then shook his head.

"Always thinking huh?"

"And still breathing." Frank answered.

"So how long you got to retire?"

"I told you before, fuck off!"

"Ya know, after you left and I went back into the

Chief's office."

"Yeah what'd he tell ya? That deep down I had a charming personality and warm, friendly demeanor?"

"He said to keep my mouth shut, do what I was told and I'd not only get through this, but learn more in six months with you than I would in two years with most other cops." Mahone stared expressionless through the windshield.

Remembering what he had learned in prisoner psychology class and how prisoners reacted with silence at first but eventually gave in to talking to their cell mates when locked in the bugged cells for prolonged periods, McCray decided he'd wait for the silent treatment to pass.

The evening traffic was light on Eighth Avenue, but Mahone drove as if he were on his way to dinner at his in-laws. A long fifteen minutes and thirty-two blocks later Frank broke the awkward silence.

"Three years, nine months, two weeks, three days and seven hours. But who's counting? What's your sob story?" Frank finally piped up.

McCray suppressed a smile.

"Short and sweet. The Navy four years, three and a half years of it with EOD. Out at twenty-three. College, pre-law then decided on the Police Academy. Finished up there then a year on the streets before transfer to Robbery-"

"Streets? Where?"

"Sutton Place. Later over at the U.N."

"All the hot spots!" Mahone sarcastically quipped. McCray continued.

"Exactly! After all the action in the Navy with EOD I needed more than just taking statements from rich people."

"Adrenaline junky huh?"

"In-between college spent the summers at Grand dad's produce stand down on Christopher Street. Figured I was obligated to come back and help him out. Worked his whole life to scrape together enough money to open that place. Couldn't bail out on him. Then one night we're havin'a drink around the corner at Eddies . . ."

"Eddies near Christopher?"

"Yeah."

"Nice joint." Frank agreed.

"So we're drinking. He says, ya know I been thinking, why the hell you hanging around here selling lettuce at inflated prices? Get the hell outta here and go make somethin' of yerself."

"So you picked cop work?"

"Had to. Failed the city sanitation exam." Frank fought the sensation of distance that swept over him and began to admire the new guy. "How "bout you? You from the City?"

"Yeah, yeah I am. Father was a cop, grandfather was a cop. Pop only did two years then set himself up a P.I. gig." McCray smiled as he looked down at the car floor.

"I know who you are." Mahone blurted out. McCray showed no reaction as he made eye contact.

"That make a difference to you?" McCray probed.

"Only if you fuck up and get me killed!"

The open police band radio crackled to life.

Two Victor Charlie, Two Victor Charlie, Dispatch. Say your Twenty please. New Guy manned the hand mike.

"Dispatch, Two Victor Charlie. We're west bound on 16th, just crossing Seventh."

Roger Two Victor Charlie. Be advised 211 in progress, Alverez's Mercado, corner West 12th and Hudson. Reports single perpetrator, possible firearm. How copy?

"Good copy Dispatch. Two Victor Charlie enroute. We're presently moving west along Fourteenth, ETA one minute. Request back-up, caution responding units two plain clothes on scene. How copy Dispatch?"

Good copy Two Victor Charlie. Use caution. Dispatch out.

McCray had already buckled his seat belt and was placing the hand held, magnetic blue light on the passenger's side roof.

"I buy sandwiches in this place sometime." Mahone began. "We'll come around and head south on the Greenwich Street, keep on his blind side. I'll drop you in the alley behind the dry cleaners. Take the hand-held. Break squelch twice when you're behind the mercado."

"How will I know it from behind? I've never been in that alley."

"It's the next to the last door before you hit

Hudson."

"Right. Wait! Why the hell you takin' the risk goin' in through the front?"

"Sixteen years, two months, two weeks, four days and one hour. That's why."

"Beer's on me tonight." McCray offered by way of encouragement as they pulled up and he hopped out.

"I don't drink beer. Go!"

"Of course not."

They made the four block run fast but without siren so McCray was able to slip out of the car and make it undetected up the back alley. Or so he thought.

Neither of the two noticed the teenage girl across the street from the row of stores chatting away on her cell phone, deeply engrossed in an animated conversation. Until the unmarked cruiser pulled up. Instantly her tone changed to one of restrained alarm.

"Oye, Luis! El tocino, tocino apurate!"

Cuantos cerdos? Came the response.

"Dos! Luis, por favor, vamonos rápido vato!"

Mahone slowly cruised around the corner, seatbelt off and door half opened. Leaving the car on the far corner he made for the store entrance. In a well-rehearsed routine, he pulled his Glock 9, opened the safety and quietly chambered a round. Approaching the front door Frank cautiously peered through the front window to assess the situation.

Due to the over stocked, dark little shop it was

difficult to discern exactly what was happening.

With any luck he grabbed the cash, got away and no one was hurt! He quietly hoped.

However, as the Irish used to say, we live in hope and die in despair.

A woman's scream pierced the air and two shots rang out in rapid succession.

SHIT! It's show time!

Squatting low Mahone scurried across the front window and through the front door. He rapidly scanned the shop and immediately realized his day was going to get a lot worse before it got any better.

"Hi Ruiz!" Frank greeted the known felon. Ruiz cowered behind a hostage, a woman, thirty-ish. They were between the checkout counter where the clerk lay and the first aisle.

Maintaining a bead on the thug Frank attempted to visually assess the severity of the clerk's wounds who lay slumped and gasping for breath off to the side of the checkout counter to his left. The look of panic in his young eyes compelled Frank to signal him with his hand that all would be okay.

Ruiz had a hand firmly pressed over the woman's mouth from behind, gun to her head.

"Ce paso, officer Krupke?" Ruiz greeted with a smile.

"Been busy hey Ruiz? Why don't you put the gun down Vato?!"

"Fuck jew, putto! Jew put jour gun down!"

"Just put the gun down before someone else gets hurt, and everything'll be okay. I'll tell the DA you let her go. I'll won't tell him she was a hostage. Come on man, this is your third strike. I'm tryin' ta work with ya here." Ruiz became more visibly irritated.

"FUCK JEW MANG! I ain't playin' witch jew! Drop it or I drop the bitch!" Ruiz cocked his gun. "I swear ta God mang, I'll venerate her fucking head!" Mahone smiled but was careful to maintain his bead on Ruiz's exposed right upper quadrant.

"Jew dink dis is funny, putto!"

"It's ventilate Ruiz. Ven-til-ate. No wonder you Spic ass holes can't make it here. You're too fuckin" thick to learn English!"

The desired effect was immediate. Ruiz turned beet red, swung his weapon to draw a bead on Mahone but never heard the shots, just felt the burning sensation in his right wrist, forearm and shoulder as two rapid rounds caused his weapon to go flying and his hand and fingers to go numb while blood pulsed from his forearm.

He slowly collapsed to his knees staring at the bloody, mangled arm in disbelief as the terrified hostage ran past Mahone and out onto the street screaming.

Frank approached the fallen criminal maintaining his bead and kicking the gun away from the now medically retired thief.

Reaching in his pocket for a handkerchief he tossed it on the floor in front of the kneeling Ruiz.

"Here's a bandage. Soon as I get minute I'll call for an ambu . . ."

CRACK! CRACK! CRACK!

Mahone watched himself stumble backwards through the display of soap powder and dish liquid, then felt his chest refuse to expand in respiration.

But, was it really him or was he floating above himself in a dream? Everything snapped back into focus, no longer in slow motion. Then, suddenly . . . *Who the hell hit fast forward?*

A second thief stepped out from behind the end cap further down the aisle.

"You are the only one who's going in an ambulance, Officer Krupke!" The voice echoed in his ears from everywhere.

Through the whirling haze of pain as he tried to catch his breath, Mahone watched the unknown figure walk around the still kneeling Ruiz, approach him and stop in front of his own supine form.

Squatting down next to the stunned officer buttons flew as the second gunman ripped open Mahone's shirt and spied the detective's bullet proof vest. The unknown figure spoke.

"Vest hey vato? Very wise!" At point blank, the man fired a single round into Frank's right shoulder where there was no Kevlar to insure his immobility prior to his impending execution.

In one clean jerk, forcing Mahone to cry out in pain, the second assailant opened the cop's shirt further and lifted his vest. Prying Frank's Glock from his numbed hand, the man checked there was a round chambered and placed it at Mahone's sternum.

"Where's jew vest now, pendajo?"

"Drop your weapon asshole!" McCray's high pitched voice squealed out from behind.

With impressive reflexes the gunman spun on one knee with both pistols held in outstretched arms at eye level firing at McCray as he spun.

Mahone's newest partner barely had time to hit the deck behind the aisle and cover his head as the firing continued in short controlled discharges.

The bastard's counting his rounds! Mahone observed.

Frank, now able to partially regain his breath, struggled to raise his head. The gunman turned back towards him with a raised weapon.

Fully accepting that his time was over, Mahone thought only of his partner and was able to see a third perpetrator, a girl, behind McCray, pistol raised at his back. Frank raised his hand to point.

Two gun blasts in rapid succession registered yet another deafening report and Mahone's would-be executioner lurched forward and crumpled to the floor to land on top of Mahone.

The female screamed, and ignoring McCray ran past the now unconscious but still bleeding Ruiz and ran towards Frank and the dead thug.

The wounded store clerk, now propped up on the blood stained cash register lowered his wheel gun and managed a smile as he mumbled through blue lips.

"Pendajo thought he was El Mariachi!" The clerk dropped his weapon, passed out and fell back behind the counter.

Seeing her thug boyfriend shot, the girl screamed for the last time in her young life as she ran towards her compadre, 9mm in hand but was felled from behind as McCray emptied four rounds into her.

Frank with his one good arm shoved hard to push the glassy-eyed corpse off him as he struggled with the pain of his wound. With his face only inches from the gunman, Frank swore he saw a smile creep across the tattooed face.

CRACK! Everything went silent, but he was still conscious and could see clearly. A salty taste welled in his mouth and the pain in his shoulder subsided.

What the hell's happening now?! His mind raced

Glancing down his body, Frank watched in fascination as blood oozed from his stomach.

That doesn't look so good.

He heard steps scurry up next to him.

"Shit! Shit! You're gonna be alright!" McCray's face came into partial focus. "You're gonna be alright! Shit, shit, shit!"

Mahone noticed both McCray's hands were empty as he reached to lift Mahone's head.

"Where's . . . your weapon rookie!" Frank chastised as his vision faded out again, but his hearing was still intact.

"What?"

"There might . . . be more of them. Find . . . your weapon."

"There are no more of them man. We got them all."

"Like . . . basketball. Zone defense. Never get them . . . all. Just the one's . . . in your. . ."

"Don't die man! Please don't fuckin' die!"

"Jan's not gonna . . . like this." Frank mumbled.

"What the hell are you people looking at!? Call an ambulance!" McCray shouted at the few passers-by gathered in the doorway.

The wail of sirens became louder.

"Not gonna like it. Not one . . . little . . . bit."

Easing his head back onto the floor, Frank's mind was suddenly overtaken by a sea of calm. Sirens floated dully in the background. A blue light joined the red one already dancing off the walls.

Noises, footsteps, shouting. Must be somewhere else. Too dull to be in this room. Whatever's happening must be good. The pain's going away.

Like the iris of a camera the tunnel of light Frank saw in front of him began to slowly close until there was only black.

*** * ***

CHAPTER FIVE

St. Vincent's Hospital
Lower East Side, NYC
22:37, Tuesday

For about the fifth time in the last half hour Chief Wachowski, glanced up at one of the half dozen plastic engraved signs above the rows of seats in the spacious room:

Emergency Room Waiting Area.
NO SMOKING

"Shit! I hate these god damned places!" Wachowski mumbled to himself. The stench of antiseptic filled his nostrils and the inane chatter in a half dozen languages was starting to wear on his nerves. Standing against the far wall of the room he was momentarily distracted.

A male patient was wheeled into treatment bay #3 and helped up onto the bed by a nurse who was having great difficulty maintaining her composure. Sitting on the bed the man, middle-aged, was in considerable pain as he held his towel-draped crotch. The older nurse had to fight back the laughter as she drew the full length curtain around the bed.

As she returned from the area and walked towards the nurse's station Wachowski was compelled to question her.

"Hey, what's with him?"

"Penis stuck in a wine bottle." She whispered as she moved passed him.

"Fer Christ's sake!" The Chief mumbled.

"Captain Wachowski?" He turned to face a tired looking, grey-haired doctor who had obviously just come out of surgery. Over the left breast pocket of his pale green scrubs was stenciled, 'St. Vincent's Hosp.'

"Yeah?"

"I'm the attending on officer Frank Mahone."

"I'm all ears, Doc."

"Doc? You must be ex-military."

"Former Marine, but how 'bout we play *What's My Line* a little later and skip right to the part where you tell me if I got a broke cop or not."

"He's definitely not out of the woods yet but he's also definitely not a cop anymore."

"Shit!" Wachowski let out a prolonged sigh.

"The shoulder wound's a clean through-and-through. It'll heal up in a month or so. So no real concern there. The body shot on the other hand . . ."

"Is he gonna make it?!"

"It grazed the abdominal artery, he lost a helluv'a lot'a blood before we got him and the lower lobe of the lung was punctured."

"Doc! His chances?!"

"Fifty-fifty at best. The body shot went through the intestines and up through the lung. We were able to sew up his gut but I can't guarantee he'll ever have full use of his lower left lung again."

"Anything else?"

"To maybe put his situation more in perspective, the human body holds 5-6 liters of blood. We needed 8 liters for the surgery, he's in post op now receiving another liter along with a saline drip and I've got three liters typed and cross matched standing by in the lab in case."

"Enough guys show up to donate?"

"Only about . . ." He flipped through some notes. ". . . only about seventy-six." The elderly surgeon shook something in his hand like a die.

"And?"

"He's lost about three feet of intestine, but the re-anastomosis was text book. The bullet missed the spine, came out through the left kidney. If he makes it through his patrol days are over though."

"When's he outta the woods?"

"We'll know in about 48 hours. If he comes out of it, he might want this." The surgeon offered the item he had been holding in his hand. "Soldiers and cops usually do." It was a 9mm slug.

"Now if you'll excuse me, I have to go talk to his wife."

"Uh Doc. If it's okay with you . . . I'd rather talk to her."

"You're funeral Chief." The surgeon nodded and left.

"Nice choice of words!" Wachowski grunted.

The Chief went through the double doors to his right and out into the ambulance bays. He stood

Paddy Kelly

there observing a woman pacing the length of the small parking area attempting to light one cigarette with the smoldering butt of another. It was the same woman who was at the funeral last week.

A young nurse came out and approached her.

"Are you alright Ma'am? Can I get you something? Coffee, tea, Coke?"

"Lemme ask you something." The woman flicked the butt off to the side and picked a fleck of tobacco off her tongue. "You have a basic medical education, right?"

The young nurse nodded in agreement and tilted her head in curiosity. The woman took a deep drag on her new unfiltered cigarette.

"Then why the fuck would you think I need MORE CAFFIENE?!" The woman, partially shrouded in an eerie haze of cigarette smoke glared unblinkingly at the young nurse. "Thank you! You may go now." The stunned nurse paced quickly away and back through the door which the Chief was holding open.

"Once more into the breach!" Chief mumbled as he made his way over to the woman.

"How're ya holdin' up Jan?"

"Where's his new partner?!" She snapped. "Aren't partners supposed to be together all the time?" The Chief fished into his hip pocket then held out McCray's badge.

"Third time's a charm, huh?" Wachowski snarked.

"So now he's pissed off the Mayor's family?"

99

Jan snapped.

"The kid said he wasn't cut out for it. Going try teaching school."

"Glad somebody in this insane asylum has half a brain!"

"Jan . . ."

"Don't Ralph! I heard all this macho, soap opera bullshit before." She turned and made her way to the side of a parked ambulance and started to shake uncontrollably. Finally she let her dangling cigarette fall from between her fingers and completely broke down. Wachowski moved to her, offered his handkerchief and held her from behind by the shoulders.

"I don't want a fucking flag! You got that, God-damn it?! That's all I ask! NO FUCKING FLAGS!!"

****

10:38, Friday, July 12th

"Why 12:01 for fuck's sake?" Frank bitched from his hospital bed. I could'a been outta here two hours ago!"

"You're a detective, you figure it out." The nurse answered as she unfolded a wheelchair next to his bed. "It's so we can charge you for an extra day's stay."

A Doctor in surgical scrubs who Mahone had never met entered the room with a sheaf of papers in hand. Crossing the room to the bed next to him the doctor simultaneously undid her mask and consulted a clip board as she approached the small group of anxious people huddled around a young mother. The haggard people quickly exchanged worried glances.

"Who is Martha?"

"There is no one here by that name doctor." The old woman answered.

"I'm Mary." The young mother replied.

The doctor lifted a page on the pad and scribbled something before she spoke.

"I'm afraid I have bad news Mary. Your son has passed. He never really regained consciousness." The woman looked away from the doctor then at her family and quietly began to sob.

"One of the nursing staff reported that the last thing he said was, tell Mary I love her." The woman began to cry openly. The doctor took two prepared prescriptions from a pad in her pocket and handed it to one of the young men.

"Tell me if you need that renewed. The Chaplin will be up shortly." The surgeon paused. "I'm sorry we couldn't have done more." She said as she drew the privacy curtain around the bereaved family.

Preoccupied and with fatigue written all over her face, the over worked surgeon made her way across the room to where Frank sat quietly in his wheelchair.

"Isn't that illegal or unethical or something?" He quietly challenged.

"Isn't what illegal?"

"Lying to family members about last words and all."

She raised her head up from his chart and made eye contact.

"What makes you think I was lying?"

"You pretended to have the wrong name when you told her about his last words, but you had the script all made out. If you didn't know the name how could that be?"

"You should have been a cop, officer Mahone." In an obviously agitated state, the doctor scrawled her signature across several forms then handed them to Mahone. "Next time you need advice on how to beat a confession out of a suspect gimme me a call!" She made no attempt to mask her contempt. "An attendant will be with you shortly to take you down." The doctor faded into the maze of corridors.

"Doctors, no sense of humor!" Frank mumbled.

Fifteen minutes later Mahone was being wheeled out of the hospital via wheelchair by an orderly.

As he came through the front door a taxi from the waiting rank a hundred yards away pulled up in front of them. The Seik driver looked into his rear view mirror when he heard the short, shrill screech of a police siren from behind him and saw a black Chevy with flashing blue light on the dashboard and a big cop waving him away.

The annoyed cab driver sped off and Chief Wachowski's car slid up to the curb.

"Cop's salary not enough to meet your gambling

habits, now you gotta moonlight as a hacky?" Frank badgered.

"Fuck you smart ass. Get in or walk home. That is if your broke ass can still walk!"

"Warm as ever Wachowski!"

The attendant folded up the wheel chair, helped Frank climb in and they were off. Nearly a half hour later they pulled up to the curb in front of Frank's place.

Reaching in the glove box Wachowski retrieved a foot long cardboard placard: NYPD POLICE EMERGENCY! And tossed it on the dash in the front windshield.

Wachowski walked Frank up the stairs and as Mahone opened the front door Wachowski stepped into the front room and stared.

"Jesus Frank, half you're shit's gone! You been robbed!"

Frank didn't respond he just limped over to the wide screen T.V. and ripped off the note Scotch taped to the screen. Jan was gone.

"Yeah, looks like I been ripped off." Frank agreed. Wachowski peered over his shoulder and read the note.

"Jesus Frank, tough break amigo!"

"Fuck it! Less shit to worry about! You want a beer?" He limped out to the kitchen and opened the fridge door.

"SON-OF-A-BITCH!"

"What?"

"Bitch took the beer!"

****

"Chief, the truth is after reviewing Detective Mahone's overall performance through the last few years, I've decided not to recommend him to continue on active duty."

Smartly dressed in a sensible dark pants suit, a pastel blouse and wearing sensible ear rings Wachowski couldn't help notice the forty-something wore no wedding ring and avoided eye contact as she spoke to him.

"Why not? Based on what?"

"As I just said Chief Wachowski, based on his overall performance since the first shooting incident."

Wachowski glanced at the poster of the Tabby cat hanging from the tree branch on the wall behind her.

Hang in there Baby, Friday's Coming.

"His overall performance has been exemplary and you know it!"

"You are not the final arbiter in this!"

"No I'm not. But my endorsement is-"
She calmly shrugged.

"Lemme ask you something, you enjoy your work?"

"Helping officers and their families is very rewarding, yes."

"You ever read Rosenthal and Bernstein?"

"Never heard of them!"

"A pair of police psychologists who wrote a paper. Their thesis on the negative effects on peer standing in the community when a cop's career is terminated, especially by a bad or trivial decision, and the adverse effects following unpopular decisions."

"Any career when prematurely terminated is bound to have negative effects on the subject."

"But they didn't focus on the cops. Their study dealt with police psychologists' decisions. Primarily those aimed at forwarding one's own status in the professional community that they themselves never really had the guts to sign up for by making decisions based on 'the safety of others'."

"The best I can do is recommend him an administrative position until retirement."

"He'll quit first."

"That's not under my control. My job is to protect the other officers."

"Really? I thought your job was to help the cops who are having bad time of it. My mistake." Sensing he was about to lose his temper, Wachowski stood to leave but stopped at the door.

"You know, I like movies, a lot. And I can't think of a single cop film where you guys are portrayed in a positive light. Can you? I wonder why that is?"

"This is the real world Chief! Not the movies!"

He forgot to close the door when he left.

****

Monday morning roll call at the 13th Precinct was 08:00 sharp. At the podium in front of the assembled shift the burly Watch Commander launched off into his morning spiel.

"Morning crew. As we can see this morning the weather has turned so bring your light rain gear out with you today. To start off with I have some good news and some bad news. The good news is Downtown has okayed overtime for the next month. Foot patrols only!" The sporadic chatter generated by the announcement quickly died down.

"What's the bad news?" An officer in the front row asked.

Suddenly there was a small disturbance in the back of the briefing room. At exactly one minute after the hour Frank Mahone hobbled through the door on crutches.

"Never mind Sarge, bad news just showed up!" Someone else called out as Mahone took a seat off to the side.

"What the hell you doin' here?" The Sergeant challenged. "I thought you wuz broke?"

"They fixed me. Now I ain't broke." Carefully setting his crutches aside he perused the entire room turned and staring back at him. "I ain't as broke."

"Chief Wachowski warned me you might pull something stupid. You're supposed to be on convalescent leave."

"Consider me convalesced."

"Go see the Chief. He said to send you in when

you showed up."

Frank pushed to his feet, grabbed his crutches and turned to leave. "Hey Mahone. Good job on the Mercado robbery." The sergeant called back to him.

A uniformed female officer which Frank was once forced to help break-in was the first to stand and start clapping. As the others followed suit she moved forward and hugged him.

"We all thought you were dead." She whispered.

"Yeah, that's why as soon as word went out I was hospitalized you assholes started a pool!" She shrugged and began to blush. Frank made eye contact with her. "Hey, sorry about the 'twat' thing." He said by way of a sincere apology. The faces of the other half dozen detectives standing around registered shock at the apology.

"Fuck you guys!" She said, making eye contact as she addressed Mahone. "Well, I was a bit shocked at the word. I'd have called me an asshole for not listening to you." Frank felt a physical pang in his gut as he began to realize exactly what he was going to miss.

Not doing a very good job of fighting back the tears welling in her eyes, the female officer took his face in both her hands.

"You gonna be alright?"

"No. But fuck it."

"I know about you had to be ordered to ride with me on my rookie week." She said.

"No idea what you're talkin' about."

"The bet, asshole! I know you lost the bet with

107

Franzetti." Frank couldn't remember being this disarmed.

"Fuck all you people." He perused the room before he turned to leave. The standing ovation continued until he was out of the room. Mahone held his smile until he was out the door.

Hobbling over to the Chief's office he knocked once then entered.

Wachowski was on the phone as Mahone came in but signed off as soon as Frank entered.

"Word around the squad room has it you had a pow wow with the shrink." Frank challenged.

"Cops! Gossip more than a Mormon sewing circle! And I wouldn't be too critical there Quick Draw! The shrink actually vouched for your dumb ass." Wachowski lied. "How you feeling?" He asked as a bottle of whiskey appeared on the desk along with a pair of glasses.

"You got any idea what time it is?" Frank asked not bothering to reach for his glass as Wachowski poured two shots.

"Fuck it. It's five o'clock somewhere!" Wachowski shrugged and downed his drink.

"You gonna put in for early retirement?" He asked Frank.

"What the hell for? I'll be back in two weeks, three tops."

"The shrink thinks it's a bad idea. She nixed your R-TAD." Mahone's face turned serious as he ground is teeth.

"So I don't get a return to active duty because

some twat who doesn't even go out on the fucking streets thinks I don't belong out there!"

"People like them don't wanna know that people like us are still around Frank." Chief poured himself one more. "We're old school, dangerous. Now days it's more important to be touchy feely then to be smart and brave."

"And drink nothing but soy milk? Fuck that!" Frank reached for his drink. "Voluntary?" He asked.

"Mandatory/voluntary." Wachowski added. Frank fell back in his chair.

"I'll go the union."

"Thought you hated the unions?"

"I'll request a board."

"Your choice. I mean, I know you'll be back 100% but your chances of a handful of board members risking their advancements, their reps or maybe even their jobs to back you is pretty slim."

"You tryin' to tell me in a nice way I'm fucked?"

"Not necessarily. I might have an out for ya."

Frank downed his drink.

"I ain't interested in flying a desk down at Police Plaza! Desks are for losers and invalids!"

"Really?"

"You know what I mean!" Frank weakly defended,

"Calm the fuck down cowboy! Nobody said anything about Police Plaza!"

"Just not interested in a desk."

"Not interested in flying a desk even if it's in Merry Old England?"

"What the hell you talking about?"

"Ever been to Europe?" Chief asked.

"Europe?! I don't even go to New Jersey unless I have to!"

"There's a slot coming open in the next two weeks in an exchange program."

"Why me? You tryin' to get rid of me?"

"Not really, that's just a perk. But also we need a good cop and I hear Tom Selleck's not available."

"England huh?" Mahone replaced his empty glass back on the desk.

"Plus you'd get a chance to visit the 'Auld Country! Drink some Guinness!"

"I don't drink stout and I have no interest in going to Ireland. Beside, my mother was a Pollock."

"Sorry about that."

"What'd theoretically be my job?"

"Who the hell knows and who the hell cares?! At least you're still on the payroll, you get to chase bad guys and maybe you'll accidently pick up some culture! Might even bring back something might help The Department. That is after all what the program is supposed to be for."

"Is it true their cops don't carry guns?"

"Yeah, so what?"

"How ya supposed to kill people?!"

"I understand they're pretty good with the language, maybe they talk 'em to death! Plus they all carry umbrellas. You in or out?"

"I'll give it a think."

"Yeah, you do that. But don't think too long,

there's a list a mile long to get in on this and people pay thousands to vacation in Europe!" Wachowski refilled Frank's glass.

"Vacation? What's that?" Frank reached over to the desk and lifted his drink. They toasted. Frank threw his back and pushed the glass back across the desk as Wachowski recapped the bottle.

"You not gonna have another?" Frank asked.

"Nah, I'm tryin' to cut down, three's my limit for breakfast." The Chief grumbled as he restowed the bottle in his bottom desk drawer.

Frank rose to leave. As he reached the door Wachowski called after him.

"Mahone!" Frank turned to face him. "FYI, there's more than one asshole around here layin' odds on exactly when you're gonna fall flat on your face!"

"Put me down for twenty. I'm good for it." Mahone quipped.

"Twenty?! Ya cheap bastard! I'm in for thirty!"

"Then put me in for fifty."

"Don't ferget to pack an umbrella!" Wachowski called after him as the door closed over.

*

Two days after separation from his wife Frank had found a newly refurbished one bedroom on the Upper East Side but was still living out of the dozen cardboard boxes he and a couple of friends had dropped off weeks ago.

One afternoon, returning home after a drink and a film he unlocked the door and was greeted with an empty apartment.

"Son-of-a-bitch! Twice in one month!" He checked the kitchen cabinets and found two cans of soup, three cans of beans, and the half loaf of stale bread next to the half bottle of Jameson's. He rinsed out a glass in the sink, uncapped the bottle, poured a drink and sat next to what had to be one of the last land line phones in New York City.

He dialed a call.

"I'd like to report a 211."

What exactly has been stolen sir? The voice on the other end asked. Frank perused the empty apartment and sardonically chuckled.

"Everything."

On entering the front door, an hour and a half later, a Lieutenant from Robbery took immediate charge of the crime scene stationing a man at the door and then directing the single forensics tech where to begin. Mahone smiled to himself as he instantly recognized the gruff voice punctuated by the heavy Brooklyn accent throwing orders at the investigative team now invading his apartment.

"Head of the department in person. Now that's service!" Frank spouted over his shoulder.

"You okay Mahone?" The lieutenant asked not bothering to temper the sincerity in his voice.

"Ecstatic."

Should have known better, the Lieutenant thought to himself.

"What's missing?"

"Don't know."

"What'a ya mean ya don't know? Didn't you bother to look around?" He asked, any trace of amazement in his voice, well camouflaged by annoyance.

"Didn't have time." Mahone replied.

The uniformed officer with them stopped what he was doing and glanced over at the pair.

"You saw them?! You chased them?!" The lieutenant asked as the uniformed cop approached him with a cellular phone.

Frank shrugged. "I'm a cop."

"Call in on the precinct phone sir. It's from the street team, Lieutenant." The uniform informed the Lieutenant.

"Tell them hold one. Frank, what do you mean you didn't have time?"

"Didn't have time. Had to start drinking." Holding up the near empty bottle of whiskey.

"You're some kind of an asshole, ya know that?! I thought you were goin' to AA?"

"Summer recess."

"If you keep feelin' sorry for yer self, pretty soon nobody else is gonna."

"Thank you Doctor Phil! Ain't you got some finger prints ta take before you tell me you probably ain't gonna find these pricks?"

"Sir, you'll want to take this." The Patrolman once again offered the small Nokia to the Lieutenant, who grabbed it.

"Lieutenant Nicholson. What'a ya got?" After a brief moment, Nicholson assumed an animated smirk and held the expression after hanging up the phone and taking a seat opposite Mahone.

"Too cheap to have your own cell phone, ya tight bastard?" Mahone challenged.

"Don't want my own cell phone! Fuckin' electronic
babysitter! Besides, damn things give ya brain cancer." Nicholson leaned forward in his seat. "Brace yerself, wise guy." Nicholson warned. Frank lifted his glass.

"Fer what?" Mahone remained as he had since Gene Nicholson and his team arrived, completely expressionless and staring through his former colleague.

"Fer ta go down ta the property room and I.D. yer shit!"

Frank lowered the rocks glass from his lips before he could drink and Gene watched with satisfaction as Frank's eyes focused on his own.

Pointing at the Lieutenant with his index finger while still holding the glass of whiskey Frank made his feelings clear.

"Don't fuck with me Gene!"

"We caught them. Recovered all your shit! Everything you own. Took two large garbage bags. Sounds to me like we got all of it."

"That doesn't make sense." Frank sat his drink on the pressed wood coffee table separating the two cops and sat back on the sofa.

"No it doesn't make sense." Nicholson picked up the glass, threw back Frank's drink and smirked again. "Usually takes us a day or so before we recover the stuff, but seein' as how your shit was so valuable we put a rush order in."

Twenty minutes later Frank was again alone in his apartment.

As he poured the last of his whiskey he stood staring out the single window down onto Second Avenue as a city bus pulled out from a stop.

Looks like I'm going to fuckin' England. He mused.

*

CHAPTER SIX

Terminal 2
Heathrow International
Sunday, 21 July: 20:15

United's 12:45 from New York landed right on time and at thirty-seven years of age Frank Mahone, save for a drunken weekend in Tijuana while he was in the Navy, stepped off the plane and into a foreign country for the first time in his damaged life.

Due to increased security at the baggage claim, compounded by a Nigerian gentleman who objected to immigration control arresting him for his forged passport and the two and a half kilos of coke they found in the lining of his baggage, it was the better part of an hour before Mahone was able to claim his single suitcase, locate a cab at the taxi rank and climb into a black Hackney to head east into the city.

"Fielding Hotel please. Do you know it?"

"Not a clue Gov'nor, but 'at's why we has these little beauties!" The chubby driver jubilantly declared as he punched some buttons on his dash mounted GPS device.

Hearing the American accent the driver's mouth watered at the possibility of affording an extra pint later that night.

"Coventry! You must be one of them high up

execs from the States, eh?" They pulled out into the light traffic.

"Coventry a well-to-do town is it?"

"Not a town Mate, it's a borough, like youse 'ave over in New York."

"Ahh!"

"Over for 'oliday are we?"

"Training program, sort of an international exchange thing. Your government and the AOEP office cut us a deal on housing for the time I'm here."

"Police eh? You'll not find too many active officers over here mate! Bank on that! Tits on a bull so they are most of 'em."

"So you don't like cops?"

"Most of 'em's good people to be sure, but try and find one when you needs 'em! At's all I'm sayin'."

People bitchin' about cops! Maybe England's not so different. Frank mused.

Given the moderate traffic it was about thirty minutes outside the city on the Cromwell Road when they hit the Belgravia district and were held up by a police road block on an overpass which afforded them a vista down into the town square.

"'At's gonna get quite ugly real soon so it is!" The driver declared as he peered out his side window and down from the overpass.

"What's going on?" Frank asked as he slid over and leaned forward in his seat for a better view.

Down on the shop-lined street a small line of

officers were unsuccessfully attempting to control a much larger crowd of ethnic Muslims as they aggressively yelled, beat on parked cars and slowly pushed the police line back.

"Bloody Joe Dakis!" The driver declared.

"What?"

"Joe Dakis, Pakis! Fuckin' Mussis tryin' to take over everything." The driver informed. "Half of 'em's illegal the other half's just wantin' to oust the rest of us and take over the whole bleedin' country!" The driver spat out.

Having been called to any number of racially fueled riots in the various New York boroughs back when he was in uniform Frank reserved comment.

As they sat on the road awaiting the all clear several more police vehicles pulled up from both sides of the demonstration, now turning violent and waded into the fray.

Tear gas was fired and the mob began to fracture and run as the arrests started.

Frank noticed that one of the Bobbies appeared to be a Pakistani or perhaps Indian.

"Poor bastard!" Frank quietly mumbled to himself.

Ten minutes later the traffic cops on the road ahead finally pulled the road barrier aside and waved them on.

"I read about the immigration problems over here."

"You ain't read the 'alf of it Mate! They filter the news sumthin' terrible here in this country so's you never get the real story."

"Join the fuckin' club friend! Ever heard of CNN?" Mahone coughed out.

"Oh yeah! Over here we spell it BBC."

Half an hour later the cab pulled into a narrow laneway in an urban area and Mahone hopped out in front of a white cottage styled building conspicuously looking out of place situated in the middle of a Twentieth Century, city's residential area.

After some confusion about exactly which pictures of British royalty he was to hand over to the cab driver Frank grabbed his luggage and made his way to the front desk.

Mahone didn't recognize any of the pictures on the banknotes but he could read numbers as well as the next guy and so the driver's attempt at tipping himself more than what was intended was unsuccessful.

The Fielding Hotel in Coventry is a well-appointed, medium priced affair and Mahone was too tired to duel with the grumpy, middle-aged, woman who glanced down her nose at him while he scratched out his details in the thick log book and slid his passport across the desk.

"Can I have a wake-up call for six-thirty, please?"

As he signed in she burped a quiet harrumph before she spun the register book around and scanned it to be sure he had supplied all the required information.

"You are in room 7A Mr. Mahone and I'm afraid we don't do 'wake-up calls' sir."

"I see."

"Perhaps you might use your mobile." She curtly suggested.

"My mobile what?"

"Your mobile phone, sir."

He was amused by the old styled skeleton key to his room and smiled at the woman he arbitrarily decided to name Jacob Marley as he left the small, well-appointed lobby and headed down the well-appointed hall to his room.

As he unlocked the door and stepped into the well-appointed en-suite he nodded his approval, fell onto the bed and initiated a conversation with himself.

"Trucks are lorries, French fries are chips, stores are shops and phones are 'mobiles'. Huh?! And I thought I already spoke English!"

Twenty minutes later Mahone fell asleep trying to figure out how to set the alarm on his 'mobile' phone.

*

Next morning Frank awoke to the sounds of a couple arguing out in the hall, rolled over and glanced up at his Casio G-Shock. 06:37.

Coffee fixings in the room was a nice surprise as was the notice on the wall above the tea kettle that a complimentary breakfast was served in the 'dining hall' from six until eight.

Twenty minutes later, following a shower and a shave, Frank was taking a seat at a corner table in the small but well-appointed dining room.

Tem minutes after ordering, a plate appeared in front of him.

"Excuse me ma'am, what's this?" He poked at the small black patty on his plate next to the two large sausages, two fried eggs, two fried rashers, a large pile of beans and four wedges of toast.

"That would be black pudding sir." The server politely answered.

"Ahh." Frank quietly commented as he sliced a small piece off the patty with his fork and popped it into his mouth. "Interesting. Pudding and sweets are usually for after the meal in New York." He polity commented in between chews.

"Actually sir, it's not sweet. It's fried coagulated pig's blood."

Mahone immediately spit the masticated remnants back onto his plate.

"Christ! What'a you people vampires?"

"The other one is white pudding as well if you like sir!" She politely pointed to the white patty on his plate. "There's no blood in that. It's only pig's fat."

"Thanks, I'll pass." He said after gulping his glass of orange juice in one go.

Out at the front desk he found an attractive day receptionist, who bore a striking resemblance to a young Cameron Diaz.

"Good morning Mr. Mahone. I trust you slept well!"

"Very well thanks for asking."

"How may I help you?"

"I'd like to –" Suddenly, in his pocket, his I-phone alarm went off. He fished through his pocket, found the phone and, with some a help from the receptionist, shut it off. The medium built, dusky blond, who had an infectious smile. Handed him back his phone.

"Gift from the guys before I let New York." He explained. "Due at the office at nine." He played it off. "Could you tell me the best way to get to Scotland Yard? Other than getting arrested I mean."

"Actually sir, were you to get arrested you'd likely be taken to Holborn Station or Charring Cross. The Yard is reserved for significant cases."

"I see."

"If you want to take the Tube, that would be the Covent Garden station to the Westminster Station Mr. Mahone."

"For you I could be Frank."

"Well that's very kind, but I am also being frank when I tell you I'm engaged." She brandished her diamond ring.

"Trust me sweetheart, with me you're safe as a bottle of whiskey at an AA meeting!"

"Sorry?"

"Going through a particularly nasty divorce. Definitely not looking. At least for the moment."

"I see. Then a date for dinner is definitely out of

the question?" She teased.

"No, but very kind of you to ask. Scotland Yard?"

"The Hotel to the Yard is approximately five miles and four to six pounds will get you there by ferry. The bus cost you three pounds, while the Tube will set you back two to three pounds. Or you, being a somewhat healthy middle-aged, moderately good looking man, for a Yank I mean, could walk."

She'd fit right in back in New York! Frank mused as he thanked her and headed out and down the street.

****

The short walk from the Westminster Tube station to the Yard led Mahone to the entrance where he couldn't resist stopping just under the world renown triangular sign and looking up.

"That's what all the movies are about?" He said out loud.

As he pushed through the front doors the busy atmosphere of foot traffic, phones ringing and noisy lobby chatter filling the modern glass and chrome area was reminiscent of One Police Plaza in Lower Manhattan.

Impressive! Frank mumbled as he turned and entered through the turnstiles and stepped up to the X-ray conveyor. Familiar with the routine it was out of habit that he flashed his badge which back in the New York would have gotten him waved past security.

The officer behind the barrier leaned in, perused the badge and smiled.

"Thank you sir. Please place it in the basket with any other metallic items you may be carrying and step through the metal detector." It was then that it hit home.

Back in New York he may have been a decorated robbery or homicide detective, but here he was just another tourist.

On the other side of the conveyor the policeman handed Mahone the basket.

"Thank you sir. Welcome to Scotland Yard."

"Could you direct me to administration?"

"Which administration would that be sir?" She pleasantly inquired.

"I need to get some information about where to go."

"Oh then you'll be wanting Information sir."

"Yes, information, about where I need to go."

"No sir, I mean the Information desk. You'll want to go to the Information desk. Just down the hall on the left."

"Thanks."

"You're very welcome. Enjoy your visit."

At the info window Frank repeated his question.

"Where can I find the Administration office, I'm supposed to check in?"

"Which division would that be sir?"

"I'm not sure."

"The Scotland Yard Division, Executive Branch

Administration, Governmental Division, NHL, U.S. Justice Division which includes the FBI, Met administration, or the IHOP Division?"

"IHOP?! You sell pancakes here?"

"IHOP would be the international division sir."

"I'm supposed to meet with an Inspector Morrissey?"

She attacked her key board and found the name.

"Inspector Morrissey Special Homicide Investigation Team, room 601. That would be floor six sir. Lift is to the right in the center."

"Thanks."

"You're quite welcomed sir, happy to have helped."

Seriously, the SHIT squad?! They really do have a different take on the lingo over here! Bunch of really polite fuckers though I'll give 'em that!

Minutes later stepping off the elevator Frank found 601, knocked and entered. A civilian woman sat behind a large desk and two officers were in the far corner of the spacious room. Several desks sat unoccupied.

"Hi. I'm looking for the . . . uh, Special Homicide Squad?"

"Ah yes, the SHITS. They've temporarily relocated down the hall. Third door on our left. It's marked AV Room."

"Thank you."

I hope the fuck these people find criminals a helluv'a lot faster than it takes to find their fuckin' offices!

At the AV Room Frank let himself in to find Sergeant Heath, the only occupant, working with a slide tray on the overhead projector.

"Any idea where I can find Inspector Morrissey?"

"Depends who's looking." Heath replied without looking over.

"Frank Mahone, NYPD. I'm here for the exchange program."

"Oh, hi. Name's Franklin, Franklin Heath." He extended hand. "Part of the Special Squad. Welcome to England!"

"Thanks!" He perused the over-sized but empty room. "Where is everybody?"

"Most of the Squad are down in Brixton, probably be there well past lunch. You're welcome to hang around here or I can arrange a car to take you down there if you like."

"How long to get down there?"

"Half an hour or so depending on motorway traffic."

"I'd kind'a like to get right into it if that's okay."

"Eager beaver 'ey? Skipper'll like that. No problem. Give us a minute to wrap this up and I'll drive you down meself."

"Much appreciate it."

126

*

There was a knock at the door and Chief Wachowski's secretary popped her head in.

"Chief?"

"Yeah?"

"The Watch Commander just called up, that FBI guy's here." She informed the Chief.

"Send him in when he shows up."

A minute later a somewhat jaunty, thirty-ish, overly groomed man in a charcoal grey suit and dark blue tie introduced himself.

"Chief Wachowski, Special Agent Willis, FBI, Local Forces Liaison."

"What can I do for you today agent Willis?"

"Like to ask you a couple of questions about one of your men."

"One of my guys fuck up?"

"I don't think so Chief, least I hope not." The Liaison slid a photo copy of a passport across the desk. It was Frank Mahone.

"You know this officer?"

"Yeah. He's some kind'a of hero or something isn't he? This, a joke?"

"Now Chief, we don't want to step on anybody's toes here. That's why we came straight to you."

"And?"

"We understand that you put in a special re-activation request for Detective Mahone?"

"That's right. A few weeks ago."

"Any special reason?"

127

"Only one. He's the best man for the job."

"But he was medically retired only two weeks ago."

"That paper work is yet to be approved by higher so right now he's not medically retired anymore."

"That's not the information we have Chief."

"You second guessing my judgment or you saying I'm lying?"

Willis realized how crucial it was to maintain and control the course of the interview suddenly gone reverse interrogation.

"How's he been since he's off the force?"

"No job, no wife no future. Then he got to move into a neighborhood where instead of a welcome wagon they cleaned out his apartment for him first week he was there. On top of that the day after he leaves for England his apartment gets robbed again. Other than that he's doing fine."

The agent shifted position and briefly glanced down. Willis might have been formally educated on how to conduct interviews, but he was well out of his league on covert interrogations. There was a reason the guest chair sat directly in front the Chief's desk and was three inches lower.

"Actually, we don't think he was robbed."

"That was you pricks?!" Chief declared.

"Couple of over enthusiastic young agents. They've been re-assigned. Everything was returned in good order I trust?" Chief wasn't quite sure how to take this guy. But knew he only wanted to take him in short doses.

"Why all the charades? Why not just pull his file? Why not use his academy photo instead'a making him look like a criminal with this photo copy of his passport photo?!" Chief asked.

"The kind'a stuff we want to know about him isn't in his file."

"Like what?"

"Like personal habits. Idiosyncrasies, likes and dislikes. Sexual preferences."

"Did your mother drop you?! What the hell significance is shit like that?" Willis gained confidence as Chief was caught off guard.

"We need to know if he can be blackmailed, bribed, corrupted in any way." The Liaison continued to enjoy the protracted silence. He stared at Mahone's supervisor before he spoke again. "Well?"

"Well what?" Chief was finding it more difficult to contain his anger.

"Well is he crooked?"

"That guy's a hell of a lot cleaner than anybody you people have down in D,C., I'll tell ya that!"

"Was he ever on the take?"

"Not a chance!"

"How can you be so sure?"

"I knew him and his father since before he was on the force. His grandfather was a cop, his father was a cop, his uncle was a cop and now he's a cop. He's clean as a whistle."

"His uncle was only a cop for a couple of years. Had some problems according to our files."

"Don't bullshit a bull shitter Special Agent Willis. You ain't got no files on his father or his grandfather." Chief had had enough. He leaned forward in his chair, folded his arms on his desk and peered at the FBI representative. "His uncle's the one brought down your crooked Treasury agent counterfeiting ring in D.C. Took out four or five of the bastards so the story goes. And as long as we're being up front with one another, is it really true the FBI worked on that counterfeiting case for nine months and couldn't get anything on those guys? Imagine that. All it took was one New York City Cop to break one of the biggest criminal cases of the war." The strategy worked. Willis shifted again.

"How do you know there are no files?" Willis challenged.

"Because the operation associated with all that mess probably went all the way to the top. And nobody wants anybody to look bad, now do they?" Wachowski sat back in his chair. "Just too bad nobody told your ex-boss Comey how things work, huh?" Willis suddenly realized that he was not getting anywhere and probably wasn't going to. "What's the matter, don't watch the nightly news?" Chief added.

Willis also had a short tolerance for sarcasm.

"Anything you could help us with would be sorely appreciated Chief Wachowski."

"Sure thing! You let me in on the big secret, tell me what this is all about and I'll see what I can do."

"We're just following leads Chief, that's all."

"Door swings both ways, Bruce. You got something on Mahone now's the time to either come clean or -"

"Or what?" Willis challenged in no uncertain terms.

"Or next time you come back here you give adequate notice, submit the proper request forms and know there'll be people here from I.A., the Commissioner's office and the union. Have a nice day Agent Willis."

Willis smugly concealed his anger as he turned to leave.

"By the way, name's not Bruce! It's Richard. We'll be in touch." The office door closed over behind him.

"Look forward to it! Don't forget to write, Dick!" Wachowski watched the agent make his way through the maze of desks which lined the squad room then called out to the senior clerk who was talking to a detective a few desks down. He motioned the clerk into his office and closed the door over.

"Shirl, find out what hotel Mahone's stayin' in over in London and get me a contact number." The clerk had barley turned to leave when Chief grabbed her arm and stopped her. "Never mind the hotel number. Get me a copy of Captain Dietrich's message, the one he asked where to assign that Bobby from the London Metro. Then get a hold of me."

"The exchange cop?"

"Yeah. I think he was assigned somewhere over in the 10th." The clerk shuffled through her clip board searching for her copy of the memo. She couldn't find it.

"I'll have to get on the computer and look for it Chief."

Wachowski didn't bother to tell her there was no hard copy memo about the Chief's request to assign Mahone the coveted exchange program position. He never issued one. For fear of disapproval, Wachowski had filled out and approved the request himself without submitting it to the Downtown district office. Wachowski placed a hand on the board and halted the clerk's shuffling.

"You know what, don't go through any trouble."

"It's no trouble Chief, I just have to-"

"No really Shirley, just find the English cop and tell him I'd like to see him. Better yet, get me a contact number for him. There's a couple of inter-precinct S.O.P.'s I have to give him." For the third time the clerk went to walk away and was brought back. "Do it yourself. Don't let anyone else do it. I'm worried they'll forget again. Got it?"

"Yeah. I got it." She said. The Chief headed back to his desk while the clerk just stood there. As Wachowski turned to sit he looked at the clerk who still hadn't moved.

"Why are you still standing here?"

"Because."

"Because why?"

"Because one more instant replay and I'm gonna

get whiplash. Are we through?"

"Get the hell outta here!" Chief took his seat as she left and closed the door. "Wise ass!" He chuckled.

*** * ***

Later that afternoon PC John Hedge, the Englishman who temporarily swapped places with Mahone, called Chief Wachowski's office where he was casually invited to meet the Chief and a couple of the guys after work for a beer.

Only a few blocks north the precinct PC Hedge found the place no trouble, Molly's on 3rd Avenue, and made his way into the moderately full, long, narrow pub and eatery.

The tall, handsome twenty-three year old was surprised however when the fifty-something barmaid waved to get his attention and then pointed to a booth in the far rear corner where only Chief Wachowski sat. He was surprised because Wachowski was the only one there.

"Evening Chief."

"Officer Hedge. What'a ya having?"

"Pint of pale ale, please." He looked around then posed his question. "I thought there'd be others?"

The Chief waved at the barmaid who scurried over to the end of the bar and nodded.

"TWO SAM ADAMS MAGGIE!"

"TAP OR BOTTLES?" She called back.

"TAP!" He yelled back. She signaled back with a

thumbs up.

"Yeah the others kinda got delayed." Wachowski bullshitted. "So how ya getting' on over at the Tenth?"

"Hugely impressed by the cordiality of everyone. All the lads are very helpful."

"Don't let it fool ya! They're only being nice 'cause yer an outsider. It's when they start being assholes ya now they've really accepted you!"

"I rekin it's no different for your detective over at The Yard." Hedge responded.

The pints arrived.

"Cheers!"

"Cheers!"

They made small talk but after the third round of beers arrived Wachowski estimated it was time to spring the trap.

"PC Hedge-"

"You're welcome to call me John if you like."

"Okay, John it is. John I need a little help, if you're up for it."

"What can I do to help Chief?"

"I've run into a departmental problem, channels-wise that is, and you're in a unique position to help out."

"Never turn down a chance to score points with the boss, that's what me da always said anyway."

"Well, technically I'm not your boss Captain Dietrich is-"

"You catch me drift. Tell us what you need!"

"Do you happen to have any connections at

Scotland Yard?"

"Yeah, I've a mate in admin actually."

"I need a small favor. Only it has to be on the QT."

"Sure thing Chief! What's a 'QT'?"

****

CHAPTER SEVEN

**Bob Marley Way
Brixton, London**

Morrissey stared straight at it. The twitch in the big, uniformed officer's left eye as he spoke without reading from the small note pad he held in his hand.

Bob Marley Way is a short, two lane, residential road ending in a dead end 'T' junction. The two car garage where the armored van had been found was attached to the rear of a three story, very old, run-down Georgian apartment building.

Morrissey and the large, older PC who greeted him next to the detective's car now stood in the middle of the single lane road.

The big sergeant launched straight into his report.

"Armored van number 1-9-8-9, involved in what was known as the 19-89 case-"

"Creative, except that it occurred in 19-99." Morrissey interjected.

"Actually reported missing on New Year's Day 2000 sir, along with both guards. Search officially ended one year later when Lloyd's paid off the insurance claim. The money was stashed because the theory was that if the Y2K virus jimmied up the bank's computers –"

"The bankers would still have some cash on hand

with which to do business next day."

"Yes sir. #1989 was the only armored vehicle not accounted for-"

"There were others?!"

"Three others from this company and as many as a couple of dozen or so across the U.K., so the popular press reported."

"Remarkable!" Morrissey stared down wide-eyed at the macadam road. "Banks stashing cash like so many misers!"

"Yes sir. At any rate, the guards and approximately half a billion pounds in used notes were never found." The tall sergeant looked down at Morrissey.

"Billion, with a B?" Morrissey clarified.

"Yes sir, billion with a B."

"Had no idea you could stuff that much dosh into one vehicle!"

"As I was saying Inspector, never found."

"Uh huh." Morrissey stared up at the older PC. "Sergeant, you ascertained all that in the short time since you've responded to this call?!"

"Negative Inspector. I clearly remembers the case. I was a probationary PC at the time, followed it quite closely so I did! They still use it occasionally at the academy as the premier robbery case except this lot got away with twenty-five times what Ronnie Biggs and his lot did."

"Fascinating. Anything else?"

"If memory serves Inspector, there were two guards, they signed out at around 22:30, checked in when they reached their first two check points then at around 22:50 reported they were all secure and in their final hide. Next morning they nor the van was no where's to be found."

"This wasn't their final hide?"

"Not according to reports Inspector."

"Where were they supposed to be?"

"Somewhere up in Haggerston, in the Whiston Road area, I think. There were farmlands up there at one time. Can't say what might be there these days."

"Does that computer memory of yours happen to recall the approximate time of their last communication?"

"That was just it sir. According to the reports they was to radio in again sometime after one a.m. and every hour thereafter. When they didn't 'e, the dispatcher that is, put it down to atmospherics on account'a all the fireworks and such. Wasn't till several hours later they went lookin' and discovered everything, them poor guards included, was missing."

"Anybody look inside the van yet?"

'Negative Inspector, still locked up. Call only came in eight minutes ago, we was only just up the road and so was the first to respond."

"I see. Owner of the space?"

"Don't know but the Hamlet Agency's been notified sir." The sergeant informed and was met with a quizzical look. "Owners of the van sir."

"Ahh! Of course."

"One of their agents is in route."

"Who called it in?"

"Indian gentleman over there in the . . . the funny long shirt speakin' wit the female inspector sir." He pointed to a 30-something Indian speaking with Dunn in front of the double door garage.

"It's called a sherwani PC." Morrissey corrected.

"Yes sir. The Shit-wani gentleman inspector."

"No, the shirt Sergeant. It's known as a sherwani shirt. The inspector is a 'woman' inspector."

"As you say Inspector."

"Anything else?"

"No Inspector, that's all we've been able to ascertain at the moment."

"Thank you PC, good work, excellent report. Set up barricades at the end of the street, post a man there and have one or two wander up and down to keep the rubber-neckers away. No one breaches the perimeter until you hear from me personally."

"Yes Inspector."

Just then Dunn, the only member of the SHIT Squad at the scene besides Morrissey, approached.

"Right, everything's sealed off. Fella in the sherwani says his brother rented the garage several years back sight unseen. Lives in America, all done on the internet. The brother says -"

"Name?"

"Rohan Khan."

"Any relation to-"

"I asked, he said no."

"Can't say as I blame him, I'd say no too. Go

139

on."

"Mr. Khan says his brother passed away last week, heart attack. They're down from Manchester just getting around to settling his affairs."

"Did his brother happen to own an armored van?"

"Not that he knew of. Businessman in New York, Teledyne Corporation, junior exec of some sort."

"Notify the lab we need a forensics team down here."

"Will we treat this as a homicide?" She inquired.

"There's no body yet, at least no one reports smelling anything."

"What else?" She asked.

"We'll need ownership records of this garage as far back as the records go. Trace the chain of custody, then assemble a comprehensive list of their contact numbers. Also we'll want all POC's of the . . ." He peeked into the open garage. "Hamlet Security agency going back to anyone who worked for the company from 1998 on, '97 would be . . . are you actually on your mobile while we're responding to a case?!"

"Pause." Dunn said into her mobile. "I'm recording all your instructions while simultaneously transmitting on line to Dragon."

"Transmitting what, for God's sake?! And who the hell is Dragon?"

"Transmitting back to my desk top and onto my computer via voice recognition. The program is called Dragon."

"Why?!"

"For later reference and so the whole squad can be briefed. Eliminates errors, omissions plus slashes my research time." Dunn explained.

"Not sure that's such a good idea. I-"

"And eliminates most all the required typing for AA reports."

"You mean this Dragon program can type too?!"

"It's recording as we speak and all we need do is add the heading and the conclusion of the report which can also be done with VR."

"Voice Recognition?!"

"Yes."

"No more typing reports?"

"Once the program is accustomed to your voice speech patterns, completely unnecessary!"

"George Orwell, here we come! Very well. Carry on."

Dunn reactivated her phone and continued. "I've instructed the uniforms to ring in for back-up and to start canvassing the flats for witnesses." She informed.

"Good idea but not likely anyone's gonna remember anything from 1999, even if they were here or want to talk to us."

As neighbors began to slowly seep from the surrounding homes and apartments Morrissey did a cursory check around the outside of the garage entrance. Like the Georgian building it was attached to, the double wide, two door, dilapidated garage was not well maintained but secure and had stood unnoticed for years as everyone in the neighborhood assumed it belonged to someone else.

"Why weren't they traced by the main office's GPS?" Morrissey wondered out loud.

"Couldn't, not in 1999." Dunn quickly informed him. "Except for in the spy films GPS hadn't developed to the point of that accurate tracking."

"I knew that." Morrissey shot back.

As they moved over into the garage a Vauxhall Corsa patrol car cruised up to the end road, was waved through by the officer and drove down the narrow two lane street to pull up in front of the garage.

Heath and Mahone climbed out.

"Inspector, may I present our American cousin who was supposed to be here last week, Lieutenant Detective Frank Mahone. Detective Mahone, Inspector Nigel Morrissey." Heath introduced. They shook hands.

"Sorry I got hung up leaving New York, I had to stick around and sign some papers."

"Never mind the Nigel bit. Call me Morrissey."

"Call me Frank."

"Heath, we'll be needing someone on late watch next week. Might as well be you."

Heath began to seethe. Not at the shit assignment, but at the fact that he forgot yet another unwritten rule. Nobody refers to Inspector Morrissey by the 'N' word.

"Well Detective, you're right on time. We're

about to dive into a cold case." Morrissey directed them over to the garage. "First strong lead in eighteen years." Not yet fully recovered from his injuries, Frank limped slightly as they moved along.

"Nineteen years sir." Dunn corrected.

"I knew that. Dunn fill our guest in. Heath give us a hand, grab the other door." Morrissey with Heath in tow, pushed back the two tall, heavy wooden doors and they made their way into the two car garage. They circled the tall van as Dunn disseminated what little they knew to date.

"Uh huh." Mahone nodded as Dunn led him into the garage space behind the others as she talked.

Scraps of cigarette butts, several empty Coke cans and chocolate bar wrappers as well as the snipped ends of black zip ties littered the concrete floor.

"Whoever they were they were amateurs about cleaning up after themselves." Heath added.

"Not necessarily." Dunn corrected, now standing behind them.

"How so?"

"It's possible they want us to think they were amateurs."

'Possibly." Morrissey conceded. "Or they could just be a bunch of arrogant pricks and not give a fuck if we know it was them or not." Mahone added. The other three stared. Trading glances, Frank looked back. "You know, just your garden variety collection of scumbags." He shrugged.

Heath shook his head, Dunn smiled and

Morrissey stared at the floor.

"Officer Mahone a word if you please." Morrissey asked. They stepped aside into a corner where Morrissey spoke in a hushed tone.

"Do all New York police officers engage in such extensive levels of profanity?" He asked. Frank responded in the same hushed pitch.

"Oh fuck no! It's against fuckin' departmental policy." Mahone limped back over to the crime scene where Heath and Dunn donned their rubber gloves and tried the passenger's side door. It opened.

"Jesus, something stinks!" Heath immediately declared.

"Probably a dead rat." Dunn suggested.

"I thought it was locked?!" Morrissey said.

"Apparently just the cargo compartment, Chief." Dunn added "But if I may make a suggestion? Regardless of what we find, in the press release we say it was amateurs, an amateur job."

"Let's get a solid handle on what we're dealing with before we start writing our own obituary, shall we?"

Frank smiled at Morrissey's remark.

Just then another vehicle pulled up out on the street. Two suits stepped out. Heath and Morrissey stared at the new arrivals as they approached.

"Sergeant Heath, remind me to submit another complaint to the chief Inspector regarding foreign interference of U. K. domestic investigations."

"Right Chief."

"They should wear signs. Save us all time." Dunn quipped as she watched the two suits cross the road.

"Special Agent Sims, how not so very nice to see you. I see you brought reinforcements." Morrissey greeted.

"This is Agent Bubba Cortland." Sims casually introduced. Heath, Dunn and Mahone gathered round.

"Been monitoring our radio traffic again Sims?" Morrissey challenged.

"Aw come on Nigel-"

"Inspector Morrissey, if you please, Sims." He corrected.

"Oh come, no need to be so formal we're on the same-" He was cut off as he eye balled Mahone leaning against the cargo compartment of the van. Morrissey noticed him looking.

"Sims, this is my new faithful, assistant, Doctor Watson." Mahone smiled and waved with his fingertips at Sims. Morrissey continued. "We were told you chaps might pop by for a gander."

"Really?!" The pugnacious looking suit next to Sims spoke up. "I thought ya'll just talked that way in the movies!" Cortland blurted out with a smirk.

"I do believe e"s 'av'in a go at us mate!" Heath said to the two new American arrivals.

Cortland leaned into Sims and whispered.

"What language is that?" He asked.

"Thick bastard!" Heath mumbled under his breath as he stepped away from the two agents.

"I understood you two were trained in homicide not robbery?" Morrissey threw the first dart.

"Well, there's two bodies, ain't there?" Cortland blurted out as he and Sims did a preliminary walk around observing the exterior of the van.

"Dunn, go and see how the uniforms are getting on. Heath call in and get us an ETA on the Hamlet tech getting here."

"Yes sir."

"Right." Dunn answered, Heath went out and Mahone stepped to the side with Morrissey. Mahone shrugged and nodded in the direction of the two suits now on the passenger's side of the van.

"FBI. London office." Quietly Morrissey informed him.

"Any good information for us yet?" Sims asked over not really expecting an answer. He called from around the van as he pointed down to the dash board inside the van. Cortland nodded, looked immediately to the dash board and examined the three inch diameter hole.

"Nigel, what'a ya make of this hole in the dashboard?" Sims yelled over as he leaned in and perused the slightly mangled, ten inch, perfectly round hole in the dashboard. Cortland moved quickly to measure the hole with a small pocket tape he produced from his jacket pocket.

"Coffee cup holder I reckon." Morrissey called back.

Dunn returned. "All's well Inspector." She reported. "FBI, geniuses ain't they?" Dunn remarked as she stood off to the side next to Mahone who shook his head.

"Now Dunn, they're your American cousins, we must treat them with due respect." Frank said without a trace of respect.

"Lincoln!" Dunn said to Mahone.

"What?"

"*Our American Cousins*. The name of the play Mary Todd dragged Lincoln to when he was assassinated." She said.

"Good to know. Never know when that might come in handy." Frank complimented her.

Cortland and Sims wandered around to the opposite side of the van.

"What'a you think?" Cortland quietly asked Sims as they stared at the dash board, the other four out of ear shot

"I think the eggheads back at D.C. were right. It's the only thing missin' outta the dash. The model 3.2-89 was the largest contemporary model at the time and this hole is about the right size."

"Maybe they wrapped it in sum kind'a casing? You know, ta make it look bigger. Kind'a like, a dee-squise?" Cortland suggested.

"Maybe. Maybe not. Get some photos, re-measure the gap to be sure and let's get the hell outta here. I'll keep inspector Morse busy."

To buy time for Courtland, Sims wandered back around the other side of the van.

"Find something interesting Mr. Sims?" Morrissey probed.

"Agent Sims. **Special** Agent Sims, Mr. Morrissey."

"Mister Morrissey?! Let's don't be so formal, Jeremy. Call me Inspector."

Seconds later Cortland appeared and nodded at Sims.

"Well, not much we can do here. I guess we'll mosey along." Sims casually said. "Good day Nigel. Don't forget to let us know if there's anything we can do to help out. After all, we're on the same team ya know."

"Good-bye Sims, lovely to see you again. Leaving that is." Morrissey quipped.

The two agents headed back out to their car.

"By the way, there's a new donut shop opened on Canary Wharf." Dunn called after them.

They all watched as the two climbed into their car and drove off.

"What the fuck was that all about?" Frank inquired.

"He's FBI?!" Heath declared his interrogative.

"Not just FBI. Head of a special task force." Dunn informed.

"Now he knows that we know who he is."

"How?" Frank questioned.

"I have a friend in MI5, I asked him to pull the local FBI files before I left the Yard this morning." Morrissey explained.

"What kind of task force?"

"We don't know but apparently he's been around the Bureau for donkey's ears but was pulled off whatever he was doing someplace else to look in on us."

"Should we be flattered?" Dunn cracked.

"What difference can it make and what the fuck is 'donkey's ears'?" Mahone asked.

"It means for a very long time." Dunn informed.

"The difference is the FBI don't like their shroud of mystery stripped away from them. Feeds into their paranoia that they're not immortal"

"You don't trust these assholes?!" Mahone asked.

"He told me there were 'bodies'."

"So?"

"So unless the American Government has lately taken to issuing X-Ray vision to equip her FBI agents, he had no way to know there was more than one body involved here. The 614 merely stated homicide, not multiple homicides."

"They could have researched the records?" Frank suggested.

"If they did they would have had to use our records. It's a U. K. domestic case, the Yanks wouldn't keep records of it unless it went through INTERPOL. I checked, Sims didn't access The Met or INTERPOL and they couldn't have talked to Hamlet or they would have mentioned it when they were called by us to send an agent down here. They don't care about the money or the guards. There's something else." Morrissey opined.

"Too bad we can't have them followed!" Frank remarked. "What about tailing them for a little while? See where they go?"

Morrissey smiled at Heath who nodded back.

"No need" Dunn added.

"What the hell you people up to?!" Mahone asked.

"I put it in the rear, left wheel well." Heath boasted to Morrissey.

"Huh! A little James Bond shit!" Frank said as he realized the Feds had been tagged with a tracker. "Hat's off to you guys!"

They turned their attention back to the van.

Morrissey crouched and picked up one of the cut ends of the black zip ties.

"Is it feasible that someone stumbled over the van while dodging the coppers?"

"Not a chance." Frank said. "This job was carefully planned well in advance. Including the part where they probably killed the first guard then forced the other one to drive here."

"Forced to drive here at gun point before they whacked him." Heath added.

"Whacked? Suddenly we're in The Sopranos?" Dunn chided Heath.

"How the hell did they drive at all? This Batmobile hasn't even got an ignition slot for a key!" Heath observed.

"Inspector!" It was Dunn calling from the other side of the cab. "Think I found what's causing the smell." When the others approached she pointed down under the passenger's seat, to the decaying remnants of human hand.

"Wonder if that's all that's left of the bodies?" She asked.

"Well there's no doubt it belonged to one of the guards." Mahone affirmed as he wrapped a handkerchief around his hand, picked it up and examined it.

"How the hell do you know that and why in God's name would they cut off his hand?" Dunn challenged.

Mahone pointed to the faded scar on the skin flap between the thumb and forefinger. He double checked that the parking brake was on and applied the hand to a small metal plate on the right side of the steering column. He had to reach in and pump the gas pedal a few times but as he did the van's engine coughed and sputtered to life.

"Surgically embedded microchip." He reapplied the hand to shut down the engine. "Turns the motor off the same way." He informed them before he tossed the hand back to Heath who quickly threw his hands in the air and back peddled causing it to bounce off his chest and fall to the floor.

"You're a proper arsehole you are!" The big man spat.

"Why are there no blood stains? Even after eighteen years-" Heath asked.

"Nineteen." Dunn corrected.

"Even after so many years there should be remnants of stains at least."

"They killed him first then took their time driving the van here."

"Likely took three maybe four men the better part of twenty to thirty minutes to unload over five hundred million in dosh." Morrissey elaborated.

"Dosh?" Mahone asked.

"Cash, money." Dunn explained.

"Any you guys seen *Witness*?" Frank asked.

"What is it?"

"A film." He answered.

"Why?" Heath jumped in.

"Took an army of skilled people over twelve years to bring that film to the big screen."

"So what's your point?" Heath pushed.

"You can't rush perfection!" Frank boasted. "We'll catch these assholes. They're too fucking stupid not to get caught."

"Nuthin' like a cocky Yank to boost morale, eh?" Heath commented.

"Well boys and girl, we can't wait all day for this Hamlet fella. Detective Mahone and I will stand-by here, Dunn, you and Heath check to see if the uniforms have uncovered anything then take the patrol car, get back to the Yard and get to work tracking down the leads I've given you. Detective Mahone and myself will ride back in my car."

"Should we notify PR so they can prepare a statement for the press?" Dunn asked.

"We won't have to."

"Why's that?" Heath inquired.

"The FBI lads will do it for us. They'll leak the discovery." Morrissey said.

"Why would they do that?" Dunn asked.

"Wantin' to grab the PR for themselves. God knows they need it these days!" Frank offered.

"Plus they're probably hoping to drop as many obstacles in our path as possible." Morrissey added as he perused Mahone.

"They're hiding something." Frank added.

"Such as?" Dunn asked.

"No idea." Morrissey said. "Detective Mahone, I don't suppose there's anything you can do about our FBI friends?"

"Inspector, by virtue of the fact they have nearly unlimited resources with upwards of 40,000 personnel on the books they are the premier law enforcement agency in the world. But the reality is the home office can't keep tabs on all the rouge agents that are out there. Those facts combined with all the political shit they're wrapped in now days . . ."

"I see. Okay, you two'd better shove off." Morrissey instructed.

"Yes sir. Heath, let's go." Dunn nodded. The two left.

"Detective Mahone, would you like a coffee?"

"Isn't it a little warm for coffee?"

"I thought all you New York police types always drank coffee when you were standing around working on a big case?"

"It's 'on the job' and this ain't *NYPD Blue*, and call me Frank. We just gonna leave the scene and stroll off for a coffee?"

"Oh, God no! We'll send a PC!"

Just then a black Lexus pulled up to the barricade up the road and was waved through.

"He must have heard us. We'll have to forgo the coffee." Morrissey sighed.

The vehicle drove the short way down to the garage and delivered a diminutive, middle-aged man in a rumpled suit who presented I.D. to the effect of the Head of Internal Security for Hamlet Security Limited.

Without discussion the three proceeded to the rear of the van and the small man produced a key ring with two long, custom made keys and a third, shorter key with teeth on both edges. After unlocking the rear door he used the double edged key to unlock the narrow, floor to ceiling, rotating personnel compartment leading into the main cargo bay which allowed only one man at a time to enter. The man went through first then Morrissey followed by Mahone.

Once Frank squeezed through the space he found Morrissey and the Hamlet exec standing staring, speechless at what they saw.

"I heard you guys were good but, finding the property before the suspects steal it!" Frank quipped. All the three could do was stare. "What's your best guess?" Mahone idly queried.

"The butler in the parlor with a spanner!" Morrissey quipped.

"Uh huh. What the fuck's a spanner?"

"Mister Higgins, any educated guesses?" Morrissey ventured to the Hamlet rep.

"Excuse me gentlemen." The exec mumbled as he squeezed past the two cops back through the rotating door and went out into the street while dialing his mobile.

"Put Banbury on the line, immediately!" He commanded as he stepped further into the street to be certain he was out of ear shot. There was a pause on the other end of the line.

Hello. Hello?!

"Mr. Banbury, Higgins here! You're not going to believe what they found!"

Tell us.

"It's all there!"

What's all there? Stop speaking in riddles man!

"The money! It all appears to be there. Still paletted and on the original racks!"

On the other end the exec herd the phone drop.

CHAPTER EIGHT

22 Bishopsgate
The Square Mile,
London

The as of yet to be completed Bishopsgate Development is a mixed use, sixty-two storey glass and steel structure on the eastern edge of the financial district.

England's latest effort to compete with Manhattan as the financial center of the western world, Bishopsgate, although not yet finished, was rapidly rising to add to the eclectic London skyline.

Engulfed by controversy since day one nearly a decade ago, #22 now has only the top few floors remaining to be completed and with most of the corporate tenants occupying the lower floors and settled in, the upper floors had been designated as 'luxury' apartments, meaning prospective tenants were required to give their first born as collateral before moving in, and so were as of yet unoccupied.

That morning the spacious lobby was alive with activity.

At the circular reception/security desk, centered in the spacious lobby, phones rang almost continuously while people scurried in and out of the street level doors.

Having risen from an innocuous little warehouse in the borough of Holborn, Hamlet Security now occupied the north east corner of the third floor of the behemoth structure now commonly being referred to simply as "Number 22".

The same morning of the van's discovery, actually less than an hour after, the *BBC Breakfast* program on BBC One broke the story that Hamlet's long missing security van had been found.

On hearing the news Anakin Banbury was motivated to call an urgent meeting at the head office in Number 22.

Fortunately for Banbury he was able to organize the informal but urgent get together on short notice because, just as predicted, the BBC News broadcast's breaking story all through the day was that a missing armored van belonging to the Hamlet Security Ltd firm had been found. That's all. Strangely enough the fact that the missing money had also been found wasn't made public.

For reasons he explained to no one, Morrissey ordered that news of the cash not be released and a twenty-four hour armed guard put on the van after forensics had cleared the scene and the vehicle had been towed to undisclosed police impound.

Also unexplained was his order that one of the SHIT Squad's inspectors be continually stationed in rotating 12 hour shifts with the van at the impound office.

The Hamlet security tech who unlocked the van was sworn to secrecy under penalty of prosecution and Franklin Heath drew the first shift.

Back at Number 22 Peter Grahams, now

ambulating via an electric wheel chair, steered himself off the lift, down the hall and as the receptionist held the door open for him, entered Anakin's office.

His salt and pepper hair betraying signs of his age, Anakin sat comfortably but nervously behind his large, Louis XIV desk when his now retired GM entered.

"Morning Boss."

"Morning Peter."

"You heard?"

"Put the telly on as soon as you rang." Anakin shot back "Drink?" He asked as he moved toward the small bar off to side of his corner desk.

"Bit early for me mate. Besides, Judy's been on to me about quitting."

"Kidneys acting up again?"

"Waiting on the results of the last scan."

Anakin iced his double scotch and returned to his desk then plopped back down taking full advantage of his overstuffed, his high back chair.

"Who did we have those vans insured with?" Grahams queried.

"RSA through Lloyds."

"What have they said, I mean what's their position?"

"No way to know." Anakin spouted.

"What do you mean? Why not?"

"The Met apparently haven't contacted them yet."

"You sure?" Peter queried.

Paddy Kelly

"I rang them right after you rang me and asked if there was anything I needed to know before I went into the morning board meeting. They said there was nothing out of the ordinary." Anakin sat back and thought. "If the BEEB's gotten a hold of the story, that must mean someone, a third party leaked it." He deduced.

"Either that or the BBC's gotten onto a bad source." Grahams proposed.

"Given the hubbub over the Fake News epidemic now days there's little chance they're not double checking their sources. Besides, it's not CNN we're talkin' about, it's the BBC!"

"Given their recent propensity to follow the American left wing media trend I wouldn't put too much stock in that!" Grahams countered.

"Point taken." Anakin added. "The obvious deduction then is the insurance agent at RSA must be lying about not knowing."

"Which in turn means the coppers have told them to lie." Peter suggested.

"Is that what you think?!" Panic tainted Anakin's voice. "Why would the Met want to hide what they found?"

"Not a clue. What'd they say when they called here?" Grahams probed.

"They just wanted someone to come and let them into the van."

"Who'd you send down?" Peter asked.

"Higgins."

"Higgins is a good man. He'll know to keep it

159

quiet until we say otherwise." Peter threw out. "Maybe they got suspicious when you didn't show up?"

"Not necessarily. They weren't initially looking for the head man, just to get into the van."

"Why didn't you go, just out of curiosity?" Peter asked.

"Wouldn't look too good. Look too suspicious, too concerned. Besides, there was no reason for me to go."

He held his tongue but Grahams was puzzled at this last statement. Anakin turned to his intercom.

"Janeen, call down to records and have them pull the log books from 1999."

All of them sir?

"No, just the ones you haven't become emotionally attached to. Yes all of them!" Grahams threw him a dirty look. Banbury buzzed the secretary back. "Yes please Janeen. All of them. Thank you love."

"Shouldn't we contact the Met and ask some questions?" Grahams asked.

"Like what?"

"Like exactly what they found? Where they found it, what if anything they've uncovered about the two thievin' bastard guards that took our money and our van?"

"Why the urgency? So they found the van! We've been paid. The insurance company retrieves their money along with a profitable interest check based on the inflationary rates since 2000. At some point I'll make a speech about how great the Met is and we all carry on as usual."

"And when people start asking questions about why you risked hiding so much money?"

"Because it was either that or risk there being no money at one minute after midnight due to a possibly unsolvable computer virus! No cash at the banks, no cash at the ATM's and, only days later, no cash in anyone's pocket. No cash to buy food water or other life-saving necessities."

Anakin prepared another drink. "You remember that disaster film where the meteor is hurtling towards the earth and there's panic in the streets? It would be a bit like that only not as much fun."

"I'm thinking about the guards' families. To have all this dragged up again after twenty years!" Peter argued.

"It's only been nineteen years." Anakin corrected.

"At the very least they'll have some kind of closure. Plus, now it's only a matter of time before the authorities find and catch those two and whoever else was in on this."

Anakin came around from behind his desk.

"Peter, why do you think I decided to by-pass the stockholders in the first place? Running it through the Board would have taken ages and after they realized we were-"

"You were!" Peter interjected to Anakin's surprise.

"Acting in their best interest. Even then they

would probably have approved it anyway." He poured a second drink as there was a knock on the door.

"Yes you explained this to me back in '99."

"Enter." It was his secretary with an arm full of hard bound log books.

"The Met's just rang in. They want to drop by and have a chat." She added.

"Not like they weren't unexpected." He said to Peter. "Thank you. And Janeen!"

"Yes sir?"

"Sorry I snapped at you. I've been a bit edgy lately. A bit concerned over this new merger deal."

"I understand Mister Banbury. Don't give it a second thought."

"Thanks Janeen." She left.

Peter steered his chair closer to Anakin's desk.

"Anakin?"

"Yes Peter?"

"Whatever you did you did and that's in the past. But what I need explained to me, and it need never leave this room, is exactly how you kept your position in this firm after instituting *Operation Hide & Seek* without telling the Board, losing well over half a billion Sterling and two fully vetted guards when the Board obviously had the option of preferring grand larceny charges and possibly accessory to murder against you if the guards' bodies were found?"

"That's a more than fair question Chumly! Sure you don't care for a scotch?"

Grahams shook his head no as Banbury fixed himself his third in last twenty minutes.

"At first they were going to prefer charges and quite possibly even murder charges. They even went so far as to hire a few Pinkerton's out of Boundary House. But when I quietly explained, in private, to the two largest shareholders, that I may have overestimated on the insurance–"

"You mean lied?" Grahams snapped.

"Accidently-on purpose overestimated on the insurance amount required and if, despite the extremely remote possibility of anything happening something did happen, we would stand to pocket an extra twenty-five per cent on our principle . . . well . . . they quite quickly came around to more clearly see my way of thinking."

"And if it wasn't a scare, and the virus did hit?" Grahams pushed.

"And if it wasn't a scare and the mythical Y2K virus had hit, we would have been one of the only games in town able to guarantee our clients cash-on-hand for the inevitable run on the banks which would occur once word got out. Which would not only enable us and our clients to carry on, but put Hamlet in the extremely enviable position to-"

"To dictate the market standard for cash!" Grahams suddenly realized.

"Until some whiz kids banged away day and night and figured out a solution, yes. Now you're thinking strategically Peter."

In an almost congratulatory manner Banbury

finished his drink.

"And if all went as per scenario, which it did, the insurance paid off, as it did, and our clients were still able to conduct business, which they were and three-hundred and seventy-five million quid extra went to Hamlet Ltd., a tidy profit which insured that Hamlet had operating cash until the Y2K thing got sorted, which it did and we-"

"You! Pocketed an eight per cent bonus of 30 million!"

"Are the toast of the town for having such foresight!"

Though still not in full agreement Grahams began to soften his tone.

"But all that was for naught, Peter Old Boy. Dust in the wind as it were. There was no Y2K virus." He sipped at his scotch.

"All that happened was a half billion went missing!" Grahams sarcastically pointed out.

"Temporarily misplaced."

"And the extra insurance money payoff in the event it all went south? How in God's name did you convince those geezers at Lloyd's to insure over one and a half billion hidden in armored vans?"

"Geezer, singular. I might have forgotten to tell them about the armored vans bit. They assumed I was relocating the cash somewhere else in the facility out of the time lock vaults where access wouldn't be affected by the virus and I simply neglected to correct them."

"But . . ."

"Their marine division alone does twice that in any given quarter. I made an arrangement with Thurston Howell at Lloyd's who manages all eighty-five syndicates."

"Syndicates! Appropriate name for those gangsters!"

"Agreed!" Anakin raised his glass. "Eighty-five syndicates worth untold billions, all handled by only about fifty managers. But all those managers are required to file quarterly reports with monthly updates. All to one man."

"Let me guess, Mr. Thurston Howell?" Peter quipped.

"Howell saw the writing on the wall when the trouble with Sterling Underwriting started."

"In the Summer of '99! I remember that."

"Exactly. He 'called the ball' as it were and saw the shutdown coming."

"Okay." Peter was immersed in these fresh revelations.

"So even today the managers of all eighty-five syndicates all submit their quarterlies to one office, run by our man."

"Thurston Howell III. But that's today."

"Yes, and our man is still in the game! How do you think Howell has lasted so long and climbed to the top?"

"Never gave it much thought but I've a creeping feeling you're going to tell me that by August of '99 Howell had correctly guessed what was going on with the Sterling mess?"

"He didn't need to guess! He was sitting on inside information that Sterling were going to be shutdown which would have devastated his portfolio! That on top of the pending Y2K scare . . ."

"Raped his portfolio more like! That very ballsy call brought Thurston to the attention of the suits at Lloyds and the rest is history." Anakin triumphantly concluded.

"The 529 Syndicate scandal! No wonder there was such an abrupt change of command and it hardly garnered a headline."

"As I said, three hundred and seventy-five million profit is nothing to thumb your nose at Peter! Surely even a moralist like yourself must see that?!"

"Maybe I'll have that drink after all." Anakin gladly poured Peter a measure of the twenty-five year old and they toasted.

"I've a doctor's appointment at half one but I'm free all day afterwards, if there's anything you need or-"

"I'll keep you up to date on everything as it unfolds, word of honor Peter! You just relax and enjoy your day."

"See ya then." Peter finished his drink and headed for the door as Anakin scurried to hold it open.

"Best to Judy!"

Grahams made his way through the large oak door and before the door closed over behind him

Anakin was back at his desk dialling an overseas number on his private land line. The line rang once before someone picked up.

"Señor Diaz por favor." Anakin said as he began rapidly pumping his leg. There was a pause and a voice came on the line.

"Si?"

"Diaz?! Recibe un mensaje para N. M. Necesito hacer una reunión!"

"¿Cuándo?"

"!Lo antes posible!" Anakin insisted.

"Nos pondremos en contacto con usted." The voice informed him.

Why Banbury needed so urgently to meet with Diaz was clear to only two people – Diaz and Banbury.

*** * ***

Mahone was the last to arrive that morning to the AV
room on the sixth floor of the Yard where he was to meet up with Morrissey and for the first time, the entire SHIT Squad. Instead he found a note telling him they were all to meet down in the waiting area of the Interview Rooms.

Dunn, Heath and Enfield had already arrived and were milling around outside the small waiting area nursing their coffees. The tag of a tea bag dangled from Dunn's cup.

"Where's the Inspector?" Frank asked.

"Requisitioning the prisoners." Dunn informed him.

"So today we get a two-fer, huh?" Mahone blurted out. The others exchanged glances and stared blankly. "Two-fer!" He repeated. "You know when you get two for the price of one? A two-fer?"

Dunn, ignoring the awkward silence, pressed on with the introductions.

"This is Enfield, you met Heath down in Brixton." Heath and Mahone traded nods as Enfield lunged at Frank with an extended hand, an ear-to-ear grin and all the enthusiasm of a child meeting his favorite super hero for the first time.

"Where's the Interrogation rooms?" Frank asked.

"As we don't beat confessions out of prisoners here Detective Mahone, we refer to them as Interview Rooms." Heath snipped.

"How polite!" Mahone mumbled.

"Interview Room B is ours." Dunn clutching a pair of police records took it on herself to fill Frank in. "We'll be talking to two prisoners this morning, Detective Mahone-"

"Frank."

"What?"

"Call me Frank." He perused the others. "You guys are all on a first name basis aren't you?"

"Actually the department discourages the use of Christian names while on duty." Enfield informed. "Unprofessional! So they claim." He added.

"The Inspector has taken it upon himself to rechristen us with nicknames." Dunn explained.

"He's our newest addition so he's FNG. Heath's Mohammad Ali-"

"We're you a boxer?" Mahone inquired.

"No. Outside of primary school football I've never played sports."

"Rohan's off doing-" She added.

"Rohan?"

"Rohan Rankor, he's the fourth Musketeer as it were. Gunga Din. He's off doing something for The Inspector."

"And yourself Miss Dunn?"

"Token, as in Token Female and it's a long time since I'm a 'Miss', but thanks for the compliment."

"Individual handles! I think I like this guy." Mahone complimented.

"What about you? How long are we graced with your presence here Detective?" Heath inquired.

"Orders say minimum three months, ninety days. We have the option to quit and go home early but-"

"But that would go over like a fart in church." Enfield interjected.

"Yeah. But, not an issue. I don't quit. Additionally we have the option of extending another ninety days, depending on our fitness reports."

"Reports?"

"The Inspector is supposed to send my boss in New York monthly-"

"Not an issue Frank old boy!" Enfield declared.

"Definitely not an issue!" Heath added.

"Old Crater Face hates doing paper-" Enfield

was cut off as the hall door suddenly opened and Morrissey came in.

"To quote a renown sports announcer, 'and a hushed silence came over the crowd'." Dunn whispered.

"PC Enfield, you were saying?" The Inspector coaxed.

"I was just . . . I'm not a PC, I'm a-"

Dunn elbowed passed him as she moved in to bail him out.

"I was just explaining to Detective Mahone what the agenda for this morning is, Inspector." Frank was already perusing one of the police records.

"Please carry on Token. Unless any of you'd prefer to hand it over to Old Crater Face?"

"Thank you Inspector." Dunn resumed. "There's a James Franklin, an IC3, currently charged with Receiving Stolen Property, B&E and Fencing. But he's really here because Special Unit found this in his flat." She passed Frank a photo of the canvas money bag with '#09361-99' stamped across it.

"A serial number?" Frank inquired.

"A serial number we traced to a bank which combed their records and came up with an account at Lloyd's owned by . . . three guesses and the first two don't count!"

"Hamlet Security." Frank smirked. "Can we connect it to the armored car case?"

"Probably, not sure. But something on Rankor's to do list is to get over to Hamlet in The Square Mile and have Hamlet confirm that this cash bag came from van #1989. Meanwhile we'll see what happens this morning. Our first contestant, also an IC3 is-"

"IC3?" Mahone inquired.

"Individual of Caribbean or African origin. Fella named Axel, refuses to give his correct family name, changes it every time someone asks him. We're running his prints now. Speeding while intoxicated. On a motorcycle."

"What'a ya mean 'not known' to you? You've got his jacket right in front of you." Frank pushed.

"Just means he's not a recidivist!" Dunn clarified.

"Why was he brought in instead of just being ticketed?" Frank asked.

"He's a known running mate of Franklin." She brandished the other police report as she spoke. "This knacker did some time for grand theft, possession of stolen goods and fencing. May or may not be a connection but Inspector Morrissey thought it worth the gamble."

Just then a uniformed PC popped into the room.

"Prisoner's in Interview Room B Inspector."

"Thank you Sergeant. Right folks, contestant number one, let's start with Axel." Morrissey turned to Mahone as the entourage was buzzed through the heavy security door and made their way down the long narrow hall. "You'll enjoy this one." Morrissey quipped. "Suddenly became a revolutionary 'brother' activist and a Muslim when they impounded his motorcycle for the first time three months ago."

"Drugs?"

'None that we've found."

"FNG, go and fetch Franklin out of the custody suite, have them put him in the room C. We'll need to compare their stories as we go." Morrissey directed pointing to the adjoining room. "See if we can't get at least one of these two lovelies to cough something up." He added.

Frank spied the sign on the door: 'Taped Interview Room'.

"One way glass, we can see in, he can't see out." Enfield informed Mahone as he turned to leave. Dunn rolled her eyes and shook her head.

"Yeah, I seen it once on CSI." Frank replied. From inside the room Axel waved at the four of them. "What'a we need outta this guy?" Frank asked Morrissey.

"Ideally anything we can get out of him that may lead us to anything regarding the van heist." Morrissey answered.

"You think these two were in on the job?"

"Oh God no! This one's a penny ante operator and the other one well, if his brain were donated to science they'd likely send it back. Postpaid."

"In the Navy they always taught us by making us do it."

"Your point being?" Morrissey challenged.

"I didn't come all this way to be a spectator. My accent might throw him off balance. Make him think there's something bigger going on than just a robbery rap."

Morrissey glanced at Heath then Dunn. Both shrugged.

"Okay." The Inspector nodded.

"Are the rooms AV equipped?" Mahone asked.

"England's over a hundred centuries old but we do have some technology." Heath snapped.

"I ask because in some jurisdictions in the States CCTV is outlawed in the interrogation rooms." Mahone calmly answered as he finally sensed Heath's simmering hostility.

"We have CCTV." Dunn interrupted. "As long as the little gerbil runs fast enough on the wheel to keep the generator going." She jumped on board.

"You sure you're not from New York?" Frank asked her. "When was that money bag found? The one the Special Unit found in Franklin's apartment?"

"A day or so ago."

"Okay. Anything else?"

"After Axel did his time he went straight as far as we know. Kept parole, kept his nose clean, found a job and so forth." Dunn informed.

"That'd be with this Waxman fella?" Mahone asked pointing at the file.

"Yes."

"Anything else I should know?"

"No Dirty Harry tactics! This isn't America." Heath snapped.

"Yeah, no English cop ever beat a confession out of an Irish suspect." Frank quipped. Dunn stifled a laugh, Heath wasn't amused.

"Let me have that photo." Frank requested. Dunn handed it over and winced when he folded it over and stuffed it in his inside breast pocket.

"Perhaps I'd better hide in the corner. Just in case." Morrissey suggested by way of maintaining control on the situation. The others waited outside the observation window as Mahone and Morrissey went in.

Sitting behind the table of the small room Axel smiled as they entered the dimly lit space. Outside Dunn turned the dimmer switch up to brighten the room for the CCTV. Axel sat back and slipped into 'cool mode'.

"Ahh! The B side has arrived!" He quipped.

"Morning Axel." Morrissey greeted.

"Well this is quite convenient! Two arsholes, no waiting!"

"This is a detective Axel, a detective from America." Morrissey remained cordial as he took the lead. "You don't mind if he asks you a few questions, do you now?"

"Sub-contractin' our work to Third World countries are we Inspector?" Noting no reaction from Mahone Axel decided to try again. "Sorry detective, I meant to say the Colonies."

Showing no emotion Frank took a seat at the table directly across from Axel while Morrissey quietly receded to the corner. Over the next ten, long minutes Frank sat and slowly perused Axel's jacket one page at a time in front of the cocky mullato. He then slowly closed over the folder and took a deep breath. He motioned as if to speak, hesitated and then reopened the folder and continued to read again.

Axel slid forward in his chair, cocked his head, and glanced over at Morrissey who stood arms folded leaning against the side wall. Morrissey smiled back and shrugged.

"What's 'is then? Good cop Stupid cop?" Axel again probed. "Failed the readin' portion of our Leaving Cert did we Detective?" Realizing he got through to Axel after another long wait Mahone closed the folder over and pushed it to the center of the table before he spoke.

"Wife, kid, apartment, in a nice neighborhood." Frank reopened the folder for a quick glance. "A bike. A Ducati! That's gotta be what? Twenty thousand bucks! What's that in Sterling?" He asked over his shoulder.

"A Ducati? What model?" Morrissey played along.

"Says here it's a Panigale."

"A Panigale! Ought'a be in the neighborhood of around sixteen, sixteen and a half thousand pounds I'd venture."

"WOW! A guy's gotta be impressed by that! How fast's it go?" Mahone asked.

Axel just rolled his eyes, crossed his arms and slid back down in his chair. Mahone went back to the folder.

"So . . . you're a member of the Taimas it says

here, are you?" Frank casually mentioned. The suddenly less cocky man adjusted in his seat.

"Oy! Don't try pinnin' nunna that gang sheit on me mate! I ain't never run with no gang bangers in me life! I don't know no Taimas!"

Mahone nodded, sighed and paused before speaking again.

"You know Axel, you almost got away with it, almost. And probably would have too, if only the bills weren't marked."

"What fuckin' bills you on about Yank?!" Axel snapped.

Outside Dunn and Heath exchanged glances just as Enfield returned.

"There's no way those bills were marked!" Heath protested to Dunn. "Were they marked?" He added.

"What'd I miss? What'd I miss?!" The slightly out of breath Enfield pushed.

"There was over five hundred million pounds in that van! No way could they have marked and recorded each and every note back then!" Heath blurted out.

"He don't know that." Dunn smiled.

"He won't fall for it! He's not that stupid!" Heath argued.

"Twenty quid says he will." Dunn, mesmerized by the show, challenged.

"You're on!" Heath shot back. He and Dunn shook on it.

"Count me in on that." Enfield imposed. "What'a

we betting on?" Enfield asked.

"The Yanks yankin' his chain." Dunn said.

"Is that where the word Yank comes from?" No one answered Enfield.

Back inside the atmosphere had developed a palpability as Mahone continued.

"Axel, even though there' a 10-20% loss of resolution on VHS magnetic tapes over the years since the Waxman thing, we were still able to-"

"What da fuck do Waxman got to do wif anything? I saved that old geeza's life now you bringin' it back to 'frow it in me face?"

"I was just going to say that I know you've been keeping your nose clean after a small mistake all those years ago and just wanted to know if you would try and help us with another case. That's all."

"What's old man Waxman got to do wif anything?!"

"Well as I was about to tell you, you know, so maybe you could help us out, Special Unit raided a flat over in . . . in . . ."

"Hackney." Morrissey volunteered.

"Hackney. Guess what they found?"

"Let me guess! The missing dosh from the Great Train Robbery? Amelia Earhart? 'illary Clinton's missing emails? Whatever it was it's got nuffin' ta do wif me!"

Just then, the security door out at the end of the hall opened and the sergeant PC came down with a three page report and approached Dunn.

"This addendum just came in from Central

Records."

"Thank you Sergeant." Dunn accepted it and immediately went to the sheets and read.

"This wanker apparently had some good in him at one point." She declared.

"How's that?" Heath asked. She showed him the report.

"Bloody hell! Fought off and killed three raiders and saved his boss' life!"

It was then that Mahone reached into his pocket and produced the photo of the money bag found in Franklin's flat, at first holding it so Axel couldn't see it.

"Son-of-a-bitch!" Mahone cursed as he turned in his chair to see Morrissey. "Inspector, here's that photo we were looking for all day yesterday! It was in my pocket the whole time!"

"Son-of-a-gun!" Morrissey declared with a smirk as he moved towards the table.

"Some pair youse two are! Can't even find a bloody photo in yer own bleedin' pocket!" Axel taunted.

Mahone unfolded it and laid it off to the side on the table face up then feigned rifling through his other pockets. Axel leaned forward and glanced at the bait.

"What's 'at supposed to be then?"

"That? Oh nothing, must have picked it up by accident. It has do with another case, guy named Frankwell, Frankincense, Frankenstein . . . something like that."

"Franklin, James Franklin." Morrissey again quietly volunteered from the shadows.

Axel's facial features melted before their very eyes.

"Axel! You okay? You look like you just saw a ghost!" Morrissey taunted as he stepped out of the corner. Frank remained expressionless.

Axel experienced the longest, loudest silence he had ever known as his whole life evaporated before his eyes.

"Axel?" Frank coaxed.

"Franklin you donkey!" Axel softly whispered. "What 'ave you gone and done? Donald Ducked us for certain, so you 'ave!" Even as he fell back in his chair Axel kept his eyes glued to the glossy, creased, photo. "Shove me fist right up your deaf and dumb so I will!" He swore.

Out in the hall Heath turned to Dunn.

"Was that some kind of confession we just got out of that guy?" Heath implored.

"Some kind of confession **the Yank** just yanked outta that guy!" Dunn corrected.

"Give us a fag, will ya?!" With the tone of a defeated man Axel quietly requested. Morrissey stepped forward tossed a pack of *John Player Blues* on the table followed by his lighter and Axel lit up before he opened up.

"It was a few weeks after the raid, after I slaughter housed them geezas in Old Man Waxman's chemists."

'Yeah." Frank said. All ears perked up and,

outside the room Dunn double checked that the digital recorder light was lit. "In mid-January of 2000?" Mahone confirmed.

As if entering into an out of body experience, Axel slumped in his chair, absentmindedly fondled the lighter and slipped into a haze as he quietly described the events from eighteen years ago. Events that would now land him in jail for most of the remainder of his useful adult life.

"A day or so after Waxman gets out of 'ospital 'e sends for me. I shows up and he 'rewards' me for riskin' my life to save his. A whole fifty pound sterling! 'Ats what my life is worf to that old fuck!"

"But you went back? A few weeks later." Mahone prodded.

"We was going back to get the rest of my dosh. Supposed to be like ducks matin', know-what-I-mean? Simple in and out! Grab the dosh and make the squash!"

"But it didn't go that way?"

"'E's fuckin' dead in't 'e?!"

"Who's dead?" Outside in the hall Enfield asked. "Who's dead? Who they talking about?!"

"Enfield, try and keep up with the plot, will ya?!" Dunn snapped. Inside Axel continued.

"Was me, Franklin, Jimy, a fella named Nathan and some bird we was tryin' to impress.

'Why we gotta come all the way over here to hit a chemist's?' Nathan asks me, leaning over the front seat the car. 'At was a good set o' wheels 'at was.

I knew 'Whiston Road was the only Pharmco

Waxman ain't put a silent alarm in.' I explains. 'If you would be so kind as to turn off here just under the A204 Franklin.' I tells 'im. So 'e does.

'You know who's on the till tonight?' Nathan asks me. 'E was always wif the questions, hoped more information would steady 'is nerves I reckon. Quite obviously it didn't, did it?

'Don't matter.' I says.

'Why not?' 'E says.

'Because my 'alf breed friend, we're going in frew the back. Jimy you and Mel is going in frew the front . . .' I says.

'Why the fuck we got'a . . .'

'SHUT UP!' I says."

"Where was the girl?" Mahone interrupted.

"Twixt meself and Franklin in front. 'Turns me on when you get mad!' She says. Playin' us two against each other like a coupl'a ping pong balls so she was.

'Youse two are goin' in frew the front.' I tells 'im. 'Try and attempt to look like a respectable couple.' I warns 'em. So Jimy begins tuckin' in his black leather shirt and metal studded vest.

"What'd the girl say?"

"Nuffin'. Just adjusted her chrome choker chain and checked her face rings in the mirror then smiled.

Nathan, Franklin and meself was to admit ourselves through the rear fire door.

So I tells him to park 'round back. A certain party was given twenty quid to make sure the fire door was unlocked for the precise period we was to be there. It was late enough so Old Man Waxman would'a been there. Only we shows up and the bloody door 'in't unlocked now, is it?

'Nathan would you be so kind as to go and tell my brother that the fire door seems to have been OVERLOOKED!' I tells 'im. A minute later Franklin appears in the back and we was inside the office rifling through the cabinets and desks."

"What were you looking for?" Frank asked.

"I'm gettin' to it, I'm gettin to it! 'You take that side I'll look along here.' I directs Nathan. And doesn't Franklin pick this time to decide 'e 'as to 'ave a piss?!

'What we looking for?' Asks Nathan.

I quickly rummages frew the largest desk wif no joy and then switches to the green metal file cabinet. Noticing Nathan down on 'is knees underneath the work table, I opens my mouth to chastise him when me fingers finds their goal. A small steel cash box where old man Waxman stashes the real cash.

Goin' about me business I proudly holds up the cash box. 'Nice one!' Nathan congratulates.

Suddenly and wif out warnin' we hears the sound of a gunshot echoin' off the wall out in the toilets. Some old bird up the front of the shop screams and Nathan and I legs it outta there. I comes out of the corner office and over to the jacks and there's Franklin, all slumped over like his best bird just ditched him. Then he opens that fuckin' stupid mouth of 'is."

Axel assumed a mock voice as he continued.

"'I thought the loo was empty!' 'E babbles. 'It looked empty but when I . . .' E says, and 'e looks like sheit!

I goes up to 'im and takes the pistol from 'is hand and smells it. Sure enough, it's been fired. Next I tries pushin' open the toilet door only it don't open, do it? Not all the way I mean. 'Alf way open it thumps against somefin'. That something was Old Man Waxman. At least what used to be Waxman."

"What happened then?" Morrissey asked.

"I sez, 'Franklin! What 'ave you gone and done, you fuckin' stupid twat?!' Then 'e starts makin' stupid excuses.

Axel resumed the mock voice.

'I needed take a piss . . . I didn't know . . . he just burst out'a the stall and . . . ya can't just burst in on a man when he's doin' a raid now, can ya?!'

'JUST GOT 'IMSELF KILLED DEAD! 'AT'S WHAT 'E DID DIDN'T 'E?!' I yells."

All three sat quietly while Axel lit another cigarette and composed himself.

"Nathan goes all quiet like and stares off into the distance.

"What can you remember happened then?" Frank asked. Axel didn't respond.

"Take your time man." Frank encouraged.

"At's when we heard sirens closin' in and legged it out the back."

Out in the hall Dunn held out her hand then

politely thanked Heath as he handed her a twenty pound note.

"Next Nathan asks me; 'Axel, what's that mean?' as he points to the L.E.D. panel readout on the wall as it flashes, 'SILENT ALARM ACTIVATED'.

'It's a good thing there's no silent alarm!' Nathan, in an extremely rare moment of lucidity gobs out. Suddenly the sirens in the distance didn't sound that distant. So we runs out just in time.

"How much was in the metal box?"

"Bit over a two grand."

The three took a breath and sat quietly for a long moment.

"Any chance of a coffee lads?" Axel asked. Morrissey signaled to the guys outside the room and they sent Enfield for coffee.

"At this point I suppose we right panicked and a second police car came screamin' from the other direction.

We was lucky because we dodged the coppers and drove round to the Mammoth Sports Ground to the other side of the rail tracks and into an alleyway. It was an area we scoped out the day before in case it all went pear shaped."

"Bob Marley Way?" Mahone ventured and even Heath was impressed.

"Yeah. Franklin found it. 'E's a big fan of reggae. At that point we was just searchin' fer some place to get out of sight for a bit when, Jimy who walked a little ways down the alley yells over, 'This one's opened!'

"Now you're still on Bob Marley Way?" Morrissey interrupted.

"Yeah. So I drives the car down where Jimy's standin' and by now he's inside. So I goes inside, and . . . fuck me! I sees this armored van parked all funny like, like they was in a 'urry or sumfin' when they parked it."

"Anybody in the van?"

"Wait'll I tell ya! I pulls Franklin aside and says: 'I thought you said you scoped this area out and there was nuffin' here?!" I says.

'Well there wasn't was there?' 'E says.

'Nathan, give us a hand, the bloody door's stuck!' Franklin says. So they both pulls and on the second tug the air tight gasket gives way and the door swings open.

"BLOODY HELL!" Franklin yells.

'What's wrong?' I says

'There's a bloody hand on the floor!' 'E says.

'What ja'mean a hand on the floor?!'

'I mean like a fuckin' corpse only from here down! All the bits from here up is missin'!' 'E daftly explains.

'DON'T TOUCH NUFFIN!" I tells everyone. 'I ain't goin' down fer no murder gig, incasin' there's bodies in back there you savvy?!' I says. That's when Nathan notices a bag of bangers n' mash spilt out on the front seat."

"Food in the van?" Mahone queried.

"'Ear Morrissey, where'd you get this Old Bill?

It means cash ya Turkish!"

Mahone turned to Morrissey and asked. "Should I be offended?"

"Not really. Carry on Axel, you're doing good."

"Cheers Gov! So, 'We gotta take the dosh!' They insists, meanin' the cash bag. So I says we split it up with the Waxman dosh later. Right now we're gonna leg it outta Brixton all together, over to Franklin's place where we'll settle things up there."

"Why'd you guys tear up the dashboard?"

"This more of your copper psychology Captain America?"

"No, I'm being serious. Why'd your guys tear up the dash on the armored car? Was there something of value mounted there or something, were you looking for a key to the back?"

"Look mate, we didn't do nuffin' ta that fuckin' van 'ceptin' lift a bit of cash in bag, that's it! Once we felt the coppers had cleared out we legged it! Besides, we figured the geezas what did the heist took all the cash. 'ceptin' what they forgot in the front."

"Okay. I believe you. Just one more thing, now that the cards are on the table."

Outside Enfield finally arrived with a carrier tray of coffees and handed them out.

"What's your real name? We have your prints, we'll find out eventually."

"It ain't exactly a name I want gettin' around, if ya know-what-I-mean!" Axel demanded.

"My word as a man. Never leaves this room."

Mahone pledged.

"Reginald. Reginald van Gleason, The Third."

"Kind'a royal! Ain't it?" Morrissey remarked.

Following his cup of coffee Reginald was booked into custody as an accessory to murder. James Franklin and his other two running mates were in custody twenty-four hours later.

The SHIT squad eventually discovered the girl was traced and found to have died a few years after of an overdose three days shy of her 22nd birthday. When her parents were contacted to I.D. the body they had no idea she was a drug addict.

"The parents didn't know she was an addict?" Frank asked.

"Found out the day they showed up to I.D. the body." Morrissey informed.

"Not much different than back in New York."

"Just one thing I'm not sure of." Morrissey said.

"Yeah, what's that?" Frank answered.

"What's a Taima?"

"It's the mascot for the Seattle Seahawks."

"The American football team?"

"Yeah."

"I get the feeling you've done this before"

"Saw it on an episode of CSI Miami."

**

187

The Galileo Project

CHAPTER NINE

AV Room
The Yard

That afternoon just after lunch Rohan Rankor returned to the squad's office in the AV room to report what he had found down at Hamlet Security in Bishopsgate during his interview with Anakin Banbury. Morrissey wanted a debriefing before Rohan typed out his report.

With Mahone sitting in it was just the three of them gathered around one of the smaller tables.

"Did you confront him about not initially reporting the van missing, but waiting until that Tuesday to notify us?" Morrissey asked.

"Yes, and he said it was company policy to immediately launch their own investigation to definitively determine if there had in fact been a crime committed." Rohan informed his boss.

"If there had been a crime committed?! What the fuck did he think? The guards were taking their time at Starbucks?!"

"Frank, language please! Go on, Din." Morrissey calmly chirped.

"They are a security company and **not** calling the police when you're victimized is something which they certainly have the right to do."

"Was there anybody else there when you questioned him?" Mahone asked.

188

"Frank, we don't 'question' witnesses, we question suspects, witnesses we interview. Din, was there anyone else in the room when you interviewed him?"

"No sir, we were alone. Mr. Banbury then went on to state that by that Sunday night they concluded it was a heist and that in all likelihood, one or both of the guards were involved."

"Were there only two guards?" Morrissey asked.

"Yes sir."

"You believe him as he spoke?" Frank pushed.

"Wouldn't be the first time an armored car heist was engineered form the inside and there was, is, certainly enough money to hire outside muscle and brains." Rohan surmised.

"True, but now that we found the money we have to readjust our thinking." Mahone added. "Was there anything that aroused your suspicions?"

"Well, at first there didn't appear to be anything out of the ordinary but when I asked him specifically about the money he said something that was out of sync."

"Like what?" Morrissey asked.

"I asked him, 'can you think of a reason why there might be any significant amount of cash in the front compartment?' He answered, 'Why? Did you find a money bag in the front seat?' 'No', I answered, but we have reason to believe there might have been some money taken."

"Good answer." Morrissey encouraged.

"What's out of sync about that?" Frank asked.

"There are about half a dozen ways cash can be packed for storage or shipment in armored vans, lock boxes, cello wrapped, canvas bags, marked crates."

"Okay."

"I never said anything about 'a bag'."

Frank and Morrissey exchanged glances.

"Interesting my dear Watson!" Morrissey cracked.

"Who's Watson?" Rohan asked.

"Just an expression sergeant." Morrissey told him. "So we're back to one of our original questions, why would there be cash in the front seat?" Frank asked.

"The guards having a little fun with the money?" Rohan suggested.

"And then what? One guard cut the other guard's hand off on a dare? Doesn't fit." Frank argued.

"If we go on the premise that the guards were clean my guess would be whoever did this left the money and bag there to throw suspicion on one of the guards." Frank postulated.

"Well money obviously wasn't their priority." Rankor added.

"Do we know if all the cash was recovered from the back?" Mahone asked.

"Before I left him I told Banbury we'd need a certified statement with the exact amount and anything else that was in the van the night they dispatched it from the garage. Meanwhile we're waiting on an exact count from forensics. Heath and

Enfield are over at the impound now trying to find out why the dashboard was damaged."

"Get us the forensic photos as soon as they're ready." Morrissey instructed.

"You'll have a complete file to date by five, half past at the latest." Din agreed.

"Well done. Dunn's on guard duty and Din I need you, to leg it over to the insurance company, you did get the details of the insurance company?"

"AXA, through Lloyd's." Rohan rattled off.

"Good, leg it over to AXA to see what they know so far then over to the bank, get the name of whoever Hamlet normally deals with at the bank and see what you can get out of the Moneychangers. Above all make sure you get exact figures in writing from them both!"

"And don't let on that you've 'interviewed' both or how much each told you there was missing." Mahone added.

Rohan glanced at Morrissey who nodded his consent.

"You think there's a chance the numbers won't jive?" Din asked.

"We're dealing with hundreds of millions of pounds sergeant, you savvy?" Frank responded.

"Point taken."

"Inspector, why use all your troops? Why not just let Dunn do what needs to be done at the impound since she's there already?"

"Because my dear American cousin, what you have no way of knowing is that there is no shortage of individuals who would be delighted to see our little collection of cause oriented coppers fail and fail spectacularly. Sergeant Dunn's assigned task is guarding that van until relived at which time another member of our intrepid force will take over. I don't want that vehicle left without a baby sitter for one minute while its down at vehicle impound. Din, are you relatively confident we'll get an accurate figure from Banbury?"

"He said he'd have his people pull the logs today, notify his accountancy firm and get it to us first thing in the morning."

"He doesn't seem overly concerned for a guy who lost a half billion in cash." Frank threw out.

"With that Y2K thing and the panic it caused he has a legitimate excuse for doing what he did." Morrissey defended. "Any significant friction is strictly between him and his board of trustees. Still, we should nose a little deeper into what security precautions he took."

"And who else could have known." Frank again chimed in.

"Is there anything else Din?"

"No sir, just the usual array of dates times, names and places. I'll be sure they're all included in the report."

"Well done Din."

Rankor rose to leave then hesitated.

"Something more Din?" Morrissey asked.

"For some reason walking back from there an old Hindi proverb came to mind." He blurted out.

"Lay it on us Bro!" Frank encouraged but was met with a quizzical stare by Rohan.

"I think he means for you to allocate to us your random thought." Morrissey interpreted.

"Yeah, what he said." Frank clarified.

"When we were children and we'd do something wrong my Nana would tell us, I am a good enough person to forgive you, but not a stupid enough person to trust you again."

"Okay. Do you trust him?" Frank asked. Rohan folded his hands over each other in front of himself before answering.

"I readily accept that Mr. Anakin Bradbury is a well-established member of the community. A hard working businessman who brought himself up by the bootstraps from a small one or two vehicle operation to a position of respect and esteem in the London corporate world as is evidenced by his company's standing on the FTSE."

"So **do you** trust him?" Frank pushed.

"Not as far as I can throw him."

****

The female PC poked her head in through the door of the AV room, looked around and caught Frank's eye.

"Detective Mahone, you have a call from America."

"Thanks."

"You can take it on line three." She added and

Frank moved to Morrissey's table at the head of the room.

"Frank Mahone speaking."

You havin' a cup-o-tea with some fish-o-chips mate? He immediately recognized Chief Wachowski's voice.

"Wow, for a minute there I thought I was talking to that famous actor, My Cocaine!"

Fuck you asshole! How are ya getting' on over there?

"Good not much, routine stuff. Good people. One semi-interesting case. A twenty year old heist job. Pretty big too, half a bill in English pounds."

Yeah I read something about that. I thought it was only seventeen years ago?

"Okay, eighteen years ago. Probably won't lead to anything. They collected the insurance, their stock temporarily dipped and they recovered. Case was essentially closed until a few days ago when some gangbangers inadvertently led us to the armored car."

What about the perps?

"Probably the guards or the guards in on it with some gang. We're still working it."

You need anything from over here let us know.

"Thanks Chief, but the FBI office is just down the road and these guys seem to have a pretty good liaison with them."

Yeah, about that. Frank listen, as long as I got you on the phone I should let you know there was an FBI guy here a few days ago asking about you.

"Askin' about **me**?! What the hell about?"

Don't know partner. Frank, is there anything I need to know? Anything that's gonna come up from behind and whack the back of my head off when I'm not looking?

"How long you known me?"

Long enough to know to ask what I'm askin'! You got any skeletons in the closet I need to know about, now's the time!

"Fuck no there's nothing!"

If there was-

"If there was you'd be the second . . . maybe the fourth to know about it." There was silence on the other end. "I'd tell ya!"

Good enough for me.

"You get that fed's name?"

Yeah, Agent Willis, Special Agent Willis.

"First name Bruce?"

Richard. You want me to ask around?

"No. Don't bring any heat on yourself. Besides it might tip the bastards off that we know they're snoopin' around for a sucker for something."

Just watch your ass over there that's all I'm sayin'!

"Yes mommy!"

Hey wiseass, in case you're not up on the news the FBI upper echelons ain't exactly scorin' any points with John Q. Public these days which is makin' the whole organization look bad! Between Comey letting' Killary off, McCabe lyin' under oath and Mueller lookin' to knock Trump outta' the box-

"Yeah, yeah, I get it. Same circus different clowns."

Don't push this aside! This sounds like a potentially high profile case you're on and someone could be lookin' to score big points, especially after the press gets wind of it or any progress you might accidently make!

"Chief I appreciate your vote of confidence but -"

Add to which Americans aren't exactly the most popular people in the world right now and it's a different planet over there.

"Okay Chief. Look I gotta go. It's almost tea time."

Just keep in mind, they think different than we do.

"Think different? You should hear the sons-of-bitches talk!"

****

Town Hall
The Queen's Walk, London

Confusing as it may seem to some, London does not have a single mayor. There are a small collection of Mayors running the city of London under one man they call 'mayor'.

Unlike cities of similar size such as New York where there are five borough chiefs but one Mayor, the British capital has a collection of mayors.

There is an elected mayor who also acts as the ceremonial Lord Mayor of Greater London as well as a ceremonial mayor for each borough while additionally the boroughs of Hackney, Tower Hamlets, Lewisham and Newham have their own elected mayors.

Despite this top heavy collection of administrative bureaucrats it is ultimately the voter, driven by popular public opinion, who calls the shots.

That morning, Sadiq Khan leading his loyal entourage of lackeys, made his way through the steel and glass hallways of The Neo-Futuristic Norman Foster Building, sarcastically called The Beehive, to the large town hall briefing room.

He was surprised to see a collection of about twenty secondary school students who were on a field trip, seated across the back of the room.

"Who the hell are they?!" Khan demanded from one of his two trailing Pakistani lackeys, one male one female.

"Students sir."

"I can bloody see they're students what the hell are they doing here in chambers?!"

"You invited them sir."

"I invited them?!"

"Yes sir, last week. To observe how their government works sir."

Khan waved and smiled at the students as he swore under his breath and took his seat at the head of the five meter long table.

Commissioner Cressida Dick, Commissioner of the Metropolitan Police Service had already arrived and was there, seated to Khan's right to render her briefing on second quarter crime statistics in London.

The meeting was the fairly standard policy info dissemination business sprinkled with the occasional Q&A, some financial info the mayor had requested and the borough heads exchanging ideas and promises to 'do more' on whatever the topic d'jour was.

Finally the increasingly negative crime PR was brought up and through an increasingly heated debate about patrolling, police overtime and pretty much a laundry list of band aides which would have little or no effect on the rising crime rates in greater London, Khan sought to cut the meeting off and adjourn.

"I think that about wraps it up for today's meeting." Khan's assistant announced and they all started to wrap things up.

"Lord Mayor, we still have the crime reports to-" Commissioner Dick attempted.

Khan nodded to his assistants who thanked the students for coming then quickly began to usher them out of the room. Once the kids were gone Khan stood and addressed the others.

"People," Khan started. ". . . given that parts of our city such as Newham and Tower Hamlets have reached 25% according to-"

"Sir, Newham is thirty-two percent and Tower

Hamlets is now 45% up five percent from 2011, particularly in the Muslim neighborhoods."

"Muslim crimes are not to be given to the press! As a matter of fact, no ethnicities or ethnic data are to be leaked under any circumstances, only crime types. And those given judiciously!" Khan sternly ordered.

"Yes sir." Dick said. "What about terror incidents and or threats?"

"Maintain silence on the ethnicity of the perpetrators and release their names only twenty-four to forty-eight hours after they are known."

"Anything else?"

"Yes, these idiots zipping around the streets on motor scooters throwing acid in people's faces do we really want to classify that as an act of terrorism?"

"We may or may not want to Lord Mayor, but the twelve poor blithers affected by people like this Croydon character certainly would."

"Knife crime?"

"12,980 in the first two quarters, up nearly 2,500 from last year."

Ninety minutes after starting, other than Khan's order to politically spin the crime stats, nothing of any significance had been resolved and so the meeting was finally adjourned. Again.

As the meeting broke up it was out in the hallway that Khan cornered his top cop.

"A word please Commissioner." They stepped aside.

"Yes Mayor."

"Knife crime, acid flingers, Russians executing their spies in my city and what do I have to contend with? A twenty year van heist that happened years before I even entered politics!"

"Actually Mayor, it's only an eighteen year old case."

"I don't give a bloody sheit! Bad enough we've now surpassed New York City in murders! I want this fucking fiasco contained do you understand?! I'll be the laughing stock of the civilized world! 'There goes the Mayor who let them get away with forty times what the Great Train Robbers got away with!'"

"Actually Your Honor, we still don't have the final tally on the Hamlet Heist. We think it only tallies to about thirty eight and a half times what the Great-"

"Get your people together and do what you have to do! Make it happen Commissioner!" Khan demanded as he stormed away down the hall.

****

Paddy Kelly

CHAPTER TEN

Woldingham School for Girls
Woldingham, Surrey
Monday 29 July

Deep inside the rolling hills and lush valleys of Morgan Park, Surrey The Woldingham Catholic Boarding & Day School for Girls is something right out of a Charlotte Brontë novel.

Founded in 1842 the 700 plus acres of the Woldingham's devotion to tradition is patently obvious from the first time you step onto the grounds.

Immaculately manicured lawns surrounded by meticulously trimmed hedgerows lead up gently sloping hills to a Gothic Revival building, known as The Mansion which is tastefully designed in red brick, slate tile and over-sized chimneys.

Multi-paned windows and terraced archways give way to an interior of marbled floors and oak festooned lecture halls and classrooms while traditional English school girls in uniform pepper the grounds and permeate the buildings' interiors.

Unfortunately this Victorian attention to elaborate setting and detail belays the ability to maintain what, in a modern day mindset, can be considered as a wholly secure environment.

The Sainsbury's Bread delivery van was halted

at the electronic, wrought iron gates while the overweight security guard struggled up off his stool and waddled out of the shack, clipboard in hand and up to the driver's side.

"Morning!" He merrily spewed to the rugged looking, thirty-something, Hispanic driver.

"Morning sir!" The driver smiled back.

"Watch the match over the weekend?" He handed the driver a clip board.

"I would not miss it, for sure." He replied scribbling his signature across the bottom of the delivery log-in form.

"Rangers pulled it through in the last minute!" The guard boasted as if an actual member of the team.

"Yes but Villarreal will get it next time, I am certain!" The driver defended.

The guard smiled and waved the bread truck through and less than a half mile down the long, tree lined road The Mansion perched high on the hill crept into view.

The driver slowed his vehicle produced a GoPro camera from his jacket side pocket and quickly snapped a few photos.

Restowing the camera he drove on and around behind Main House to where he spotted what appeared to be the building housing the dining hall and pulled over and took several more snap shots. The school's two blue and white Vauxhall people carriers were backed into their usual parking places behind the kitchen.

For the next fifteen to twenty minutes the truck's skulking around the grounds went nearly unnoticed. Nearly, until Dr. Wilson the Sixth Form chemistry teacher noticed the uniformed man bending underneath the rear of one of the people carriers and stepped out of a doorway in the back of the Marden Building.

The professor watched as the man stood and walked back over to his delivery van.

Wilson flagged him down as he slowly drove back out in the direction of the main road.

"You seem to be lost. May I help you?"

"Sorry, it is first day on this job." Wilson thought he detected a trace of an Hispanic accent. "I just delivered some of the breads and am trying to find back the main road out."

"Well you're heading in the right direction. Simply drive straight on and you'll come to it."

"Thank you sir."

"Not at all."

At the risk of thinking the terrorist jihadists will have won another one should he report a false incident, the professor considered notifying security but put it to the back of his mind as he watched the truck drive off.

What would I report anyway? He mused. *I caught a bread van delivery driver looking at a twenty-four pack school bus? Look pretty damned foolish!* He told himself.

He strolled back into his office.

The Galileo Project

*** * ***

Frank Mahone stepped out of the pedestrian turbulence and din of the London traffic and into the big red call box on the busy street corner outside Charring Cross Underground Station. He fished through his pocket for a handful of coins and spread them across the small metal tray next to the bulky pay phone.

Left standing to heed the calls of the tourist-o-crats in government after the mobile phone revolution raced to invent ever new and more expensive toys to satiate the voracious appetite of a gadget oriented public, a handful of the iconic, bright red London phone boxes could still be found sprinkled around the city.

After several failed attempts at feeding the phone then trying to dial direct, Frank gave up and dialed the operator.

Good afternoon, thank you for using BT Communications. How may I help you?

"Operator, I'm trying to call the United States. Can you connect me?"

Sir you can dial that call directly by using the country code followed by-

"I appreciate that operator but I'm-"

O, I'm sorry, you're disabled! I'm so sorry! She blurted out.

"Yeah, disabled. Lost my right hand in the war. Sorry to be a bother." He jumped in.

Certainly sir! What's the number?

"Zero one, two-one-two, four-seven-seven, seven-four-one-one."

Ahh! New York City! We were there once on 'oliday, me and my 'usband.

"How did you like it?" Frank cordially asked.

We was mugged! Your call is through sir.

"Thank you ma'am. Sorry about your-" The sharp bite of a click signaled she had hung up.

Thirteenth precinct. How may I direct your call?

"Chief Wachowski's office please."

Please hold.

Major Crimes, Chief Wachowski.

"Hey fat boy!"

Fuck you Mahone. What the hell you want and where the hell are you?! Sounds like you're in the middle of Midtown at rush hour fer Christ's sake?!

"I'm in a call box outside the Underground."

What the hell's a 'call box'?

"It's a phone booth! Ain't you never seen no movies?"

Not since Fast and Furious 12! What'a you calling about?

"This FBI guy-"

Willis.

"Yeah. You got any more dope on him?"

His name is Willis and he's an FBI guy.

"Outstanding report! I see why you made Chief. I need some skinny on him."

Frank you're not working on getting your ass in a sling again are you?

"Not consciously no."

205

So what'a you sayin', now you want me to milk this guy for info?

"Milk him for all he's worth."

Okay.

"Just like that? Okay?"

Yeah, okay. But you gotta seduce me first. Wachowski seductively chided.

"As long as I don't havet'a take you to dinner! I seen you eat!"

Okay deal. What'a ya got?

"An armored car stuffed with a half billion in cash disappears in 1999. Twenty years later-"

I heard it was nineteen years later.

"Fuck you!"

I read the story.

"It's discovered nineteen years later when some not-so-bright gang bangers trip over it while trying to dodge the local police. The ringer is, the money's all still there and the only thing missing is the guards."

Money's still there?!

"Yeah, but keep that under your hat for now."

The hoods jacked the van, got spooked and headed for the hills?

"I considered that but ruled it out. Too clean. Besides these gang bangers didn't exactly just step out of a Di nero film even before he contracted TDS."

Where'd ya find the van?

"Across town, some place where it wasn't supposed to be."

And nothin' missing?! That's a bit hard to swallow.

"Nothing missin' except for a bag of cash the gang bangers probably lifted after they found the armored car."

So what'a you thinking? The guards did a deal with some locals and it went bad? Never came to fruition?

"THE BAG! That's it! It's gotta be something with the bag!" Mahone declared.

Like what? It's a money bag! Is there something special about English money bags?

"Yeah, according to Morrissey they're half as full as they used to be!"

How much was in this money bag?

"Forty, fifty grand, same as our banks back there, only in Pounds."

Sounds like whatever you think you're onto Pisano find out what's missing' and you'll crack your case. Where do you stand with it now?

"I don't know, but throw in one dodgy security firm owner and a pair of squirrely FBI field agents and it makes no sense what so ever, which is why I think it smells worse than Hillary explaining about Benghazi! Which is why I need the scoop on this FBI guy snoopin' around the precinct."

I'll see what I can find out from Willis. Maybe invite him back for a meet outside the office and see if I can fish around.

"Just be careful, he may be dumb but he's probably not stupid!" Mahone cautioned.

"You tryin' to say I don't know how to work people?"

"No, why would I think that?! Look how well my marriage worked out after you introduced me to Jan."

Yeah, sorry about that. Just watch your ass over there. You're in somebody else's playground! Your primary mission is to observe and on top of that, we're not exactly their favorite brand of people!

"I appreciate the help Chief. I'll ring back in a week or so."

Don't you mean fortnight, mate?

"Fuck you. Sir."

****

CHAPTER ELEVEN

London City Cruises
Westminster Pier
The Thames

It was a soft, warm evening with a light breeze drifting out over the Thames and through the Westminster Pier when a uniformed deck hand was just about to take up the bow line from the starboard side bollard and cast off.

The gently bobbing tourist cruise liner was three quarters full and the merriment had already begun.

Mentally wrestling with whether or not he should bother getting up in the morning to attend his Economics class the young deck hand looked down the dock to see a well-dressed, young couple frantically racing towards him. He momentarily considered tossing the large mooring hawser up onto the deck and telling them they just missed the boat, but found himself transfixed by the rhythm of the girl's breasts inside her low cut, red dress as she ran towards him hand-in-hand with her date.

He was snapped out of it when they suddenly stood before him.

"Are we too late?" The out-of-breath boyfriend asked.

"No . . . no! Not at all mate! Climb aboard" He took their tickets. Ahhh! Big spender you've got here miss! Window seats!" He quipped.

"Cheers!" The guy grumbled.

London City Cruises' standard offer was a three course dinner and a show for sixty-five pounds. But as this was a special occasion the dapper young gentleman decided to spring for the extra five pounds and get them both window seats.

They found their seats, had a nice meal and enjoyed the first half of the *Elvis Dinner Cruise* as per scenario.

It was five minutes into the show's half time when her date suggested they go out on the fantail.

"It's cold out there!" She objected.

"Bring your coat." He countered.

"But it's so nice in here! And I don't want to miss him sing *In the Ghetto*! That song brings tears to me eyes."

"That's why I took the Elvis option! So's you could cry!"

"Don't be a bollocks!" She punched him in the arm.

"All I'm sayin' is it's more romantic out there! Come on. I'll get us some more drinks"

"All right but if I miss work in the mornin' cause'a your carry-on . . ." She warned.

"They'll find someone else to do all those old birds' nails that's what! Come on!"

They made their way out onto the aft deck of the fantail and the colorful glow of the Tower Bridge and the London skyline in the background where only a handful of passengers stood scattered around smoking.

With the cruiser gently drifting through the water he set his drink aside, took her by the hand, turned her to face him then dropped to one knee.

She gasped loudly.

Clumsily fishing through his side jacket pocket he produced a ring box and looked up to her.

"Donna Melisa Abernathy, would you do me the great honor of becoming my . . . ?"

Staring down in disbelief the young girl suddenly brought both hands to her face and screamed in abject horror.

"AAGGGHHH! OH MY GOD!" She quickly covered her mouth and began to violently cough up and gag. She attracted no small amount of attention as she backed away from her kneeling boyfriend, scurried to the rail and vomited up her dinner.

"Jesus Donna! You could've just said no!" He sulked.

Another couple tossed their half smoked cigarettes over the side as the woman ran to Donna and the man drifted over to the still kneeling, dumfounded ring holder.

"I'm not sure mate but, I don't think she's not all that gone on the idea!" He tapped the guy on the shoulder.

Just then the woman comforting Donna also let out an ear shattering wail while pointing down at the water off the port rail.

Along with several other passengers the fiancée stood, moved to the rail and spotted what the two women had seen.

It appeared to be a copse tightly wrapped in partially tattered, heavy clear plastic tarp. The half fish eaten, mutilated face was partially visible and, as if waving goodbye one arm gently bobbed on the surface.

Their continued wailing alerted everyone within a half mile radius including the couples across the river on shore strolling the docks.

A nearby crew member came bolting down the starboard side promenade, crossed the stern and bellied up to the rail.

Fifteen minutes later a pair of police boats were tied off alongside the pleasure cruiser, which now sat dead in the water. Two of the police crew were grappling with the body using gaff poles to guide it into one of the skiffs.

The number of rubber-neckers at the aft rail of the pleasure boat gradually swelled to gawk and watch as the river patrol tied the plastic wrapped corpse off to their stern ramp.

"Met River Patrol Three calling Central."

Go ahead Three.

"We are currently opposite Church Hills Gardens just east of the Chelsea Bridge and have found the reported object. It appears to be a corpse alright. We're securing it now. Over."

Roger Three. Can you identify? Over.

"Corpse is enclosed in some sort of plastic wrapping dispatch, Stand by."

Roger three.

Once the body was close up to the stern ramp of

the patrol boat one of the crew produced a pocket knife and carefully cut away some of the damaged plastic wrapping to more completely reveal the partially decayed face but still rendering immediate I.D. impossible.

Cutting further down, the corpse was discovered to be wearing a uniform of some sort. The boat commander radioed back in.

"Dispatch Patrol Three."

Go Three.

"Believe we may have a partial, tentative I.D on the body."

Ready to copy Three.

"Deceased appears to be male, thirty to forty wearing some sort of uniform."

Can you say type? Is it military?

"Negative dispatch, civilian. Insignia appears too mucked up to identify. "

Stand-by I'll notify the Met.

"Right. Shall we bring him in to station?" There was a short pause before the dispatcher came back.

Negative Three. We're in contact with The Met now. They've asked us to hold.

"Right, Patrol Three standing by."

The patrol boat commander ordered the two man crew to haul the body up over the stern ramp and on board for a better look. A speed boat appeared ripping through the water and down the central laneway of the river to disappear under the bridge. The other patrol boat slammed into gear, pushed off and gave chase to the drunken boaters.

Patrol Three, Dispatch.

"Go ahead Dispatch."

How many hands has your corpse got?

"What? Say again Dispatch."

The deceased! They want to know how many hands has he got?

"Hands?'

Look at your arm Patrol Three! See that thing at the end of it with the fingers sticking out? That's a hand. How many of those has your corpse got?

"Stand by!"

The patrol boat diver took the knife from his belt scabbard and carefully sliced a slit on either side of the plastic wrapping.

"Dispatch, Patrol Three."

Go ahead Three.

"One hand Dispatch. Deceased has only one hand. Missing the right hand."

Very good Patrol. Obtain witness statements and bring him in. Will have an ambulance standing by up river. Dispatch out.

Patrol Three, out.

Another twenty minutes later the police patrol boat had recovered its bow line from the pleasure cruiser and cast off back up the Thames.

It was close to midnight before the young couple along with the rest of the passengers, were back on Westminster Pier.

"What's that boat?" The distraught girl in the red dress asked the gangplank attendant indicating the ornately lit long boat moored just behind them.

"That Ma'am is the R.S. Hispaniola. It's very fine restaurant but it's permanently moored. She never goes out."

"Herbert?" She asked as they shuffled down the gangplank.

"Yes love?"

"Maybe next time we eat at the Hispaniola?!"

"Whatever you say love."

Later, on their way home in the taxi, with an evening to remember, she said yes.

*** * ***

CHAPTER TWELVE

**Woldingham School for Girls
Woldingham, Surrey
Monday, 5 August; 08:15**

The two dozen school girls, glad to be out of uniform and in casual attire, made no conscious effort to lower the noise level of their random chatter as they leisurely filed out of the back door of the main building and into one of the school's new custom made Vauxhall, twenty-four pack buses. Most left the building and took their seats on the smaller of the two busses as they were preoccupied with their nubile young faces buried in their mobile phones. Those that weren't, once on board, instantly joined ranks.

"Jennifer, are you alright?" Dr. Bowridge, dutifully standing by the door counting heads enquired.

"Yes Dr. B! Why?"

"You've severed your umbilical cord!" The petite student shot her professor a quizzical glance. "You're not surgically attached to your mobile this morning." The prof clarified.

"My mother confiscated it." The girl pouted. "Said the bill was too high last month."

"AHH! Fiscal responsibility! A very important lesson to learn early on." The middle-aged, well groomed woman cheerfully encouraged.

"Yeah, good lesson until there's an emergency!" She angrily snipped as she stepped up onto the bus.

"I tell you what dear, if we're hijacked you can use my phone to ring your mom."

Janet Bowridge's biology class was gearing up for their monthly day trip this time to further their knowledge of British fauna and flora.

Once on the bus the constant chatting continued. In between texts of course. Although they were all top students and conscientiously applied themselves to all their studies, they were after all first and foremost, teenage girls.

With everyone neatly packed on board Dr. Bowridge signalled the driver they were ready to leave and the Vauxhall backed out, made a two point turn and headed up the road and out the main gate.

Today's excursion would take them about thirty to forty minutes south of the school to the woods of the Westerham district where they would have a one hour trek through the forest, collect some plant and insect specimens and following a leisurely lunch, return home with their botanical and entomological treasures.

Thirty-five minutes into the trip they were turning off on to a side road just off the M25 and heading south into a remote wooded area where Bowridge had conducted many classes before.

Only minutes down that single lane, macadam road the bus suddenly slowed and turned right at a four way intersection.

"Ellen what's wrong?" Bowridge asked the driver as she lay down her book and sat up in the jump seat.

"What'a you mean?"

"Why are you turning right?"

"Just following the GPS. We want the Cloverfield clearing don't we?"

"Yes, but I've always taken them straight on."

"Sorry Dr. Bowridge, this is only my second time on this trip and I wasn't the driver last year. I'm just following the course we plotted before we left." She nodded at the GPS unit in the dashboard.

After making the turn Ellen slowed the bus and Bowridge stepped over to the dash and looked at the built-in GPS unit beside the speedometer. The red tracking line on the small screen in the map traced from the M25, ran through their present current position, indicated a right turn where they were and continued straight on to a point labelled 'Cloverfield'.

"Huh?!" Bowridge quizzically huffed. "I must be getting old."

"As are we all dear! Perhaps there's just a bit of road works on the other road or they've just rerouted the way."

"Could be I suppose." Bowridge accepted.

"So?"

"So, lead on McDuff!" The prof teased.

"And damn'd be him who first cries 'HOLD ENOUGH!'" Ellen playfully answered.

Several students up front shook their heads at the

two crazy ladies.

They continued on uneventfully for the next twenty minutes when the driver again slowed down, this time pointing ahead through the windshield to the ten meter high mound of rock and dirt rising nearly vertically, straight up from the ground and blocking the road.

"Well judging from the heavy overgrowth that mound was not put there yesterday!" Bowridge commented.

"Which means-"

"Which means two things: it's been there for some time and we've gone the wrong way."

It was then that a tall dark stranger entered into their lives. And not in a good way.

Dressed in a khaki shirt, camouflaged trousers, black combat boots and a shin-length black leather jacket, he made no attempt to hide his face but casually stepped out of the woods and in front of the bus.

Totally void of expression he withdrew a 9mm pistol from his waist belt and quickly shot out the front left tire which immediately sputtered flat.

Screams rang out from both women and chatter inside the bus immediately stopped as most of the girls ripped off their headphones or looked up from their mobiles. As faces peaked up over seat backs more screams filled the cabin of the Vauxhall. Bowridge clamped a death grip on the driver's arm and they both froze solid.

"Right on time." The man mumbled.

Slowly and deliberately, keeping his 9mm levelled at the driver, the highwayman made his way around to the passenger door and with the muzzle, tapped on the glass.

The terrified women exchanged glances and Bowridge nodded to the driver who opened the door. The man stepped up to the first step and perused inside.

"Good morning ladies, good morning. Sorry to interrupt your school excursion. We are about to take a little detour and I'm sure you will also find it very educational." He blithely announced.

Fear silenced the girls and women alike.

*

Main Switchboard
Scotland Yard

1936 London was the time and place of the establishment of the world's first automatic telephone connect system to the public and the emergency services. The Yard has helped lead the world of law enforcement in communications ever since.

PC Stewart, assigned to the central switchboard that morning had just started her shift and sat perusing the night log when the phone rang.

"Scotland Yard, central desk. Which service do you require, police, fire or ambulance?"

The female voice that responded on the other end

was laced with shear panic.

The Captain says . . . you're . . . you're to put some-someone in . . . in charge on the line!

"Ma'am, please try to calm down. What is your name location and the nature of your emergency?" Stewart could hear faint whispering in the background.

You're to put some-someone in . . . charge on the line! Please do it now or . . . the Captain says he'll kill one of us!

"Ma'am I need you to-" On the other end a shot was heard and the line went dead.

Upstairs in the AV room the SHIT Squad had mustered up and were about half an hour into the start of their day.

Dunn picked up the in-house line when it rang.

"Special Homicide, Sergeant Dunn speaking." She listened, nodded then hit the hold button before calling over to the two figures seated at the back of the room as she headed back to her work table. "Inspector, call for you. Line three."

"Who is it?"

"It's the Chief Inspector." Morrissey left Mahone and went to his large table-come-desk.

"Inspector Morrissey speaking."

Nigel, gather your people, have them stand by and meet me down in the situation room in five minutes. The Boss has just ordered an emergency task force be assembled and I need you in the main briefing room immediately.

"Will do Chief Inspector." He hung up and

turned to the group. "Token find FNG tell him to report here as soon as possible. Meanwhile you, Ali and Gunga stand by here till I return. Detective Mahone, care to join me?"

"What's up?"

"It seems we've been beckoned."

"What's the buzz Inspector?" Ali asked as Morrissey and Mahone were heading out the door.

"Not sure. Keep everyone here until I return to fill you in."

A couple of minutes later, along with two dozen other assorted personnel, Morrissey and Mahone were packed into the main briefing room where a temporary command and communications center was in the process of being hurriedly thrown together.

They took a seat and along with the others gave the Chief Inspector their undivided attention as the tall slender C.I. stood behind a metal podium.

"At exactly nine minutes past ten this morning we received a phone call from a somewhat distraught school bus driver." He read from a report sheet. "The driver, who apparently was forced to place the call under noticeable duress, uttered the phrase, 'He says you're to put some-someone in . . . in charge on the line!' and then hung up. The speaker was audibly distraught."

Some of the officers took notes on their hand-held, police issue note pads.

"Cut off or hung up?" Frank, not taking notes, called out. He could feel Morrissey's hand on his forearm even before the words were out of his mouth.

"Kindly hold your questions until I've finished bringing you up to speed! Thank you."

"Sorry Chief Inspector." Morrissey quickly apologized as the C.I. leaned in to get a better look at the guy in the second row next to Morrissey.

"Who exactly is that?" The C.I. asked.

"Detective Mahone Sir, he's American."

"Oh, I see. May I continue?"

"By all means Chief Inspector. Sorry once again." Morrissey reiterated his apology.

"The PC taking the call reported she could hear faint whispering in the background before the message was repeated. 'You're to put some-someone in . . . in charge on the line! Please do it now or the Captain says he'll kill one of us!' When queried about her location the PC taking the call reports she heard a shot and the call was terminated."

Murmurs wafted across the assembled crew.

"Apparently it's a school bus situation of some sort as one of the school girls managed to get a text off to her mother who contacted the school who in turn called here minutes ago. What we've learned in the last twenty to thirty minutes is that while on a field science excursion a Professor Bowridge's biology class from the Woldingham Catholic Academy for Girls appears to have been hijacked in a vicinity yet to be determined. Onboard the blue and white Vauxhall 24 pack people carrier were twenty-two to twenty-four schoolgirls between the ages of sixteen to eighteen, the bus driver, a longtime employee of the academy and a Professor Janet Bowridge. The vehicle **is** equipped with a GPS location device and we are currently attempting to ascertain a possible location. Ladies and gentlemen, questions?"

"The call, hung up or cut off?" Frank Again called out.

"Can't tell but sounded as though hung up."

"Which, taken in conjunction with the shot heard, means the perp or perps were listening in and likely present?" Mahone pushed.

"Yes, the 'perp' or 'perps' as you so creatively put it, were likely present." The C.I. responded.

"This 'Captain' fella, any indication captain of what?" Morrissey asked.

"Industry? The bus Captain at the local Hilton?" Mahone quietly cracked.

"We're running a scan for all known aliases or variations." The C.I. answered.

"We get these nut cases all the time." Frank indelicately added. "Didn't get enough attention from his father, delusions of grandeur. This guy's probably from the Bronx!" Mahone's comments were met with groans of disapproval.

"Vehicle make and model, on the Vauxhall confirmed sir?" A female PC in the back asked.

"Yes along with the driver and teacher, still waiting on verification of all the occupants. Plate number as reported by the school is PA 52 SMR"

The C.I. answered.

"Sit-rep on the Flying Squad sir?" Another officer asked.

"Anti-terror has been notified and are standing by to be dispatched as soon as we have a location."

The Q&A was interrupted when another officer snuck through the side door and quietly walked over to the Chief Inspector, handing him a message.

"Where's the hell's Woldingham?" Frank quietly asked as he leaned over to Morrissey, realizing his second faux pas at his first Metropolitan Police briefing.

"It's an upscale London suburb out in Surrey, about 30 minutes from Victoria. Most of the houses start at a million and go up from there."

"So when you get up into that price bracket you've got-" Mahone started. Morrissey finished his thought.

"Prominent Middle Easterners with kids attending private schools, Russian diplomats and oligarchs, rich footballers, celebrities-"

"Kids who every time one of their parents shits the FTSE spikes?" Mahone added.

"How colorful. You ever considered a career as a television commentator?" Morrissey quipped.

"No, but I got an aunt in Queens who's a telephone operator, sooo . . ."

"Well at least you have something to fall back on after you're suspended."

They were cut off when the C.I. again spoke.

"Ladies and gentlemen, you too Detective

Malone . . ."

"Mahone sir. Lieutenant Detective Frank Mahone, Thirteenth Pre-"

"Yes thank you. Full C.V. not required." The Chief Inspector grumbled. Now it was Morrissey's turn to lean over and whisper to Frank.

"You're quickly scoring points!"

"Ladies and gentlemen, I've got to duck out for a moment, please remain seated." The Chief Inspector announced. "Inspector Morrissey, a word if you please." Morrissey stepped over to where the C.I. had moved away from the podium.

"Yes sir?"

"Be in my office in five minutes." He quietly ordered.

"Yes sir."

The C.I. turned and addressed the rest of the gathering.

"Ladies and gentlemen, Assistant Chief Inspector Sommers will assign you your duties, and pending any significant occurrences, we'll meet again for an update in one hour. Call home, plan on extra hours tonight!" He added just as he stepped through the door.

Leaving Sommers to organize the group the C.I. gathered his notes and headed up to his office.

"Am I fucked?" Frank asked as Morrissey returned to his seat.

"We prefer the word 'banjaxed' and no, not yet. But you're making considerable progress."

✱

"QUIET! QUIET DOWN!" Back in the bus, still brandishing his weapon the hijacker motioned for Bowridge to take her seat.

Now that she was able to get a closer look at him, the professor made an effort to memorize the details of his physical features.

Easily six foot tall, a bit over. Good posture, possibly military or ex, particularly dressed like some sort of fascist. Ninety to ninety-two kilos, dark hair, brown eyes, square jaw. No visible scars.

Then it occurred to her that as he showed no effort to hide his face the possibility existed that he intended to kill them all. At least likely not to hesitate shooting anyone who disobeyed him. But her fears were partially allayed as she studied his jaw line while he rummaged through an inside pocket for something.

"You wanted them to think you shot one of us!" Bowridge challenged the hijacker.

"I see why you are the professor. Now let's see if you can maintain your line of intelligent reasoning and do as you are told before I am compelled to actually do it! Driver, you have the tools to change out that puncture?"

Bowridge listened closely to his pronunciation. Controlled yet slightly stilted. English good but definitely not native British.

"Yes!" Ellen fought back her anger as she rose from the seat and went to leave. "I'll get the jack."

She resignedly grumbled.

"Do it quickly!" He ordered.

"I'll calm the kids." Bowridge answered and stood to reassure her students.

"Leave the keys in the ignition and give me your phone!" He ordered the driver. "Now kindly get to it. And don't dally we have a schedule to keep."

He pronounced 'schedule' with a 'K', not as a Brit would say it. Only people from the Americas do that. But surely he's not a Yank! Her internal dialogue was running at full speed as was her brain.

He then turned to the students.

"Ladies! You will deposit your mobile phones in this bag. Cooperate and no one gets hurt!" Continually brandishing the pistol he then produced a black cloth bag and handed it to Bowridge. "Professor be so kind as to collect the girls' cell phones and do it quickly!"

Cell phones, not mobiles. Bowridge noted.

The earlier screams in the bus had been replaced with sporadic sobs and although none dare ask, questions abounded.

As Bowridge made her way down the aisle and the terrified girls obediently deposited their phones into the black sack, their assailant watched her as he reached over and bashed the built-in GPS device on the dashboard with the butt of his pistol then reached underneath and jimmied it lose ripping it from its plastic frame.

A dark haired student near the back, holding her phone low below the seats, quickly scrolled through her apps to the Waze location app and activated it.

"C'omon Malinda! He said **all** phones!" Bowridge coaxed, purposely speaking a bit more loudly than necessary.

"Yes Doctor Bowridge."

The young student smiled as she flashed the phone in front of Bowridge then carefully dropped it into the bag. Bowridge smiled and nodded back before returning up the aisle and handing him the bag.

"What if he checks them and turns them off?!" The student next to Malinda whispered.

"It stays activated no matter what!" Malinda whispered back.

"What about when the battery runs out?" There was no answer.

Finished re-stowing the damaged tire on the rear of the bus the driver returned to the cabin.

"Well done! Any feminist would be proud!" He mocked. "Now back this thing up into that clearing and turn it around."

"Where are we going?" She asked not really expecting any sort of informative answer.

"Your job is to drive so, drive!"

Glancing at her wristwatch Bowridge noted the exact time they backed up and turned.

Keeping to single lane dirt roads it was about twenty minutes later when they were deep in the forest and pulled into a small, cleared space amongst the large pine trees. The kidnapped teacher and students had no way of knowing it but they were only a few miles away from the old, single runway Biggin Hill Airport.

"Pay attention ladies! We are going to be spending some time here. You will dismount the bus all holding hands! You will keep moving and enter through the door in that concrete structure!" He nodded out the window to the only structure for as far as could be seen in the densely wooded area.

"Any foolish attempt at escape and the two girls next to you will be shot! Dr. Bowridge if you can be so kind lead them in. Driver you'll be last in line. You'll find a single light switch on the left at the bottom of the stair. Move!"

From the outside all that could be seen was a small, six foot square, non-descript concrete building heavily overgrown with weeds. The single door which had been kicked in and now hung by one hinge, and the unfinished nature of the structure rendered it to look like a 1940's style public toilet entrance.

On entering the professor and the girls found the long abandoned bunker a dark, rank smelling experience. Just inside the damaged door a long, iron spiral staircase led down over three dozen or so steps to a dirt floor.

The location, obviously scouted out some time before, suited his purposes explicitly. One way in and one way out.

Once off the last stair Bowridge halted the girls on the staircase and felt around the damp wall and located a toggle switch.

Throwing it open, it was under the iridescent yellowish glow of improvised lighting that the eerie specter of a WWII air raid shelter appeared.

At the base of the stairs a pair of the girls screamed as several large rats scurried in front of them disappearing into a hole in the base of the wall opposite.

"Don't be afraid Eunice! They're more scared of us then we are of them." Bowridge shakily encouraged.

"I seriously doubt that Miss!" Eunice's mate shot back.

The interior of the near century old shelter was an even more striking apparition.

Long dirt strewn corridors, no more than two and a half meters wide, were lined with dilapidated period bunk beds of which only rusting metal frames and springs remained. They were stacked three high and ran the entire length of the two meter high tunnel. The odd, rotting sign giving directions accompanied by sporadic graffiti on the walls was all that was recognizable as reminders of the hundreds of residents who gathered there each night during the relentless bombings which claimed thousands across England.

Their kidnapper followed them down and spoke in a loud clear voice.

"Make yourselves comfortable ladies! And I shouldn't be too anxious to explore any alternative means of escape. These tunnels are over eighty years old, in poor repair and some of the rear areas are attached to unfinished mine shafts hundreds of feet deep. If you fall into a pit or partially excavated area . . . I'm afraid you will have discovered your grave!"

He was pleased to see the intended effect was apparent on the faces of the young girls.

"What do you want with us?!" The Professor demanded.

"From you, nothing really. If the police do the right thing you'll all be home for dinner with mommy and daddy this evening. If not . . ." He backed out of the steel door and, after he closed it over, the girls could hear a large timber being dropped into the iron cleats bolted into either side of the metal doorway followed by heavy chains being wrapped around the rusting panic bar.

He then made his way back upstairs to the wooded area and placed a phone call.

****

"Is it absolutely necessary **he** be here?" The C.I. challenged as Mahone came into the office in front of Morrissey.

"Afraid so sir. Rules of the international agreement are quite clear. He's essentially my shadow."

Mahone made a mental note to later thank Morrissey for bullshitting his boss.

"Very well. Try not to get in the way Marone-"

"Sir it's Ma-"

"And please refrain from any sordid levity at future briefings! However street-wise you and your colleagues back in New York may be, in this country we maintain decorum and professionalism at all times! Do I make myself clear!"

"Crystal clear Chief Inspector. Yes." Frank politely responded. "I'll do my best Chief Inspector. And may I say what a pleasure it is to be here working with London's finest -"

"Morrissey, take a seat." The C.I. gestured for Morrissey to take the one chair beside the desk and like Marie Antoinette's head, Frank's mocking attempt at appeasement was whacked off.

"Our man's rung back and repeated his demand. This time with a slight twist. Now he's identified himself as a Richard Phillips! Claims he is 'the Captain'."

"This asshole's got a sense of humor!" Frank quietly quipped.

"Something to contribute Marone?"

"Richard Phillips! The *Alabama Maersk*. Somali pirates?!" Frank quickly synopsized for the Chief.

"I don't watch Arnold Swarzenegger films Detective." The C.I. passed a sheet of paper to Morrissey. "Either of these names ring a bell?"

"Kevin Michaels, Josh Hartley? No sir. Should they?"

"Just a long shot. About fifteen minutes ago this Captain fellow contacted Her Majesty's prison Wakefield-" He was interrupted as his desk phone rang and he picked up. "Chief Inspector, yes?"

Sir, it's him again.

"Is the trace set?"

Yes Chief.

"Then put him through." The C.I. put them on speaker phone and the connection was immediate. "Chief Inspector Lister speaking."

Chief Inspector Lister, sorry to ring you directly but I couldn't find a listing for the Mayor's new Wonder Boy Inspector Nigel Morrissey. Could you arrange for me to speak with him?

In shock the C.I.'s eyes shot to Morrissey.

"Actually, he's right here with me."

How convenient! Would you be so nice as to put him on to the line please?

"We're on speaker phone Captain Phillips."

Is there anyone else present?

"No!" Morrissey quickly answered while the C.I. signalled for Mahone to be quiet.

"Morrissey here."

Inspector Morrissey, so good to make your acquaintance. Congratulations on finding the Hamlet armored car! Have you any suspects? Has any of the money been traced?"

"Thank you. No and no. Have we met Mr.? Mr. . .?"

"Captain, Captain Richard Phillips, but time for idle chat later. I have some guests with me, several young ladies, two dozen in fact. If you wish to see them again you will follow my instructions. Are you understanding me?

"I'm listening, but you'll have to understand-"

Earlier I sent a text to the Met. You will arrange the release of Mr. Josh Hartley and Kevin Michaels who are currently being held as political prisoners in Wakefield prison.

"We don't have that auth-"

Nigel, I have it on good information that you had quite a privileged upbringing, yes?

"Your point being?"

You should know better than to interrupt! Please avoid it in the future! Michaels and Hartley are currently in Her Majesty's custody at HMP Wakefield. You will release them to a rendezvous point to be designated and in exchange your school children will be set free. In addition to my colleagues you will arrange for a payment of 100,000 pounds Sterling. Be so good as to put that in small bills if you don't mind.

After I have sent you the rendezvous point you will take my colleagues there with the money and your policemen will leave.

Any attempts to stall and two of the lovely young girls, who are under close guard by two heavily armed associates, will die. Any attempts at deception and two of them die. Any sign of observers, snipers or tails and the blood will be on your head. And Nigel, do not try and be clever by putting in a homing devices, dye markers or any of those little toys you use to catch the stupido street bandits. The delivery case will be scanned and your men will be under constant surveillance at the drop off point.

Morrissey glanced over at the C.I. who nodded in return.

"That'll take some time."

Take all the time you like, just keep in mind it's a beautiful Summer's day as we speak however, come nightfall in the wilderness these beautiful little children are going to get very cold and very hungry come sundown.

"What about the meet point?"

All in good time Nigel. The line went dead.

Mahone immediately checked his watch.

"It's nine thirty-seven that gives us eleven to twelve hours before sundown."

The C.I. immediately picked up and speed dialled the switchboard.

"Any luck on the trace?" The C.I. asked of the tech.

All we could get sir was that he's south of the city within a 30 kilometer radius before we lost contact. He's scrambled the signal about three to five seconds after we answered the call.

The C.I. slammed down the receiver.

"My ten year old niece can locate the nearest bloody shopping mall in 4.9 seconds flat on her mobile and all the modern electronic gear in England can't pinpoint one deranged lunatic!"

Just as he finished the phone rang again. On the off chance it was Phillips again the C.I. allowed it to ring three times to allow the trace to be set.

"Chief Inspector Lister."

Sir, it's Bangor in communications again.

"Yes Bangor what is it?!"

Sir we were just guessing at suitable hiding places large enough to hide two dozen students and a Vauxhall bus.

"Well, what in bloody hell are you waiting for, trumpets?! What is it?"

Sir, with no discernable abandoned buildings, factories or such, we're thinking fallout shelters or bunkers.

"Go on!"

Belsize Park, Camden Town, Chancery Lane, Clapham Common, Clapham North, Clapham South, Goodge Street and Stockwell tube stations all have fallout bunkers left over from the war.

"Dispatch units on silent alarms immediately to all those areas, order them to report when they are in site of the bunkers. Use unmarked units where available and get back to me with how many air mobile units we have available."

Yes Chief Inspector!

"Tell them not to approach until they've called back in! We'll be standing by! Also get that list to Morrissey and his Shitters immediately!"

Yes Chief Inspector!

"And Bangor!"

Yes Chief Inspector?

"Well done!"

Thank you sir.

"That means if he's in a remote location in or around one of those bomb shelters he's using a portable scrambler." Frank pointed out.

"Possibly military." Morrissey suggested.

"Yeah, and it also means he's definitely in the vicinity of the girls." Frank reinforced.

"Right, Morrissey looks as though you and your squad have an assignment. Let me know what you need."

"We'll have a strategy drawn up in the next quarter of an hour sir!" Morrissey assured his boss as he and Mahone left the office.

Lister reached for the phone and again called down to communications.

"Bangor, contact the school, see if they've heard anything from the girls' phones, the GPS tracker on the bus or anything else." Lister instructed.

I'm on it Inspector. The PC on the other end assured.

In the lift Mahone and Morrissey batted around ideas.

"He mentioned the 'wilderness'. He must be holding them in a wooded area somewhere."

"Possibly. Could've been a slip of the tongue or could've been a plant to throw us off." Frank suggested.

"Do we know the purpose of the field trip?" Frank asked.

"Bowridge teaches biology."

"Good! Then we know what time they left the school, what time we first learned of the hijack and we can safely assume they're somewhere in a wooded sector, within an hour of the school! We should be able to narrow the search area!"

"Good point. Save for small patches, all the wooded areas are well outside the sixty kilometre mark!" Morrissey noted.

"He wasn't just making small talk either. He was fishing." Mahone declared.

They stepped off the lift and headed down the hall.

"How do you mean?"

"About the van."

"Yes but he also indicated he didn't know about the money and he asked about suspects."

"False flags. If he's involved in the robbery he knows the money was left behind and so odds are he knows who did it! Was probably in on it one way or another. The question is why? Why in the hell would somebody go through all the planning, all the risk to heist a half billion in small bills and then leave it behind?"

"Apparently they got spooked."

"That's the obvious answer." Frank blurted out. "But someone with that much planning and balls to pull off a heist that size is not likely to be spooked that easily.

They entered the AV Room.

"Well what's your insightful answer that we are so **obviously** missing Detective?"

"I don't have an answer. But I do have another question."

"And that would be?"

"Why the hell is the FBI interested in a twenty year old-"

239

"Nineteen year old."

"Yeah, yeah, nineteen year old robbery case?"

"You're referring to the two who showed up at the van scene?"

"Yes. And where the hell do twenty schoolgirls fit into the plot?"

"I don't have an answer. There are twenty-six hostages and the answer is likely that they are pawns in order to spring these two geezers from Wakefield who will no doubt lead us to the actual perpetrators-"

"Perps!" Frank corrected.

"Yes of course, perps!"

***

HM Prison Wakefield
Wakefield, Yorkshire

At that moment the inmates were being herded out of the dining hall from their breakfast.

Josh Hartley had skipped the morning meal and instead remained in the common area playing cards.

The small pile of filtered cigarettes in the center of the circular table gradually grew as each of the six inmates seated at the table anted up for the next hand.

While Hartley was collecting his winnings Kevin Michaels was also occupied with one of his more favorite past times - beating the shit out of another inmate.

As they filed out of the dining hall an altercation broke out leading Michaels to man a metal serving tray and whack another inmate across the head. Michaels then used the bent over metal dinner tray edge-on to attack the Rastafarian's nose cracking bone and cartilage with one well-placed whack.

Blood gushed from his nostrils as he sank to his knees then fell over onto his side writhing in agony. Two others, one black one white, quickly joined in and as it looked as if a full blown riot was about to erupt Michaels cleverly faded to the perimeter of the ruckus just as the riot squad guards beat the four other prisoners unconscious and dragged them away.

Josh Hartley and Kevin Michaels were behind bars in Wakefield, alias 'Murder Mansion' for crimes Jack The Ripper would find too horrifying.

Between them they had taken nine lives, most in the commission of a secondary crime.

Armed robbery, robbery, extortion, blackmail, grand theft auto, arson and of course murder. As they were both professionals, they were what the Americans would call first degree repeat felons.

At 10:47 the guard at the back gate was occupied watching BBC Two's morning report.

Reliable sources indicate that up to twenty-four young students from the Woldingham Catholic Academy for Girls have disappeared while on a school excursion in the Surrey area south of London . . .

The guard in the control cage looked up at the telly in the upper corner of the small booth as he made an routine entry in the logbook. When finished he then peered out through bullet proof glass as the two thugs were being escorted through the outer holding area and towards a waiting, unmarked police van idling just inside the large iron gate.

In an effort to preoccupy and disrupt the London Met's attempts to engage in an all-out man hunt, news of the kidnapping and hostage crises had been leaked to the all-too-eager-for-sordid-stories press. The 'anonymous' tip had been phoned in to induce panic and overload the Met with more than they could deal with in a short time.

Now dressed in non-descript, street clothes the two career criminals were being briefed by the warden before being allowed to depart.

"This is the situation. We've a terrorist who's requested you two by name to deliver a package."

'What's in this here all important package Gov'nor?" Hartley grumbled.

"Something of no value to you!" Prisoner Hartley

"Which terrorist? I know lots of terrorists!" Michaels' quip which earned him a thump in the back by the shotgun wielding guard behind him.

"It's been explained to you that if you cooperate fully you both will be considered to be transferred to a softer facility?"

"How do we know you'll hold up your end of the deal?"

"Because Hartley, unlike you two recidivists, I can be trusted! Any other questions?" The cons exchanged glances but remained silent. "Good. Now then follow the instructions of the head guard and we expect you'll be back here nice and cosy in your cells by nightfall." He reached in his jacket side pocket and produced a mobile phone. "This phone has a full charge and is pre-programmed to my direct line. As soon as he, the Captain as he calls himself, has the satchel you are to ring me. We'll be watching you so stay where you are and someone will come to collect you immediately. Any questions?"

"Yeah! What's this all about? You owe us that!" Hartley pushed.

"There are lives at stake here Hartley. Many lives. You men are being given a chance to prove to Her Majesty your lives are redeemable. A chance to make some amends for your crimes. My advice is carpe the diem!" He walked away as their handcuffs were removed and they were immediately herded out the door by two of the other shotgun wielding guards.

"What the fuck is a carpe diem?" Michaels asked.

"It's Latin. It means go fuck yourself!" Hartley answered.

The head guard pulled the warden aside as the prisoners

were brought out to the yard.

"Yes Jenkins?"

"Sir, what about an escort? I mean after we let them go with the money? They find out or even suspect what's in that case and we'll never see them or the hostages again!"

"No escort this time Jenkins." He addressed the tall armed guard. "Orders from the minister himself. This has to be as low profile as possible."

"But after we release them to the terrorist how will we -"

"In coordination with the Met we are going to track them and relay their coordinates the entire time they are at large. They'll never be more than a kilometre away!" The guard looked puzzled. With a James Bond-like flare the warden lifted the hem of his own coat. "Tracking devices." He whispered. "On loan from MI5! Both of their coats, wired for sound, so to speak! As is the satchel."

The warden patted him on the shoulder and confidently walked away.

Being led out of the block with a six man escort the two cons were brought up into a six pack van and seated in the very back. Along with the driver waiting inside the armored transport was another officer with a brown leather satchel cuffed to his wrist with a second 16 gauge carrying officer bringing the on board escort to four. All officers were additionally equipped with a side arms.

Being under relentless scrutiny until they were escorted into the back of the vehicle the two rough looking cons had no chance to interact, until seated and the van was on its way.

As they drove out the massive main gate they looked at each other quizzically.

A short time later, as they crested the top of a hill an airfield appeared in the distance a few miles down the road. In a low voice one of them finally spoke up.

"Hartley." He introduced himself and they traded nods.

"Josh Hartley?"

"Yeah."

"Kevin Michaels. Any idea what this is about?"

"Not a fuckin' hint mate."

Save for serving several consecutive life sentences each in Her Majesty's Prison at Wakefield, Yorkshire, Joshua Hartley and Kevin Michaels had little else in common, had never crossed paths and had no clue who Captain Richard Phillips was. All that would soon be rectified.

"OY! You two, shut it!" Jenkins, the head guard who sat behind the diver and facing them yelled down the aisle.

"This better not be a Jekyll!" Michaels leaned in and whispered.

"We'll soon find out if it is!" Michaels was right to fear a double cross. But for the wrong reason.

Out on the small airfield the blades of a military Bell UH-1, with the pilots already on board, emitted a high pitched scream as its rotor started to kick over.

The police van drove across the tarmac, the five passengers climbed aboard the chopper and the van driver parked off to the side and wandered into the two story control tower to await their return at some unknown time that afternoon. Minutes later the chopper was airborne.

The general direction of the rendezvous had been passed by phone to the Met and about an hour and fifty-five minutes into the monotonous flight the chopper's radio unexpectedly crackled to life with an unrecognized voice.

Rescue One, Rescue One do you read me?

"This is Rescue One, we read you, over."

Rescue one you will proceed to the following coordinates.

"Unknown caller, identify please. What is your call sign?"

Rescue One you may call me the Captain. Please report when you have reached the following coordinates: 51.33° N, 0.02° E. I repeat, 51.33° N, 0.02° E

"Captain, Captain this is Rescue One do you read?" There was no response "Captain, Captain this is Rescue One can you repeat -?" Again there was no response. "How the hell did he get our freq?" The co-pilot asked.

"Got me mate! But sounds like he knows what he's doing!"

"You mean he knows what we're doin'! Did you get those coords?" The pilot asked.

"Yeah. He's got us heading due south south-east"

They flew as directed and ten minutes later the mysterious Captain's voice radioed them instructions to set down in a clearing near a small public park. They complied and three or four minutes later police sirens were screaming down on the chopper. Instantly the radio crackled back to life and he radioed a new set of coordinates.

The cop cars watched helplessly as the chopper again lifted off.

This pattern of instructions repeated twice more until . . .

"Let's just hope this guy's not some terrorist fanatic just playing with us!"

"No! It's using false insert maneuvers! We used to use it in the Royal Marines. You make two or three false drops miles apart when you're infiltrating a recon team! It's to confuse the enemy. This guy's definitely military. Or ex-military."

You will now proceed to –

"Look whoever you are you're obviously ex-military so you know this bird doesn't have an unlimited fuel supply! So either-"

You will now proceed to 51.3320° N, 0.0291° E. I repeat, proceed to 51.3320° N, 0.0291° E and set down on the west side of the motorway. There is a car parked in the clearing. You will deposit my two passengers along with my money and clear the area along with the lucky members of the London Met who have been treated to a lovely day out.

As he spoke the co-pilot tapped his C.O. on the shoulder and pointed out the window to the airstrip of

Biggin Hill Airport which ran roughly parallel to the A233 just west of it. The Captain's instructions continued.

You will have one minute to clear the area. And make no mistake gentlemen and officers of the London Met, we are watching!

"What are the instructions to the two men once they have located the car?"

They will know what to do. Captain out!

"Thinks he's bloody Hans Gruber so he does!" The pilot quipped as he guided the chopper down and onto the designated spot opposite the motorway.

Once on the ground the two cons were let out, handed the satchel and given instructions by the pilot.

"He says about a hundred meters down the road there's a black sedan parked off to the side. Key is in the glove box."

"Then what? Drive to fuckin' McDonalds?!" Hartley challenged.

"He says you'll know what to do!" The Huey driver shouted over the din of the rotors. He then pulled back on the collective and lifted off to head back north.

Hartley and Michaels headed down the one lane, dirt road where they found the sedan as promised. Inside the glove box they found the key and a note with instructions.

'You have made it this far. Well done! The GPS

*device on the dash has been pre-set. Just press the
start button and follow the directions. For your
efforts you will be taken care of for the rest of your
lives. You have my word.'*

The cons exchanged glances and smiled.

The Air Traffic Controller on duty in the control
tower at Biggin was puzzled as he turned his binos
south and watched the Huey slowly rise out of the
trees and make a steep bank north in the direction of
the motorway.

With no prior notice of clearance filed and the
fact that helicopters didn't regularly land and take
off from the direction of a busy motorway, he rang
his supervisor who immediately contacted the
police. The local police contacted the Met and the
info was put out over the police net.

"They've touched down!" The plain clothes
detective seated next to the MI5 agent in the
unmarked, green Ford Corolla, designated Bird Dog
Three, listened as they heard the info coming in
from the Met H.Q. "Package appears to have been
delivered!" They were just over one kilometre
away.

"I'll radio the other units to converge." The MI5
agent manned the car's radio handset. As he lifted it
from the hook a bizarre kind of static filled the air.
He switched channels. The static changed frequency
but remained. Flipping through the channels didn't
help.

His radio freqs were being jammed by bad pop

music.

"It's fucking Lady Ga Ga!" The agent declared. No message was sent from Bird Dog Three.

At the same time up in London, in MI5 H.Q. agents were dutifully observing a moving blip as they manned a tracking console. The black sedan had been bugged with tracking devices.

Unknown to Hartley and Michaels, earlier that morning an eighty-five year old local, who was out for his morning constitutional, had stumbled on the black sedan parked out of place just off to the side of the one lane dirt road he had been walking on.

Police were notified, the car was searched and based on the note found took action. The MI5 agents withdrew and all was left in place with one small addition – two tracking bugs were planted in two different places on the car.

"Bird Dog One this is Bird Dog Three, we got them!" An alternate team three kilometres away from the drop reported. "Notify the lads at the Met Bird Dog Three has the signal and is in pursuit!" The agent tracking the blips on his lap top reported. "They're heading south on the A223. They're really pushing it hard! Looks like they're heading for the coast."

"Maybe they have a boat waiting down there, intending to make their escape by sea!"

"Only place they're making their escape to is straight back to the jug!" The other agent grunted as they took off south along the motorway.

*

Meanwhile, down in the cold, damp darkness of the bomb shelter . . .

"Well ladies it appears all is going to plan." The Captain happily announced.

"What do you want with us! You can't just randomly kidnap –"

SLAP! The attack with his backhand was unexpected but not as brutal as it could have been. Bowridge fell back onto one of the rusty bunks rubbing her cheek but refused to cry.

"That Professor was to get your attention. Now be a good little girl and remain quiet!"

Once again he resorted to his phone, dialing a preset number as he stepped to the side to speak but made no attempt to hide his short conversation.

"¿Hiciste le llamada?"

Si!

"Bueno! Enviame un mensaje de texto cuando estés alli!"

Okay, I will.

Straining to listen one of the students who was in her third year of Spanish at the academy, understood the conversation. She leaned over and whispered to her roommate.

"He's an accomplice."

"To what?"

"Don't know. He asked if he made the phone call. About a meeting, they're going to a meeting. They're to meet with another guy somewhere. He's waiting on a text."

It was nearly seven that night when the Captain ordered Bowridge to keep the girls down stairs while he made another phone call telling them that he would be back in ten to fifteen minutes.

By nine forty-five it started to dawn on the girls that their kidnapper probably wasn't coming back and that, perhaps they had been abandoned.

"That doesn't make sense!" One of the girls said.

"Maybe they caught him and he's in jail!" Another speculated.

In the now increasingly cold shelter Ellen the driver volunteered to venture upstairs. Finding the steel door unbarred and no one or nothing upstairs she returned back down to the shelter and gave the welcomed news to cold, tired and hungry students.

The school bus was gone along with the black sedan and all their mobiles.

After some thought Dr. Bowridge authorized two of the girls to go with Ellen, find a road and find help.

✳

At the same time, along with the plain clothes detective seated next to the MI5 agent in the unmarked car, Bird Dog Three along with a half dozen other squad cars and two police helicopters had converged on the parking area of the Royal Pavilion in the beach resort town of Brighton well south of the capital, two hours away.

An hour and a half later, near dark, when they had found nothing, they realized that they had been led on a wild goose chase.

*

"He's not gonna be there." Frank confidently declared as they sped towards the Biggin airfield across the open tarmac.

"What makes you so sure?" Morrissey asked.

"I know his kind. This isn't about money."

"You expect the money will still be there?"

"Since he asked for small bills, not likely." Frank opined.

"What is it about then?"

"No fucking idea, but it's not about the van money."

"Do your clairvoyant powers tell us if the schoolgirls are alright?" Morrissey mocked. Frank silently glanced out the window.

There was a police helo already hovering overhead to spot any movement away from the target area which incidentally helped them pinpoint their destination.

After being assured by the medics that, aside from being cold hungry and scared, all the girls were alright, the first person they sought to interview was Dr. Bowridge.

"There was only the one that we saw but I'm certain from his actions there were others. Additionally when one of the girls overheard him arranging a rendezvous with someone he spoke

Spanish. But he certainly appeared to be in charge."
Dr. Bowridge, sitting in the rear of a patrol car
wrapped in a blanket calmly informed.

"Can you give us any hint about who he spoke
with? Or who they might have been?" Morrissey
squatting outside the car asked.

"Only that he had no qualms about us seeing his
face which was very unnerving, and that the two he
spoke with on the phone were very rough sounding
and the one in charge was definitely not English."

Frank and Morrissey exchanged glances.

"How do you know he wasn't?" Morrissey
pushed.

"His English was not British. More American."

"Yes, we've had an influx of criminals from the
United States recently." Morrissey dryly quipped as
he smirked at Mahone.

"No he wasn't from The States. From one of the
South American countries, but not Brazil. More
likely one of the Spanish speaking countries."

"How do you know he wasn't from the U.S.?"
Frank returned the smirk

"His misuse of prepositions. His English was
very good but not dialectically fluent. The
Brazilians use a unique syntax in sentence structure.
Completely unlike Spanish speakers. He was
definitely from one of the Spanish speaking, South
American countries."

"Or Mexico?" Frank prompted.

"Possibly, I can't say to that level of detail."

"Dr. Bowridge we know who the two

Englishmen he was speaking with are but a PC will want to get as detailed a description from you as possible about the third fellow. Then I promise you we'll get you a ride back home straight away. Is that acceptable?"

"Yes, I understand. And the girls?" She asked.

"Their phones are all missing so we're taking them all back to the school to make it as convenient as possible for their parents to collect them."

"I will need to go with them and be sure they're all reunited." Bowridge added.

"Perfectly understandable. Let the officer know what you need." Morrissey assured her. They turned to go.

"And Inspector?" On the verge of tears she tugged at Mahone's arm as he stepped away.

"Yes Ma'am?"

"Thank you!"

Morrissey and Mahone headed back to their car.

"Thank you Gov'nor! You're so bloody courageous!" Frank mocked in a stilted Cockney dialect.

"Was that supposed to be a British accent?" Morrissey challenged.

"Just trying to fit in!"

"Don't. That was appalling! You sounded like some knacker out of a Guy Ricthie film! Like a drunk Alec Guinness. Worse!"

"I suppose we should talk to the driver too." Frank suggested.

"I'll talk to the driver! You take notes! And take

them in proper English please!" Morrissey insisted.

"What? You don't be thinkin' I ain't gots no 'bility ta writes in good English n' shit dawg?" Morrissey, still struggling to form an opinion of the American shook his head in disgust.

They found the heavy set driver sitting at the back of one of the ambulances, an oxygen mask over her face.

"Excuse me miss, you are the driver?"

"Yeah."

"I'm Inspector Morrissey assigned to this case and this is a . . . a rookie intern sent us by Social Services on the work-release program. Do you mind if we ask you a few questions?"

"Absolutely not! We have to catch these fucking bastards! Kidnapping school kids and holding 'em hostage! Get the UKIP's into office and they'll sort's this kind of sheit out!"

"I'm sure they will! Okay, let's start with anything unusual?"

"You mean other than shooting out my tire, kidnapping everybody, locking us all in a hundred year old underground bunker and threatening us with death? No not really. Just another day on the job!"

"Miss-"

"Ellen, youse can call me Ellen."

"Ellen, if we really are going to catch these bastards, we'll really need your help. So, once again, anything unusual? In their behavior? Actions? Speech patterns?"

"The guy in charge."

"What about him?"

"He kept referencing some kind of electronic gadget."

"What did it look like? Did it look to be a weapon of some sort?"

"No his weapon was an H&K 9mm. A VP9 I think." Mahone and Morrissey both stared at her. "Father's ex-military. Fought in the Falkland's War with Two Para." Both cops were impressed.

"Can you describe the gadget?"

"Like I said, it was a gadget looking thing about the size of a sheet of paper."

"A4 paper?" Morrissey sought to confirm.

"Yeah and thin, about the thickness of an I-pad."

"But definitely wasn't an I-pad?"

"Definitely not, no."

"Had you ever seen anything like it?"

"No never. I thought it was maybe a new kind of lap top but it looked way too small and way too thin and had a weird feature attached."

"Such as?"

"An antenna. Like on the old T.V. sets or portable radios. Remember those?" She asked.

"I don't but he does." Frank jumped to respond.

Just then a PC approached holding out a mobile phone.

"Inspector Morrissey, it's the C.I. on the horn for you.

"Thanks." He took the phone. "Morrissey here."

Morrissey, We've just located what we believe

are two of the hijackers. Found the bus too.

"Are they talking sir?"

Not likely. Both DOA at the scene.

"Found, the two cons, both DOA." He relayed to Frank who stood next to him.

Abandoned mining pit just south of Croydon. Get up there soon as you can and take charge. Report to me as soon as you're back in London.

"That might not be until quite late sir."

No matter. This thing is spiraling out of control! This sociopath strikes again before we get a clue as to who the hell he is and the next victims might not be as lucky!

"Roger that Chief Inspector. We're enroute."

"Ask him how they bought it." Mahone nudged and whispered to Morrissey who shrugged at not understanding the reference. "Die! How were they killed?" Frank clarified.

"May I ask the cause of death sir?"

Both GSW to the head.

"Both GSW's?" Morrissey repeated aloud for Frank's benefit.

Yes, both. Is that Yank detective there with you?

"Ah yes sir. He's wandering about observing procedure." Morrissey shoed Frank away as he spoke.

Well just be certain he doesn't muck anything up by tainting any evidence!

"One to the head two to the body?" Frank quietly pushed now standing directly behind Morrissey.

"I'll keep a close eye on him Chief Inspector.

Sir, were each of the suspects shot three times?"

Yes. Why? How'd you know?

"How'd you know?" Morrissey mouthed to Frank as he nodded yes.

"Lucky guess." Frank mouthed back.

"Ah, lucky guess Chief Inspector."

You really are quite sharp Morrissey! Kudos!

"Thank Chief Inspector. Comes from years of experience sir. Be in touch when we're back sir." He signed off and turned to Frank. "What was that about?"

"Mozambiqued!" Frank declared. "One to the head two to the chest. This Captain, whoever he is, is a pro. And he's definitely ex-military."

****

CHAPTER THIRTEEN

Brixton Quarry
SW Biggin Hill
South of London

After heading north up the A212 it was thirty minutes later that Morrissey and Mahone arrived at the open quarry now turned police crime scene.

A heavy duty, Transtar 35 ton wrecker was in the process of hauling the mangled carcass of the blue and white Vauxhall people carrier out of the water and up the hill side. The detectives arrived just as the bus creaked up over the edge and into the noise of a generator truck and the illumination of several portable, tripod mounted flood lights.

Water continued to run from the under the door of the bus as the wreck rolled up level with the ground while the dozen or so police and medics stood amongst half a dozen emergency vehicles and watched.

In a well-organized routine, as soon as they got the 'all clear', forensic techs in Tyvex suits, masks, gloves and booties got to work taking pictures, applying swabs of luminol on the dry areas of the vehicle and taking notes while the line of PC's, working shoulder width apart and manning flashlights methodically scoured the area.

Token and Ali were already there to greet

Mahone and their boss as the two pulled up in their car.

"Evening Chief." Ali greeted.

"Catch me up."

"School bus from the academy. A group of local kids came down for a late swim and spotted the bodies over there and called it in."

"JESUS! Bodies?! How many bodies!" Morrissey panicked.

"Two."

"Only two students' bodies?"

"No Boss, convicts, the messengers he picked to deliver the money."

"Two dead convicts. Well that's okay then."

"We've got uniforms sweeping the area but don't expect to find much. Looks like he popped them someplace else, carried the bodies over by that clearing, then came back and shoved the bus over the edge with another vehicle."

"Why not put the bodies in the bus first?" Morrissey questioned.

"Time? Too much work? No idea but they were definitely killed outside the bus. But a second set of tire tracks indicate he used a second vehicle to push the bus."

"Impressions?"

"We took impressions of the front and rear of both vehicles and I've ordered them sent up to London as soon as they dry. What about the students?" Dunn asked.

"Cold, tired and scared but all accounted for.

Any word from the pursuit teams?" Frank asked.

"Dead end down in a Brighton shopping center." She informed him.

"You mean they got away?" Frank jumped in.

"Well they did and they didn't. 33% of them did." Ali nodded over to where a pair of police medics were arranging Harley and Michaels' bodies on gurneys next to a double bay ambulance.

"I don't get it! Then what the hell were we chasing all this time? We were tracking them the whole time!" Mahone asked to no one in particular.

The four made their way over to the ambulance. Frank pulled back one sheet while Morrissey gently lifted the other. They exchanged glances. Both corpses had two holes in the heart area and one in the forehead.

"You called it Frank!" Morrissey credited. "Mozambiqued."

"Must have had stooge one distracted when he popped him then when stooge two turned around he finished the job with one each in the head."

"At least he's tidy!" Dunn commented.

"Where the hell do you suppose these two fit in?" Dunn queried.

"They don't." Mahone answered.

"How do you mean?"

"They were used as McGuffins."

It was then they noticed the Harley and Michaels were dressed in Man United tee shirts.

"Why the hell would the warden send two cons out in gym clothes?"

"He didn't! Son-of-a-bitch had them strip and gave them new clothes to eliminate the possibility they were bugged!"

The group were approached by a PC.

"Inspector, we've found this." He held a broken open brown satchel dripping with water.

"Probably the bag given them by the warden at Wakefield." Morrissey observed as he and Mahone moved over to the bus.

As the tow truck driver grappled with the chains and tow bar to allow access inside the wrecked vehicle they ripped open the jammed door to afford entrance and made their way across the partially flooded floor searching the seats as they went.

"Eureka!" Morrissey exclaimed as he lifted the dripping black sack of mobile phones from the floor just as Mahone called over to him.

"Morrissey! Come here."

"What?"

"See anything that rings a bell?" Frank pointed down into the driver's compartment. Morrissey scanned the dashboard.

"The hole!" Morrissey declared.

"Wow done you old geez'a you!" Frank said in mock Cockney.

"Don't do that!"

"Tell us why not mayte?" Frank kept on in a British accent picked up from bad American movies.

"Because your inability to do dialects is as bad as your sense of humor, that's why." Morrissey chastised.

"Dollars to donuts there used to be a GPS tracker in that hole!" Mahone declared. "Can we think of any other recently discovered vehicle also involved in a crime with a similar anomaly?"

They exchanged glances.

*

AV Room
Scotland Yard

As they didn't finish at the quarry until after midnight the Chief Inspector ordered that Morrissey and the squad take the next day off while the evidence they had recovered was being processed.

Of his own volition, true to form, Morrissey decided to pop into the office that afternoon anyway. When he got there he was surprised to see Mahone, Dunn, FNG and Gunga all at their stations working away.

Suppressing his surprise Morrissey casually opened then tossed the copy of the *The Times* he carried onto the center table. They all drifted over to have a look.

Hero Met Team Saves School Girls!

The headlines blasted across the front page read.

Dunn quickly dug into her handbag and came up with the morning's copy of *The Independent* featuring the headline

MET TEAM TO THE RESCUE!

While Gunga Din matched the tabloid poker game by tossing a copy of *The Guardian* with similar headlines onto the pile.

All the morning papers featured the team as front page news accompanied by detailed stories of the squad's "incredible exploits" while the tabloids featured step by step, numbered graphics of the eighteen hour ordeal.

Finally, from under his table, Frank produced a copy of the *New York Times* and ceremoniously laid it across the table over the rest of the dailies.

"Beat that!" He proudly declared.

STORMY DANIELS SPEAKS!

"What the hell is a Stormy Daniels?" Gunga queried.

"You trying to tell us something Detective Mahone?" Morrissey challenged as he perused the front page of the *New York Times* which brandished the rumoured, lurid details of a story about the pop prostitute and a man now known as Creepy Porn Lawyer.

"Yeah." Frank blurted. "The significance attributed to all major social events directly reflects the values of that society. Basically it all comes down to culture."

"What the hell is the hold up on those tire impressions?" Morrissey complained. "We sent those to the FBI lab nearly 20 hours ago?"

"No idea Chief. I've rung over twice and they say they'll get back to us as soon as they've written their report."

"Well ring them again damn it!"

"Yes Inspector." Enfield snapped.

"Hey boss, I just remembered!" Dunn blurted. "Glad you came in." She scurried to her table and returned with a palm-sized electronic item. "This was in the bag with the kids' phones." Dunn handed the mobile phone-sized device to her boss.

"What exactly is it?" He asked.

"Near as the lads in tech can figure it's some sort of jamming device. He must have wanted to be sure none of the kids surreptitiously switched on the tracker devices on their phones."

"So that taken in conjunction with the missing GPS tracker says this clown-" Frank begun to add.

"The Captain!" Gunga mockingly corrected.

"Of course, The Captain! Has a proficiency in electronics."

"Not just electronics, but electronic communications." Dunn extrapolated.

"So, ex-military. Commo man. Speaks English with a slight Spanish, or Central or South American accent. That's only nineteen countries!" Morrissey observed.

"Minus Brazil is eighteen."

"Plus Mexico is again nineteen." Mahone added.

"Narrows it down to only about four hundred and twenty-three million suspects!"

"Minus the civilians!" Din again added.

"But since everybody in those countries seems to be military that only leaves about three hundred million." Dunn cracked.

"That's a relief!" Din cracked.

"What have we found out about these two clowns?" Frank nodded to a pair of mug shots of the two Wakefield cons on the table. Dunn picked up the ball.

"Michaels and Hartley, both multiple convictions, career criminals. But their A game is Grand Larceny, arson with intent to do bodily harm. Both carried multiple GBH and murder charges."

"What do they have in common?"

"They're both multiple murderers. Both are varsity league players."

"Varsity league players?" Din questioned.

"Both have killed police." Dunn explained.

"So we won't be sending flowers to their funerals?" Frank commented. "Anything else?" Frank asked. Dunn continued.

"One of the PC's doing the routine questioning says a teacher, a Dr. Wilson, remembered seeing a suspicious guy last week in a bread truck cruising around the back of the campus. The teacher let it go at the time but called it in when he heard the midday BBC radio broadcast yesterday. Says he remembered the reg number. They ran it down. Belongs to a rental company who says a guy paid in advance by Pay Pal and picked the car up one night just before closing. Still had the magnetic bread sign on the sides. Says he told them he needed it for an advert shoot."

"He return it personally?"

"As a matter of fact, no. Left it parked outside the next morning, keys under the mat."

"Presumably they got a photocopy of his fake driver's license?" Frank queried.

"Yes, they did."

"This teacher off-handedly remembered a random license plate number?" Mahone challenged.

"Chemistry professor. Apparently the fella has a photographic memory for letters and numbers." Dunn informed them.

"You mean an eidetic memory." FNG proudly corrected.

"Does that mean he remembers things?" Dunn coyly asked.

"Well yes."

"Then he bloody remembers things thank you very much Sheldon Cooper!" She snapped.

"Morrissey, has that armored car been returned to Hamlet Security yet?" Mahone asked.

"Money's been locked away but the van no, not yet. They're due to come collect it before lunch."

"Cancel that and get a judge to order them to hold it in impound until we can examine it again."

"What'a you thinking?"

"Let you know if I'm right. If I'm wrong no harm done. Meanwhile can you get a judge's order in time?"

"Judge? An order? This isn't America Old Boy!" Morrissey picked up the phone, dialed and spoke into the receiver.

"Julie, Morrissey here. Be a dear and cancel that release order for the Hamlet van would you love? Cheers. Best to Jerry and the kids." He hung up and turned to Frank. "You're in a free society now."

"Don't think I haven't noticed!" Mahone replied.

"Well, boys and girl, it's nearly happy hour and I recommend we reanudamos mañana! Or go for a pint."

"Boss, reanudamos is the third plural, so no need to say 'we'."

"Inspector Enfield?"

"Yes Boss?"

"No one likes a smart ass."

"Got it Boss."

As the four moved to the elevator the Chief Inspector rounded the corner and called Morrissey aside.

"Where are we off to Morrissey?"

"Bringing the lads out for a pint sir."

"Okay, but as much as I appreciate the boost to camaraderie, I need your people to understand that under no circumstances is this to be made public!" He tapped the black, cake-sized box Morrissey had tucked under his arm.

"I understand Sir! I'll pass the word." Morrissey quickly caught up to the others as they piled into the lift.

"What was that all about?" Din asked as he and Dunn moved to the back of the car. She surreptitiously pointed to the black box but responded loudly and clearly as Morrissey and Mahone stepped in front of them.

"I just remembered I should text Ali to meet us." She broadcast.

"No need." Morrissey called over his shoulder. Dunn and Rankor got quiet. "Already done. I've got you all on speed dial."

After drizzling through the main door the SHIT Squad huddled up outside in the slowly fading, dusk light.

"See you guys same time tomorrow." Frank signed off and turned to head towards the Tube station. In the group evil smiles crept across their faces as they looked around and exchanged glances.

"Detective Mahone!" Morrissey called over to him. "No time spent at the Met would be complete without at least one trip to the highest holy of all squad rooms."

"Time we showed you a bit of British hospitality, shall we Detective Mahone?" Dunn challenged as she optioned in the opposite direction.

"Meaning?"

"Meaning the Inspector is looking for an excuse." Rankor answered.

"Excuse for what?" Frank asked.

"Suggestions?" Morrissey opened the floor for input.

"*The Silent Wife*?" Rankor was the first with a

suggestion.

"Typical married man!" Dunn attacked. "*The Bull and Shirt*!" She donated.

"I vote *The Brazen Head*!" Rankor suggested.

"RIGHT! *Dirty Dick's* it is then!" Morrissey declared as he led them off across the Embankment along Westminster Pier past the Tube station and onto Great George Street. The smallish pub was wedged in between two glass and chrome business buildings and the after work crowd was nearly in full swing.

Din nudged Dunn, smiled and nodded back as they piled through the front door. Frank was standing out on the walk staring up at Big Ben.

"Kind'a big ain't she?" Dunn goaded.

"I suppose she is. For an English clock." Mahone retorted. He held the door open for her and perused the place as he entered. "*Dirty Dick's* huh? Sounds classy!" Frank sarcastically complimented.

The business crowd already occupied the bar proper so they squeezed through the pack to a booth against the back wall and settled in. Morrissey counted heads and mumbled to himself as no one spoke.

"What are we doing?" Frank asked. FNG filled him in. "It's called 'rounds'. Chief's the only officer to have ever aced all three advancement exams for promotion. He's got a photographic memory for laws and regs so he does!"

"More like pornographic memory!" The only one to laugh, FNG's juvenile joked scored him no points.

"He throws out obscure codes or regs and whoever gets it wrong buys the first round."

"How quaint." Mahone commented.

"PCSO?" Morrissey threw out.

"Police Communications Support Officer!" Enfield blurted out.

"Police **Community** Support Officer!" Rankor corrected. I'll have a pint of bitters thank you very much Sergeant Enfield."

"Who the hell knows that?" Enfield complained as he rose to go to the bar.

Just then Ali came through the crowd and spotted them. He took a short stool outside the booth.

"Don't forget the Yank!" Rankor added as Enfield moved to the bar.

"What'a havin' Mahone?" Enfield asked.

"Lager."

"Get him a Smithwick's." Dunn, who sat next to Frank, advised. Then she leaned in and spoke to him. "Unlike youse lot we use vocab in lieu of numbers to describe regs and so forth. So a 'Dipper' is a pickpocket. A 'Dancer' means someone's done a runner.

"Someone escaped?" Frank clarified.

"Ran away. Exactly."

"IC9?" Morrissey again challenged.

"Person of Unknown description!" Rankor shot out.

"Who the **hell** knows that? 'Ave you no life outside the Yard?" Heath challenged.

"There's a reason Indians score the highest on the Leavin' cert Franklin."

"Watch that Franklin shit, Gunga!"

"Heath doesn't like his given name." Dunn explained.

"Help me out here." Mahone said. "In New York we've got the NYPD. In the NYPD, a city department, we have several units, homicide, robbery bunko, and each unit has squads."

"Sounds simple enough." She conceded.

"Here I'm confused as hell about the how the police are organized!"

"Most of the time we're not." Dunn quipped.

"Here, here!" Rankor concurred.

"Now, now Token, don't let's give our Colonial colleague the wrong impression of our fine organization." Morrissey interjected.

"So the Metropolitan Police Force are you guys?" Mahone pointed around the table.

"Metropolitan Police Service! We are not a 'force'. That's for Yanks." Ali added.

"The Metropolitan Police Service is the formal name but most just use the informal name, The Met." Dunn continued.

"Which used to be called the Metropolitan Police Force." Ali added.

"Informally referred to as the Met."

"That's an old reference though as we are only responsible for The Metropolitan Police Force, the Met whose old name is the Territorial Police of Greater London." Morrissey added.

"Except inside the 'Square Mile', formally known as the City of London." Ali added.

"They are the territorial police force responsible for the greater London area." Dunn added.

"Excluding the Square Mile of course." Din added as Enfield returned with the pints.

"Now you assholes are just fucking with me!" Frank challenged.

"Told you, Yanks only like things simple!" Ali mocked.

"What the hell is the 'Square Mile'?" Frank asked grabbing his pint of lager.

"The original area known as Greater London, or just simply the 'City of London'."

"Well who polices that?" Mahone asked.

"The City of London Police, of course." FNG answered.

"Of course. Stupid question." Mahone shrugged.

"There are no stupid questions, mate. Usually. Any more questions?"

"Yeah! How many fucking police forces does one city need?"

"Well, taking into account the population of Greater London is eight and a half million-" FNG started.

"Legally speaking!" Dunn added.

"The population of Greater New York is over twenty million and has over 130 square miles less than greater London. One police force." Frank held up one finger for emphasis.

"Wow! That's quite smaller than I thought!"

"That's what she said!" FNG quickly spit out.

"Don't start that shit!" Dunn chastised.

"Small? You want to talk small? Manningtree is small!" FNG only finishing off his first pint but with the tolerance for alcohol akin to the tolerance of an Eskimo to the Serengeti at noon in the middle of Summer, already began to slur his speech.

"Where the hell is Manningtree?" Ali challenged.

"Essex. It's where I grew up. Seven hundred people, 307 sheep and fifty-seven cows all spread over 20 hectares!"

"Sounds painfully small!" Dunn criticised.

"Let's just say that what happens in Vegas may stay in Vegas, but what happens in Manningtree is-" Enfield stopped talking as he stared, moving his head in unison with a pretty, blond secretary in a tight skirt swimming through the crowd. Dunn leaned over and slapped him in back of the head.

"-public knowledge within the hour!" FNG finished. "Slag it if you like but a big advantage of living in a small town is that when I don't know what I'm doing everyone else does." Enfield defended.

"CHEERS!" Morrissey lifted his glass.

"Here's to international police cooperation! Cheers!" FNG proposed.

"Sláinte!" Frank called out.

"Sláinte!" Dunn echoed with a broad smile.

Sitting next to Frank she struck up the first casual conversation he'd had since arriving in

England.

"Why homicide?" She asked.

"Well, I was temporarily transferred to Robbery, pending some administrative issues, homicide actually wasn't my original choice. I was originally assigned the Bunko squad."

"What's 'bunko'?"

"Bunk's an older polite word for crap, shit. Worthless things. Back during the Depression grifters latched onto various scams like selling fake Bibles and such. Scams we call them now days."

"Dodges, we call 'em dodges. To set up a dodge'. 'Do a dodge'. Like that." She explained.

"Din another round son!" Morrissey commanded.

"On it Boss!"

Frank leaned in to Dunn and whispered to her.

"Why does Morrissey change Rankor's name all the time?"

"How do mean?"

"Sometimes he calls him Gunga Din other times he calls him 'Rohan the Barbarian' Is that because the little guy is a scraper in a fight?"

She laughed out loud.

"Scrapper? I doubt he's ever raised his fists in anger."

"Then why Rohan the Barbarian?"

"Ever seen him eat?" She finished off her pint. "What about you. What's your story? Why'd you volunteer for this sort of work?"

"Near the end of my second year on the force

wife stopped watching the news. Said it scared her too much."

"What'd she do instead?"

"Stared watching crime shows. Said it calmed her down. Then she lost twenty-five pounds worrying about me coming home in one piece so, she pulled the plug and bailed."

"Then?"

"Then fast forward eleven years later and wife number two who recently bailed and here we are at *Dirty Dicks* in the middle of London."

"How incredibly cliché."

"Why thank you Doctor Ruth! You mocking my life's failures? What's your excuse for being here?"

"Husband. Married nine years. He's in the, emergency services. No kids."

"Drives an ambulance?"

"No. Qualified M.D. and pilots an emergency evac helicopter for the Special Boat Squadron, in the reserves."

"M.D., SBS, chopper pilot! What a loser! No wonder you've no time for kids!"

The ting of a butter knife tapping on a pint glass interrupted the conversations. With no attempt to hide his animated gesticulations Morrissey stood to make an announcement.

"Lady, gentlemen. Others. May I have your attention please?" He cleared his throat. "Now I think, to quote the most culturally significant literary geniuses of British culture, *It's Time For Something Completely Different!*"

There was mild applause as he produced the black box from under his coat draped across the back of the booth.

"On behalf of the fifth month anniversary of the Special Homicide Investigation Team . . ." Fumbling through the box as he spoke and in cadence with his speech, Morrissey unwrapped and removed the item. ". . . and the outstanding work you have all done together, The Chief Inspector has authorised me to present you with this award." He brandished a bronze plated roll of toilet paper mounted on a small walnut plague. "Allow me to read!" He recited the inscription on the bronze plate. "When the case stinks of subversion or smells of deception there's only one team to wipe it clean! The SHIT Squad!"

"How utterly professional!" Dunn commented.

"I don't think Agatha would approve." Ali added.

"Neither did the Chief Inspector completely, so we're to keep this quiet!" He cautioned as they passed the small trophy around the table.

Twenty minutes later, following the third round of pints tongues started to loosen. By the fifth round they had coagulated into three groups. Morrissey, still undecided as to whether or not he liked Mahone, was intent on exploring him more deeply.

"What are you so deep in thought about?" Morrissey tentatively probed.

"Anything strike you strange about this asshole's ransom demands?" Frank answered.

"You mean besides the fact that he asked for so little? Maybe he hasn't seen the same films we have and didn't know he could have asked for more?" Morrissey postulated.

"A hundred grand? That's peanuts for the relative risk. My life's worth a lot more than a hundred G." Mahone declared.

"What on earth is a 'G'?"

"Not important."

"What then?"

"A bus load of kids whose parents are filthy rich and all he asks for is a hundred thousand pounds?" Frank explained.

"One hundred thousand pounds would be enough for most people to start a new life on. What's your point?" Morrissey pointed out.

"In the past when hijackers, kidnappers, your garden variety, run-of-the-mill scumbsgs do something for the money, for ransom, if they ask for too much they're not really serious and will eventually come down on their demands. They know they're not gonna get what they asked for. But if they ask for too little they're either amateur or don't give a fuck about the money."

"I agree. You think he didn't care about the money?"

"Who else apparently didn't give a fuck about the money?" Frank asked.

"What'a you getting' at?" Mahone asked.

Morrissey sat back and pondered. Mahone watched as the wheels turned. Suddenly a bell rung!

"The Hamlet van! You think there's a connection?"

"It's the second thing we've found in connection to the Hamlet job, what'a you think?" Frank reiterated.

"I think there's at least a good chance there's a connection. What'a you think?"

"I think there's a connection! Maybe a tenuous one but I think there's a connection."

"Okay so we agree there's a connection. Now what?"

Half the crowded bar turned and stared as a tall, svelte blond in a charcoal grey business suit and skirt entered. She stood in the doorway scanning the pack.

In her late twenties early thirties, she stepped through the door but held onto the handle to let the door close over gently and carefully perused the bar room more closely as she did.

With a short smile she headed directly for the cops' table in the back by the window.

"Hi. I'm looking for a Detective Frank Mahone." She looked straight at Frank as the words, tinged with a slight Slavic or Russian accent, came out of her mouth.

"And who shall I say is asking?" Frank shot back.

"Irina, Irina Kuksova."

"And what exactly is it you're here to sell me Miss Eye-reena Kuksova?"

"Actually it's pronounced EEE-REENA. But you got the Kuksova part right."

"Our abject apologies Miss EEE-REENA Kuksova. Please don't take this the wrong way but, we're in the middle of something here." Dunn politely informed. "We're kind'a celebrating and you're kind'a interruptin' is what the man is trying to tell you missy." On her forth pint little Dunn made no attempt to be polite. "So if you don't mind, there are plenty of other seats to have your pint." They both perused the now packed pub. "So maybe you can sell your wares down the road in the *Horse and Hogg*?" The remainder of the table also smelled the stench of government on the blond but sat amused and silent as the alpha hens faced off.

'Yes you're here celebrating having saved that school bus load of kids someone tried to hijack and probably hold for ransom. Well done by the way. However my business is with Homicide detective Mahone PC Dunn and with your permission Inspector Morrissey, I would like to borrow the detective for a brief, private chat."

Knowing everyone by name changed the flavor of the conversation as everyone, save Dunn, looked around at each other.

"Well Miss Kuksova-" Morrissey started.

"It's Agent Kuksova actually. Field Agent Kuksova, Federal Bureau of Investigation, London office."

"As I was about to say Field Agent Kuksova, that would be up to the good detective. What's your pleasure Frank old boy?"

"Oh I doubt we'll get as far as my pleasure

Inspector, but maybe I should see what Field Agent EEREENA Kuksova of the FBI wants. Excuse me."

Snide remarks, comments as well as a few contorted faces behind their backs were passed as Mahone and Kuksova made their way out to the end of the long bar just in from the vestibule where there was a small unoccupied snug.

"A Russian FBI agent? I'd say the American democrats are taking this diversity thing a bit far, don't you think?" Heath said.

"How did she know where to find us?" Back at the table Enfield queried.

"She's FBI. Probably used a drone!" Dunn snarked.

"Sorry to pull you away from the party." Kuksova explained.

"No you're not sorry."

"You're right I could care less but good job on the hijacked school bus case anyway."

"Thank you. Now what can I do for you and I have to tell you up front, I'm a married man."

"Yeah married, but not so's anyone would notice."

"What's that supposed to mean?!" He challenged.

"It means that we know your wife's left you, has filed for divorce proceedings and will likely take you for everything you have. Which isn't much."

"Does James Comey or whoever the hell is running the FBI this week know you came all the way over here on the taxpayer's dime just to insult me?"

"I didn't come **just** to insult you, that's a bonus. I came here because I need your help."

Frank eyed her with even more suspicion then when she first approached.

"You need my help you must be in some deep shit lady. What'a you want?"

"We can't talk here better if we meet later."

"Ferget it doll, I'm on holiday. What'a you want?"

"We need someone whose on the inside with these Bobbies."

Without comment Mahone got up and turned to walk away. Kuksova called after him.

"You know we could have this assignment pulled and have you shipped back to the States and put on desk duty till you retire. Word is the NYPD shrink has already drawn up your paperwork." He stopped dead, hesitated then turned back towards her moving in close right up to her face.

"So you ask for help, I decline and you threaten me? No wonder you assholes are always on the front pages of the papers for the wrong reasons! Who's brainstorm was this anyway? Send in a pair of tits and a pretty face and he'll jump through hoops? Wise up Sweetheart! I'm not sixteen years old and it's 2019, men are wise to that sex ploy shit by now! You vamps are gonna havt'a find yourselves a new strategy to get what you want!" He walked away but half turned as he did. "By the way nice job on that *Fast and Furious operation*!

Not as messy as *Ruby Ridge* mind you, but way cleaner than *Waco*!" He called over his shoulder. Yeah, I'm a big fan of your work."

Irina stared blankly as she watched the last of Mahone weave his way back through the crowd.

"Wow! Short fuse on that guy!" She mumbled to herself "Shit!" She kicked the wall and cursed. "That could've gone better!" She said aloud.

A bearded Hipster in Louis Vuitton jeans who witnessed the scene smoothly moved in on Kuksova and went for it.

"Excuse me. . ." He creatively started one arm on the wall, pint in hand. "I saw what happened and if he's not interested I certainly would be happy to-" His Dutch courage instantly became flaccid as Kuksova flashed her badge.

"That's a pretty beard. Shame they'd have to shave it off in prison."

Pint between two fingers and both hands in the air he back peddled back over to the bar.

***

Paddy Kelly

CHAPTER FOURTEEN

Jomo Kenyata Inter'l Airport
Nairobi, Kenya
Monday 12 August; 10:45 Local

The glass and aluminium forming the neat clean lines of the modern décor of the new terminal in Jomo Kenyatta International is a pleasant surprise to most first time visitors.

Unfortunately for Big Peter Krige, now standing at the sole kiosk to be found, international flights that week came through the old, run down terminal still only partially refurbished after the devastating fire of 2013.

"Lager please." He ordered from the headphone adorned emaciated teen behind the counter. The much too narrow counter was packed with various packaged snacks, pulp reading material and pouches of tobacco.

"That'll be 200 ZAR." The boy informed him as he set a warm can of beer on the counter.

"What?! 200 ZAR for a beer?!"

"Dat's de price brother."

"Fuck off you! Find yourself another sucker!" Krige's six four frame lumbered away back across the terminal to where he had been standing with his lady friend in between baggage handlers competing to see who could move slower.

"Where's your beer?" She asked.

"Bloody bastard wanted 27 Rand for a pint! Don't need a beer that bad!"

Krige and his fiancée Nadine Zuma, two South Africans were flying out to meet some relatives in Johannesburg.

The new terminal was much more well maintained but the overcrowded, shabby lounge they were now compelled to stand in, the largest space in the old terminal, with its woeful lack of seats, was reminiscent of something out of the '50's.

They had decided to take the next British Airways flight from Nairobi south to J-burg on the last three days of their holiday break and were forced to stop over in Nairobi when their plane was grounded due to high winds. Their ultimate goal was to visit relatives who operated a farm down south near De Deur.

An hour later they made it to their gate where boarding proceeded without incident and following a short delay they were in the air.

About an hour into the flight however, the aircraft suddenly banked hard to the left, climbed several thousand feet and levelled off.

The captain's voice was not as calm as passengers would have liked as he instructed them to sit up straight, buckle up and obey the flight crew. A minute later and with more of a panic in their voices, the crew instructed the passengers to remain in their seats.

In short order word was passed to assume the

crash position.

"Nairobi Tower this is BA714, Nairobi Tower this is BA714."

Nairobi tower go ahead BA714.

"Tower be advised we think there's-" Static filled the airwaves.

BA714 this is Nairobi Tower do you read?

There was no response.

BA714 this is Nairobi Tower do you read?

Following fifteen minutes more of fruitless attempts at radio contact search and rescue were notified.

***

The AV Room
Tuesday· 14:35 Local

"Dunn, the report on those tire impressions on the phantom vehicle come back yet?" Ali called over from his table on the opposite side of the room.

"Report's in your in-basket Big Man." She responded making her way over to her table.

"Thank you love."

With the exception of Morrissey who hadn't come in yet the entire squad were already scattered around their tables hard at work when Mahone popped through the door. He was greeted by Dunn.

"Morning Ian Fleming, message for you." She handed him a sealed, standard envelope.

"What's this?"

"Classified, from your FBI girlfriend." She ribbed. "For your eyes only! Show her our golden gun last night did we?"

"You kiss your mother with that mouth Dunn?"

Dunn assumed a morose face.

"My mum's only just passed away last week Mahone! Me being an only child we were very close. It was quite difficult." She chastised as she walked away.

"Shit! Sorry Token. I mean Maureen." He immediately answered with an embarrassment tinged apology.

Unseen by him Enfield sniggered behind his computer screen.

Mahone took a seat at his table and opened the sealed message.

Passenger airliner out of Nairobi enroute south to Johannesburg went down in Burundi mountain range. Call me.

"Hey Dunn, where's the Burundi mountain range?" Frank called over as he sat, puzzled more than before he opened the note.

"I imagine, **detective**, in Burundi."

"Thanks for clearing that up."

"Anytime."

"It's on the country's western border detective Mahone. Near Uganda."

"Thanks Enfield."

"The actual mountain range is shared by-"

"Thanks Enfield."

"But Detective Mahone , I was gonna-"

"Thank you Enfield. Thank you very much."

"Boy's slower than a politician giving answers at an inquiry!" Dunn shook her head and mumbled to no one in particular.

Frank pulled out his phone and dialled. Kuksova answered on the first ring.

"Got your note. This your way of asking for a date?"

The plane crashed some place called mount Elgon.

"Where the hell is that?"

Like it says in the note - in Burundi!

"Africa! So?"

Left Nairobi and crashed into a mountain in Burundi?! She spoke slowly to emphasize.

"Do I look like I watch the *National Geographic Channel* even during *Shark Week*?" He snapped.

*Burundi is west of Kenya my geographically challenged detective. **Miles** west of Kenya. Johannesburg is in South Africa. Not even remotely in their flight path.*

Mahone digested the information.

"You think . . .? What part of town you in?"

No. Tonight. Pick you up at eight. Be ready. She hung up.

"Wow! She takes that secret agent shit real serious! First time a woman's ever **ordered** me on a date." He mumbled into the phone as he took his jacket back off the rear of his chair and made for the door.

"Hey Dunn!"

"Yeah Mahone?"

"I gotta go out for a bit. Inspector Morrissey comes in tell him I'll be back in a bit."

"Will do."

"And Dunn?"

"Yes Mahone?"

"Say hi to your mom next time you see her." He snarked as he left.

He was less than a minute out the door when Ali sounded off.

"Hey Dunn!" He called over to her.

"WHAT THE HELL IS THIS TODAY?! THE HEY DUNN PROGRAM?! **WHAT?!**" She called out from her workstation just as Morrissey came through the door.

"We've got a brand and make on the tire treads from the phantom car the Captain used." Ali called over brandishing the tire report he'd asked about.

"Congratulations Ali! Now 'Hey Dunn' me when you've tracked down all the possible makes and models of all the cars the tires they could have possibly belonged to!" She shot back.

"Hey Dunn!" Ali immediately called.

"Bastard! WHAT?!" She yelled back just as Morrissey walked through the door.

"Inspector Dunn, is there a reasonable explanation for your being so loud at this un-godly hour of the morning?" Morrissey demanded one hand on his head.

"Sorry Inspector!" She apologized. "Ali got a lead on the tire tracks from the unknown getaway car in the bus hijack case."

"Well that's something to yell about. Give it to us Ali!" Morrissey ordered.

"The car was apparently a late model Fiat 500X, probably 2018 fitted with 215/60R17's and of all eleven models only one is classified as All-Wheel Drive."

"Well that's god news! I think." Dunn opined.

"There's better news!" Ali added.

"What?" She pushed.

"Left rear was a spare. An asymmetrical spare with a defect on the #2 inside valley on the contact patch. One and a half centimetre chunk of rubber missing. Must have run over a stone in the road or something in its past life."

"Dunn!"

"Inspector Morrissey?"

"Get on the horn and get me the Honcho at FIAT Britain. If some minion says he's in a meeting tell him he has a choice, interrupt it or schedule his next meeting at the Old Bailey!"

"Got it!"

"Enfield get in the game over here!" Morrissey called over to FNG who was tinkering around at the coffee station in back of the room.

"I'm all ears Chief!"

"Get those details from Ali, and you and he get on the phone and get us a list of all the car rental agencies that have, use or rent FIAT 500X models in the greater London area. Then expand the list to all of South England if need be. Ali, get us the same data for car dealerships. Also inquire about recently fitted spares."

"Roger that Boss Man! The SHIT squad is in the house Baby!" Ali declared as he moon walked back to his table.

"I could never get the hang of that!" Morrissey declared as he clumsily attempted the same manoeuvre. Dunn looked on in pain before commenting.

"Hey Boss! Please don't!"

*

That evening Kuksova's red Audi A3 turned into the narrow laneway and pulled up outside the Fielding Hotel in Coventry at eight on the dot as arranged. Mahone was waiting outside and hopped in.

"Where to?" He asked.

"Someplace just out of town. I don't want to chance being seen with you."

"Huh! I've never heard that line from a girl before."

"I very much doubt that Cowboy!" She quipped. "When you say girls you mean never heard it from wives or daughters?"

"Both actually."

She showed no response but rummaged through the glove box as they came out onto the main road.

"Here, put this on." She tossed him a striped tie.
"We on a date are we?"

"As if! I didn't wear a three hundred pound dress and two hundred pound heels to be seen with a guy looks like I found him busking outside Victoria Station."

"What are you talking about? This is my best bowling shirt! £10.95, straight from the Charlie Sheen collection!"

"Great! A comedian." They sat in awkward silence for a short time until she spoke again. "How's your accommodation?"

"Well appointed."

Aside from a smidge of small talk there was no real chit chat for the next half hour as Kuksova took them south on the A203 turning off and heading into Dulwich Village.

She took them to a small mom and pop styled restaurant called Franklin's on a corner just off the main drag.

Taking a booth in the back corner and the fact that she demonstrated good trade craft by sitting against the back wall facing towards the front door wasn't lost on Mahone. The nearest diners were several tables away.

They waited to speak until the waiter dropped by with menus and water.

"Give us some time. We'll signal when we're ready." Frank relayed to the middle aged, balding waiter.

"Very well sir." He smirked while his eyes

roamed over Kuksova.

Frank leaned in and opened the foray.

"Okay, let's pow wow. The FBI doesn't just show up at a crime scene with a missing armored car, two missing guards that vanished into thin air twenty years ago. Especially one that's full of cash. What'a you guys hiding?"

"Look, Mahone don't ever feel like you have to hold back with me. Just say what's on your mind."

"I will."

"And it was nineteen years ago."

"Meanwhile, if you have even the slightest faint of a hope of getting one scintilla of cooperation from me I wanna know what's going on. No bullshit."

She sighed in exasperation but Kuksova was on a mission, losing her composure wasn't an option.

"Alright. To start the short, slinky skirt in the pub was a bad-"

"Lemme guess. It was your fifty-five year old boss's idea who's seen too many spy movies."

"No. It was my idea."

"Well in that case, can't blame you for trying."

"You have any kind of clearance?" She asked.

"You now damn well I don't! They revoke it when you leave the service. Clearance or no clearance this is not up for discussion. I know what I'm involved in or I walk."

Kuksova put both arms on the table and leaned in as much to keep her voice down as to fool the other handful of diners that her and her date were being intimate.

"What I'm about to tell you is-"

"I know, classified and when you're done you'll have to cut my head off and put it in a safe."

"You ever take anything serious?"

"Not if I can help it."

"Pay attention Seinfeld. There's something going on in D.C. and whatever it is, the Bureau's in deep."

"Congrats, you discovered the FBI higher up's are fuckin' up. Again! Not exactly up on current events are we Agent K.?"

"Lower your voice!"

"What's this gotta do with me?"

"Nothing yet. But whatever it is it's bad and I can't crack it alone."

"Which is why you want my help?"

"**Need** your help!"

"Why me?"

"You're an American cop, you're on this van case and you've got an in with the Yard. And I can't be seen to be meddling in a U.K. case or things will start to melt away and they'll get away with whatever it is they're planning."

"Whose 'they'?"

Kuksova let her gaze drop as she answered.

"I don't know."

"What are 'they' trying to get away with?"

"I . . . I'm not exactly sure."

"Jesus woman! What the hell you want me to do? Watch the front door while you rob the place? Gimme a break!"

Kuksova may have been maintaining her composure but at the same time was just now, as she said it out loud for the first time, realizing just how desperate she really was. Compounded by the fact that she was coming off like a complete idiot it was time to shift gears.

"Back in June of 2008 Columbian Special Forces staged a raid on a FARC camp over the border just west of San Cristobol where they seized a laptop and some documents."

By this time Frank was struggling to pretend to be listening.

"Among other incriminating evidence linking FARC to cooperating with the ELN, the lap top clearly showed safe havens over in Venezuela which, because they were located in and around fairly populated towns, could only have been safe if the Venezuelan government sanctioned them."

"Okay, I've heard of the FARC. Me and a partner rode shotgun once on a DEA raid up in Spanish Harlem. Who the hell are the ELN?"

"National Liberation Army of Columbia. Bunch of left wing socio-communist fanatics about 3,000 strong as far as we can tell. We collar the occasional one in the U. S. trying to collect donations for 'The Cause'"

"I thought all those commie nuts in South America died out in the Sixties?"

"Unfortunately not. While the U.S. and the U.K. are busy with the crazy Arabs over here, the security services down there've got their hands full

296

Paddy Kelly

with the crazy commie/socialist wanna-bes."

"Enough fanatics to go around hey?"

"Exactly. So, a year later, agitated by plenty of press, the local row escalated when ambassadors from both countries were recalled and the Organization of American States had to get involved. They asked the U.S. State Department under Clinton to moderate."

"Hilary Clinton?"

"Yes."

"Huh!"

"The intel was verified and the OAS issued a statement to the effect that Maduro's people were guilty of violating several international treaties which forbid the shelter of known terrorist groups."

"Okay." Frank slowly began to pay attention.

"Maduro was the Venezuelan Foreign Minister at the time." She continued.

"So Hilary stepped in and it was our crook against their crook! Huh, Maduro didn't stand a chance."

"The escalation sparked international speculation of a war."

"Well there was no war, so how'd it end?" He asked.

"The Clinton State Department couldn't get anything accomplished-"

"Imagine that!" Frank smirked.

". . . they pulled out and by the time tempers reached boiling point the Union of South American Nations got involved. A short time later Juan

The Galileo Project

Manuel Santos was elected as Columbia's new president and the UNASUR guys, by-passing Maduro completely because they knew they couldn't trust him, arranged for Santos and Hugo Chávez to meet face-to-face. Santos agreed to turn over the laptops to a third party. Diplomatic relations were restored and everybody kissed and made up."

"Jees, ya miss the Six O'clock news one day and all hell breaks loose!"

Irina stared blankly at him.

"You've got a mind like a steel trap Mahone."

"Thank you." He smiled.

"Anything gets in it gets mangled beyond recognition."

"You know if we're going to be friends you can call me Frank."

"As I was saying, Mahone –" She started. But Mahone was just as prepared to shift back into cop mode.

"Okay." He nodded and sat back. "That is an outstanding report Columbo. Where do I fit in?"

"Two of the most unstable countries in South America right now are Columbia and Venezuela. My suspicion is our boy is an agent working for one of the two and if I'm right-"

"If you're right?"

"Three guesses who one of those laptops belonged to."

"Venezuelans aligned with the Columbians."

"How'd you know?"

298

"Lucky guess based on the tons of drugs Columbia ships to the U.S. every year. Besides, I'm a cop remember?"

She pulled an I-phone from her purse and called up a series of B&W photos which were obviously taken from cover at a distance.

Mahone took the phone and scrolled through the photos stopping on one to enlarge it. It showed Maduro on a large, elaborately decorated, outdoor stage in front of a crowd. Mahone read the Spanish language banner across the risers as well as several of the crowd held signs.

"You speak Spanish?"

"I'm a New York cop, what'a you think?"

"Oh."

"Why was Maduro at Santos' inauguration? I thought he was a diehard Chavez man?"

"Congratulations Detective Mahone. You are now caught up on Twenty First Century Third World politics in South America!"

He passed the phone back to her, sat back in his chair and sucked in a deep breath.

"Thanks for the education but, I ain't the CIA and you ain't MI6! This is way above our pay grade!"

"Did anyone on that bus say anything about getting lost? A wrong turn, sign posts in the wrong place or missing? Anything of that sort?"

"Yeah, the driver." Frank's became a little more interested. "Why?"

"Whoever hijacked that school bus and

kidnapped those students had access to advanced navigational technology which is how they sent the Yard's men two hours to the south of the country and so far out of the way."

"Obviously. So?"

"How would you feel if that school bus was hijacked in Queens?"

"I'd put it down to another day in New York."

Her realization of misjudging Mahone, that he would be all gung-ho to jump on board but obviously was not, aggravated by her lack of progress in winning him over had begun to boil over. Her face hardened as she fought to keep her temper.

"If that's your honest sentiment, then fair enough. Now that you're in this, if for any reason you feel compelled to pack your bags and fly back to New York, no hard feelings and bon voyage! But that school bus was hijacked in my assigned district on my watch and these local yokels have two chances of catching this guy, slim and none, and it appears Slim just left town!"

"These 'yokels' are Scotland Yard. Maybe you've heard of them?" Frank's sudden defense was unexpected by both parties.

"Well Sherlock Holmes and Doctor Watson haven't done very well so far with the radical Muslim factions here –"

"That's because they've got a Muslim mayor who's more preoccupied with putting up giant balloons mocking president and telling Londoners that terrorism is just something 'they have to learn to live with' backed by a PM who's one step above a meat puppet and has one foot out on the street!"

Though not yelling, their voices gradually reached the point where they grabbed the attention of the other half dozen diners in the place. The half-asleep waiter was startled and scurried over.

"Is everything all right sir?"

"Do you like tips?" Irina jumped to reply.

"Yes of course."

"Then here's one; do as the gentleman requested and go away until we are ready!"

The waiter skulked back to his corner station to languor in his boredom.

"So you don't mind spit in your food?" Frank asked.

"I damn well intend to find the son-of-a-bitch that hijacked those girls and I intend to stop him before we have a full blown terrorist incident on our hands and the Bureau –"

"Gets yet another black eye? Okay I get that. But let's take it down a notch. Or three. We're attracting attention."

She looked around at the two tables glancing their way and responded with a sarcastic smile.

Mahone was completely taken aback but impressed by Kuksova's passion and was temporarily at a loss as to where to go next.

"Okay. So what'a ya want from me?"

"On the 27TH of June last year FARC

surrendered all their arms to the U.N peacekeepers and reformed as the CARF, the Common Alternative Revolutionary Force. I think there's a strong possibility that not all of their upper echelon membership was happy with the peace treaty they signed."

"Well if this is them then what the hell do they want now?"

"What do they all want? Power, money, control? Recognition. I figure the ransom money was to re-finance the operation which was probably running out of gas."

"What about the armored car job? That was twenty years ago-" Mahone insisted.

"Nineteen."

"Eighteen and a half and the money was still there."

"Near as I can figure something went bad and the perps, whoever they were, opted to stay alive rather than get caught." She suggested.

"Or go back and face their boss?"

"Could be. But regardless we need the connect between the van and the bus to find who these guys are to uncover the operation."

"What operation?"

"I don't know. I'm at a dead end and I can't work within the London office."

"Why not?" His question was answered with a prolonged blank stare.

"You telling me you want in?" She challenged.

"Maybe. But I need to know why you suspect the

Bureau."

"I can't really talk about it."

"You're losing me again sister."

"Word of honor, when I can I will."

Mahone sat back in his chair and sighed.

"So you're at a dead end?"

"Not completely I could still-"

Frank glanced around the room, reached in his jacket pocket and came up with a small calculator-sized gadget, slightly thicker, wrapped in a clean chamois cloth. He laid it on the table in front of her.

Immediately suspecting what it was Kuksova picked it up an causally examined it.

"Where'd you get this?!"

"Off the right rear quarter panel of the school shuttle bus. Druggies back in New York use hide-away, magnetic key boxes to quickly hide drugs if they smell a cop. Most common place was under the rear quarter panels on the nearest parked car. The bottom plate of this thing is magnetic."

"Does Morrissey know about this?"

"No."

"Why keep it from him? Don't you trust him?"

"I'm a two time divorcee, I don't trust anybody, but that's besides the point. I'm not really keeping it from him. I just haven't shown it to him yet." She handed it back.

"It's a kind of navigational device." She casually threw out.

"Yeah I know. I took it around today to a few places in town. Nobody seemed to know what exactly it was for, but a Chinese guy in Maplin's Electronics on Oxford Street said he thought it might be some kind of false echo location device."

"Then why the hell'd you ask me?"

"I'm a cop, remember? Needed to see if our story jived with his."

"Well it does, and at this size with the capability it apparently has, it's bad. Especially if they've found a way to by-pass magnetic interference!"

"How bad is bad? Exactly." He asked.

"You know all that research Kim Jong-il is spending millions on to develop nuclear missiles, the research that's slowly creeping forward while the politicians stroke him off?"

"Yeah."

"And those nuclear missiles being built by the Ayatollah Khemani in Iran, the ones Obama helped pay for? The ones the Israelis keep trying to stop?"

"Yeah."

"Put those two together and its more dangerous than that." She said. Frank fell back in his chair.

"That little thing?" He asked.

"Not the device itself but the technology used to develop it."

"What the hell is more dangerous than that?"

"A magnetic wave tolerant spoofer."

"Who the fu. . . heck are spoofers?"

"**What** the fuck are spoofers detective, not who. Spoofers were developed after we learned how to defeat advanced jamming devices. They are able to send out a false signal which can alter not only the actual location but the time signature of the cargo or whatever the criminals are looking to hide, hijack or destroy."

"A mimicked translocation signal! False echo, like with what some insects so they can avoid bats."

"You're not as dumb as you look!" She remarked.

"That's just a disguise. So the real threat of spoofers is they can waste millions of dollars and hundreds of man hours in tracking down the real location of whatever it is we're looking for?"

"You should be a cop."

"Thought about it. The pay's lousy and the hours even worse." He rewrapped and stashed the spoofer back in his pocket.

"I'm gonna need that Detective!" She insisted.

"That's up to Morrissey."

"Morrissey's cops, I'm federal!"

"Not here Baby doll! Over here you and me is just another pair of tin badges unless we have permission from Big Mama to do something. That is to say, Her Royal Majesty's Coppers!"

"I could make you give it to me." She pushed. In response he reached into his breast pocket and produced a hand-held Dictaphone which had been running the whole time.

"And I could make sure this reaches the right ears. How'd your boss feel about that?"

"YOU SON-OF-A-BITCH!" The others in the place looked, the waiter snapped awake again and she stood to leave.

Frank pocketed the tape recorder and smiled.

"Sit down!" She continued to collect her things. "Come on, sit." After a short stare-off she complied. "Not my first rodeo Sister! Don't worry, I'll erase it later. Just needed to be convinced what side you were playing on. Besides can you blame me?"

"I need a drink." She spat. He signaled and the waiter slowly sashayed over. Frank ordered.

"White wine and a whiskey neat please. White wine okay?" He asked Kuksova.

"Yeah." Frank waited until the server was again out of earshot.

"What about you? Why the Bureau?"

She took her time answering, licked her lips, sighed and forced herself to recompose.

"I had just finished my degree in software engineering with a minor in programming-"

"Don't tell me! Harvard? Yale? MIT?"

"Pittsburgh."

"PITTSBURGH?! Pittsburgh as in Three Rivers Stadium, steel factories, The Pirates and a shit load of bridges?"

"The factories are mostly gone now, replaced by Google, IBM and Apple but it's also a center for military tech and nuclear research. Both my parents are engineers-"

"Of course they are!"

"Things were getting uncertain in the Ukraine and my parents didn't want to have kids under a communist government, so they emigrated here in the Eighties following the last of the Cold War flare-ups. P.A.'s got a large Eastern European population, good schools et cetra."

"I know."

"You've been?"

"No, but I seen *Flashdance*." He confidently relayed. Irina shook her head.

"The Bureau sounded exciting, they were recruiting so I signed on. I didn't want to start my career a tiny cog in a massive tech wheel in an office full of geeks sitting behind desks for twenty years like a field of mushrooms. FBI sounded more interesting. Besides, gotta start your career somewhere."

"Pretty big decision no?"

"Not really. " The wine came, she downed half her glass and Frank mimed a toast then sipped his whiskey.

"Now back to business Detective.-"

"Sorry to keep interrupting but, if you're a tech engineer for the Bureau, what'a you doin' in the field?"

"You really are a cop, aren't you?"

"Just askin'! You don't have to answer any questions without a lawyer present!" He joked.

"I temporarily got assigned to encryption translation. Most of the stuff we get to go through is still generated in Russian."

"Makes sense."

"We think Iran used this spoofer tactic to lead a couple of Navy patrol boats astray last year which they consequently captured."

"That sucks!" He snapped.

"My kid brother was on one of those boats."

"That really sucks!"

Her wine glass now empty, Frank signaled for two more drinks.

"That thing off?" She cautioned referring to the tape recorder. With the wine she seemed more visibly settled as she continued.

"Yes."

"Fourteen of the sixteen critical services in the U.S. to include transportation, communication, the power grid and global finance all depend on GPS.

"Everybody knows about communications and I knew about transport and the power grid but finance? That's new."

"Homeland Security's working with a scenario where-by terrorists through spoofers, feed fake data into electrical sub-stations in one or more of the metro areas and overheat power lines, blow the transformers and cause wide-spread power outages."

"Sounds like a fucking Jason Statham movie!"

"Who's Jason Strathman?"

"Statham! Not important."

"In their theoretical scenario, at the same time spoofers feed fake data into electrical sub-stations, multiple hidden jammers cripple cell phone service and other communications. Fire, police emergency and medical services are then all forced to revert to single channel radio communications, which are much more simple to intercept. This in turn will keep the bad guys fully appraised of what we're doing all the time."

"Wow! That kind of attack would also take out ATM's and limit people's ability to get essentials such as food and water unless they had significant cash stash!" Frank added. "Which nobody does!"

"Exactly!" She conceded. "Best case scenario estimates have it at a minimum of thirty days before we could locate and disable the jammers. But the longer we took the more systems could be compromised!"

"And large swathes of Western civilization would come to a screeching halt!"

"Bingo." She mouthed. "Pretty scary shit huh?"

"So, other than that how'd you like the play Mrs. Lincoln?" Mahone declared as he threw back his second whiskey, fell back in his seat and stared. "I feel like I just been epiphanized."

"I . . . don't think that's a word." She challenged.

"It is now." Frank signaled and the waiter reappeared.

"Will you be eating tonight sir?" He asked. Frank glanced over at Irina.

"I'll have the fish please." Irina ordered.

"For you sir?"

"The lamb, no wine sauce." Pleased that his life once again had meaning, the waiter scurried happily away.

"Now that that's out of the way, where were we?" She said.

"You think these guys are planning something

that big?" Frank probed.

"To date all attempts at interfering with GPS signals have involved two approaches: Interoperability, mainly against the Russian system GLOSNAS or the European's Galileo and the Chinese system all of which are planned to be up and running by 2020. But countermeasures were able to defeat all attempts . . . so far."

"What's the other approach?"

"Clocks."

"You mean like disrupt all the clocks to cause chaos in the computer systems?"

"No, it's still about disrupting navigation."

A good looking woman with brains! And here I thought they were an extinct species. Frank mused as she spoke. For the first time in recent memory Mahone found himself being truly enamored by something he previously had no interest in; technology.

"You see clocks-" She started before Mahone cut her off.

"Ho, ho, hold it! My damn' head is about to explode!" He blurted. Irina suddenly blushed a deep red and slowly sat back in her chair. Having had little or no time for relationships during four years at university and three years advanced training with the Bureau, this was actually the first time she was ever in a position to share what her life's work and passion were with a man.

Frank stared at her for a long time. She stared back then finally broke her silence.

"What?! What is it now?" She probed.

"Did you join the Bureau for hot dogs, mom's apple pie and love of country or was it something else?" His sarcasm was barley hidden. Her resultant ire as not.

"I joined to catch bastards! Bastards like these guys!" She shot back. Frank smiled over propped up elbows on the table. "And . . ." She downed the rest of her second glass of wine. "I'm sick of the Bureau getting kicked around in the Press because of a couple of twisted up bureaucrats at the top suddenly deciding that the American people were too stupid to elect their own leader! And getting political then selling us all down the river to cover their own asses!"

Frank nodded then slowly pulled the Dictaphone back out of his pocket, ejected the tape and slid it across the table to her.

"Okay then." He said quietly. "I'm in."

She stared in shock.

"You sure?"

"You convinced me, I'm in. Where do we start?"

She stared down at the tape took a deep breath and smiled.

"You tell me." She said.

"I'd say the plane crash, it's the most recent event and so our hottest clue right now. To start we need to know as much as possible about that African airliner crash. In particular was it the work of our illustrious perp, 'the Captain' or an actual accident. If there's a link we need to find it."

"The NTSB report'd be the best place to start for that."

"Can you access that?" He asked.

"Only if I can justify it but that might attract a lot of attention. Let me sleep on it."

"Find us the info in that report and when you do contact me at this number day or night as soon as you do." With his pen he scribbled across a serviette as he spoke then slid it over to her. She perused the number.

"This is a disposable cell phone." She observed.

"Yeah, bought it when I first arrived here but haven't had a chance to use it yet. Better not to use government issue gear when possible."

"Good thinking Batman!" She joked.

"And the Ice Queen melteth!"

"What's that supposed to mean?!"

"Underneath that tempered, steel shell there is a girl with a sense of humor!"

"I have a sense of everything!"

"Fair enough."

"I should be able to dig up the whereabouts of the report in a day or so, then we'll have to figure out how to access it. I'll call as soon as I've got something."

The waiter reset the table for their food as they continued with small talk.

"I'll drop you back after we eat. What's on your agenda for tomorrow?" Irina asked.

"I gotta talk with Bruce Willis." He quipped.

"Bruce Willis is a friend of yours?!"

"Probably not."

Finally content with something to do, the waiter served the dinner and they ate.

****

CHAPTER FIFTEEN

AV Room
Scotland Yard
Friday, 16 August; 11:47

Ripping a piece of note paper from his desk pad and holding it high Ali stood and proudly made an announcement to the whole room.

"Thrifty Car Rental near Tower Bridge!" He firmly declared.

The tire treads on the getaway vehicle used in the bus hijacking were traced and potential matches of the car had been located.

"Isn't that handy?" Morrissey observed. "Just down the road!"

Twenty minutes later Morrissey accompanied by Ali and Dunn walked through the front door of the Tower Bridge show room of the Thrifty Rental Agency.

"May I speak with Mr. Billings please?" Morrissey asked the young service clerk.

The well-dressed gentleman that emerged from the back could only have been a Mr. Billings. Tweed coat, plaid waistcoat, corduroy trousers and brown vintage Corframs.

"Yes, may I help you?"

"Inspector Morrissey, The Met, Sergeants Heath and Dunn. My associate rang in earlier and was told although a car may have not been rented at this office you have access to the central data bank for all London rentals in the last month?"

"Yes of course Inspector. Shall we speak in my office?"

"Not necessary. I just have a few questions if that's not a bother."

"Not at all! How can I help?"

"How many model 500X's do you have on inventory?"

"City-wide four at present. They're quite popular."

"Any rentals of that model within the last month?" Billings stepped behind the counter and manned the nearest keyboard and quickly zeroed in on the required window.

"We've had several rentals ahh . . . seventeen by my count. If you're seeking a particular vehicle can you narrow it down? Time, day, week? Color perhaps?"

"Afraid not. Anything at all stand out about any of the renters? Name, age nationality perhaps?" Dunn asked.

"Let's see . . . ahh . . . 11 British. Three American. One couple from Japan, one woman from Germany and we had one rental, huh! Only one from South America!"

"May I have his details please?"

"He registered as a Dr. Gorge Menendez in on business from Santiago."

"And you're certain he rented a 500X model?"

"Perfectly certain."

"Had it recently been fitted with a spare?"

Billings again typed away.

"As a matter of fact yes it had! You blokes really are as good as they say you are!"

"Actually, no we aren't. We're better!" Dunn quipped.

"You've been around that Yank to long!" Ali accused.

"We've just fitted it with a proper replacement. If you'd like to inspect it I'm afraid it's out at the moment."

"To whom has it been rented?"

"That particular vehicle to a Mrs. Peckwith. Seventy-two year old pensioner from Leeds. I can notify you when she returns it. It's due back day after tomorrow."

"That won't be necessary. You photostat your clients' I.D.?" Ali asked.

In lieu of an answer Billings again manned the keyboard and called up Dr. Menendez's licence photo and turned the screen so Morrissey could see it.

"Do you have any kind of paperwork from the transaction? Anything at all?"

"Yes, we have the insurance agreement he signed."

"The guy bought fucking insurance!" Billings and the young female desk clerk standing next to him were taken off guard by Dunn's profanity.

"She's Irish." Morrissey explained.

"I see." Billings quietly commented.

"From Dublin." She added.

"I see. I'll just fetch the paperwork."

"Thank you but, could you be careful handling it? We'll need to get it back to the labs for prints."

"Of course!"

As Billings headed back to the office Dunn disappeared out the front door, went to the unmarked police unit parked in the drive and returned with a small black case.

"Sir?" Morrissey turned to see Dunn holding a portable print kit. "Packed it along just in case, sir."

"Nobody likes a smartass Token!" Morrissey quipped. "But remind me to buy you a pint."

"That's three this month sir."

Billings returned gingerly holding the rental form by a single corner and carefully set it on the counter in front of Morrissey who slid it across the desk to Token.

"Who else could have handled this form Mr. Billings?"

"It would appear I was the agent on duty that day! So, just myself."

"I'll need Sergeant Dunn to take your prints for comparison, if you don't mind."

"Of course not."

Fifteen minutes later a useable set of prints had been lifted and faxed off to INTERPOL Headquarters in Lyon.

"France? Why not send it to their office here?" The rental clerk asked over Morrissey's shoulder.

"Because their office here would have to send it to Lyon there and that would take longer."

"Oh." She whispered. "Now what?"

"Now we wait." Dunn explained.

Forty-five minutes later a name along with a photo arrived form INTERPOL H.Q. in Lyon to the Scotland Yard Intel desk and was immediately e-mailed over to the car rental agency where Morrissey et al waited. The manager printed it off and brought it out from his office to the customer lounge where Morrissey and Dunn were flipping through some old magazines to kill time. Ali was watching a replay of a Chelsea match.

"This just in Inspector."

"Thank you Mr. Billings."

"May we have the envelope please?" Ali quietly announced as he stood and moved closer to Morrissey.

"And the winner is . . ." Dunn added.

"Ladies and gentlemen, the winner is a Raymundo Cancalo Jordão Battesta!" Morrissey read as he held up an accompanying full color photo sent by the French.

"Very interesting!" Ali declared as he read it then passed the document to Dunn.

The picture of a 40ish, Hispanic man with one brown eye and one blue eye was accented by the tracings of a moustache and a barely noticeable scar on his left forehead.

"Is he wearing one contact lens?" Ali asked.

"Heterochromia iridium." Morrissey

volunteered. It's a rare genetic anomaly. Prevalent in less than one per cent of the population."

"Oh yeah! That's what I was gonna say." Dunn mocked.

"Apparently **Captain** Battesta is the former head of State Security."

"In Brazil? That is very interesting!" Ali added.

"In Venezuela."

While the members of the SHIT squad were yelling and high fiving each other in front of the main counter out on the rental floor, an old couple shuffled through the front door of the rental agency.

Spotting the rabble rousers causing a ruckus at the front desk, they hesitated, did a slow about face and went back out.

*** *** ***

Merchant Street
London's East End

José Santiago, Erik Mathias, Sebastian Coro and Raymundo Cancalo Jordão Battesta were in the process of casually packing their carry-on luggage in the non-descript East End safe house off the A11 which they had occupied for the last five days.

José Santiago, the only one in the spy cell not packing, was busy comprising a report for transmission back to their handlers when he could hold his tongue no longer and spoke up.

"Raymundo, why did you start us out on this

wild duck chase?!" Spinning in his seat to face his leader he also gauged the reaction of his two comrades across the room. "I don't understand why the African airliner isn't enough." Santiago protested.

"I tell you why José." Not seriously concerned with his communications specialist questioning his orders Raymundo continued gathering personal belongings from around the room. "We now have the upper hand."

"How, exactly?"

"Now that they realize we are not small fish trying to play at a big game, we have their attention. The Americans and the Brits like to publically brag they will not bargain with our kind. But they do. They just don't do it where their public can see them. However, sometimes they have to be shown that there is no option." Battesta calmly answered.

"Goose chase you idiot! It's goose chase, not duck chase!" Erik Mathias, not a patient man, stood in front of the mirror methodically rewrapping his man bun.

Mathias was a former hit man for the Venezuelan internal security force known as the SEBIN, Venezuela's answer to Himmler's SS, only not as warm and cuddly.

Born in Brazil of German immigrant parents, he was a promising mechanical engineer who became politically radicalized while attending U.C. Berkley in the U.S.

Upon returning to Rio De Janeiro he fell in with

the *A Frente do Povo*, The People's Front, eventually abandoning his pursuit of engineering altogether.

During the 2016 presidential election riots at Berkley, after being arrested for participating in a fire bombing incident is when he graduated to the FBI's TSDB or Terrorist Screening Data Base list.

Mathias gladly extended Raymundo's reasoning. "Everything's developing exactly the way that old communist Brezmenov said it would! The useful idiot' plan is working beautifully! Their mainstream press have all but collapsed, the professors and feminists are undermining the educational system disrupting and rewriting their history, that country has never been more polarized! There's even a Marxist in the U.S. Senate for the first time ever!"

"That idiot Ocasio Cortez?" Santiago countered. "She's a buffoon! Every time she opens her mouth she reminds the world of how stupid she is."

"She may be a buffoon but at least it was money well spent to get her in!" Mathias commented.

"For once Putin's people did something right!" Sebastian Coro added. Mathias continued.

"That political prostitute Cortez along with the puppet Sanders is useful enough to help destabilize the already dishevelled democrats leaving America with one functioning political party!" Raymundo approved.

"My question is why were we sidetracked into this technological sabotage bullshit?" Santiago pushed. "Our mission was to undermine one of the world's largest oil reserves so Moscow could come to the rescue of the Venezuelan people after Maduro went to them for help."

"Yes, and of course that's exactly what Putin is going to do' 'Come to our rescue' he sarcastically mocked. How old are you Santiago?" Battesta chastised.

"I meant it as a euphemism." José defended.

"Do you think for a minute Putin is going to shift resources from his own spheres of influence to help us? He'll be preoccupied with Syria for the next decade, is busy keeping his eye on the Ukraine and with the other arm is wrestling with China who's struggling to keep a leash in that megalomaniac in North Korea! Besides the idiot Germans just signed a multi-billion Euro deal with him to buy gas! Putin no more needs Venezuelan oil then Trump needs bad press!"

"Besides Trump would never allow so many Russians so close to his own country." Coro joined in.

"Then if you believe Putin will not aide us, who-" José challenged Battesta.

"The one man who is at the head of the only country who has the ability to help us!"

"Trump?! You're insane!" José Santiago argued.

"Not Trump you donkey! Bolsonaro. Brasil backed by the U.S. They will use the same ploy Putin's people are trying to use in Venezuela now. But Putin's people will fail. With so many Americans in the dark, uneducated about world affairs-"

"As they invariably are!" Mathias interjected.

"Precisely! With so many uneducated in world affairs the unending attacks by the press on the White House will allow the people to side with Trump. We must be alert to all that is happening in the world stage as well as in the headlines!" Battesta continued the ideological narrative.

"Once we guarantee the Americans complete secrecy so there is no political embarrassment to them or to Venezuela, once they are completely convinced of our abilities, they will bargain!"

"How do you know?!" José challenged.

"Roosevelt did it with Emmanuel of Italy in 1943. Kissinger did it with Ho Chi Min and Reagan did it with Gorbachov! Negotiation works! So long as you have a something to bargain with!" Battesta argued.

Revealing his distaste for the mission to date Santiago opened up.

"And tell me Erik, what more will we do to finally show them our capability? Hijack another school bus? Crash more airplanes? And Raymundo, whose idea was it to kidnap the bus load of schoolgirls, to divert the headlines?"

"Where were your vehement protests when the money was delivered José Santiago? When the last operational funds from Moscow or Caracas didn't arrive what were we supposed to do? Form a fucking boy band and take to the streets busking?"

"My question still stands! What are we, much

less Moscow to gain from this James Bond shit?" José Santiago insisted.

In a time honored male challenge dating back to the origin of man Raymundo Battesta quietly made eye contact and stared at Santiago.

"I don't give a fuck about all that ideological subversion bullshit! Do you understand?!" His red face standing as a warning to the others, Battesta moved in to stand face to face with Santiago. "I want Maduro!" He backed off and collected himself. "You are free to go home any time you like José Santiago."

A long silence blanketed the room. There was no doubt in anyone's mind that they needed some sort of victory if the mission was to continue. Finally Battesta once again spoke.

"The world looks at our people, the Venezuelans like a ragged collection of Third World peasants! We were one of the richest countries in the world! But our great savior Chavez had us well and truly fooled! I followed him, same as all the rest. We trusted him with big boy toys but, little could we know he had the mentality of a child. So what did he do? Led us to a 90% poverty and a 4,000% inflation rate! Our people are eating from garbage cans! I will remedy that!"

Raymundo grabbed his suitcase and back pack and left.

"Erik, I've finished testing this spoofer device. Where do you want it?" José Santiago asked.

****

U.S. Consulate
Nine Elms District
Wandsworth, London
16:57 Saturday, 17 August

At 14:10 Irina Kuksova, FBI researcher, acting American undercover agent and Russian by birth stepped off the Tube at the Battersea station on the North line extension of the London Underground and walked the short distance to the new embassy building opposite St. George's Square on the south bank of the Thames.

Approaching the building, which looked for all the world like a giant, twelve story high ice cube, she pushed through the double glass doors, flashed her I.D. and badge to the Marine in his class C uniform who stood at the turnstile before she faced the security camera and assumed a neutral expression.

The perfectly starched and groomed Marine behind the desk activated the facial recognition software and perused the monitor behind the desk.

"Good evening Ms. Kuksova."

"Good evening Corporal."

"Purpose of your visit today Ma'am?"

"I have some paperwork to wrap up for tomorrow's meeting." There was no need for him to write anything down, the entire conversation had been recorded, dated and filed before Irina stepped through the eight foot tall metal detector.

He scanned the screen on his desk and waved her through.

"You have a nice evening Agent Kuksova."

"Thank you Corporal."

Kuksova might have been FBI currently holding a TS level clearance and had access to most of the departments and offices in the embassy however, she nor anyone else, the Ambassador included, had unfettered access to all the offices in the Consulate building.

As there are no National Transportation Safety Board offices overseas, agents of the NTSB branch usually worked out of the local embassies, so she realized she would have to get her information from one of the stateside offices.

Unfortunately flying to D.C. and back again would be too ponderous, too time consuming, too complicated and far too risky. So, the next logical thing; intercept the report before it got to D.C.

The accident site, now only about 56 hours old, should have just been reached two days ago by the Italian team she knew to be in Rome at the time investigating a small train wreck which they by now had concluded.

Familiar with their S.O.P. and the fact that rather than prep and fly a whole new team from D.C. to Africa, Irina knew they would have flown the closest team, the one in Rome, down to Nairobi.

As using the FBI's dedicated office wasn't a good idea access to the currently unoccupied office of the Agricultural Secretary was easy enough and she got to work immediately hacking into the D.C. files.

Her first task was to track down the name of the lead investigator of the train wreck team. Simple enough.

After finding the name then confirming the whereabouts of the Rome team through the GAO accounting office and finding the team in Rome had indeed been ordered to Nairobi, she moved to the NTSB current files sector and searched 'Accidents, Aircraft'.

Two minutes later she smiled and mumbled *Eureka!* Then . . .

"Son-of-a-bitch!" She cursed out loud.

The report was marked, 'Cc'd to FBI office, London. To the Attention of Special Agent Sims'.

Suddenly she heard the office door open behind her.

"Is there something I can help you with Agent Kuksova?" She was careful not to betray being startled by not turning around immediately. It was the Assistant Secretary to the Consulate General, Lawson, the number two man in the embassy.

"Just finishing up a PR blurt for Woody."

Assuming she meant Woody Johnson, the current Ambassador, as she knew he would, it gave him pause.

"I see. What blurt exactly?" He grunted. She added the icing.

"Since the latest street stabbings, the D.C. office

wants weekly reports from our office on the street crime situation over here."

"And why exactly are we not using our own office agent? The F.B.I. office which was installed at an additional cost of 2.7 million dollars, security measures included?"

Irina took in a deep breath, let it out and slowly spun around in her chair as she assumed just the right amount of faux irritated defiance. She purposely allowed her skirt to slide halfway up her thigh. He ignored the sexual bait.

Must be gay! She thought to herself.

"I'm fully aware of the cost of our suite Mr. Secretary. However, when you build a building at the cost of a billion dollars, the most expensive embassy in the world ever built, and the builder goes with the cheapest IT company even though they have all the necessary clearances, your ASCII files are bound to get crossed with your BCP circuits when you initiate your Hayes Command Set, ergo temporarily rendering your particular IT lines inoperative until the glitch can be found and rectified! It's basic Boolean logic! But of course then . . . you know that don't you?"

He stared blankly.

"Uh huh." He grunted.

She turned and resumed her work, quickly opening a new window to camouflage her NTSB window. "Things were much simpler before we moved over here. Back when we were still in Westminster, I mean." She said.

"Yes, quite." Not completely convinced but with no angle from which to further his attack the Assistant Secretary turned and left.

"Fuckin' pencil neck!" She mumbled and produced a USB tab from the lining in her handbag.

By 17:32 Special Agent Irina Kuksova was passing through the front door with what she came for and was back out on Nine Elms Lane heading for dinner.

Maybe Mahone's right! The sex angle DOESN'T work anymore! She thought to herself as she turned the corner onto the quays

****

"The Fielding Hotel in Coventry, this is reception. How may I help you?" The receptionist answered.

Room 7A please.

"Certainly."

"Hello." Mahone answered.

Frank, it's me.

"Hey, good evening Doll!"

Cool it Romeo!

"Okay, what's the plan?"

Victoria and Albert Museum, in Knightsbridge. Tomorrow, half one. Don't be late!

"Should I pack a lunch?"

No. We can stop for a Happy Meal on the way! I'll be at the statue of David. Be on time! Irina hung up.

Jesus! Will this guy ever grow up?! She said to herself.

Holding the phone's receiver at arm's length Frank spoke to himself.

"Jesus! I've met corpses with better senses of humor!" He climbed into bed, switched off the lamp and went to sleep.

＊

Knightsbridge, London
The Cromwell Road
Sunday 12:25

Frank stood in front of the one meter by two meter wall poster of a pair of radioactively deformed spiders with multi-colored legs apparently having sex with each other. The red, white and blue logo below was simply labelled 'Underground'

"Looks like somebody gave a kid a box of Crayolas, a shot of whiskey and told him to have at it!" He shook his head then traced the train lines on the wall poster of the Underground until he located Knightsbridge.

It was a relatively short ride and along with a battalion of shoppers Mahone disembarked at the South Kensington station, rode the travelator to the exit and headed north back towards the museum.

When he was nearly through the ornate, sprawling front entrance of the museum, he stopped and looked down at the ground. "Son-of-a-bitch!"

330

He quietly cursed. "If I don't do it I'll never hear the end of it!"

Moving back down the steps and out about fifty yards back up the main path, he pulled out his phone, took several pictures of the entrance then headed back up and into the museum.

Inside he made his way to the desk, collected a brochure with the floor layout from the rack and located the Sculpture Room.

He was surprised to see Kuksova dressed in a flowered dress, a sun hat and draped in a light jacket, smiling and waving happily from across the floor by the Michelangelo replica as she made her way towards him.

"Hug me." She said in a loud whisper.

"What?"

"Hug me asshole!" He complied. "We're supposed to be intimates."

"Better kiss then you know, to make it look real."

"We're not that intimate!" She pushed him away then took his arm and led him across the floor instead. "Let's go look at something I know a New York Homicide detective will be interested in.

She appeared to know the layout well and led him through the warren of corridors and exhibit halls directly into a spacious, ballroom-like display area with multiple, giant bell jar displays of ornately dressed mannequins.

"The fucking Victorian evening gown collection?! Are you serious?!" He declared.

Evilly smirking, Irina congratulated herself on evading any tails there might have been while simultaneously perpetrating her prank on Mahone.

"What's the matter, not Butch enough for you?" She challenged as he stared and walked around one of the large glass enclosed displays of cumbersome, colourful and ornate dresses.

"No, not that at all! I'm overwhelmed!" He stepped close into the nearest display and closely examined it. "How did you know my mother was a seamstress?! I was very close to my mother. She would have loved to have seen these. Thank you!" He declared skirting around and wistfully perusing another of the displays. "Thank you Agent Kuksova!"

"Hey, Bonehead! Cool it with the 'Agent' shit! We're supposed to be undercover."

"Get serious! This place is like a church on Super Bowl Sunday. There's nobody here who cares what we're sayin'."

After scanning for anyone following them anyway, she retook his arm and led them slowly towards a side exit.

"Okay, petty gags aside, how'd you make out?" He quietly asked.

"I'm pretty sure I got what we need. All that was in the NTSB file anyway."

"How the hell did you manage that?!"

"Don't ask."

"Okay I won't. You looked at it?"

"A quick glance is all I had time for. But we

can't examine it here."

"Where to?"

"My car. I feel safer outside the city."

"Okay." Frank readily agreed but his Spidy sense immediately began tingling with the suggestion of getting out of town. He quickly got to work formulating a plan and waited until they were down on the ground floor of the museum when he spotted a men's room under the staircase by the exit.

"I need to see a man about a horse before we shove off." He nodded towards the loo but was careful to make eye contact with her.

"I'll wait by the door." She let him know without reacting to his eye contact.

Once inside the toilet he quickly manned his phone.

"Morrissey?"

Frank! What's got you so bored that you're ringing me on a Sunday afternoon?

"Pay attention, I don't have a lot of time! I'm with Kuksova-"

The FBI bird?!

"Yeah."

Mahone what the hell are you-

"Listen to me, we're heading out of town-"

Where to?

"Don't know but keep your phone on. I'll text you when we get there. This chick is into something and I don't know what it is but it stinks seven ways from Sunday!"

I assume that means it's bad?

333

"That's exactly why you'll make Chief Inspector someday! If you don't hear from me by nine or ten tonight send in the cavalry, you got that?"

You don't honestly think-

"This is the FBI brother, Fastly Being Integrated into a missing person is their motto! I'll text you by ten."

Stepping over to the row of sinks and quickly running a comb through his hair to make it look like he was sprucing up, he met Kuksova in the vestibule of the side exit and they made their way to her car.

Once on the road Frank decided to probe for intel.

"Where to this time?" He casually asked.

"I rented a room for the night in a little dive out near Brentford just off the A1."

"Really?! A hotel room?"

"Keep it in your pants Charlie Sheen! It's because we'll be working late and I don't want to do this around the embassy office. We need to keep this away from official channels."

"Oh? Why?"

"For now I mean. At least until we're sure of our hand."

"**You** rented a room? How come you're footing the bill? Don't you guys get an expense account" He probed.

"Tonight's not on the books." She said.

His suspicions rose. Kuksova paying would leave no paper trail. He decided on a distraction maneuver.

"Explain to me, in plain speak please, the connection of GPS with world finance, because I gotta be honest I never heard anything about that."

"You're not alone. Joe Citizen doesn't realize-"

"You learn all this in FBI school?" She ignored his interruption as she drove.

"Joe Citizen doesn't realize the extent to which the GPS timing signal is critical for ATM transactions and literally every point-of-sale transaction conducted in the United States and throughout most of the rest of the world."

"So how do we defend against an asshole who can bring the world's economic system to near collapse from the safety of his mom's fucking basement?"

"What the hell do you think **we're** doing?!"

"Ah hah! So what you're saying is . . . it's you and me against the world Baby?"

She pulled back and stared blankly at him.

"How in God's name did someone with your maturity level rise to the responsible position of Lieutenant Detective in the Homicide Division in the largest police force in the Western world?"

"Guy in front of me for promotion got killed responding to a 211. I got bumped up." He shrugged.

She stared. He assumed a dopey smile and shrugged again.

"Hey, don't blame me! That's the system Baby!."

She exuded a deep sigh of frustration.

"Can we get back to work please?"

"Sorry."

"And stop calling me Baby! It's sexist."

"Oh Christ! You're not one'a those are you?"

"One'a what?!" She demanded.

"Nothing, nothing. Let's get this figured out. There's a cricket match that I have to fall asleep to later. I'm an insomniac, it's the only cure." She suppressed a laugh.

"The van job was probably because he needed more operational cash." Irina continued.

"Okay, we thought the same."

"My suspicions are, now that we know what we know, is that the BA airliner hijack was to test some newly designed spoofer."

"Sounds logical. And extremely threatening. If this asshole can do that to **one** airplane-"

"Exactly! It gives terrorism a whole new dimension."

"But that still leaves us with two big questions - is this Jamoke working alone and does he have some big Dr. Evil plan?"

"What's a Jamoke?!" She asked.

"A jerk. A loser. You know, an asshole."

"You really are from New York aren't you?"

They reached the small, out of town hotel by half past four and checked in.

He held the room door for her then, coming in behind her slipped the 'Do Not Disturb' sign on the outside of the door and locked it after himself.

As he watched her slip off her jacket and shoes she cleared the coffee table, dumped her purse out and open it all the way.

"I only snagged the NTSB report. There were a handful of other documents in the file but none of which related to our case."

She knelt on the floor at the large coffee table in front of the couch and opened her laptop.

He didn't completely buy her story but could think of no real reason to question whether or not there were any other papers in the NTSB file.

He sat beside her on the plaid coved couch and watched as she pulled open a Velcro pouch to reveal a false bottom in her large, patent leather handbag and then pull out several electronic items amongst which were several small, flat USB sticks and an item the size of two small fingers. Mahone picked up it and examined it.

"What the hell is this thing?"

"It's a low light camera." She took it back off him and placed it in her purse.

"So that's where my tax dollars go?"

She plugged in one of the flat USB's and waited for the files to come upon her laptop.

"You don't wanna know where your tax dollars go Detective. Trust me!" She quipped.

"Why all the Jane Bond gear?"

"Because I'm not supposed to have this so if certain people became suspicious enough to detain me the first thing they'd nab would be my phone along with the evidence in said phone. Providing we have any evidence." The window opened. "This is the first page of a ten page report." Scrolling past the first two pages of the report she informed him. He readjusted himself sitting on the couch behind her to better view the screen.

"It says twelve pages." He questioned.

"First page is the cover page and the next is just instructions."

"I always thought these things were bigger. Longer I mean."

"Yeah, like I always thought the black box was black." She adjusted the screen and focused on the first actual page of information. "Length of the report depends on the incident. But that's not normal!" She declared as she used the cursor to point to the 'NTSB EYES ONLY!' stamped in the four corners of the cover page

"'Eyes Only!', that's a higher classification level than Secret." Frank observed. "So what'a we looking at?"

She scrolled down.

"This is the AAR1809, the *Collision with Terrain Accident Report* for this specific incident."

They spent about thirty minutes carefully perusing all ten pages and every detail of the report. They found nothing that seemed out of the ordinary.

"Except for the EYES ONLY thing it looks like an accident report to me." Frank commented.

"Shit! I was sure there'd be something in here!" Irina declared as she scrolled back through it.

Mahone rose and moved to the honor bar and

poured himself a whiskey.

"You want a drink?"

"White wine, thank you."

"What's the weather box say again?" He asked.

"It's Central Africa. Clear and sunny."

"No bird strike, mechanical malfunction?"

"No, it's clear, pilot error."

"If this place Burnandi-"

"How are you a detective? It's Berundi!"

"I told you, I-"

"Never mind! I remember."

"Berundi is mountainous country, isn't it?'

"Like the Rockies."

"So there's no way in hell anybody was able to get a team out there in a matter of a day or so to go over the wreckage."

"Not one day. Two maybe." She added.

Drinks in hand he retook his seat on the couch. "You snag anything else from that file?"

"Not from the file but I found a 6120 memo to British Air from the NTSB inspector promising an estimated date and time for the report."

"What's on that?"

"Essentially the same info. Date, time, location. Number of casualties, probable cause."

"No difference?"

"Only the names of the official recipients who are supposed to get a copy of the report."

"We missed something. Go back to the copies of the two inspector's papers." She typed in the names and waited. "Now back through to the 1809." He instructed.

"Got it."

"That's timed and dated, yeah?" He affirmed.

"13:10, 12 August."

"That the date of submission?"

"No, it's the date the report was filled out. It wouldn't have been submitted until the next day."

"And the bus hijack incident, there was no sign of anything in the file you saw?"

"You know there's not. We already went that route."

"Now flip back to that FBI memo we thought was irrelevant, the one requesting NTSB sign off on the bus incident." She did and seconds later her head snapped up from her computer screen.

"18:10, Monday, 12 August!" She read aloud.

"The highjack was over two weeks earlier, at the end of July!" He added. "The twelfth's' gotta be the evening the NTSB inspector came through London." Mahone guessed.

"But why would he sign off on an incident without actually seeing-?"

"Because he didn't see it! Someone's trying to bury the bus report."

"Why?" She questioned.

"Someone from the London office must have requested the NTSB to send a rep after the bus hijack was over." He affirmed.

"You lost me." She said.

"The bus report's in that file somewhere!" He insisted

"But I had time to search that whole file. It wasn't there." Irina insisted.

"It was there. It just wasn't labelled as a bus/road incident." He theorized.

"Why would an NTSB inspector, the same NTSB inspector, be carrying a report on the bus hijack?"

"It was probably fed to him to bury it as an accident. Probably to divert attention from the fact that it was a hijacking."

"It was all over the news!" She insisted. "You can't hide it was a hijack, not something that big!"

"It was big over here, for about two hours, until it was time for the next big story. The folks stateside have no idea what the hell happens over here unless it involves America. And even if they do it's forgotten by the next morning."

"Okay, but more importantly, how can two reports on the same exact incident, filed by a member of the same exact inspection team have two different times on them seven hours apart?"

"They can't." Frank declared. "My theory is if we track this guy to or from the bus hijack to the plane incident we can track who he is and possibly where's he's based."

"If he's actually based anywhere." She challenged.

"He has to be. He has too much material support to be a lone wolf."

"That stands to reason, but between London and D.C. there are over two dozen agents working on this case and it's gonna be a real rodeo beating them to the punch while still trying to remain invisible. How do we connect the two without raising red flags?"

"Look at the time on the 1809." She scrolled back. "Now look at the time on the memo."

"They're off by seven hours!" She observed.

"BINGO! Plenty of time to jiggle the facts around and get it to D.C. before it was submitted to the authorities in Nairobi." Frank opened another of the small bottles. "The discrepancies in times backed by the fact that somebody in D.C. saw it before anybody in Nairobi definitely means somebody, probably the London people, are hiding something!" He added.

"Not to mention the 'EYES ONLY' stamp on it. There's no reason to classify a routine air accident that high." She reinforced.

"Unless it wasn't routine!"

"Or worse yet, something that wasn't an accident!"

"What'a ya wanna bet that 'something' can only be someone in the FBI person who knows there was a spoofer used to crash that BA flight!" Mahone concluded their deductions.

It was well over an hour since they had started and both appeared ready for a breather.

"I'd say that calls for a drink!" Irina declared as she rose from the floor and made her way over to the bar.

"I agree. But let's not rest on our laurels, time's

becoming a factor. Let's push on. When you first attacked me in the pub-

"You mean when I first approached you as a fellow professional and you so rudely shunned me!"

"Sorry, I must have misremembered. When we talked you mentioned something about GPS and finance."

"Yeah. Besides being used to operate ATM's, route your phone calls and cash register transactions, GPS is used to send power to your house and business from the public electrical grid. Also the Stock Exchange uses it to regulate the trades that go into investment funds and portfolios."

"GPS does all that shit?!"

"When you pull cash from an ATM or swipe your card at the coffee shop, the machine needs to determine the precise time that the transaction occurs to, for example, prevent it from being over-drawn. Since digital money moves faster than humans can think, banks and regulators rely on time stamps to monitor transactions and make sure the right people get paid. More importantly to catch fraud. But, over time, even the most precise clocks start to differ from one another.

Time doesn't much matter when you're meeting me for lunch at noon, but if you're timing transactions down to the microsecond, which is the standard now used in bank's electronic networks, tiny differences can screw up your whole operation. What makes the Global Positioning System so crucial then, isn't in the 'positioning' part. It's the ability to make machines all over the planet agree on exactly what time it is."

"You mentioned the Stock Exchange?"

"What about it?"

"You reckon there's a connection with FARC as part of the deal for them to help to attack Wall Street?"

"That's certainly one possible scenario." She nodded.

"Jesus! How deep's this rabbit hole go?"

"Deep!"

He fell back and laid on the floor to stare at the ceiling.

"Look, we're not going to get much else done tonight, so why don't we just talk." He offered.

She peered at him not trusting his motives. "At least try to become friends!" He insisted

"Me thinketh thou hat an anterior motive dear sir!" She teased as she opened another mini-bottle of Cabernet Sauvignon.

"Jesus! Two jokes in one week!"

Kuksova slowly flipped him the bird, British style.

"You **have** been here too log!" He quipped.

It was after her third drink that Kuksova began to loosen up. She fell into a slumped seat on the couch.

"All right, you wore me down. True Confessions time." She blurted out. Frank adjusted himself up on one elbow.

"Okay, deal. You tell me yours and I'll tell you mine."

"OOOKAYY?!" Came her confused reply. "You remember an agent named Sims?"

"Can't say as I do."

The hallmark of a man who has reached the point where he trusts no one is that he has no desire to reveal anything to anybody unless absolutely necessary. The hallmark of woman who is on a mission to corral a man into telling her what she wants to know is her tenacity.

"You were visited at the Hamlet van crime scene by two agents, one tall and slender, one big and stocky. Both not very bright looking. The tall mouth breather was Special Agent Sims."

"Ahh! Mouth breather, that rings a bell." He waited for her to volunteer more info. She wasn't about to. "So you're working for Sims?"

"Sims?! Christ no! He's robbery and fraud I'm assigned Counter Intel. Sims! If he actually had a brain he'd be dangerous to himself and the community! No, not working for or with the asshole known as Sims."

"So how do you really feel about him?"

"Special Agent Sims trained under former Director Comey where he picked up some very bad habits. One of which was playing both sides of the fence. I don't have any idea what he's up to now, but whatever it is it's wrong, it's bad and probably illegal. And, as you've so astutely pointed out, before the Bureau gets another black eye, I intend to –"

"HOLD ON CHICK!" He stopped her. "Don't

go sharing any classified shit I don't need to know which is gonna bring the fucking NSA busting in my house in the middle of the night and drag me off to some secret safe house that doesn't exist according to *Sixty Minutes*!"

"Too late for that dude! You became a player the moment I approached you in *Dirty Dick's*. Classy place by the way."

"Great! Just what I fuckin' need on top of everything else!"

"Why's that?'

"I'm two steps away from mandatory retirement because there's a middle-aged shrink who's pissed off she never became a homicide detective and so thinks because I'm too dumb to get shot and killed but still keep catching bad guys that she's compelled to make it her mission to get me booted off the force.

"I see. What's your plan?"

"I fully intend to exploit this gift from the cop gods and nail this fuck!"

"You intend to do this despite the fact that you have no real jurisdiction, it's not an NYPD or an FBI matter because it's international and therefore falls under the jurisdiction of INTERPOL and is currently being led by the London Met? And oh yeah, you don't even have a gun."

Frank smiled as he choose his words.

"My father always said there's nothing like an impossible task to force a good man to rise to the challenge!"

"Sounds like he was either crazy or a good man."

"He was a good man. A very good man. Just born out of time." Frank finished his drink and returned to the bar. "Why have you got such a hard-on for this asshole Sims?"

Kuksova chose her words before answering.

"My father once told me that right is right no matter if nobody does it and wrong is wrong no matter if everybody does it. Sims is as crooked as five miles of country road! A Clinton hold-over from the bad old days! Assholes like him are what give us, the Bureau, a bad name. Sims is just wrong!"

Mahone was amused in a good way at her apparent dedication.

"May I propose a proposal?" He offered. She turned towards him, made eye contact and became more attentive.

"Okay."

"You help me nail my asshole and I'll help make sure you nail yours. Deal, Agent Kuksova?"

Appearing to be mulling it over she was, in reality, soaking in the moment.

"Deal, Detective Mahone!" She nodded in assurance.

Now with the last of the wine in her glass and Mahone lifting the last of the whiskey from the honor bar the clock was nearing midnight when Irina excused herself and headed into the en suite bathroom.

Frank lay back on the floor and stared up at

nothing and let his mind wander.

For the first time since Ciccione's funeral he was moved to give some weight to his own long term future.

Should he stay in London and see this thing through? The relevance of the outcome had certainly taken on new significance now that he was 'on the inside' so to speak.

Or should he go back to New York? New York and the 13th Precinct? Where Agnes the receptionist for the Homicide squad made coffee so bad the Hispanic cleaning staff used it to clean the staircase after hours.

Go back to the 13th and do what? Retire? Fly a desk? Fight the shrink? Stay in The City and find another apartment to get robbed in?

His last thought before hearing the bathroom door open was thank god his marriage was over and thank, thank God they had no kids!

It was only ten minutes after she went in that Irina finally emerged from the bathroom. She had changed into a robe and slide on pumps.

Frank had stood and was preparing to leave.

"Why don't you stay?" She asked.

He turned and stared but suppressed his surprise.

"I'd love to Sweetheart, I really would. But truth is I'm not quite over my divorce. Maybe at a later date I can reconsider how I feel about it."

"Maybe this will help you get over it!" Suddenly she dropped her robe to expose a very revealing skimpy top and panties. Mahone nodded and smiled curtly.

"Very kind of you to offer and the underwear is lovely but. . . I'm not quite ready."

"Underwear?! These are Victoria's Secret, French cut, and satin thonged briefs! $62.50 with tax!"

"I'm sorry Irina, I . . . just . . ." He quickly made for the door and disappeared into the hall.

She stood and stared in utter disbelief.

"SON-OF-A-BITCH!" She stomped her foot walked over to and fell back on the couch. "Did not even see that coming!" She glanced over at the empty mini-wine bottles scattered across the counter. "This all your fault, ya little bastards!"

Still struggling to process the fact that her plan crashed and burned so suddenly, Irina started to pack up her laptop when the room door slowly creaked back open and Mahone stepped back in.

"Okay, I reconsidered!" He shrugged as he peeled off his jacket which he draped over a chair. "But only conversation. No sex!"

He was just fast enough to dodge the shoe which shot past his head.

****

Mahone rolled over, checked his watch on the night stand and tapped Irina on her upturned hip. She began to stir.

"Morning Sunshine." He said quietly.

"Coffee!" She quietly mumbled into her pillow.

Suddenly there was a vigorous knock against the front door backed by several male voices whispering loudly out in the hallway.

Frank jumped from the bed, pulled on his underwear, grabbed Irina's Walther PPK from her purse and headed to the vestibule. Pulling on her hotel robe Irina was right behind him. He listened carefully to the hushed voices just outside.

"Sounds like they're giving each other instructions." He whispered to her. He listened more closely, then held up four fingers to indicate the probable number outside the door. Noticing the weight of the pistol felt light he ejected the magazine. It was empty. He looked back questioningly at her.

"I've never had to use it!" She whispered back in defense.

Just then the door was slammed open and three heavily armed police piled into the narrow hall. One of them instantly drew a bead on Mahone who dropped the pistol and raised his hands as the others dispersed into the room.

Behind the breech team Morrissey, hands in pockets, appeared in the doorway. He perused the two in their night clothes, smiled and nodded.

"Are we interrupting Detective Mahone, Agent Kuksova?"

Irina ignored him and headed back into the bedroom to dress.

After he dismissed the uniforms Morrissey

headed out behind them.

"Shall we be expecting you at the office today Detective?" He asked from the doorway.

"Possibly later this afternoon, Inspector. The lady and I will be going to brunch." Mahone replied retrieving the pistol.

Checking to be sure Irina was out of ear shot Morrissey quietly asked Mahone.

"Anything I need to know?"

"I'll send you a memo." He forcibly guided Morrissey back towards the door. "I thought you were supposed to be here last night?"

"I thought you were supposed to text me last night."

"Shit sorry! I was otherwise engaged." Mahone pushed him out the door and closed it over. Irina appeared from the bathroom now dressed.

"What the hell was that all about?" She restrained herself but made it clear she wanted an explanation.

"We're friends . . . colleagues."

"I know who he is. He was at the pub with you."

"We sometimes work together. I was supposed to check in last night but forgot." Mahone awkwardly explained.

"That was Morrissey. What exactly the hell is going on with you and that character?"

"Nothing. We need to decide on a plan of action. You want breakfast?"

"First coffee!" She lifted the phone to rang room service.

"I've got a pretty full day! What time is getting to be?"

"It's just after eight." She told him.

"What time's check out?"

"Ten, ten-thirty. Why?"

Frank made his way over to her, took the receiver from her hand and . . .

Later that morning . . .

It was ten fifty-five when they made their way through the hotel lobby and, on the suggestion of the concierge they found a small village café and sat outside in the sun.

"Monday morning brunch on Uncle Sam's dime. Thank you very much!" Frank boasted.

"Risking your life for eggs Benedict and strawberry daiquiris? It seems worth it." She said. They toasted.

"The African plane crash thing?" He opened.

"Oh yeah! Sorry I forgot."

"No wonder! Your brain's nearly full up with all that technology shit!"

"I'll take that as a compliment."

"You should. Quick recap. Airplane crash-Africa. And let's keep it simple please."

"Simple enough that even a cop could understand?" She jabbed as she moved the plates and set up her lap top on the table again calling up the report. She read through the addendum notes added by the NTSB inspector.

"Touché." Frank replied.

"By the notes it appears both African embassies immediately agreed to host an NTSB team. The report states pilot error in navigational malfunction of unknown origin."

"How long had the co-pilot and pilot been flying?"

She read from the screen as she answered.

"It was their first flight of the day but time at the stick, eighteen and twenty-one years respectively. Both with more than ten years on the Nairobi to J-burg run."

"I'd say that pretty much 86's the pilot error theory." Frank emphasized.

"Agreed." She added.

"A terrorist would have attacked a larger international flight not just a small plane on a short domestic hop. Generally they want us to know who they are. Additionally no one has claimed responsibility." Frank observed.

"Yet." She countered.

"It's coming up on a full week, if this were your run-of-the-mill yellow-bellied, towel-head terrorists they'd have sent a message praising Allah along with all their other bullshit by now."

"I get the impression you've got a beef with terrorists?" She queried.

"I'm from New York City. Maybe you heard, we had an incident once."

"Sorry, forgot. But why a BA flight? Why not a South African Airways?" She wondered out loud.

"To make a point. An African plane crashes it gets a mention. A British airliner goes into a mountain and it makes the front pages internationally as a terrorist attack."

"There's something else. Something weird."

"Like what?"

"Weird thing is the U.S. embassy in Nairobi contacted the Burundi and Kenyan governments to offer help. Normally when a plane crash comes over the wire the State Department waits to be contacted by the host nation asking for help, then notifies us when the NTSB is sent out."

"So it's not standard protocol for D.C. to offer help in such cases?" Frank probed.

"Not unless it's an American airliner, some big international case or a significant number of Americans are involved. Or . . ." She leaned over to the window and stared out.

"Or what? Don't leave me hanging!"

"Or unless somebody in D.C. wants something from somebody."

"What would anyone in D.C. want from Nairobi or Bujamba, Bujambubu, bujam-"

"Bujumbura."

"I knew that! I was just giving you a chance to show off."

"We find out the 'who' we'll find out the 'what'." She observed.

"Huh! Definitely smells like somebody else is chasing our man. Can you access some more info?" Frank asked.

"Depends. Like what?"

"Find out if the exact chain of commo from the time of the crash, how soon the NTSB team were dispatched and how long it took for them to get findings to Nairobi."

"I can do that."

"Most importantly, verify that the final report went through D.C. first before it was sent to Nairobi."

"Of course not! By law NTSB has to give the final report to the host or requesting nation before anyone else! Nairobi would have to deal with the friends and relatives."

"Exactly which is why I think we might find a surprise."

"I just thought of something else." She blurted out.

"What?"

"If someone in the government is involved why are they being so sneaky about it?"

"Probably because they're friends with Hilary Clinton."

"Hey! I voted for her!"

"Not your fault. I'm just sayin'!" He shrugged.

*** ✳ ***

"Seventh floor, Section three please." Irina spoke clearly into the transceiver.

The foot traffic in the lobby of the Kensington *London Hilton* was light but the old styled, closed

355

off phone booths afforded the privacy Kuksova needed for her short call. Secrecy wasn't a consideration but quiet was.

Not ten minutes after Mahone and her parted company at the restaurant Kuksova located a pay phone and placed a call to her boss.

Clearance please? The operator asked.

"TS, level seven. Agent I.D. 0763."

Key word please?

"Cookie Monster."

Hold please. She heard the line click through.

Kuksova?

"Yes sir."

Where the hell you been?! You should'a called in two days ago! The male voice on the other end made no attempt to hide his irritation.

"These things take time, sir."

What have you got?

"It's definitely Sims. He's still snooping around the armored van case."

What about the loser detective?

"He's hesitating but I'll get him on board."

Make sure you do! The President's summit and trade negotiations meeting with the E.U. has been announced. It's set for September the ninth just before he flies back to New York for the 9-11 Memorial.

"Got it!."

If he's not on board I want to know pronto! I don't want some flat-footed Seamus fucking this up!

"He'll come on board sir!"

We have to give the Secretary something to convince the Europeans to delay the launch of the last of the few . . .

"Sir, the Galileo program is pretty far along to think they're going to-"

I could give a shit about all that scientific technical mumbo jumbo! My job is to get them Muesli-eating, non-English speaking liberals to delay activating the Galileo system until we can develop the GPS's blocking capability! The POTUS has to know where we stand no later than Monday the ninth!

"I'll have you a full report before that."

Make sure this Mahoney clown's not stringin' you along! He's not a player hence wasn't written into the script from the start!"

"His name's Mahone sir."

Who gives a fuck?!

"Sir?"

What?

"I need to know about Sims."

Don't worry about Sims, just focus on your mission! And Kuksova?

"Sir?"

Don't fuck this up!

The line went dead.

"No pressure, huh?" She mumbled.

**

CHAPTER SIXTEEN

St. Albans Grove
South Kensington
Wednesday, 21 August

Approaching the granite steps of the elaborate red brick entrance Mahone perused the intricate stone work of the largest building, one of three on the expansive, open grounds.

"This . . . is . . . the main residence?" Frank asked slightly winded.

"Yes, why?" Morrissey confirmed.

"They should have . . . a . . . fucking taxi service from the main gate to here!"

"Most callers to this address don't have to walk." He noticed Mahone's mildly labored breathing. "Feeling our age are we old boy? One too many whiskies?"

"One too many bullets to the chest! Still working with a partially collapsed lung."

"Oh, sorry mate!" His embarrassment laced apology was sincere.

"Not your fault. So what'a we doing here?" Frank asked as he realized that, except for the rose bushes, he didn't recognize any of the other dozen various shrubbery ornamenting the hundred meter long perimeter of the nearly two hundred year old Goddard styled building.

"We're meeting a man who originally worked under a gentleman named Herman Goldstine, one of the originators of the GPS theories."

"Okay."

"His name's Dr. Stoli, Aron Stoli. Was in on the ground floor of the tech revolution back after the war. Actually met Thomas Edison at an event once."

"So he's named for Russian vodka and is getting ready to celebrate his thousandth birthday? Should I be impressed?"

"Yes, you should."

"Ya know, I met Linda Lovelace once. That was like thirty years after she became famous for *Deepthroat*. She didn't hold up so good as you might think."

Morrissey shook his head as he rang the door chime.

"What's he a doctor of, what'd he do his degree in?"

"He never did an undergraduate degree."

Frank reached in to man the large brass knocker but before he could the door opened.

"Then what the hell did he -?"

Mahone was cut off as a well postured, middle-aged butler who looked like Andre the Giant and Dwayne Johnson had a kid stood in the doorway.

"Good afternoon." Morrissey looked up and greeted.

"Good afternoon gentlemen, how may I help you?" He answered with an indiscernible accent.

"I'm Inspector Nigel Morrissey, of the Met and

this is Detective Mahone of the NY . . . ah, here to observe how we do things. We have an appointment with the doctor."

"Do come in."

Through a short hallway, off to the left they entered the study where Frank was distracted by the collection of degrees, awards and photos of famous people he never heard of plastered across the wall.

"I'll inform the doctor you've arrived. Please make yourselves comfortable."

Frank was administering a close-up exam of a large parchment degree with a red wax seal over a blue ribbon when Morrissey drifted over to him.

"Thought you said he didn't go to college?" Frank quietly whispered.

"He didn't. Didn't have to until he enrolled in graduate school after skipping an undergrad degree when he was eighteen. There was nothing the professors could teach him. He practically invented astro-communications."

Morrissey also perused the library shelves.

"How is he a doctor then?" Frank pushed.

"He has half a dozen honorary Ph.D.'s from several universities in three different countries."

"Humph! Show-off." Mahone mumbled as he attempted to decipher the Latin inscription on one of the degrees.

"Esse audi-tum a sae cu lo . . . samis honor-eye-bus . . ."

"Summis honoribus. With highest honors!"

"Okay, so he got good grades!"

The butler reappeared and they were shown next door into an office space. The over-sized servant asked if they desired anything to drink. Both declined. He pulled the French doors behind him as he backed out and they were left on their own amongst the photos, yet more awards and books. Lots and lots of books.

From a second door on the opposite wall a motorized wheel chair rolled into the room.

The heavy set old man seated in it expertly maneuvered around and parked behind the large, mahogany desk and adjusted the heavy wool blanket covering his lower half. His rat's nest of grey hair, blotchy skin and faded blue eyes revealed he was in the late stages of isotope toxicity.

"Professor, it's an honor to meet you." Morrissey greeted. Mahone concentrated on not concentrating on staring while focusing on not calling him Professor Xavier as they shook hands.

"Gentlemen." He nodded. "I assume you're here to question me about something?"

"Information Professor. Just seeking a bit of information."

"You are policemen, that's your job. My job is to finish my final text on Radiological Initiation of Ontological Modeling before I go tits up and assume room temperature! So let's get on with it, shall we?"

Morrissey was slightly put off. Mahone was impressed.

"You worked with a researcher named Dr.

Goldstine?" Morrissey queried.

"In 1939 Goldstine took a position teaching at University of Michigan where I was studying. I became his T.A."

"T.A.?" Mahone questioned.

"Teaching Assistant." Morrissey informed. Frank continued.

"Okay, so he's teaching, you're helping him teach. Who's' actually doing something?"

Stoli leaned back in his wheel chair, grunted and shook his head. Morrissey sighed.

"Ever heard of the Atom Bomb Detective Mahone?" Stoli challenged.

"I seen it in a John Wayne movie once." Frank quipped a second before Morrissey's face dropped into his hand.

"**That's** something **we** were doing Mr. Mahone."

Frank looked over at Morrissey. "Remember I asked you if I should be impressed?" Morrissey shrugged in response. "I'm impressed." Mahone declared. Stoli continued.

"Dr. Stoli," Morrissey moved in to continue the questions. ". . . we're trying to find out as much as we can with regards to the background of the GPS system. There was an incident recently with a school bus -"

"The academy school bus hijacking, yes. I follow the BBC."

"We have reason to believe-"

"Am I or my servant a suspect in any way?" Stoli pushed. Morrissey was again put off. Again Frank was impressed that Stoli didn't mince words.

"Well, no, of course not."

"Then I don't care about the details. Would you like me to continue with everything I know?"

"Please do." Morrissey took a seat as Mahone perused the large room to see that the inspector had taken the only chair.

"A gentleman working at Los Alamos became involved with the ENIAC project and arranged it so the ballistics could be calculated by computer rather than the old cumbersome artillery tables." Dr. Stoli elaborated.

"Ballistics? I thought they just took the bomb up in an airplane and dumped it?" Frank blabbed out.

"When you're bombing with conventional ordinance at ten or twenty thousand feet Mr. Mahone, you can afford to just 'dump' the bombs and continue on your way. But when you release your payload of sixty-four kilos in excess of 31,000 feet in the air which must detonate at exactly two thousand feet above target and which will create a shock wave felt nineteen to twenty kilometers away with a blast radius of over a mile in diameter, well . . . I think even you get the point, detective."

"Sixty-four kilos. How much is that in real weight?" Frank purposely agitated.

"Enough to kill more than 150,000 people and level a city the size of Hiroshima." Stoli blurted out.

"Or Nagasaki." Frank chimed in.

"Actually Kyoto was supposed to be the second target on the list. We only bombed Nagasaki because Secretary of War Stimson spent his honeymoon in Kyoto before the war." Stoli added.

"So what exactly was your connection to the project?" Frank asked.

"The Ballistic Research Lab was the sponsor of the ENIAC project when John Von Neuman out at Los Alamos working on the Manhattan Project realized computers would have unlimited potential if applied to ballistics and so became involved. So involved in fact that the first test problem for the atomic bomb, which was supposed to be run using military artillery tables, was actually run on a prototype of ENIAC."

"Why not on the artillery tables?" Mahone probed.

"Would have taken over a million cards."

"Yikes!" Frank commented.

"Calculating and programming exact coordinates eventually led to the evolution of programmes for S.A. technology."

"Okay, since we've established I'm the stupid one," Mahone interjected. "What's S.A.?"

"By applying Selective Availability, normally used with satellites, the U.S. military can make GPS inaccurate in selected areas of the globe." Stoli pulled back on the chair's toggle and maneuvered it around the desk and out onto the floor as he spoke. "When the war broke out Dr. Goldstine enlisted and was assigned to be an ordinance mathematician."

From a bookshelf Stoli picked a framed picture of two men standing together at a desert military compound and passed it to Morrissey. Both were in short sleeved shirts with dark goggles pulled back onto their foreheads

"This is he." Stoli pointed out. Morrissey perused it and recognized it was at the Aberdeen Proving Grounds in the American west. Stoli took it back from Morrissey and replaced it on the shelf ignoring Mahone's out stretched hand.

"Firing tables took thousands of women, human computers they were called, to do the work required. It took about 750 separate calculations to compute a single high velocity trajectory."

"So that's where the word 'computers' came from?" Mahone deduced. The other two looked over at him. "See, I'm not as dumb as you guys think I am!" Frank's self-deprecating sarcasm was lost on them both.

"It took upwards of six hours of calculations by one woman to calculate a single trajectory. In addition, there were thousands of possible trajectories."

"And Goldstine?" Mahone pushed.

"Dr. Goldstine became the liaison between the ballistics research labs and the university. A friend suggested Goldstine visit a physics teacher who had an idea to use vacuum tubes to speed up the process. They met, a proposal was written and in June of 1943 funding came through. The result was The ENIAC."

"What's an ENIAC?" Mahone asked.

"The first operational computer." Morrissey

informed.

"Well we appreciate the history lesson Doctor Stoli, but how exactly does this relate to the problem of satellite navigation?"

"Do you actually solve crimes Mr. Mahone?" Stoli commented.

"Only when we can't beat a confession out of someone Doc."

"How very American."

"Please ignore him Doctor. He's from New York." Morrissey interjected.

"Oh, sorry, I didn't realize." Stoli slowly maneuvered back to his desk. "Synchronization Mr. Mahone. Synchronization is the key to all computations, particularly with respect to speed and accuracy. While GPS was initially conceived to aid navigation, globally synchronized time is now a much more critical function of the system. Telecom networks rely on GPS clocks to keep cell towers synchronized so calls can be passed between them. Electrical power grids use the clocks in equipment that fine-tune current flow in overloaded networks. The financial sector use GPS-derived timing systems to time stamp ATM, credit card, and high-speed market transactions. Computer network synchronization, digital television and radio, Doppler radar weather reporting, seismic monitoring. Even multi-camera sequencing for film production. GPS clocks have a hand in it all."

Stoli maneuvered back to his desk.

"So, what I'm getting is GPS clocks are

important?"

"Gentlemen, if there's nothing else . . ."

"Doc let me throw one thing at ya."

Stoli stared over at Morrissey and shrugged that he didn't understand.

"He's asking permission to ask a question."

The doctor cocked his head to the side and stared at Mahone.

"Remarkable that you people are the leaders of the Free World."

"Thank you, I take that as a compliment. Word on the street is that Uncle Sam wants to stop the ESA from launching their last few, upgraded sats with improved performance capabilities so the U.S. can maintain control of navigation during national crises plus better control the international economic situation. You buy into that? Is that feasible?"

Dr. Stoli glanced first at Morrissey then back at Mahone and adjusted himself in his chair.

"As I am not involved in, nor do I plan to get involved in, the circus which is international politics I doubt there's much more I can contribute to your investigation gentlemen, so . . ."

Seconds after Stoli pressed the hidden button under the desk the doors slid open and his oversized assistant appeared.

"I take it Lurch is here to show us out?" Frank quipped.

"Show you, escort you, carry you. I like to provide my guests with options Mr. Mahone." Stoli smirked.

Once back out on the street Morrissey stopped and faced the American.

"Mahone, you do understand that we are supposed to **coerce** our witnesses into a sense of camaraderie as opposed to alienating them? Convince them that we are on **their** side? Make friends with them, that sort of thing?"

"What are you trying to say?"

"Is there **any chance** that in future, you might be a little less verbose?"

"That all depends."

"On what, exactly?"

"On what 'verbose' means."

Morrissey walked away with Frank trailing to catch up. As they walked Frank rummaged through his jacket pocket.

"This might be a good time to give you this." Mahone handed him the chamois wrapped device he had shown Kuksova back in the restaurant. Morrissey looked puzzled as he accepted it.

"I knew your time with us was nearly over, thank God, but I didn't know we were supposed to exchange gifts!" Morrissey cracked.

"So there are traces of a sense of humor beneath that crusty old exterior!"

"What's this then?" The inspector unwrapped and examined the small, calculator-sized device. He pulled out the short, portable A.M. radio styled antennae.

"Pulled it off the rear left quarter panel of the school bus."

Flabbergasted Morrissey stopped dead in his tracks, stared at the device and then at Frank.

"And what exactly is it supposed to be for?"

"Apparently it's a portable spoofer device. Used to tangle up GPS signals. Make you think they're coming from somewhere else then their actual point of origin. I figure it probably works by fucking with the satellite's clock system somehow. Probably what they used to throw your mobile units off when they sent them down to the south coast. Pretty tricky eh?"

"What the hell are you on about and what's all this *Despicable Me* gadgetry?"

"Look, you heard the crip."

"You mean Dr. Stoli?!"

"Yeah! Who else?!" Frank stopped and assumed his serious face. ". . . atomic time is the lynch pin in any of the satellite-based nav systems. Without it they'd be useless. Anyone who uses GPS benefits from atomic time. Each of the existing 24 GPS satellites carries 4 atomic clocks on board. By triangulating time signals broadcast from orbit, GPS receivers on the ground can pinpoint their own location. Tiny instabilities in those orbiting clocks contribute at least a few meters of error to any single-receiver's GPS measurement."

"How fascinating. Why did you hold on to this and when exactly did you become a bloody expert on satellite communications?"

"I wanted to have it checked out first. Spoke with some people."

"Some people or one female person?"

"I wanted to find out what it was. More importantly if there's a way to detect and then reverse that signal we might be able to find out where these arsholes are operating from!"

Morrissey realized Mahone had, at least on some level, been colluding with Kuksova on the case.

Mahone suddenly detected a slow growing anger in the man he considered his partner, however temporary.

"Do you have any idea the trouble this'll cause . . . you've caused, when I hand this in?"

"Just tell them I went back and found it."

"After a dozen officers and detectives were crawling all over the scene until the wee hours of the morning, you really believe they'll buy that?" Frank shrugged in response. "Do you understand that I'm responsible for babysitting you! You my dear boy are my punishment for refusing to accept 'promotion' to the City Offices. Perhaps where you're from –"

"New York City."

". . . perhaps in America it's perfectly fine to -"

"Are you serious?! In America cops cover for one another, that's what partners do!"

"I could have you terminated from the program for this you know?"

"Get the fuck outta here!" Frank started walking again.

"Withholding material evidence is not common practice over here, Detective!"

"What the hell you so upset about?! It's a break in the case! You should be grateful! Turn it in yourself! Tell 'em you found it!"

"GRATEFUL?! For what? Giving them an excuse for sacking me three years before retirement?!"

"They're not gonna fire you! You're one of their top guys!"

"Top guys me arse! They think no one else realizes it but this squad was slapped together by the Great Khan himself as a last-ditch measure to distract from the fact that he's getting' his ass waxed all over God's green acre by the radical Muslims! We were slapped together strictly out of political desperation."

"What'a you sayin'? The Honorable Mayor Khan and his Privy Council only really care about staying in office? That the SHIT Squad is nothing more than a political maneuver to win favor? That they don't really give a shit about protecting Londoners?"

"Exactly!"

"No shit Sherlock! THEY'RE POLITICIANS!"

Morrissey drew back and stared blankly at Mahone.

"Your acting like an arsehole in there was just an act, wasn't it?"

"Oh what, you're shocked?!" Mahone stepped closer into the inspector. "Lemme ask you something, Nigel: You a cop or just another fucking bureaucrat? Because both our towns got enough

371

bureaucrats to last for the next fifty years so make a fuckin' decision will ya! I need you to make a decision so I can make a decision! We a team? We gonna nail this bastard or you gonna throw a hissy fit every time the goin' gets tough?" Morrissey gave no reply.

Frank headed off in the opposite direction to find an Underground Station.

Morrissey headed off to find a pub.

****

AV Room
Scotland Yard
Thursday 22; 08:36

A heavy sense of urgency began to set in as the squad started their work day. First thing that morning Morrissey had briefed the squad on what he and Mahone had learned which triggered a sense that the clock was ticking. Literally.

"So what's next Chief?" Rankor inquired.

"I'll start writing my report on what we've found out concerning the gadget Mahone discovered on the bus. Meanwhile, get started on your reports. I'll need the final drafts by the end of the week." The squad members stared in shock. "I'll inform the C.I. we'll have them to him by end of the week." He turned to leave.

"Just like that? We're done?" Dunn challenged. "What about the hijackers? Or the van case? We're gonna close this out with no suspects? No arrests?"

Morrissey stopped, slump shouldered halfway to the door and spoke without turning around.

"The suspect from the van robbery and the school bus hijacker are part of the same crowd. We've identified and tracked them both and uncovered that this case is in fact an international affair. We will pass it up the ladder where it will be transferred to MI6 as per directives, and we shall then return to solving homicides as per our original directive."

"I suppose we could start with the murdered Hamlet guard from Hamlet Security." Ali suggested.

"No, that murder is part of the van investigation which is associated with the kidnapping case which is now an MI6 case." Morrissey's own sense of frustration seeped through
his words.

"But Inspector . . ."

"BUT NOTHING!" He yelled turning back and slamming the table top before taking several long, slow deep breaths. "Lads." He calmly breathed out. "Apologies for the outburst." They immediately realized Morrissey was no less perplexed at circumstances then they were. "Amongst the plethora of quaint American sayings the Yanks have is; 'Ya win some, ya lose some and some get rained out. But ya still get dressed to play for tomorrow.' This one simply got rained out. Plain and simple. Now it's time to put on our big boy pants, accept it and get back to work. Ali, let me know when Mahone gets here."

"Will do Boss." It was for a full minute they stood staring at each other before they began to disperse to their work tables.

"I wouldn't hold my breath waiting for Frank Mahone to show up." All turned towards the female voice emanating from the doorway. It was Kuksova.

"The FBI has seen fit to pay us a visit?" FNG quipped.

"I went by his hotel this morning. He's checked out." Irina explained. "Morrissey, what did you say to Frank?" Irina asked.

"Nothing of any significance. We had a disagreement about questioning a witness. More significantly what exactly are you doing here?"

"What did he do with the device?" She asked.

"He gave it to me and I was told to pass it onto MI6. Why?"

"SHIT!" She kicked a chair.

"That wasn't just any GPS tracker, was it?" Dunn deduced.

"No it wasn't. That tracker was equipped with a spoofer device!" Kuksova began to explain. "It apparently also had the ability to disrupt GPS signals and spoof their point of origin."

"Are you serious?" FNG punctuated.

"Serious as a Parliamentary session!" Irina quipped.

"So, serious in a slap stick sort of way?" Dunn replied.

"I had a drink with Frank the other night and he was pretty down about how it was going here for him."

"Well in fairness he-"

"He's used to getting things done. 'Maybe you're right. Maybe it's time I went home!' he mumbled just before leaving the pub." She added.

"You don't actually think he'd just-"

"Walk away, go back to Manhattan? Yes. Yes I do. He never volunteered for this assignment."

"Then why in hell did he come?" Ali questioned.

"Because it was this or be forced off the force and possibly lose his retirement if he tried to fight it."

It was Token who then broke the silence.

"Well how much like a useless pile of sheit does that make us feel?" She cracked. "Get kicked off the force and forfeit your pension or join us?"

"It wasn't exactly like that." Irina consoled. "He lost two partners in a short period and got himself shot up pretty good to boot."

"But I was briefed he'd also broken up a major drug ring, collared nearly half a dozen dealers and saved several civilians' lives! All in the last three years." Morrissey argued.

"And killed two other dealers." Irina added.

"Then why was the man not congratulated? Rewarded?" Ali protested.

Equating what she was about to say with most government organizations, Kuksova peered down at the floor and smirked.

"Because according to Mahone, in the NYPD no good deed goes unpunished."

"So what are we supposed to do?" Din asked as Irina turned to leave.

"Well, I just dropped in to see if you guys have heard anything from him. So, as you apparently haven't, I guess we just get back to work." No one responded. "MI6 no doubt passed the device on and it should be in D.C. and in the F.B.I. labs by this evening and hopefully they'll be something new to go on, something that'll give us a lead. Where it was made or at least where the parts were manufactured. Hopefully something to help us figure out how to defeat it." She projected.

"What are the odds of that?" FNG challenged.

"The Bureau's labs have had a pretty good hit rate in the last few years tracing explosives. It was with their help INTERPOL were able to trace the TATP used in the Parson's Greene Bombing which lead to a conviction." Irina defended. "So I guess you guys should-"

"We've been relieved of the case." Morrissey tersely pointed out. Irina was surprised but not shocked.

"Huh!" She shrugged. "Was only to be expected I guess. After the FBI lab report comes back they'll likely label it a terrorist case and take over the lead on it." She predicted. "I'll make sure I do what I can to see that you guys are given credit in the final report to the AG and the DOJ."

Leaving the dumbfounded group sitting at their

tables Irina headed out of the briefing room with no further comment.

"Bloody Yanks! Always abbreviatin' everything!" Ali snipped.

"Including important investigations!" Dunn cracked.

"Chin up lads! Here me now! We done our bit! We recovered the hostages, identified the hijacker and –"

"And threw in the bloody towel just as we were about to make the collar!" Dunn again piped up.

"You sound like Bush; 'Read my lips, no new taxes!' Just you know, just before he raised taxes." Dunn added.

"So much for that little bit of business!" Din sighed.

In what a few of them considered to be a bit melodramatic, Morrissey rose from his seat, and walked over to the door.

"Oh God! Not him too!" Ali declared as they watched what they thought was Morrissey's exit.

Instead he peered through the door, looked up and down the hall and closed it. He then went to his table, scribbled something out on a piece of white, A4 note paper and cello taped it on the outside glass of the door.

'Do Not Disturb! Conference in Session.'

Then locking the door from the inside he took a seat on the corner of his table signaling for the four of them to gather around.

"Everything I'm about to tell you stays in those room. Everything I'm about to ask you to do is completely voluntary. You must not talk about, query it or deviate from it providing you agree to participate." Uneasy looks were exchanged. Save for Dunn who fought back a smile.

"If you decline it'll not be held against you in any way." He took the silence which prevailed as consent to continue. "We are onto something that has grown much larger than first anticipated. I'm convinced that with the talent we have here in this room we can crack it wide open. And at the risk of applying excessive hyperbole, save a lot of lives in the process." Ali was the first to speak.

"Only one way to find out if we're in Chief." Ali threw out. "Try it on us and see if we run out of the room screaming." There were nods all around.

"Mahone and I believe the Hamlet van job and the school bus hijacking are not only related but may be the tip of an iceberg. An iceberg that has something to do with an international crime ring. But to get to the bottom of it we are going to have to slightly extend our own authority. Of our own volition that is. Questions, comments? Snide remarks?"

"Why not pass it on to MI5 or 6? We'll still get credit and look good. MI5 are already looking into the bus hijacking and we get to avoid stepping on any toes." FNG proposed.

"Rankor!" Morrissey called out.

"This not about looking good, Enfield!" Rohan enlightened. "It's about doing the right thing while we have the chance. This gets pushed uphill God knows where it'll wind up! And if it goes high enough it'll no doubt be squashed by someone on Westminster or Washington who are directly involved."

Morrissey spoke up again.

"Ergo, for one, I don't trust the bureaucracy to handle it. Two, because this is our case, we found it we opened it and I bloody well want us to close it. And thirdly I don't trust the bureaucracy. Anything else?"

"Ew, ew teacher, teacher! Call me! Call me!" Bouncing up and down in her seat Dunn held one arm and raised her hand.

"Yes, in the back, Mrs. Dunn?" Morrissey reluctantly played teacher.

"I just want to get this straight in my head, in case there's a test. We are a British homicide investigation unit who you are proposing to interfere with an international, terrorist investigation, stepping on the toes of the FBI, MI5, MI6 and possibly the U.S. State Department by over-stepping our jurisdiction into mainland Europe where we are not supposed to operate after the British people have voted for Brexit effectively telling said mainland Europeans to bugger off?"

"In a word . . . yes."

"A career jeopardizing move. That's all you had to say, career jeopardizing move. Thank you teacher. I love it." Dunn smiled. "Count me in!" She blurted out.

"Same here!" Ali added.

"Ditto!" FNG joined the bandwagon.

"Din?" Morrissey queried. Din sighed deeply as he looked down and thought.

"I have an uncle with a Tandoori restaurant in the East End. He is always looking for bus boys. What the hell? I'm in." Came Rankor's reply.

Having anticipated the team's response to his proposal, Morrissey quickly issued the assignments he had already preplanned.

"Right then! Dunn & FNG I need you two to get down to Paris. Get down to the bursar and tell her you need tickets and – no, never mind! Tell her you need a thousand pound withdrawal straight away, cash and that I'll be along in an hour to counter sign for it."

"Why do **I** have to go to Paris?!" FNG protested.

"You don't really **have to**. "I can reassign you to the London Kennel Club's missing poodle case." Morrissey offered.

"I always wanted to see Paris! What's in Paris?" FNG enthusiastically blurted.

"Find the ranking guy at the ESA H.Q., he's there all week prepping for a conference."

"How do you know?:

"Read it on the ESA site. Track him down and get all the info you can from him personally! No Assistant to the assistant of the helper! Understood?"

"Yes Boss. What exactly are we looking for?"

"Anything and everything on spoofer research and spoofers in general but most importantly who would have the capacity to build develop and possibly implant portable, ground-based spoofer devices especially on vehicles. Pay particular attention to confidentiality! That means the Director and the Director only! A-B conversation! Anyone else butts in you make it clear that they are to C their way out of there!"

"Got it."

"Rankor you and Ali catch up to Kuksova, let her know what we're doing minus the exact details and see if you can coax her into divulging what the FBI have on spoofers. In particular the best way to defeat them."

"Yes Sahib!"

"Everybody's mobiles topped up, batteries charged? There were nods all around. "Good, you'll maintain direct commo with me by mobile. Few people realize that the single biggest cause of casualties during the Second War was due to lack of communication! So everyone will call in here and report to me every two hours, sooner if you find something, without fail! I'll log all calls with details and no one but no one speaks with anyone outside the squad! Understood?"

"Yes Inspector."

"Inspector, what about Mahone?" Dunn threw out.

"Forget about the Yank. He appears to be well

out of the picture."

"What about you Inspector? What's your mission?" Ali asked.

"I'm going to try and buy us a little more time without letting on that we're actually going to attempt to hang ourselves. I'm going up to the Chief Inspector's office and convince him that we need to be let loose for a couple of days to chase down the other accomplices of the van job!"

"What accomplices? I thought we nicked all them geezers?!" FNG puzzled.

"Oh no! There's at least another one out in, in . . ."

"Up in Leeds?" Rankor threw out.

"Yes, exactly! Up in Leeds! Perhaps he was the ring leader. Won't know until we track him down though will we?"

"That all of it? All you're going to do?" Ali challenged.

"Yes." He moved in closer and became more serious. "Lads! It's on us now. We've no idea the end game of this geezer or why he's doing this but he's plenty ticked off at somebody and if he gets whatever toy he's developed where he wants it when he wants it, he could crash a significant portion of the Galileo and/or GPS systems and consequently create the mother of all headaches."

"No pressure though, eh Chief?!" Dunn added.

"Three things to keep in mind for the next forty-eight hours; one the security services are up to their eyeballs in their own cases. Two, we have several weeks' head start on them and three-"

"Three don't trust the bureaucracy to handle it!" Dunn, Ali and Rankor blurted out in unison.

"Right! Questions, comments snide remarks? Shut up Dunn!"

Ignoring his instruction Dunn was the one to speak up.

"Yeah Chief, what happened to that gadget Mahone took off the bus?" Token asked.

"Less than an hour after I informed the Chief Inspector I was given orders to turn it over to MI6 who, I have no doubt, consulted with our American cousins who in turn have requested, through proper diplomatic channels of course, to have it shipped to D.C. They're sending it off this morning by secure courier. So, best of luck and let's get to it!"

Out in the hallway Dunn pulled her boss aside and spoke confidentially to him.

"Had you been thinking about doing this all along or did you just pull it out of your arse at the last minute?"

Morrissey smirked, partially lifted one leg and mimed pulling something from his butt.

*

SIS Building
Albert Embankment
Vauxhall, Lambeth

As Morrissey and the SHIT Squad were

conspiring in the AV room, it was across town along the river road that a small, vetted courier van pulled into the underground parking deck of the SIS Building on Albert Embankment at Vauxhall Cross, home of MI6.

The delivery man maneuvered his unmarked, white van into one of the half dozen parking spots labeled RESERVED and shut down his van. After checking the floor and office number on the delivery docket, he grabbed the shoe box-sized package and headed across the parking deck for the basement lift.

A well-dressed man in a goatee came up beside him.

"Lift's on the blink mate. Has been since this morning." The man spoke with a cultured British accent.

"BLOODY HELL! Is there no other?" The harried courier pressed.

"Depends where you're headed." The man indirectly asked,

"Room 1217."

"OH! Twelfth floor! Hope you've a strong pair of legs. All the way up."

"Bastard!"

"Running late are we?"

"I've normally four or five deliveries a day. Today they give me six and then, to top it off, at the last minute they dump this one on me!"

"Hard go old boy! Look, I'm in 1219, right next door. I'm heading up there now. Happy to sign for it." He quickly flashed a badge and I.D. as he spoke. "Clearance and all that." He reassured. "I'll see they get it. Save you climbing twenty-four flights of stairs." There was a trace of reticence on the courier's face. "We do it all the time." The gentleman's accompanying shrug elicited the smile from the courier he'd hoped for. The delivery guy held out his electronic pad and the stranger scribbled an indiscernible signature.

"You have **no** idea what this means!" The delivery man responded passing the package.

"I think I have a pretty good idea." The courier headed back to his van while the stranger slowly ducked through the door leading to the stairwell and left the building.

Up on the second floor a secretary was in the open lift car fruitlessly pushing buttons.

Then she cursed as she fished a tissue out of her purse and peeled a wad of chewing gum plastering the 'HOLD' button in.

*

CHAPTER SEVENTEEN

European Space Agency HQ
Bertrand Building
24 Rue du Gen. Bertrand, Paris

After disembarking their plane next day at terminal 2B of the Charles DeGaulle International Dunn and Enfield grabbed their carry-ons and made their way to a curb side taxi outside the terminal and headed south on the A3 into the city.

Having flown in on the 10:45 from Heathrow the plan was to locate a Dr. Johann Dietrich Wörner, Director General of the ESA, try to get him behind closed doors and find out what they could about the current state of sat-com technology, especially spoofer development then catch a late flight back to London. Given the illegitimacy of the mission, the impromptu nature of Morrissey's plan and the urgency of info they hoped to gain, playing phone tag for a day or more, which was common when dealing with higher echelon officials, was not an option.

"You got any French?" Enfield growled from his side of the rear seat in the taxi as, approaching the city, they suddenly slowed to crawl in traffic.

"A year or two in secondary." She suddenly sat up and made no attempt to hide her excitement as the Parisian skyline came into view. "God it's great to be here!"

"How in bloody hell can you be so pumped up about a country that drives on the wrong side of the road?!' Dunn was unfazed by Enfield's expected bitching. "You're staring out the window like a kid approaching Disneyland fer fuck's sake!" He chided.

"Let's stop for a nice French breaki before we hunt this guy down!" She prodded. "There's plenty of time!"

"We ain't here on holiday Token! We've got exactly an hour and a half to get into to the city, find this Wormer geezer and pump him for all we can get out of him before we have to catch our 15:00 flight and get back to feckin' civilization!"

"It's Dr. Wörner and mind your mouth!" She chastised nodding up towards the driver.

"Highly unlikely he parlays the lingo." Enfield grunted.

"Excusez-moi monsieur, parlez voue anglais?" She asked the driver.

"No madam." He answered staring straight ahead.

"Told you!" FNG bragged.

"Lucky guess Ebenezer!"

"What's so special about a French breakfast? English food is better!" He casually commented loud enough for the driver to hear.

"Oui, oui monsieur, Et mon cul c'est du poulet!" The driver pleasantly spoke into the rear view mirror. Dunn laughed.

"What'd he say?"

"He said . . . try the chicken." She giggled.

"Fucking French! Entire language consists of an alphabet with three types of letters. 50% silent, 50% unpronounceable and a ma-wa on the end of every third word!"

"Lighten up will ya! I'm hungry and I'm gonna have some authentic French food."

"You can keep all your fu-fu French qwaay-seen! There's nothing beats a hardy English breakfast!" He continued his running grump-a-thon. "Where we gonna find a hearty English breakfast here anyway? These people never even heard of blood pudding!"

"So?! Eat a ham sandwich!" She snapped back.

"In England it's a ham sandwich, over here they put a fucking egg on it and suddenly it's the French national dish!"

"Hey Enfield, why do the French only use one egg to make an omelet?" He ignored her attempt to lighten the mood. "Because one egg is un oeuf! Ha! Get it?" She elbowed him and continued to laugh.

"I Fucking hate the French!" He crossed his arms and slumped in his seat. "Watch the meter! I don't trust this guy." He told her.

Twenty minutes later they arrived and climbing out of the taxi in front of the Bertrand Building on Rue du General Bertrand FNG again growled.

"Driver, we want a receipt."

"Oui monsieur." The driver angrily mumbled as he prepared their docket.

"Thank you driver!" Dunn thanked him with a ten Euro tip as she took the receipt.

"English food is za best! And soufflé is just eggs!" The Frenchman mumbled as he drove off. "Fucking Roast Beef!"

Dunn perused the forest of buildings surrounding them.

"We still need to find the right building, find this guy's office and hope we can pin him down." Enfield reminded.

"And hope he cooperates! Remember, we're not authorized to be here on any grounds! Legally the Gendarmerie can nab us and lock us up on jurisdictional grounds."

"So what's our cover story?"

"We're journalists writing about the recent advancements in ESA resulting from cooperation of the twenty-seven nations in the E.U." Dunn informed him.

"So it's an anti-Brexit piece?" He pushed.

"Sure, why not? You okay with that?"

"Yeah fine. Look, let's find this guy, get this done and I'll buy you all the fu-fu food you want, deal?"

"Deal!"

Finally locating the HQ building they entered a sprawling, ultra-modern lobby and approached the large semi-circular desk off to the left housing a single young receptionist.

"Bon jour."

"Bon jour."

"Excusez moi mademoiselle, parlez vous anglais?"

"Of course! How may I help you?"

"We are trying to locate the Director's office?"

"May I ask who is calling?"

"We're from the *London Daly Mail*. We're doin' a piece on the recent advancements at the ESA."

"The Director General is expecting us." FNG added.

In her best English, tinged only lightly with her natural French accent, the well-dressed secretary smiled and nodded.

"Oui! That would be Dr. Wörner. However, he is probably in the weekly departmental meeting just now. Zird floor, za auditorium is on za left. Perhaps you can catch him when za meeting iz finished."

"Thank you very much for tour help." Dunn thanked before they headed towards the elevator bank across the hall.

"Zank you! Za meeting iz on za zird floor!" Enfield quietly mocked as they waited.

"Yeah, go ahead be an asshole! But I guarantee her English is ten times better than your French." The lift arrived and they stepped on. "And of course you'd never take her to bed! Not with such poor English."

"Well in certain situations I suppose it would be rude not to overlook the accent. In the interest of international relations, of course."

"You're an asshole!"

"Who told you?"

They slipped into the rear of the small auditorium, quietly took a couple of seats in the back and tried to look as unobtrusive as possible.

An important looking guy stood at the podium addressing the twenty or thirty people concentrated down in front of the hundred and fifty seat gallery.

". . . we are compelled, therefore, to decide by the end of the month how it is we wish to respond to the American's latest proposals as regards the Galileo launch times."

Ten minutes later the gathering broke up and the two detectives ducked outside to beat the crowd out into the hall.

"And I thought Bush was a fucking cowboy!" One of the gentlemen in front of them commented in German.

"You heard any more on the rumor about the FBI visiting Wörner?" The one with the beard asked.

"No, his secretary told my girl that they had forty-five minutes blocked in but were out of his office in less than ten."

"Not a good sign!" The beard declared.

"If anything comes of it I'm sure we'll hear."

As the group filed past them Dunn and Enfield scurried up to the trailing scientist.

"Excuse me, which one of those gentlemen is Dr. Wörner?" Dunn asked.

"None. Dr. Wörner is in Iceland to taking atmospheric readings on the Aurora. Dr. Renoir is managing things while he's away. He's Dr. Wörner's chief assistant. The man on the left." He nodded up ahead of them.

"Thank you." Again they quick stepped towards the exit to catch up and stopped him at the front door.

"Dr. Renoir? We're from the *London Daily Mail* may we have a word with you?" Enfield attacked.

"I'm sorry, the press conference will be in the Fermi Room, three o'clock." He pushed through the two. The two coppers exchanged glances and shrugged.

"Doctor, I'm Inspector Dunn and this is my college, Inspector Enfield, of Scotland Yard."

"I'm very sorry, I have another meeting I must attend in –"

"It has to do with the spoofer device. The possibly of a missing spoofer device?" Dunn suddenly threw out. Enfield's eyes widened at his partner's revelation.

Already halfway through the exit Renoir stopped dead in his tracks, obviously deciding what to do next. They flashed their badges but he ignored them staring instead straight into their faces.

"We can't speak here. Follow me." He demanded more than requested.

Minutes later the three were outside the rear of the building in the garden area in an alcove tucked away from the busy floor area.

With a cluster of tall areca palms off from the rear entrance Dunn and Enfield took a seat on the bench opposite Dr. Renoir who let his eyes make occasional forays around their perimeter scanning not to be recognized.

"How do you know about the spoofer interference device?" He quickly demanded. "That information is classified by all the governments!"

"Dr. Renoir, a half billion English pounds was stolen from a security van back in 1999, the two guards vanished along with the money and possibly, we believe, a prototype spoofer device from the van." Dunn quickly filled him in.

"The missing DS14-12!" Renoir declared.

"You know about it?" Dunn pushed.

"A few of us do. But we were told it was misplaced, then, a few days later found. We heard no more about until we were eventually told the project was discontinued, a dead end to what we needed."

"To your knowledge was there ever an investigation?"

"Investigate what? As far as we were concerned we were kept up to date until it was no longer being pursued as a viable option."

"What else can you tell us?"

"In the late Nineties a tech reported a prototype of an experimental device missing but because it was so early on in the program records were not kept very well, they didn't even know if the *Galileo Project* itself would ever be approved by the parties involved. These are the days before there was an E.U. remember. Even before there was the present ASE!"

"ASE?" Enfield questioned.

"French for E.S.A." Dunn informed.

"Huh! It's like they have a different word or everything!" Enfield mumbled.

"The claims simply couldn't be traced even if someone had the inclination. Too much was happening, politically I mean. The first free elections in the Soviet Union, the Tiananmen Square massacre, the Wall coming down. Our little satellite program was a pie in the sky!"

"Doctor Renoir, we think we've stumbled onto a potential plot to disrupt or destroy some or part of the very satnav/satcom systems you people are working on."

"If you're talking about the van incident in London, that robbery was at least twenty years ago!"

"Nineteen doctor." Enfield corrected.

"About a week ago a school bus full of students was hijacked and when we recovered the bus and the students one of our detectives found-"

"He's not one of us! He's American!" Enfield again corrected.

"Bealach fada le dul to be like him, Enfield!" She chastised. "Doctor please continue."

"The dispute with the Americans is on two points: the GSL issue is one but the S.A. capabilities are the center of the main dispute."

"Clarification please? S-A and G-S-L?" Dunn interrupted.

"Guaranteed Safety of Life and Selective Application." He elaborated.

"Okay."

"Safety of Life simply means Brussels has determined that if there is a loss of life directly attributable to an error in the *Galileo* system, then compensation is due."

"And the American GPS doesn't have that?" Dunn asked.

"Not at present, no."

"Even if they did you'd likely be tied up in courts until you died!" Enfield again offered his not-so-worldly experience.

"And the S.A. feature?" Dunn pushed.

"It's being kept under wraps but my suspicion is the U.S. want to negotiate an agreement where-by they can dictate to us its restricted use in the European theatre. The politicians are dragging their feet but the ESA has no intention of agreeing to that."

"S.A. Doctor?"

"Sorry! Selective Availability. Turning the sat's navigational capability on and off when they feel threatened. Like the switch on your computer, so-to-speak."

"They can do that?" Enfield asked.

"Of course! How do you think they restricted Iraqi's maneuverability during the Iraq Wars? The Americans waited until Saddam had his troops dispersed, in route to the Saudi border then shut down the GPS in that area. In the resulting chaos of the Iraqi tank brigades the Americans attacked. Very clever actually." Renoir admitted.

"I'll bet the Republican Guard didn't think so!" FNG added. Renoir continued.

"Given the history of cooperation on the Hubble, the James Webb and other projects, between the EU through the ESA and the people at NASA, the scientists on both sides won't hear of the Galileo using S.A. on the President's orders. It's the politicians that are making the trouble."

"Politicians muckin' things up! Imagine that!" FNG said.

"There are other issues as well." Renoir added.

"Such as?"

"Such as the current system of GPS is only accurate to within about three to six meters. Less in some territories. Galileo will be accurate to within a meter to the public and accurate to within one centimeter encrypted anywhere on earth."

"ONE CENTIMETER?!" Enfield blurted out."

"Once all thirty-six satellites are in orbit, yes." Renoir qualified.

"Half an inch! No more losing the T.V. remote between the couch cushions!" FNG drew back in shock.

"Or your car keys, medications or even your pets." Renoir added as he briefly basked in Enfield's amazement. "Also it will be mostly free to non-commercial entities."

"I'd say the 'free' part's the one the Yanks are having trouble with!" Enfield interjected.

"It was the same political merde during the Cold War!" Renoir suddenly became more passionate. "If the West had teamed up with the Russians we could have had a fully functioning mining operation on the Gusev Crater by now!"

"Well, if a frog had wings he wouldn't bump his ass so much!" FNG struggled to hold is tongue.

"A frog? What has frogs to do with Mars?" Renoir queried.

"Ignore him Doctor. His mother had a difficult delivery."

"That's not nice!" Enfield protested.

"Is there anything else you can tell us Doctor?"

"Such as?"

"Who would have the capacity to build, develop and possibly implant a portable, ground-based spoofer device?"

"I don't know. Perhaps someone with a grudge or an agenda, with access to lots and lots of money!"

"Is there any way to stop or interfere with this thing?"

"Yes! A very simple way."

"What is that?"

"Find it and destroy it!" He stood to leave. "Inspectors, I am very late for my Meeting. Good luck with your mission! I will inform the Director of our talk and advise him to take every precaution we are able."

"And perhaps suggest he alert your space port in Guiana too!" Enfield advised.

"We will."

"Merci beaucoup Doctor Renoir. Thank you for

your cooperation."

"Ce n'est rien. Au revoir. I hope you find what you are looking for."

Dunn looked over to Enfield.

"Well, at least it wasn't a total waste." She surmised.

"One inch! Why would anyone want to. . ." Enfield was dumbfounded by the stat.

"Want to what?"

"Nothing. What's the time?"

"Coming onto half one."

"We'd better give Morrissey a quick ring let him know what we found out."

"Okay, let's find a land line."

They found a call box on the corner back outside the building and checked in with Morrissey.

"Sorry to say boss man but your Intel was not up to date. Dr. Wörmer is in Iceland but we managed to get some face time with his number two man a fella called Renoir."

And?

"He was very helpful on all the background stuff but two things jumped out at me."

Sergeant Dunn I await with bated breath.

"He was reluctant to talk with us at first but finally did. At that point he was very hush hush and made us retire to the back garden where no one could see him talking to us and he knew about the missing spoofer."

He knew?

"Apparently several of them did. It was

considered a minor, experimental piece of kit and, back in the day, they were doubtful whether or not Galileo would even reach its final stages. He said back in the Nineties they were told it was misplaced, then found and ultimately discarded and destroyed. Said he was told it wasn't going to be used."

I can see that I suppose, but apparently it wasn't destroyed. Back garden? Strange. Did you ask him why?

"Not necessary, it was obvious. He didn't want anyone to know he was talking to the police, afraid of being implicated."

You think he has anything to be implicated in?

"No, not really. I think he was more embarrassed then anything. The whole politics of the place. It reeks of it here. I always thought it was just about the science."

When you're dealing with six billion Euros per year shared by twenty-seven countries who were all trying to kill each other for the first half of the last century, politics are bound to creep into it.

"Point taken."

You believe he was on the straight and narrow with you?

"Absolutely. He's nothing to hide. Besides, it'll be easy enough to check his story out. We'll get Wörner's number and ask whether or not he confirms it. Renoir said he'd fill Wörner in when he got back from Iceland."

What about Enfield he agrees with your

assessment?

"Anything you want to add?" She offered the phone to FNG leaning on the wall next to her.

"Nothing that can't wait until we get back." He declined.

"We're both in agreement. What now?"

What time's your return fight?

"15:45 due in at Heathrow at 17:00. Anything yet from Ali and Din?"

Not yet no. Right then, start on your report while you're waiting around. See you two in the morning at the office. And Dunn.

"Yes Chief?"

I don't want to see any Château Lafite-Rothchild on the expense sheet when you get back! You're still on duty.

"I wouldn't dream of it Chief! But thanks for reminding me."

Well done you two. See in the morning.

Enfield glanced over as she hung up.

"What's our status?" He asked.

"We are free agents until tomorrow morning! Where to?"

"Get some coffee if you like." He offered.

Outside they walked east looking for a suitable café and came on a residential street where the road was divided by a wide median with maple trees, shrubbery and the odd bench. Finally, in the middle of the block they came on a small boulangerie across from a row of apartment buildings and went in.

Enfield settled for a coffee while Dunn took her time and finally ordered a smoked cured ham and Swiss on fresh baguette, a buttered croissant, then decided on two, a liter of fresh orange juice and a Napoleon pastry.

"You develop a tape worm in the last few hours?" Enfield asked as he stared in disbelief. Dunn smiled at him and tapped her belly.

"Are you serious? You've got a bun in the oven?!"

"Five weeks along! Just got the test results Monday."

"Congrats! What'd your better half say?"

"Doesn't know yet, he was away on maneuvers. He's back on Sunday. I'll spring it on him then."

"Well in that case, we've something more important to do just now then eat café food!"

"What's that?"

"Feed you two a proper meal! C'mon, let's find a restaurant! That little guy should know what bad food is before he's introduced to fine English cuisine! I'm buying! Let's go find ourselves some fu-fu French qway-seen!"

"My sandwich is almost ready, we have time before we have to head back out and I'd love to see more of the city before we leave. Let's eat here then wander around a bit"

"Fair enough, that's what we'll do then!"

As he paid for the food Enfield noticed Dunn gazing out the window of the small bakery, lost in her thoughts.

"You okay?"

"It will be exactly nine years ago tomorrow."

"Nine years ago for what?"

"That Jason and I were here."

"That's why you jumped on this assignment!"

"Uh huh." She nodded.

"Nine years ago?"

"Tomorrow. He proposed to me on the steps of the Rodin museum. We've never been back since. We always said we would but . . ."

With food in hand they headed for one of the benches on the wide median under a tree.

"Let's sit here." FNG, his mood by now visibly lightened, suggested as they were about halfway up the beautifully foliaged promenade.

Dunn laid out her food on the bench seat between them as if she were at an ancient Roman banquet and voraciously dug in.

"Dunn?"

"Yeah?"

"Nine years is a long time. I don't see why we can't catch a later flight back and maybe walk over to the Rodin museum, that is if you fancy." Dunn stared at her partner and for the first time saw him in a different light.

"I would like that. Thank you Enfield." She softly said. "So how is it you're not married?" Dunn probed through a mouthful of ham and cheese baguette.

"Never met the right the girl I guess."

"Too bad, you're an okay guy. Once people get

to know ya."

"Thank you. I think."

"So your husband, how does he feel about your new assignment? With the squad I mean?"

Somewhere in the distance a car backfired twice. But when a splinter of the bench rail flew up between them Enfield realized it was no car.

"Get down!" He yelled.

Enfield instinctively dropped to his knees, drew his Glock 26 and scanned the streets, saw nothing suspicious then turned his attention to the roof tops on the other side of the street. There were no more shots.

"You okay?!" He asked Dunn who still sat in place.

Off to his left he caught a fleeting glimpse of what appeared to be a man with a rifle ducking in from the railing of the roof just above the eleventh floor of the apartment building across the street on the other side of the wide promenade.

He was across the promenade and in the building's lobby in no time but was immediately confronted by the uniformed doorman as he quickly perused the massive, ornate lobby. The tall, heavy-set doorman scurried over to him.

"Puis-je vous aider? Qu'est-ce que tu veux?"

"THERE'S A GUNMAN ON THE ROOF!"

"Quoi?!"

"GUNMAN! GUNMAN!" Enfield shouted.

"Gummam? Je ne te comprends pas monsieur! Qu'est-ce que 'Gummam?"

"Gun man you dolt!! BANG BANG!" He repeated as he mimed with his fingers..

At that point Enfield brandished his weapon and mimed shooting which caused the big doorman to scream like a woman and back away. The elevator bell rang, Enfield pushed the doorman to the side and drew a bead on the elevator doors as they slid open. A mother and child stepped off the lift, spotted him and stood in shock.

It was at that moment that Enfield heard hurried footsteps coming down the back staircase and ran to rear of the lobby. Slow by only seconds he saw the rear exit door closing over. It slammed hard but through the glass panels he spied an Hispanic male sporting a man bun with a tattoo up the side of his neck who appeared unarmed.

Enfield yanked on the panic bar but discovered the door had locked when closed over.

He ran back to the front of the lobby, dragged the doorman to the back and had him unlock door. The terrified doorman fumbled to open it so Enfield again pushed him aside and fired one round shattering the glass panel then squeezed under the panic bar and out into the garden.

Out in the rear of the building Enfield was faced with a closed in rear garden surrounded by tall hedges but spotted broken branches about hallway up on the right.

Meanwhile, back outside on the bench an elderly woman walking her dog and pulling a small trolley basket had come across Dunn's slumped over body, noticed blood dripping from her hand and ran into the boulangerie to phone the Gendarme.

Enfield gave chase through the hedge rows but lost his man in heavy undergrowth between gardens.

Twenty minutes later, torn clothes and winded he made his way back out to the bench where he had left Dunn however in her place were several gendarmes taking a statement from the old woman and two other civilians with a dog. A team of paramedics were loading Dunn into an ambulance.

He headed straight for the ambulance but was blocked from getting in by one of the medics until he flashed his badge. The medic motioned him aboard just as they pulled away.

The siren blared as they sped through the lightly trafficked streets where, on board with the paramedic, was an M.D. administering an injection into an I.V. port taped to her left arm. By the I.V.'s and the electrocardiogram they had apparently been working on her for some time.

Suddenly the cardiac monitor on the shelf above her gurney beeped loudly several times then emitted a steady wail. The men went to work franticly administering CPR. The paramedic adjusted the cardiac monitor several times as the doctor alternated injections of epinephrine into the I.V. line and as a last resort Vasopressin.

The cardiac monitor remained flat lined.

Finally when the doctor placed his hand on the medic's shoulder and shook his head the young paramedic halted CPR.

"I am sorry monsieur." The doctor offered as he leaned forward and instructed the driver to switch off the siren and drive more carefully.

Enfield, slowly descending into shock, retrieved Dunn's badge and gun from her purse, stared at them then reached over and took Maureen by the hand.

"Guess we'll be taking a later flight after all." He squeezed her hand.

****

CHAPTER EIGHTTEEN

AV ROOM
Tuesday 27: 10:25

Being only days since Enfield returned alone from Paris official repercussions from Maureen Dunn's death hadn't flowed down hill yet.

The formation of the special homicide unit, though generally accepted by this point, didn't sit well with everyone at the Met when it was first conceived. Ergo the more politically minded in the upper echelons of the London police service were in the process of maneuvering to decide how best to use the tragedy to their advantage by turning it against Morrissey and the SHIT Squad.

The real battle in the Met however would take days to develop as those who initially supported the formation of the Squad and those who now retroactively opposed it split into two camps.

In the interim, liaison between the British and French police was still in the process of being sorted out.

In the Squad room the shock of the loss of Token hit the squad hard and debate raged for the better part of the next day as to whether or not they made the right call in extending their investigation to Paris.

Predictably Morrissey volunteered to take the

blame and predictably Ali, Rankor and Enfield refused to even listen to him.

Finally, realizing they were just expressing a normal healthy anger, the tragic event instead spurred them onto intensify their hunt. Particularly after they were reminded by an extremely exhausted Enfield, who had spent all of the rest of that day and the next night in Paris answering questions and seeing to Maureen's body, that the attack was absolute proof they were on the right track.

Later when emotions had settled Ali quietly approached Morrissey.

"What's the word on bringing Token home?"

"The Gendarmerie said the coroner will have his final report in the next day or so, Wednesday or Thursday the latest. Another day to arrange the paperwork and the family will fly her home on the next flight."

"Tell me the fucking Met are not picking up the tab for that?!" Enfield angrily demanded as he sat at Dunn's desk carefully organizing her belongings for packing.

"Her husband insisted on handling all the details." Morrissey informed him. "He and the sister-in-law made all the arrangements. As soon as her body is released and home I'll get everyone the funeral details."

"You think they'll ever catch that bloody bastard?" Rankor posed.

"Yes!" Enfield spat with the venom of a cobra. "I got a good look at his face. I gave a detailed description to the Gendarmes and they sent it over to INTEPOL. We'll catch him, you can take that to the bank!" No one was surprised by FNG's anger.

"Yeah but, how long could that take? He was obviously a professional and it's certain he didn't hang around Paris!" Ali insisted.

"That depends on how many tall, thin Hispanic males with neck tattoos and a scar on their cheek sporting a man bun they have in their files!" Enfield quickly added.

"Probably not too many!" Rankor conceded.

"Exactly!"

"Right then, no point in waiting around for someone from upstairs to show up with a hatchet! Until then I suggest we get back to work. There are still reports to be made out and forms to file." Morrissey directed.

Still in their shock induced stupors they drifted back to work.

But a few minutes later FNG called across the room.

"Hey Chief I think I found something."

"Enlighten us."

Holding a small sheaf of papers Enfield eased his way over to Morrissey's desk.

"What exactly am I looking at?" Morrissey asked as he adjusted his glasses.

"Something Dunn was working on before she . . . we, went to Paris. She mentioned it to me on the plane." He offered Morrissey who perused the printout "It's from the American NTSB."

"NTSB?" Morrissey questioned as he perused the five page list of over 300 entries.

"National Transportation and Safety Board."

"Are they in on this as well!?"

"No they're the world's premier accident investigation guys. Whenever there's an accident in the transport sector they're called in. If it's outside the U.S., the sovereign territory where the accident occurred has the option to ask for their help. Most do and these guys almost always find the likely cause. Pretty high speed unit from what I understand. They get over $100 million per year." Enfield added.

Morrissey pushed back in his chair, removed his glasses and stared up at the FNG.

"Enfield, how exactly do you know so many god-damned insignificant details?!"

Clearly embarrassed FNG shrugged and responded in a low tone.

"I read." He answered simply. Just then Rankor called across the room.

"Rumor has it Chief that his last unit put him in to be a contestant on *Who Wants To Be A Millionaire* but he declined!"

"Too bad Mate!" Ali added. "Could'a been a millionaire and been done with us lot a long time ago!"

"That true Enfield?" Morrissey inquired. FNG, now more embarrassed, squeaked out an even more humble retort.

"I . . . I get nervous in front of crowds!" He

apologized.

"Huh!" Morrissey grunted. "So what exactly am I looking at here?" Morrissey reiterated as he returned to the list.

"Random times, dates, locations and casualty figures of various accidents over a consecutive five year period."

"Okay." Morrissey stared up at him then re-examined the printout.

"Enfield, I appreciate what you're trying to do here and I fully understand Maureen was-"

"Go to the next to last page!" FNG directed. Morrissey complied.

"She has several entries highlighted." Morrissey noted as he scanned. "Okay, you have my attention." He conceded.

"All several of which involved vehicles that relied on GPS for navigation!" FNG emphasized.

"Coincidence?!" Morrissey tested with a shrug.

"Twelve! With at least one on each major continent?!" Enfield challenged. "Notice anything else they all have in common?" He prodded as Ali and Rankor wandered over. Morrissey studied the page more closely.

"Hmm. I see! Oh! Ahh! Yes, yes. No, I don't see anything else."

"How about column six, 'Cause of Incident?'" Enfield prompted. "It's blank. There are no entries for any of the accidents!" Enfield insisted. "They're all unaccounted for!"

"What about this Barundi flight, they have it

down as pilot 'error'." Morrissey challenged.

"'Pilot Error' followed by a capital 'P'! Which means 'Pending'! Besides, Pilot Error is the fall back conclusion the investigators label a crash with if they can't find anything else."

"I see. You have a theory I presume?"

"Twelve minor and major accidents, all in the public sector of transport, all with vehicles dependent on navigational technologies and-"

"And all with no official cause listed!" Morrissey finished. "Enfield I know you've formulated a potential next step before you brought this to my attention."

"Spoofers!"

Morrissey suddenly got a faraway look in his eyes which slowly surrendered to a broad smile.

"Spoofers with an 's'? As in the plural?"

"As in more than one yes! They're developing these things and testing them for improved capability!"

Just then Rankor joined in.

"Chief if it's one thing we've learned from the London and Paris attacks it's that terrorists may be mentally deranged but they're not stupid! If these guys are planning a major attack somewhere it stands to reason they'd try and replicate the stolen device, test it then build an 'ultimate version' for lack of a better word."

Morrissey sat back in his chair and stared at the three inspectors now gathered around his table.

"Dunn, you may have been the token female on

this squad . . ." Morrissey mumbled. "But God damn it, you're our token female!"

"Thank you for the credit, Inspector Morrissey!" FNG feigned offense as Morrissey stood.

"Oh yes, you too Enfield. Don't get a big head! Get someone to give you a hand, Ali you help him, and track down the relevant P.O.C.'s for each of these twelve 'accidents' so we can get on the horn and check if there are any updates. We need to put together a report to pass on to MI6. We need to confirm updates and whether or not they were in fact actually accidents!"

"Rankor you lend a hand."

"Right Chief! You think all these could have really been caused by the same guys, using spoofers?" Rankor challenged. Morrissey came from around his table and headed for the door as he answered.

"That's what we are going to find out my dear Din!"

"Where're you off to?" Rankor asked.

"See if I can't buy us some more time!"

Ten minutes later Morrissey had tracked down the Chief Inspector upstairs in the hallway and cornered him in the nearby men's room. Brandishing Dunn's printout, Morrissey corralled him in the far corner of the toilet and pleaded his case.

"You're asking me to interfere with the –" The C.I. shot back.

"Delay! Not interfere with sir! Delay! Two, three

days at most!"

"That's quite a big ask Morrissey!"

"Blame the delay on the French! Everyone uses them as scapegoats anyway! Say the coroner is taking his time because of the nature of the case!"

"To delay a hearing to assess culpability in the death of a Scotland Yard Inspector who was assassinated on foreign soil, possibly by terrorists?!"

"Not in so many words sir. I'm asking for a chance to let us finish something we started. If we can, finish it I mean, they'll be that much more we can pass on to MI6." The C.I.'s reticence was still obvious. "If not for me or the squad then for Inspector Dunn. If we can get to the bottom of this her memory will forever be associated with the international case she helped to crack!"

At that the C.I. narrowed his eyes momentarily offering a glimmer of hope then handed the printout back to Morrissey.

"Nigel, you lot have done a bang-up job in the short time you've been working together! You've solved literally every case you've been assigned and you should be proud of that. That Hamlet van thing was textbook! But, even as obstinate as you are, you must realize this one is clearly out of your league. I'm sorry, it's out of the question." He patted Morrissey on the shoulder as he stepped around him. "Better leave this one to the big fellas is my advice old boy." He called back over his shoulder as he exited.

Morrissey was left standing there as he watched the men's room door close over behind the C.I.

Suddenly, off to his right a toilet flushed and a portly gentlemen stepped out of the stall and stared then smiled at Morrissey.

"WHAT IN BLOODY HELL YOU LOOKING AT!?" Morrissey snapped before he stormed out.

＊

Fielding Hotel, Coventry

As Frank unlocked the door to his room after returning to his hotel from the local Cambio where he cashed in the remainder of his Sterling pounds for dollars he was compelled to scurry across the room to answer the bedside phone.

"Yes?"

I have a trunk call for Mr. Frank Mahone? A pleasant female voice on the other end requested.

"Detective Mahone speaking."

Hold please.

Following the connection he immediately recognized the caller.

What the fuck is a 'trunk' call? Wachowski barked.

"Pleasant as ever! It means long distance, overseas call. The old people here still use the phrase. Probably why she used it for you."

You're a regular Bill Burr you are!

"What's up?"

You okay to talk?

"Yeah, yeah I'm alone."

You asked me to snoop around about that FBI guy came to see me?

"Willis, yeah. What about him?"

I couldn't track down too much on him but one of his runnin' mates is apparently real chummy with Comey.

"Comey as in James Comey? Clinton's lap dog, 'Hillary's crimes weren't really criminal', that Comey?!"

One and the same!

"Jesus Christ!"

No but Clinton and Christ are often confused. There's more.

"Oh good!"

My contact here says-

The conversation was interrupted by a knock at the door.

"Hold on Chief." He said. "Place is busier than Grand Central Station!" He mumbled as he set the phone down and rolled over the bed and opened the door.

Shocked and disarmed at the sight of Irina standing there he simply walked back into the room and continued talking with Wachowski.

"Hello to you too!" Irina shrugged and entered.

"Sorry Chief, go ahead."

My contact here says one of his running buddies is now heading up the field office in-

"Wait let me guess, London!"

I knew there was a reason I okayed your promotion to Lieutenant Detective! Hedges says-

"Who's Hedges?" He asked as Irina made her way to the kettle and started a kettle of tea.

The P.C. they traded for sending you over there, we've had a few beers together. My point is watch your ass!

"Why?"

Because according to Hedges this Jamoke Sims is one bad hombre! He's got his eye on the Deputy Director's spot and will do whatever it takes to get the corner office! Word is he was drinkin' buddies not only with Comey but Strock, Page and later Cohen!

"Huh! The family that drinks together stays together! Bastard's got all the bases covered!"

I can smell your wheels turning asshole! Am I getting' through to you, you thick shit? Watch your ass!

"Don't sweat it mommy! Junior's coming home on the next flight."

Overhearing Mahone from the kitchenette Irina, though not completely shocked, looked over in surprise as Mahone continued.

What?! What the hell you talkin' about? You got at least another month or so! Stay over there, keep your head down and enjoy your vacation!

"The van case is pretty well wrapped up, I checked out how they do things over here and I'll have a full report on your desk day after tomorrow. I did what I was sent here to do."

417

Frank-

"They've got some interesting procedures and protocols over here might be of use. Fer instance did you know they're allowed to tape record their interrogations, which they call 'interviews'?"

Don't give me that horseshit! What the hell you gonna do once you get back here? Sell pencils on the street corner? May I also remind you that there's a middle-aged, sexually frustrated police psychiatrist back here that-

"Chief, somebody just came in. I gotta go! I'll get a hold of you as soon as I land."

Mahone! Listen to me. Mahone-

The last thing Wachowski heard was the click on the line being cut off.

"Tea?" Irina asked as she poured a cup and glanced at the half packed suitcase.

"Come to wish me goodbye?" Frank quipped. "I don't see any flowers."

"Ya know in most civilized societies its customary for a guy who's quitting his job to at least show up and give notice or call in. Not to skulk out in the dead of night like a disgruntled NYPD cop . . . oh, never mind."

"Calling in indicates you may intend to eventually go back." He defended.

"What the hell is that supposed to mean?"

"It means that I intend to be heading back to The States tonight."

"Tonight? Why wait? There's a flight in about an hour. Time enough to get to Heathrow!"

Frank was amused by the sarcasm masking her anger as she continued.

"You always make such life changing decisions with such nonchalance?"

"What other way is there?"

"Pity the girl that lands you!"

"That's what my future ex-wife said."

"Okay . . ."

"You had something you wanted to share with me before we were interrupted a couple of days ago?" He probed.

Taking a seat at the two seater breakfast table opposite the bed Kuksova fished some papers out of her shoulder bag before launching into her brief.

"Servicio Boliveriano de Inteligencia National, otherwise known as SEBIN."

Frank watched her face as Kuksova now calmly read to an attentive Mahone who sat next to her at the table in his well-appointed room. "SEBIN is the primary, most well financed Intel agency in Venezuela. One of the most well developed and financially supported Intel agencies in South America. Established in 1979 by President Rafeal Caldera as the National Directorate of Intelligence and Prevention Service."

"Dangerous?" He asked as he rose to pour them both more tea.

"According to several SEBIN officials who have defected to the U.S., yes. Currently SEBIN is heavily dependent on vice-president, Delcy Rodriguez. She's the subject of multiple international sanctions and has full knowledge that Maduro maintains a small but well paid, substantial network of spies in and around D.C., all supporters of or working directly for SEBIN to keep track of dissidents and folks like Ileana Ros-Lehtinen and Marco Rubio."

"Marco Rubio! The U.S. senator?! What the hell for?"

"He's Cuban American. Maybe they figure if they catch him doing some behind-the-curtain stuff they can use it. Or sell it off to the Press and collect a few bucks. The MSM pays handsomely for anything against Trump and the GOP. This blackmail approach is a strategy that's been used for some time, sell stories to the MSM outlets to help fund the 'cause'. In conjunction with open source funding it's kept them going for at least the last five years."

"A dissident terrorist group pulls in enough dosh-"

"Dosh?! What's with 'dosh'?!" She questioned.

"Americans! They never travel!" He mocked as he shook his head.

"Ya know Mahone, I can still pull strings and get you sent home. I understand they're lookin' for traffic cops in Staten Island."

"I go home who's gonna watch your back?"

"Is that what you're doing? Watching my back." She sat back and smiled at his comment.

"Somebody has to. Rookie!"

"Are you suggesting you'll still work with the

Bureau just to watch my back?"

There was a momentary silent stare-off before they leaned into each other and kissed.

"I was going to say, to make enough money to support their field operations?" He continued.

"Okay, back to business." She collected herself. "They filter their money through *Patriotas Cooperantes*. A charity organization supposedly listed as a 501C."

"Do they actually have a 501C?"

"I couldn't get into the IRS files but according to the Small Business Association, yes."

"Do we know where they work out of?"

"They've got half a dozen branch offices, mostly in run-down nighborhoods but, and this is the real reason I came over here-"

"Uh huh, I'm sure it is!"

"It is! Their H.Q. address is in New York City."

"You don't say."

"It's listed on their 501C application as 665 East 110th Street in Manhattan."

"Over on the East Side, in Spanish Harlem." Mahone pointed out. "Huh!"

She waited.

He sat for several minutes and stared.

"Huh? That's it? I come all the way over here for some analytical feedback and all I get is a caveman grunt of 'huh'!" She challenged.

"You still suspect this jamoke Sims?"

"Absolutely!" She stated. Mahone rose and donned his coat. "Where we going?" Irina asked.

"Well, when said cop decides that he is no longer making any progress-"

"Frank, there's more."

"Okay, go ahead."

"Maureen's dead."

"What?!" Mahone froze and made direct eye contact.

"Maureen Dunn. Dead. As in shot from a roof top in Paris." Frank fell back to sit on the bed.

"What the hell was she doing in Paris?!" He asked his half packed suitcase. Kuksova answered instead.

"Shortly before you decided to exit the scene the Yard decided the van case should be bumped up to the security services and the SHIT Squad should resume the mundane task of solving murders. Also, on Morrissey's glowing recommendation of you, which he sent a copy of back to the NYPD, you should be allowed to stay for an additional six months." Surprised, Frank looked over at her. "That is if you so desire. But I see that-"

"Talk to me about Dunn's murder."

Irina dragged her chair opposite the bed and cradled her tea in both hands before speaking.

"Morrissey made the very ballsy decision to split the squad up and send them on different missions to try and track down the maniacs who hijacked the students and try to confirm if there was a solid connect with the spoofer case."

"Which your guys at the bureau were going to confirm once and for all." Frank added.

"Once and for all provided we had the device to reverse engineer and discover how far ahead the bad guys might be. Except-"

"Except you lost the god damned thing! Tell me you didn't lose the damn thing?!" Mahone stared. Irina looked away.

"MI6 were charged with custody and shipment to D.C. by secure carrier after their guys had a crack at it. But it appears to have vanished before it reached them."

"Christ! You miss a couple of days at work and everything goes to hell!"

"That's what I admire most about you, Mahone! No ego."

"Walk me through the trail!"

"What?!"

"THE TRAIL, THE TRAIL! When was it last seen and where does the trail go cold?"

"You had it, I saw it, you handed it over to Morrissey, who was ordered by the C.I. to give it to MI6. It was shipped by secure courier to the SIS Building on Albert Embankment but never made it there."

"What's the courier's story?"

"He gave it to some MI6 guy who signed for it."

"Where?"

"At Albert Embankment, so he says."

"He describe the guy?"

"Tall-ish, white hair, goatee."

"Sims has it!" Mahone declared.

"Oh be serious! Besides, Sims doesn't have a

goatee." She balked.

"And after the courier gave his statement to the investigators, when they went through their files did they find anybody in MI6 who was in the building with white hair and a goatee?" Frank pushed.

"Of course! There were nearly half a dozen men white hair and-"

"Any of them unable to account for their whereabouts at the time of the delivery to the building?"

"No! As it happens there was a staff meeting that morning, they were all there. The thief probably wore a wig. And . . ." She stopped talking and stared. "Even Sims wouldn't . . . son-of-a-bitch! You really think that horse's ass-"

"One of the oldest tricks in the book! Do something illegal, frame a suitable sucker, bust said sucker, magically find the drugs, money, jewels whatever and, presto! You're the hero! No further evidence needed. Simple! People like things simple. There were over two dozen cases of false accusations of major crimes in our precinct Downtown last year alone."

"Bastard!"

"That was my Chief on the phone when you came in. Do you know why he was calling?"

"To tell you he misses you and the station house has come to a dead halt since you've been away?"

"Exactly! But also to give me a heads up about Sims!"

"How the hell does he know about Sims?!"

"NYPD Baby! We're not just for homicides anymore." Kuksova wasn't amused. "Now, there's one more important question e have to answer!" Frank pushed on as he paced.

"Which is?"

"Who's the sucker Sims planned on pinning it on? Does he know you or that you're out for him?"

The reality was quick to dawn on her.

"BASTARD, BASTARD, BATSARD!!" She threw her teacup to the floor.

Frank smiled.

"Anyone ever tell you you're kind'a sexy when you're angry?"

"I'm flattered! Now what the hell do we do about Sims? Or, since you're leaving, should I ask, 'what do **I** do about Sims'?"

"What's the time?"

"The time?" She parroted.

"Yeah, what's the time?" He repeated. She looked at her watch.

"15:50, why?"

"Good! Just in time for an after-hours drink!"

"This is England! After hours drinks are after six o'clock!"

"Well, I'm American so I don't give a shit about traditions and two, I'm still on American time."

"American time? That doesn't make any-"

He headed out the door but stopped in the threshold. "Well? You coming?"

******

425

FBI Office
U.S. Embassy, London

Chair slid back and chin resting on his folded hands flat on the top of his desk, Sims sat in his office staring at something when Bubba Cortland came in.

"What the hell is that?!" Cortland challenged.

Moving only his mouth Sims mumbled his reply. "What the hell does it look like?"

"Well, I ain't no rocket scientist but it looks like that fucking secret device that was supposed to be on the secure aircraft to Langley this morning!"

Sims sat up as he responded.

"You know Bubba, when the Director first showed me your file photo and said we were gonna be working together, my first reaction was, 'ahhh, he's probably not as dumb as he looks'. But I decided to give you the benefit of the doubt. Glad I did."

"Fuck you jerkwad. Explain yourself starting with why you intercepted that NTSB report."

"I guaranteed the Director we'd stop these Muesli eating Socialists from launching their updated version of our GPS."

"*The Galileo System*?"

"Yes, *The Galileo System*. Stupid fucking name!" Sims mumbled to himself. "And the surest way to do that is to take direct action. But in order to do that correctly, we're gonna have to-"

"Hold on there Hos! What's this 'we' shit? You got worms?"

"We're partners ain't we? We're on the same team."

"That depends!"

"Oh yeah?! On what?"

"On what you plan on doing with that thing!"

"Well, now that the pacifists in Congress have voted to eliminate the Selective Availability modes on the new satellites once those are updated there's nothing to stop these World War Two losing peaceniks from taking over the entire aero-space market! But with this little baby, they'll have no choice but to dance to our tune. Besides, with one year to retirement I need a nest egg."

"Good for you! I don't retire for another eight to ten years!"

"True, but after we pull this off, have returned the stolen deadly device, nail the people who stole it-"

"Frame someone ya mean!"

"Catch-the-thieves or more precisely, once we've put SEBIN out of commission and have made the world safe again for democracy, you'll be promoted to Senior Field Agent and retire to a three bedroom on the beach in Cabo instead of a one bedroom in Anaheim! Know-what-I-mean, Hos?" Sims maintained eye contact with the unwrapped device sitting on his desk the entire time he spoke.

"That why you didn't ship this thing back to Washington?"

"What'a you think? After what happened with the Comey circus and that pants suit wearing idiot you think I'd trust anybody else to close this case? Wise up Satch, school's out. Amateur Hour's over!"

"Does the Director know about this?" Cortland's concern level rose markedly.

"He will, soon enough. As soon as all the pieces fall into place. Now that we have the evidence," He nodded towards the device. ". . . all we gotta do is round up the SEBIN cell, arrest them and do the paperwork. Then we'll have presented the director with the perfect excuse to rack up the points the bureau so desperately needs to win back support from Congress and more importantly the American people."

"None of which makes it right!" Cortland demanded. Sims turned in his seat, readjusted and finally made eye contact with Cortland.

"Bubba, have you ever thought about how many badges we have in the U.S.?"

"Is this a test?"

"God only knows how many. City cops, county cops, sheriffs, state troopers, bailiffs, inspectors, traffic cops and meter maids. Thousands, tens of thousands. Ours is a litigious society Agent Cortland. But at the end of the day there's only one badge that really means anything." He reached into his breast pocket and brandished his open I.D. "This one!" He declared. Cortland smirked and nodded.

Sims rose from his desk, crossed the office and locked the door.

428

"Back in 2000 after the Army, I sat on the side lines for months while dozens of women and minorities were sent to Quantico for training, all well my white, male ass was passed over. Then 9/11 came and the call went out! Everybody and his brother was pushed through the program. Boneheads like Strock, McCabe and Page. Page! A fuckin' lawyer, not even an agent!"

He rose from his desk and poured a scotch from the small bar by the window as he continued his soliloquy. "Now, nineteen years later, I'm at a point where I've devoted my entire life to The Bureau, and it took me the better part of all that time to build my rep in this organization, before those self-serving, 'lawyers with badges' tore it all down in their fucked-up coup attempt! I told them it wouldn't work, but they pushed ahead, full steam!" He sipped his drink. "And where'd it get them? Sacked and knocked the FBI down to its lowest opinion rating in history, that's where."

"And some are facing jail time." Cortland interjected.

"Shit! Here's a buck, buy a clue! Nobody in Washington is going to jail, bank on that!"

"Yeah, you're probably right." Bubba conceded.

"You're probably too young to remember but they used to write books and make crime movies about us! We were the good guys! Now we're the brunt of a joke!" He finished his drink and started to slowly rewrap the device as he continued. "This is our chance to undo all that. To re-establish ourselves as what we once were, the premier law enforcement agency in the world." He paused as he stood. "Why shouldn't we reap a little bonus for the risk?"

"If you're plotting what I think you're plotting, you know any money from your little blackmail scheme here will be marked to enable an international trace."

"Which is why there's no cash involved! The electronic payment goes directly to a Swiss account."

"Which is already set up and ready to go, I assume?" Cortland challenged.

"Which is why we fake a third party stole the device, stage a negotiation to get it back, for the right price, be the heroes and make those extra few retirement bucks."

"Wait, lemme guess! The 'third party' is these SEBIN clowns?"

"That, Agent Cortland, is **exactly** why I gave you the benefit of the doubt when I first met you!"

"You made a deal with these SEBIN Bozos yet?"

"Kinda."

"Kinda'? That's not an answer. You did or you didn't."

"I'm smoking them out using another party."

"Who?"

"You don't know her. Some female from the Tech branch. Born in Russia. She makes the perfect bait! Anybody goes down, it'll be her, not us."

"There you go with that 'us' shit again."

"Cortland you remember the Y2K scare back in '99?"

"Just because you met J. Edgar Hoover back during the Depression doesn't mean I did!" Cortland shot back.

"Okay, I take that as a no. The Europeans christened their project Galileo, it stands to reason whoever these South American jokers are they would do the same kind of thing."

"What? Name it Christopher Columbus because he was Italian! They're South Americans, Hispanics, of some sort."

"Most people who went to public schools think that, but Columbus might actually have been Spanish."

"What's your point?"

"Because he took part in a revolution against King Ferdinand and lost, he escaped to Italy."

"So what are you telling me, Columbus was a fugitive?"

"Big time major felon! Then had the balls to come back years later with a complete make-over, new name, new look the whole works so he could ask for money for his voyage. We broke their codes late last year which is why we know these clowns named their mission *Operation Diego*. It was Columbus' kid's name. Because we cracked their codes we knew they had a device, we just didn't know exactly who had it. All I had to do was track it down. And I did, so now, here we be Bubba-G!"

"Fuck you, don't call me that." Cortland sat back

in his chair and stared at his partner. "You're serious about this aren't you?"

"For a potential half billion, serious as a heart attack! But you're asking the wrong question Sweetheart. The right question is . . . are you in or out?" Sims asked. Cortland continued to stare without response. "Well, I'm going to put this high tech money maker back in my wall safe and go for a liquid lunch. If you're not here when I get back I'll assume you're out." Sims explained.

"So now you're above the Law?" Cortland challenged.

"Don't be stupid Bubba, nobody's above the law! That's a founding principle of the American government. No, we're not above the law." He proceeded to carry the spoofer device in the large, clean automotive chamois cloth and placed it in the wall safe behind his desk and closed over the two foot by three foot, hinged painting of J. Edgar Hoover.

"We **are the fucking law**!" He collected his things and made for the door.

"Tell me more about these SEBIN clowns." Bubba finally asked.

Sims smiled as Cortland followed along and left with him to go for a drink.

*

The Gay Hussar Restaurant
Greek Street, Soho

Dozens of autographed pictures of known personalities plastering the walls in neat, Sardi-esque style stared out at the room while the dark, faux Tudor décor and narrow open booths of the Gay Hussar Restaurant afforded little privacy.

Save for the corner table next to the frosted window there was nowhere else to have a semi-private conversation so when Special Agent Sims and Agent Bubba Cortland entered they settled on the table to the left of the main entrance.

"Who the hell are all these people?" Cortland asked nodding at the walls as they took their seats.

"Do I look like fuckin' Stephen Fry?! Who the hell knows, famous people! Let's just eat and get back and get to work. There's a lot to do to get this thing set up! We need to have this all in place by early next week. The Director needs to be able to pass the intel to the POTUS before the 9/11 speech and meeting with these EU monkeys."

"Okay, okay! Don't be so grouchy!"

Although there was no one in the immediate area Sims leaned into the table and spoke quietly to his partner who was preoccupied with the menu.

"Cortland?"

"Yeah?"

"You made the right decision!" Sims encouraged.

"I haven't decided yet! I'm still torn."

"Between what?!"

"Between the chicken or the ham."

Sims slapped the menu in anger.

"I mean by deciding to come in with me!"

"Oh yeah, yeah. I sure as hell hope so!"

"Try the Guylás." Sims suggested.

"What's that?"

"A very tasty beef stew. It's a kind of goulash! With fresh black bread it's nice."

"Is it spicy?"

"Not really."

"What's in it?" Cortland pushed.

"What'a you twelve?! Never mind, just get a fuckin' sandwich!"

A waiter approached the table.

"Good afternoon, my name is Adami, I'll be you're server. Can I start you out with-"

Adami's over rehearsed, metronomic soliloquy was suddenly cut short as with a distinct sense of urgency two very large, dark suited men accompanied by a pair of Bobbies came through the front door, perused the room, and spotted Sims and Cortland. Moving over to their table the two men quickly flashed their badges.

"Agents Sims and Cortland?" One of them asked in a distinct New York dialect.

"Yeah, I'm Special Agent Sims. What is this? Who the hell are you two?!" Sims belligerently demanded.

"This is Inspector Lloyd, Metropolitan Police Internal Affairs and I'm Agent Dalal FBI Internal Affairs, attached to the D.O.J." He flashed his gold shield.

"Am I supposed to be impressed?" Sims challenged.

"We have a few questions." The big one said.

"Good for you! Ask Siri!" Sims challenged.

"Agent Sims, we're requesting your cooperation."

"And?"

"If you cooperate you'll be free to resume your assigned duties here." At that Sims assumed a more serious demeanor.

"And if I don't cooperate?"

"If not you'll be remanded into custody until a flight can be arranged back to Washington where you'll be more fully investigated for other suspected crimes including but not limited to extortion, obstructing a murder investigation, posing as an agent of Her Majesty's Secret Service, plotting to interfere with and interfering with said services."

It was less than an hour later, back at the AV Room that Rankor and Kuksova slid off the table and snapped to a standing position as the same two men who had confronted Sims and Cortland came through the door laughing and joking.

"Well?!" Irina anxiously demanded. The larger of the two smirked, slid his black back pack off his shoulder and tossed the chamois wrapped device to Kuksova who squealed as she reached to catch it. Inside she found the carefully, cloth wrapped spoofer.

The pair of 'agents' used to retrieve the spoofer device were actually two of Rankor's chums including Sergeants Reilly and Chowdhury, alias 'Agent Dalal' who was also a member of the London Troubadours, a Twickenham amateur theatrical group.

"Much indebted to you two lads!" Rankor thanked them.

"It was our pleasure Rohan!" He responded handing Irina back her badge. "Bloody Yanks! Always acting like they're the only ones doin' any good in the world!"

"Yeah, arrogant bastards! Present company excluded of course Miss!" Reilly backtracked and nodded to Irina.

"No problem, Sergeant." She replied. "Sometimes, with people like Sims we feel the same way! Besides, it couldn't have happened to a nicer guy!" Irina reassured him. "Pints on me at the *Dog & Hound* tonight!" She added. Reilly beamed.

"Any more covert assignments miss, I'm available!"

*** * ***

Scotland Yard
Office of the Chief Inspector

Morrissey hadn't even finished adding sugar to his coffee when a messenger appeared in the doorway of the AV Room and called over to his work table.

"Inspector Morrissey your presence is requested

up in the office of the Chief Inspector."

"What for?"

"Didn't say sir, he just grabbed the nearest peon and sent me down to tell ya."

"Thanks." Glancing over at Ali and Rankor who shot back a 'what's that all about?' face. Morrissey shrugged back as he headed for the door.

Morrissey's internal dialogue was running full speed on the way down the hall to the lift in an attempt to guess the reason for the C.I.'s beckoning first thing in the morning.

Don't tell me that useless Yank finally quit and I'm going to get me arse chewed for it!

Still pissed off at Mahon for having quit without notice and causing big headaches, Nigel's anger built. *Bloody police exchange! We're not an Erasmus Program, we're a bloody police service!* Morrissey pondered as he made his way up in the lift.

The inspector hadn't seen or talked to Mahone ever since parting company at professor Aron Stoli's residence over a week ago.

"Sir you requested to see me?"

"Morrissey, come in please, shut the door over." Before he even had a chance to close the office door the C.I. lit into him. "Well you've certainly made your mark on the Mayor's exchange program, Mr. Morrissey."

"Chief Inspector I-"

"Save it Boy-o!"

When he closed the door over he spotted Mahone

sitting on the couch behind it.

"Morning Nigel!" Mahone cheerfully greeted. Barely suppressing his anger, Morrissey avoided making eye contact.

"It's **Inspector** Morrissey, Mr. Mahone, thank you very much!" He insisted

"Morrissey, your charge here has been pleading your argument for more time and I must say I'm very disappointed that you've chosen to send him–"

"Chief, Inspector Morrissey didn't send me. He knew nothing about-" Frank interjected.

"My title is **Chief Inspector** Detective Marone. Please kindly use it!" The C.I, spouted.

Frank sat silently for a moment debating a response. But only for a very short moment as he stood from the couch.

"And my name is **Mahone,** not **Morone,** not **Malone** and not **Stallone! It's Mahone, Ma-hone**, you know as in Póg mo thón!"

"What on earth is Póg mo thón?!" The C.I. demanded as Morrissey fought back a guffaw before he quickly interjected.

"It's a traditional Gaelic greeting Sir!" Morrissey explained.

"Oh, I see."

A moment later everybody settled down and Mahone retook his seat,

"I apologize for my outburst Chief Inspector." Frank sincerely offered.

"Well . . . given the circumstances, I suppose I too should apologize. Lieutenant Detective

Mahone." Lister humbly reciprocated.

"Not necessary Chief Inspector. This case has me a bit on edge too and the fact of having to surrender it to another agency. . ."

"Yes, I completely sympathize with yours and Inspector Morrissey's situation. However, orders are orders and these come directly from the Lord Mayor's desk."

An awkward silence permeated the room when Frank spoke up.

"Chief Inspector, as I was about to inform you when **Inspector** Morrissey came in,"

At his use of the title 'Inspector' he nodded over at Morrissey who smiled and curtly nodded back.

". . . in the few days I was away I stumbled across new information that may persuade the higher ups to give us more time."

"What exactly is this new information?"

"I believe I've located our man Battesta."

Morrissey and Lister shot him a look.

"Well?" Lister insisted.

"He's working and using an apartment in Manhattan as a base. My sources say in Spanish Harlem." Mahone shot back. "I have strong reason to believe he's the actual hijacker."

"MY GOD MAN! WHY DIDN'T YOU JUST SPIT IT OUT!?" Lister grabbed the phone and started to dial. "I'll notify MI5, they can contact MI6 and –"

Frank reached over and pressed down on the hook cutting off the call.

"Not necessary Chief Inspector. My precinct has had alternating teams on stakeout watching him."

"What if they lose him?!"

"We've been on him for the last twenty-four hours. He appears stuck into a routine, probably trying to maintain a normal appearance, temporarily at least. Up in the morning, off to run errands most of the day then back to the apartment in the late afternoon where he holds up with several others."

"What about the FBI?!"

"Been notified Sir. They're involved and have been requested not to move on him until we arrive and pending positive identification and verification of other evidence."

"Located him? In Manhattan?! How in the hell did you manage to . . . ?" Morrissey blurted.

"I used up a favor from a friend in the Bureau." Frank casually informed.

"A blond-haired, blue-eyed friend of Russian stock?" Morrissey posited.

"Da comrade!" Mahone answered.

"Detective Mahone, if it's not too much of a bother, could you explain to Inspector Morrissey and myself exactly what you mean by, 'not to move on him until **we** arrive'?"

"Chief Inspector, with yours and Morrissey's help I can cut your red tape by days, catch this son-of-a-bitch and probably shut this entire ring down! All I'm asking, all we're asking for, is you to buy us a couple of extra days. Postpone the hearing on what happened in Paris by dragging out the inquiry. Tell the Supervisor you're waiting on the French, say they're dragging their feet. They gotta buy that!"

"What an original idea!" Morrissey snarked.

The C.I. sat back in his high backed chair, folded his hands over his stomach and perused the two detectives.

"It's too chancy. Sorry, but I can't."

"Chef Inspector . . . the Lord Mayor sanction this program?" Morrissey joined in the pleading.

"You know full well he did Morrissey! It was one of his bloody staff thought the whole thing up."

"Then given that the NYPD have this geezer cornered and he doesn't appear to be going anywhere anytime soon, Mahone and I could be there by late tonight, allow the American SWAT units to move in and have this bastard under the lights this time tomorrow! Possibly even coral his cohorts. How much of a boost to the Mayor's program do you suppose that would add?!" Lister looked nearly convinced. "All we're asking is for a little time!"

"Twenty-four to forty-eight hours Chief!" Frank double teamed the C.I.

Another awkward pause ensued as Lister teetered on the edge of decision.

"Chief Inspector, perhaps this will help you out." From his jacket pocket Mahone produced a letter and passed it to the C.I. Lister who unfolded and read the letter.

The Galileo Project

To: Chief Inspector Lister, Met Police, London

From: The Federal Bureau of Investigation
United States Embassy
London, England

Be it known that Detective Frank L. Mahone, Lieutenant grade, is to be commended for his unending diligence and assistance in investigation of the kidnapping and hijack of the students of the Woldingham Catholic Academy for Girls and the rescue of many students and several staff.

Additionally the Special Homicide Investigation Squad, presently under the command of Inspector Nigel H. Morrissey of Scotland Yard is to be included in this commendation.

The international cooperation between the Metropolitan Police Service of London and The Federal Bureau of Investigation, exemplified by officers Mahone and Morrissey reflect great credit upon both themselves and the joint efforts of both organizations.

Signed;

Robert Wood Johnson IV
United States Ambassador to the Court of St. James

"Huh! 'United States Ambassador to the Court of St. James!' Windy enough title!" The Chief Inspector grunted. "Doesn't this chap own a soccer team or something?"

"NFL sir, American football." Mahone corrected. "The game where they fall and don't get up unless they are actually hurt." Mahone, by-passing the political filter he didn't have, explained. "He's the great grandson of Robert Johnson, co-founder of Johnson & Johnson, thirty-seventh on the Fortune 500, a primary component of the Dow Jones."

Suddenly Frank felt Morrissey's hand on his shoulder. "He gets the point Frank!"

"A copy has been sent to FBI Director Wray in D.C. as well. I'm guessing Mayor Khan might get some political mileage out of this as well." Mahone ventured. As Lister stared down at the letter Mahone smiled at Morrissey. "I'm just saying, Chief Inspector."

"Very well. I suppose, given the importance of closing out this case and on the back of your heroic rescue of the school girls that I might be able to convince the gods of administration to give us a couple of more days." Both cops smiled. "Gentlemen, you too Mahone, as impressive as your accomplishments are bolstered by this letter of commendation, I myself helped design and endorsed the U.S.-U.K. exchange program under whose umbrella you two are currently operating. I will agree to buy you more time, however, I can't sanction Morrissey to travel to New York."

"Chief-" A deflated Mahone begun to plead.

"If I were to allow an exception in this case it would leave myself and the entire program open for criticism at the highest political levels." The C.I. reluctantly announced.

"But Chief Inspector, a letter from the Ambassador?!" Frank continued.

"Yes a letter from the Ambassador which I have no inkling of how you connived but you did. The fact remains that this is a letter of commendation not carte blanch to alter established investigative procedures. I doubt if even the U.S. ambassador would be stimulated to interfere with an MI5 investigation let alone something involving MI6!"

"But Chief-"

"Detective Mahone! This phase of the investigation, as far as you two are concerned, will run out of time two days from now at which time it will be passed upstairs to the professionals." He folded over and handed the letter back to Mahone. "Additionally, what makes you think Detective that you and the Inspector, would be permitted under any circumstances, to squander her Majesty's money on a holiday trip to America?"

Without ceremony Mahone rose to leave.

"You're welcome to keep that copy Sir." He called over his shoulder.

"You bought yourself two days Morrissey. No more!"

"Yes sir."

"Two days here in England!"

"Understood sir."

"The moment we receive word that Inspector Dunn's body is in route back I'm going to have to put in the final paperwork and initiate the investigation."

****

Covent Gardens Cocktail Lounge

After returning to his room that Thursday to retrieve his bags Frank had arranged to meet Irina for a good-bye drink a short distance from his hotel. Frank was early, on his second drink and minutes after Kuksova arrived a light drizzle started up.

The waiter brought her a white wine and they sat without conversation for the better part of ten minutes.

"Huh! Typical London!" She quietly declared. Frank didn't respond. "What time's your flight out?"

"Check in at Heathrow is seven. We're wheels up at twenty:forty-five." He informed.

"Chief Inspector Lister give Morrissey permission to go to The States?!"

"He didn't, this is a solo trip." He sat up straight and assumed a mock pompous attitude with a deep voice. "'Inspector Morrissey, I won't sanction Her Majesty paying you for a holiday trip to New York!'"

Despite her morose mood she smiled at Frank's

comical impression of Morrissey's boss.

"I take it then that the letter didn't help?"

"No, but thanks for going out of your way."

"Woody is surprisingly approachable. In spite of his status I've never seen him look down his nose at anyone!"

"Fingers crossed this asshole hangs out in Harlem until I get there."

"I still don't see the point of you going. They can nail him any time they want, they hardly need you there. I mean, what do you hope to accomplish?"

"For one thing even though I told Lister they have him staked out, I sort'a neglected to tell him that they have yet to make a positive I.D. They haven't been able to get close enough."

"And you're still flying all the way over there? Just to I. D. a possible suspect?!"

"Am I sensing a smidge of regret that I'm leaving?"

He attempted eye contact but she looked away.

"Good thing you don't have a big ego!" She snapped.

"That's a yes!"

"Okay, maybe a little." She admitted.

"I'm listed as lead on the case and since this jamoke hasn't done anything to provoke anybody in New York, at least not yet, my Chief has agreed to let me be in on the takedown."

With no choice but to accept his answer, she did but was not happy about it. She twirled her glass as the rain cold tapped a little harder at the picture window next to them.

"You and your boss are pretty tight aren't you?" She spoke into her glass.

"We have history."

"By the way, thank you for taking care of Sims."

"Well, when you get back to the U.S. maybe we can think of a way you can thank me."

"Maybe this will help." Across the table she passed him an envelope.

"What's this?" He asked as he opened it and glanced at the single sheet printout.

"A while back you said the only photos you had of this guy Battesta were the ones from INTERPOL and the one from the car rental place and both were pretty bad and looked like he was disguised."

Frank unfolded the sheet and saw a series of high resolution enhanced CCTV photos of Raymundo Battesta.

"These were taken less than forty-eight hours ago when he landed at JFK."

"Nice, these'll really come in handy. Thanks!"

Another awkward pause crept in until Kuksova spoke up.

"Okay, are you gonna ask or you gonna make me do it?"

"Ask what?"

"Seriously Mahone! Have you not one sensitive bone in your body?!"

"Seriously, what?!"

"Are we gonna see each other again?" She blurted out.

"Are we being truthful here?"

"No! I'm making small talk! What the hell do you think?"

"Okay, okay! Will we see each other again, she asks?" He took her hand. "Yes! I sure as hell hope so. I would very much like to see you again."

"Then you will."

They finished their drinks and outside the lounge, under the dry shelter of the awning they embraced with a passionate kiss. Frank flagged a black cab. Irina stood in the light rain watching as he drove off.

It was just over an hour later that Mahone finally found his gate at Heathrow and, his mind still intoxicated with thoughts of Irina, glanced across the nearly empty waiting area where, in the front row of seats, he spotted Morrissey sitting casually reading book. He approached Nigel from the side.

"Come to say good-bye Inspector?"

Morrissey casually turned, looked up and smiled.

"If I had I'd have brought flowers. By-the-way, when do you leave?"

"I'm on the eight forty-five to JFK."

"That wouldn't be flight #109 would it?"

"You're a better cop than I gave you credit for."

"What a coincidence!" From a large, brown leather satchel on the seat next to him Nigel brandished a ticket and boarding pass. Frank spotted the flight number and smiled.

"Explanation?"

"Two years, three months and some weeks since

I took a holiday. Thought it high time. Besides, all these heroics we're accused of perpetrating are wearing me out. Need a bit of a rest, quite frankly."

"Well, a premature welcome to the Big Apple Inspector!" Frank took the seat next to him.

"Does this mean when we get to America I'm going to need a translator?" Nigel asked.

"No, most people there speak English. But a couple of body guards might come in handy."

****

CHAPTER NINETEEN

13th Precinct
Gramercy Park, Manhattan
Upper East Side apartment
Friday August 30

That morning, at half past six in the morning, following an uneventful, eight hour flight from Heathrow to JFK, the alarm went off and Frank rolled over and fell from the second hand couch in his living room to the hard wood floor.

"Morning old boy!" With some difficulty he looked up from the floor. Morrissey, who had been given the bedroom, slowly came into focus. He sat at the folding aluminum table in the kitchenette, one foot on an unpacked box.

"Couldn't find anything in the cupboard so did a quick dash down the corner shop. Fancy a bagel?" He held up a white bag.

"Coffee?" Frank grumbled.

"Covered!" He proudly announced as he brandished a large container of coffee.

Mahone shook off the last of his sleep, rose to his feet and in his boxer shorts and black socks made his way across the room.

"You care for a shower? Towels are in big box." Frank offered.

"Already done. Took a crisp walk five or ten

streets to the north, stopped off at the local bakery then back. Nice enough neighborhood!"

"Yeah! As long as you're indoors between sun down and sun up!"

"So, what's the plan? Partner?" Morrissey cheerfully pushed. In between cautious sips of coffee Frank smiled.

"First order of business is to check in down at the station house and see if there's any movement on the stakeout. Also I'll introduce you to Wachowski, nice guy you'll like him. Then we'll head Uptown where we'll check in with the stakeout team and get an update and take it from there."

Frank, who had not stayed in his own place on the Upper East Side for the better part of the last two and half months, glanced around the room. The one partially unpacked box marked 'TOILET STUFF' sat atop three untouched others.

"Sorry the place is a wreck. Just moved in before I shipped out to London."

"Not a bother Mahone! I know how it is. Kudos to you for accepting the exchange of assignment! Most Yanks . . . ah Americans, don't want to leave the mother land."

"Look Morrissey, there's no way to know how long we'll be working together but it'll be a while. Call me Frank will ya?"

"Right! Very kind, 'Frank.'"

There was an awkward pause as Mahone anticipated Morrissey's reciprocation. It didn't come.

"So . . . okay if I call you Nigel?"

"Actually, no."

"No?!"

"No. Rather you didn't." He sipped the last of his tea.

"Okay, I guess."

Frank dressed and they left to catch the train Downtown.

Once out of the apartment and around the corner Morrissey suddenly stopped dead and stared across the street.

Mesmerized, the inspector watched as the corner parking lot attendant backed a car into a steel rack on top of which were stacked two other cars. When he finished parking that vehicle he got out manned a control box on the side of the tall, tubular steel rack and raised all three vehicles up to make room for a fourth. He then climbed into another car and parked it under the other three.

"What in the name of heaven . . . ?" Morrissey stood and stared at the four tiers of cars stacked one on top of the other.

Stepping to the side he saw there was an entire row of such racked cars stretched across the lot and the racks went three or four deep.

"BendPak 14000." Frank announced. "Been around for a couple of years. It's New York - if you can't go out, go up!"

"Only in America!" The Englishman shook his head.

"The rule here is compete and survive or stagnate

and die! Backbone of the free market system – competition." Mahone opined.

"Only in America." Morrissey repeated as he produced his cell phone and snapped several pictures.

The number 6 Train let them out directly onto 23rd Street and they walked the short distance to the 13th Precinct over on 21st Street.

A burly sergeant sitting behind the reception desk facing the door glanced up from his paperwork to spy Mahone and Morrissey coming through the front door.

"Jesus Christ! I didn't realize they closed Belleview!" He wise cracked as he spotted Mahone.

"At least your wife'll be glad I'm back!" Frank fired back without missing a beat as they whizzed by to the elevator.

"Not this wife brother! The last one maybe, but not this one!" The officer answered.

"Hang in there Sammy!" Frank called back.

Upstairs Frank didn't bother knocking as he burst through Chief Wachowski's office door.

Wachowski had his head down wrestling away at some paperwork and didn't even look up as the two entered.

"'Bout god damned time you showed up asshole!"

Morrissey, taken aback looked over at Mahone.

"Are you two always so cordial?"

Wachowski, who hadn't noticed Frank brought company, shot his head up to peruse the two.

"Way to make an impression Boss!" Frank greeted his Chief. "Inspector Morrissey, Chief Wachowski, Inspector the Chief. Please forgive his rudeness he's Polish."

"I see." Wachowski came out from behind his desk and they shook hands.

"You come back for holiday or you here to finally do some work?" Wachowski renewed his attack on Mahone.

Frank closed and locked the door and arranged two chairs in front of the desk.

"All joking aside Chief, we got some work to do!"

For the next twenty minutes Mahone filled him on what had happened in England and Wachowski brought the two cops up to speed on what he had learned from Hedges the Bobby and from his own poking around before he opened a desk drawer and produced a letter.

"This came in from the FBI through INTERPOL yesterday. Seems they've located a FARC fugitive through facial recognition coming into JFK."

Morrissey leaned in and read the message over Frank's shoulder.

"It's from your blond friend in the Bureau!" Morrissey said into Frank's ear. "Looks as if she's got your number mate!"

"Yeah, yeah! Don't read nothing into it! She slipped me copies of these photos in London just before I left"

"Whose your 'blond friend'?"

"Nobody Chief. An FBI agent we worked with in London."

"Worked 'with'! Is that what you guys call it England?"

"Okay, okay! Let's drop it, shall we boys?!" Frank snapped. "When'd this F.R. report come in?" He nodded at the letter

"Officially it didn't. Hedges passed it to me!"

"Who's Hedges?" Morrissey queried.

"One of yours, a Bobbie. Guy that took my place here while I was over there."

"I suppose you two should quit pissing around down here and get your asses up to Harlem." Wachowski spoke as he scribbled an address on a piece of note paper. "They've had a pair of two man teams on him for the last forty-eight hours. He's sticking to a routine. Here." He passed the address to Mahone. "It's a couple of blocks north of Tito Puente Way."

"How far east?"

"About four blocks other side of The Park. Couple of blocks from the river."

"Got it!"

"Well, shall we 'hop' a taxi as you Yanks say?"

"Taxi? This isn't England Old Boy! You're in a free country now Mr. Morrissey." Frank picked up the phone on the Chief's desk and dialed the dispatcher.

"Jenny, how are you? Yes love, it's me. Yes I'm back, but not sure for how long."

"Not long I hope!" The chief mouthed in a loud

whisper.

"Have you got anything going north up Service Area Five in the next half hour or so? Great! Be a sweetie and let them know they'll be two passengers hitching a lift, would you?"

"Advantage of having the largest police force in the Free World I guess! Always somebody going somewhere." Morrissey commented.

"We need to get up to the 23rd over on 110th." Frank explained to the dispatcher. "Cheers love! Best to Bill and the kids." He hung up and turned to a smiling Morrissey. "You're in a free society now."

"Cheers? Sounds like you were over there a bit too long!" Wachowski cracked.

"Now that I'm back I'm thinking maybe not long enough! Let's go!"

"Hey Mahone."

"Yeah Chief?"

"Good to have you back!"

"Better wait and see how the day turns out before you say anything."

Down stairs at the armory Mahone drew his service weapon, a Glock 9mm and several magazines.

"Hey Benny, any chance we can get the Scotland Yard inspector here a weapon?" He asked of the armorer.

"No kiddin'! Scotland Yard really?"

"Yeah!" Frank assured the Benny. "How about it? I'll take responsibility."

"Scotland Yard, like in the movies huh?"

"Yeah."

"Sorry Frank, no-can-do partner! Regs is Regs and all. You know the drill."

"Yeah, thanks any way Benny."

A detective unit getting off shift gave them a lift and let them off at the Housing Police Station Uptown on 99th Street to collect two uniformed patrolmen for back-up.

Although there are a few gentrified areas of Harlem their target area was not one of them so back-up was recommended.

From the Housing Police Station they took a second patrol car around the north end of Central Park and over to Tito Puente Way.

"Sergeant, cruise us up to 112th and Fifth, will ya?." Frank directed the driver.

"Yes sir."

They negotiated the Uptown traffic for the next fifteen minutes but when Frank glanced out the window and saw a shop that attracted his attention he signaled the patrolman driving to pull over.

"Come on." He tapped Morrissey as he climbed out of the unmarked cruiser.

Morrissey read the over-sized sign above the doorway as they entered.

"'Gonzales' Lucky Pawn?' What are we doing in here?"

"We need to stop in here." He replied as he led Morrissey in.

"What for?"

"You need a weapon!"

"I'm afraid I'm not very comfortable around firearms." Morrissey weakly objected. "I'm not sure I want to-"

"That's very moralistic but let me tell you an old New York Chinese proverb: It is better to have Glock nine and not need one then to need Glock nine and not have one! If you're gonna back me up, you're gonna carry."

"Am I even authorized or qualified to carry a weapon in this country?"

"You finish primary school?"

"Of course!"

"This is America. you're qualified! Com'on!"

Frank made his way to the counter and Morrissey drifted to one of the many glass cases filled with hand guns. For the third time that morning the inspector was overwhelmed by what he saw. Agog he stared at the dozens of rifles lining the wall rack, the massive collection of pistols in the half dozen glass cases and the endless stacks of ammo shelved from floor to ceiling behind the counters.

.22's, .45's and several .357 Magnums were all neatly laid out one next to the other on double shelving in the long, glass cases.

"Jesus! I'd heard you could walk into any shop and buy a gun like a loaf bread but I'd always thought it was an exaggeration!"

"It is and it isn't." Frank told him. "You see something you like?"

"This place is more well armed then the entire

Met!"

The Hispanic shop owner stared at Morrissey then Frank from behind the counter. Frank shrugged.

"Friend of mine, from England." Mahone informed the attendant as he flashed his badge. "We need something light and accurate. Something in the nine mil range."

"Mahone." Morrissey approached Mahone and quietly protested. "I've never fired a weapon in my life!"

"Not even in training?!"

"Weapons training was voluntary when I went through. You know we don't carry weapons, we have special on call weapons squads." The clerk looked up from the glass case.

"So if there's a perp with a gun you have to make a phone call?" The clerk asked.

"We have an alert code and response time is only minutes."

"Minutes is all it takes!" Frank pointed to a 9mm Glock, a Colt and a wheel gun through the glass.

The Chicano sales clerk standing behind the counter with folded arms shifted the toothpick in his mouth and shook his head.

"What about that one?" Morrissey queried and pointed.

"A Saturday Night Special, .22 caliber?!" Frank informed.

"So I take it I don't want that one?"

"Not unless you're planning on being a pimp."

Mahone added. The Chicano chuckled. Frank offered an I.D. for the clerk. "I'll sign for it. Take my badge number, anybody gives you grief tell them to contact the Thirteenth Downtown."

"You got it Lieutenant." The attendant commenced filling out the paperwork.

"We're gonna need a box of shells as well. Give him the Gould and Goodrich shoulder holster too!"

Frank paid for the gun, holster and ammo with his credit card and as Morrissey with his new toys, made their way back out to the cruiser they headed off further uptown.

"I feel like Dirty Harry!" The Inspector quipped from the back seat

"Funny, I was just gonna say that!" Missing the sarcasm Morrissey fumbled further. "It doesn't go on your belt. It's a shoulder holster." Frank explained.

"Oh. So what are the rules of engagement?"

"Only two: they shoot at you, you shoot back until they're dead and don't shoot another cop."

"Got it!" Morrissey enthusiastically replied.

The two uniforms in the front of the cruiser glanced into the rear view mirror then exchanged glances. Morrissey was still fumbling with the shoulder holster as he tried to untangle it and discover the secret of getting it on.

The ride uptown was relatively smooth by Manhattan traffic standards, but as soon as they crossed Central Park North the pedestrian traffic noticeably thickened.

As they turned the corner onto 110th Street the officer driving was compelled to slow down and before they reached the middle of the block had to pull over. The increasingly crowded sidewalks and streets impeded their driving any further.

Dozens of gaily dressed people were streaming north towards an event.

"What the hell's with all the people?" Mahone growled.

"Puerto Rican Jazz Festival." The officer behind the wheel answered.

"Four days of fun, food, fights and stabbings highlighting the traditional culture of Puerto Rico!" The sergeant next to him added with no effort to hide his sarcasm. He noticed Morrissey stiffen up a bit. "But don't worry. There's usually only one or two stabbings per year. Sometimes a shooting."

Perusing the traffic Frank cursed. "This is gonna be fun!" They got out on 111th and swam through the crowd over to the corner of 112th and Third Avenue where, with Morrissey in tow Frank was directed by a uniformed cop to the overall commander of the stakeout team, a tall, burly black man in shirt sleeves leaning on the hood of a grey Ford Taurus. The commander stared down the street where the car was parked inconspicuously off to the side as the slowly swelling crowd calmly flowed around them neither noticing the other.

"O'Hara?" Frank brandished his shield.

"Yeah." He extended his hand. "Lieutenant Detective William O'Hara, the 25th."

461

"Frank Mahone, Downtown. This is Inspector Nigel Morrissey, Scotland Yard, along for the ride."

"THE Scotland Yard?!"

"Is there another old boy?" Morrissey basked in his temporary notoriety as he finally won his wrestling match with the holster.

"You got word I was coming?" Frank asked.

"Yeah, half an hour ago. Soon as I got word I scrambled everybody. They're currently in their secondary stand-by positions waiting your word."

"How is it this street is cleared of pedestrians?"

"The stake out team notified us as soon as the festival people started arriving in this morning around half past five. I brought our assault teams undercover of the festival people and got them in position. We closed off 112th as if it was part of the festival."

"Nice move!" Frank complimented.

The uniform with O'Hara stepped around to the trunk of the Ford and retrieved two bulletproof vests, handing them to Mahone and Morrissey.

"Inspector, you're under no obligation to go in with us." Frank said.

"Yes I am." Was his terse reply.

"Okay Bill, what'a we got?" Frank asked as he removed his suit jacket and slipped on the vest then redonned the jacket over it and his waist holster. Morrissey followed suit and was aggravated that he had to first remove his shoulder holster and jacket.

O'Hara launched into a quick brief.

"Typical two lane, residential street lined with

tenement buildings along the left side all the way down to Second Ave and a federal housing project along the other."

"Have you been able to clear the housing projects?" Morrissey asked.

"Yeah, sure. All 1200 families are in protective custody down at the station! It's kind'a crowded though, we only got the one cell." O'Hara quipped.

"Sorry, stupid question." Morrissey recanted.

"Target is an old cold water walk-up, number 230 about halfway down on the left, in the back, number 67. I've got a two man team up on the seventh floor."

"Doors numbered?"

"Some of 'em." O'Hara answered.

"Elevator?"

"Yes and we're prepared to disable it one minute prior to launch."

"Good."

"The whole street's under close observation both ends. On the ground floor across the street in the Catholic school we got two plain clothes dressed as priests and backed by a couple of uniforms, out of sight in the lobby guarding the front entrance.

There's no ground floor rear exit in the tenement, you have to go down to the basement to access the back yard but there's a front and rear fire escape off each floor. I've got a full breach unit with optics standing by next door in the beauty salon and a rolling unit over on 113th in case he slips out the back. If he does he'll be trapped. We rekied the back yards. These properties are pretty old and the over growth between yards is mainly heavy thorn bushes up to six, seven feet high. No way through them without attracting attention to yourself and getting the shit cut out of you!"

"Anybody covering 111th?"

"Not yet but there's a team enroute."

"Anything else?"

"He's sticking to a routine. Out in the morning back around eleven, eleven-thirty. Only today he was out a lot earlier, six a.m."

"You think that's significant?" Mahone asked.

"We'll know if he doesn't come back."

"You think he may not come back?!" A concerned Frank asked.

O'Hara looked at his watch. "Eleven-fifty." He shrugged. "We should know any time now."

"You got the word this guy's armed and has no compunction about killing?" Frank inquired.

"Word was put out in the first morning brief. I can get another half dozen guys here in fifteen minutes if we need." O'Hara offered.

"No point, we'd just be tripping over each other. You got com with all your elements?"

O'Hara nodded and manned his car mike.

"All units, all units, this is Godfather, check in." One by one O'Hara's teams responded.

North Blockers, check.

South Blockers, in position.

Eagle's Nest, we copy.

Holy Fathers, ready for mass to start!

Breach team, standing by.
Intercept team, got our running shoes on!
"Godfather, roger all units." O'Hara confirmed. "Stand-by to move to assault positions."

Upstairs on the sixth floor, in apartment #67, José Santiago, Sebastian Coro and Erik Mathias, aka La Serpiente, were going about their daily routines while waiting for Battesta to return from contacting their handler and preparing for their final strategy briefing. Although their final target was still unknown by the police most guessed it would be somewhere in the States, probably on the east coast in a major urban area.

At the same time, down at street level, walking south along Third Avenue, casually sipping his Brazilian tea, Raymundo Battesta happened to look up through the mounting crowd and just across the street where his attention was suddenly caught by the three suspicious looking guys leaning on the trunk of the Ford Taurus on the other side of 112th Street.

Despite the heat two of them wore suit jackets and the big black guy in shirt sleeves seemed to be giving instructions to the three gringos. Suit jackets in this heat sparked his suspicions but when he caught a glimpse of the uniformed cop in the back seat. . .

Thinking quickly Battesta casually turned and made his way to the trash can on his right and dumped his drink. He then crossed Third Avenue perpendicular to 112th and kept walking west to put some distance between himself and the cops.

His suspicions were initially aroused by the suit jackets but despite the fact that there were multiple police assigned to cover the festival, he also knew, due to violent outbreaks in the past at festivals in Harlem, there was an agreement with the NYPD and community leaders that the police would stick to the perimeter of the relatively small festival unless needed so as not to provoke trouble.

These cops were significantly out of position.

As he walked further west, keeping north of 3rd Avenue, he quickly reached for his cell phone and dialed.

"Serpiente?"

"Si?"

"A polícia está aqui!"

"Where?!" Mathias barked into his phone. Picking up on the alarm in his voice the others in the apartment stopped what they were doing and listened.

"Third Avenue, on the corner." Battesta answered in a controlled voice.

Mathias hurried down through the hallway of the apartment to check the single monitor mounted on a small table in the living room. On the monitor's screen an empty hallway stared back at him. Switching channels he visualized the stairwell then the hall window outside and to the right of their apartment.

Nothing.

He cautiously peeked out and down through the

living room window curtains to street level and across to the Catholic school. He saw nothing that raised his antennae.

"Não há nada aqui! There's nothing here!" He panted into his phone.

"Perhaps not yet! Prepare to evacuate just the same. Tell the others. Meet me at the secondary assembly point this afternoon at three!"

"Okay!"

"And Serpiente, boa sorte, irmão!"

"Boa sorte irmão!"

By half past eleven the NYPD people began to get nervous and by five to twelve Frank weighed the fact that the back-up units had all been on stand-by for the last two days. The rising heat and the mounting civilian crowd in the streets added to the tension and Mahone, in a rare moment of loss of professionalism, allowed all these factors to weigh on him. Fearing time wasn't on his side he made the decision to green light the operation without waiting for Battesta to show up.

He nodded to O'Hara who manned his car mike.

"All units, move to assault positions and stand-by for count down."

"Bill, me and the Inspector'll make our way down past the school and wait. Radio the school team as soon as all your guys are set. Go ahead and get them in launch position. I'll be on point and radio back ten seconds before we go. DON'T RADIO BACK! Just break squelch twice. Ten seconds later we'll go."

"You got it."

"Also, right before we launch, radio dispatch to notify ESU to get the paramedics over here on silent alarm."

"Mahone!" O'Hara called.

"Yeah?"

"Watch your ass!"

"Appreciate it Bill!"

"Us Irish gotta stick together, brother." O'Hara chuckled and gave the black power sign as Mahone and Morrissey strolled down the street towards the Catholic academy directly across the street from the tenement.

They pretended not to notice the four man breach team hug the building as they swiftly filed out of the front door of the beauty salon across the street, up the steps and into the target tenement right next door.

As Mahone and Morrissey reached the double front doors of the school they kept walking until the last of the SWAT team disappeared into the apartment house, quickly perused the façade of #230, walked another hundred yards then crossed over. They then doubled back and also entered the building. Once inside the vestibule Frank pulled Morrissey aside.

"You stay down here." He ordered Morrissey.

"Mahone I didn't come all this way to-"

"Not my call Nigel! You get shot I'm fucked, but good! Besides you're on vacation remember?"

"And if **you** get shot?" Morrissey challenged.

"I been shot, it sucks! I don't plan on doing it again."

"Well than why the hell did I make the trip all the way over here if not to help catch this bastard?!"

"Tell ya what, walk across the street tell the stake out guys that Lieutenant O'Hara authorized you to move with them. After this thing kicks off come up with them and we'll take it from there. Good enough?"

"Right then." He reluctantly acquiesced.

With the stair well already blocked up on the seventh floor by a two man fire team, it was right behind the two man door kicking team escorting the breach team that Mahone climbed the ten flights of stairs. With much difficulty.

Once at the top, severely out of breath, he moved off to the side in an attempt to conceal the fact he still hadn't fully recovered from his healing lung.

Once in place Mahone signaled and the recon team, comprised of a camera man and an armed over watch with a 12 gauge Remington, slowly stepped past the rank of team members who stood shoulders to the right hand wall, weapons down and at the ready.

The camera operator turned his ball cap around, plugged the micro USB device into his cell phone, manned the 24 inch long camera cable and in unison the two crept around the corner and down the hall where the camera operator carefully slid up to the door.

His over watch crossed the hall and stood,

weapon poised, 45 degrees to the apartment door of number 67.

As they got into position Frank couldn't help but feel some relief when he noticed the wall he leaned on was solid stone then quickly realized the apartment walls were likely plaster.

Might as well be fuckin' cardboard! He thought to himself.

Lowering himself to his belly the camera man carefully slid the articulated cable of the borescope under the door and over the threshold then began his surveillance.

His cell phone in one hand, he gingerly manipulated the borescope in a slow circular pattern with the other while watching the phone's screen. Pressing the silent shutter on the phone he shot half a dozen stills.

The shots showed two men seated at the kitchen table and a middle–aged woman dressed in a house dress and apron moving about who was occupied serving the men fartura pastries as they sat drinking coffee and discussing something out of ear shot. Several back packs sat on the floor off to the left.

Due to the low angle of the camera he was unable to see the third coffee cup and plate at the table.

The apartment's floor plan, a straight box car arrangement, allowed the cop to see into the kitchen area ahead and by snaking the cam cable 180 to spy down the hallway with several doors off to the side.

He saw no one else and so signaled the number

'three' to his partner who in turn held up three fingers back down the hall to Mahone peaking around the corner. Mahone passed the signal to the troops lined up behind him.

Suddenly, without warning footsteps approached the door and there was not enough time to completely withdraw the borescope. The two cops froze as the phone screen displayed the shot of a man from floor level up. His arms blocked what he was doing.

The overwatch raised his weapon and both cops held their breath as between the door and the thresh hold space they could see the shadow of the man as he moved.

There was a brief fumbling on the other side of the door and the person retreated as suddenly as he appeared.

Deciding not to push their luck, the cameraman withdrew the borescope and signaled a withdrawal. He crept back past his overwatch to Mahone with the guard following while maintaining a bead on the doorway until he was back around the corner and took up position at the end of the seven man squad.

The pictures were quickly flashed through with Mahone looking on.

Also looking on were the occupants of apartment #67 via the 18 inch monitor in the back bedroom.

Not expecting so many people including a civilian woman to be in the apartment and knowing Battesta probably wasn't one of them, Mahone leaned into the wall to briefly rethink their plan but decided it was a now or never scenario.

"Signal Godfather, assault element in position. Ten seconds to breach." He quietly ordered and word was passed down the line to the last man down the stair well who radioed back to O'Hara who broke squelch twice as arranged.

In their adrenaline infused state the police failed to notice the covert, lipstick CCTV cam taped to the overhead sprinkler pipes in the hall.

Inside the apartment Mathias stood in front of the monitor, staring down at Mahone and smirked as he formed a pistol with his left hand and fired an imaginary round at Mahone's head.

José Santiago, the woman and Sebastian Coro quietly scrambled to gather up their belongings. They headed into the main bedroom and were followed by Mathias who approached the woman. As he passed by heading to the bedroom, using a remote control, Mathias hurriedly activated the IED stuck to the inside of the front door.

Looking the woman in the eye he kissed her gently on the lips, slipped her the remote and smiled.

The woman, with a distinct sense of purpose, sternly made her way back out to the kitchen.

In the hallway Mahone took the armored shield from the lead cop, and led the SWAT unit down the hall stopping off to the left side of the apartment door where he nodded to the first cop in line holding a three foot battering ram with 'KNOCK KNOCK' painted along the side.

With the butt of his Glock Mahone banged on the door three times.

"Who ez there?" A female voice called back.

"IT'S THE PLUMBER, I COME TO FIX THE SINK! WHO THE FUCK DO YOU THINK IT IS LADY?! OPEN THE GOOD DAMNED DOOR, POLICE! WE HAVE A WARRENT!" He raised the shield, shifted his stance and aimed his 9mm.

"Okay bueno, bueno! Dun shoot! Dun shoot! I come, I come." She called back in a meek voice. "I come out!" The woman called from behind the door as she opened the broom closet inside and produced a Browning Automatic Rifle and two clips of ammo which she shoved into her apron pockets. Producing the remote control from her apron, she mumbled a short prayer and pressed the red button.

Mahone's brain didn't have time to register the white flash of light before he felt his back slam against the opposite wall and lost his breath. The distinct smell of burnt C4 and seared wood filled his nostrils. When his sight and hearing slowly crept back to normal he looked up through the dust to see the last of the soldiers rushing through the seared door frame into the apartment.

The fire fight was loud and short but intense.

Mahone recognized the roar of the BAR but the continuous staccato of the 9 mils, which seemed to last forever, punctuated by the growl of the Remington, silenced the heavy weapon in quick order.

Multiple shards of door and dust slid from his

body as he slowly rose, pushed the police shield off himself and struggled to his feet. He had to rummage through the rubble to find his weapon.

By the time he shuffled from the hallway into the place the air was clouded with cordite fumes punctuated by lots of yelling as the teams systematically cleared the rooms

By the time the smoke began to dissipate two SWAT members were down with a third casualty, the woman who was hardly recognizable as a female. What was left of her was slumped in the blood stained corner of the back bedroom, the smoking B.A.R. resting across her lap.

As the cops frantically searched room to room Mahone turned around to see Morrissey, bent over hands on knees, panting for breath, pistol in hand and shuffling through the debris.

"You can holster your weapon, it's all over." Mahone said.

"Bloody stairs! Why is there . . . no lift?! You in . . . one piece . . . mate?" Morrissey inquired.

"Yeah, yeah I'm fine. Slightly deaf but okay."

"You look like shit." Morrissey commented.

"Thanks."

Several officers quickly pushed past as they evacuated their two serious casualties back downstairs to the awaiting paramedics, a third limping behind.

Mahone stood perusing the room as Morrissey surveyed the wreckage.

"Christ! Is there gun play here every day?!"

"Some days, yeah. Only we don't call it 'gun play'" Frank answered.

"What do you call it?"

"A try not to get your ass shot off day."

"Makes complete bloody sense."

"They gonna make it?" Mahone asked of the wounded officers. Neither of the cops answered. "Fuck!" Mahone mumbled half to Morrissey.

They both entered the bedroom with the mangled body slumped in the corner surrounded by dozens of bullet holes in the wall.

Now I know why they call it 'the remains'!" Morrissey commented.

"Fuckin' Ma Barker!" Mahone cursed as he kicked her foot.

"Fanatical little minx wasn't she?" Morrissey quipped.

"Not anymore!" Frank answered as he now perused the room as a SWAT member scurried up to them.

"Lieutenant, we've only got one body!"

"Recon reported three?!"

"Yes sir, but . . ."

"Check all the windows!"

"We did sir. All screwed shut. Probably to prevent clandestine entry." He presented his open palm to Mahone. "Also found a couple of these taped to the sprinkler pipes out in the hall." He held one of the lipstick cameras. Mahone looked over at Mathias' TV monitor.

"So much for the theory there wasn't a lot'a

money behind these guys!" Frank observed to Morrissey.

"Buy now they could be running low on dosh." Morrissey added. "Hence the school bus hijacking."

"Yeah, good call. But I'll be god damned if these assholes are gonna-"

He quickly joined the search team as they systematically began their sweep through the place for any intel they might use.

Just then O'Hara stepped through the doorway.

"We all good Mahone?"

"Hey Bill. One perp, female, D.O.A. pending I.D. Two of your guys hit. Three perps on the run."

"Missing?! Like they got away?!"

"Like they were here and now they're not!"

It was back in the bedroom that Frank, probing with his foot, noticed a slight lump in the well worn rug to the left of the corpse, over near the wall. He traced it to just under the woman's mangled body.

Without warning he grabbed the corpse's ankle and dragged her to the side.

"Mahone! What the hell're you doin'!? Forensics ain't got their –" O'Hara yelled in protest.

With the toe of his shoe Frank pulled back the corner of the carpet.

"SON-OF-A-BICH!" O'Hara cursed.

"What?!" Morrissey scurried over as Frank peeled back the dirty brown rug to reveal a two foot square trap door.

"A fucking spider hole!" O'Hara declared.

"What's that mean?" Morrissey asked.

"Means he probably isn't gonna get his deposit back!" Mahone spewed as he drew his pistol and ripped open the hatch. "OHARA! Alert your street units! These assholes are somewhere down on the street by now!"

"Shit!" O'Hara moved as fast as his large frame allowed and barked at a cop in the hall to hand over his shoulder mike.

"ALL UNITS, ALL UNITS! THREE PERPATRATORS EVADED RAID PARTY AND ARE BELIEVED STILL IN THE AREA! COMMENCE SEARCH IMMEDIATELY! ALL STAKEOUT UNITS TO ASSISIT! NORTH BLOCKING TEAM, MOVE TO 112TH! SCHOOL TEAM MOVE SOUTH AND HOOK UP WITH THE SECOND AVENUE BLOCKER TEAM!"

While O'Hara put out his APB Mahone dropped down through the narrow hole. Morrissey briefly peered down the hole, shook his head and made for the stairs. They met up one floor below out in the hall.

"I can't believe these bastards are gonna get away! Again!!" Frank cursed nearly the whole way down as he realized something. "SHIT, SHIT, SHIT!!"

"What now?"

"O'Hara's guys have no way to know who what these guys look like!"

"They should have the photos of Mathias and Battesta INTERPOL circulated." Morrissey protested.

477

"You're right! You should be a cop!" Frank quipped.

"Is that a compliment?!"

They finally reached the ground floor and burst out onto the front stoop when an officer standing by his cruiser, radio mike in hand, yelled up to them.

"Lieutenant! One of them has just been sighted heading east towards First Ave!"

By the time the cops realized they'd lost their prey Mathias had slowed to a jog two blocks east of the tenement.

Now walking while collecting himself, just outside Thomas Jefferson Park, two blocks away down on the Hudson River, he focused on being as calm as possible.

Battesta had been careful to make each member of the team walk out their individual escape routes a couple of days ago when they had first arrived at the safe house however back-up transport in case of emergency wasn't in the budget. Each man would have to make it to the fallback assembly point down in Greenwich Village on his own, to a location which had been pre-selected.

Each had been ordered to carry his false I.D., fake family photos and two hundred dollars in American cash on him at all times as well as the names and contact numbers of alternate safe houses and collaborators in what's known as "E&E Packs", Escape and Evasion kits.

However, in his arrogance flamed by his increasing resentment of Battesta, Mathias refused to carry his E&E pack at all times and now had carelessly left it in the apartment.

At that exact moment, back in the apartment, a SWAT officer was handing Mathias' E&E kit over to Lieutenant O'Hara.

Fortunately for Mathias it was out of habit that he never relinquished his weapon.

Being careful to keep their weapons partially out of sight Mahone and Morrissey carefully approached the west perimeter of the well groomed Jefferson park carefully scanning the few pedestrians milling about.

"Eighteen plus years on the Met in London and I never handled a weapon. I'm in New York twenty-four hours and I'm in a shootout followed by a life and death hunt for international terrorists!"

"Yeah! This a great country or what?!" Frank added.

"I never dreamt I'd say this but, I find this rather exhilarating!"

"It'll get even more exhilarating if lead starts flying this way."

"No argument there mate, but what about now?! They may not have known we were coming but they were certainly prepared for us!"

"These are some bad hombres we're dealing with here Inspector that's for sure. And they're not stupid!"

"Well there's three of them and no doubt they've split up."

"I'd venture to say that whoever it was that was

spotted in thus vicinity likely slipped into this park to collect himself and get his bearings. Shall we search the toilets?"

"No need. These mugs aren't amateurs. Only amateurs hide and try and wait it out. These clowns are gonna keep moving to get out of the area ASAP and get to the next safe house."

"Mahone!"

"What?"

"What if they're not going to another safe house? What if they're heading straight to their next target?"

Mahone briefly paused but said nothing.

The impeccably landscaped, upscale urban park which occupied only about two city blocks of space, featured a couple of baseball diamonds, a pair of tennis courts and a large, public, swimming pool. The open fields between allowed them to stalk the area and see most everything but the tall trees lining the south east end blocked vision across to the FDR Drive bordering the river.

It was here that Mathias played his chance card. Weaving through the small grove of trees behind the tennis courts and out onto the path, less than 300 yards ahead of the detectives he scanned the parking lot and spotted a mark.

A young couple fitted out in tennis outfits were unpacking the trunk of their grey BMW preparing for a leisurely, late morning match when they heard a voice from behind.

"Excuse me please." They both turned. "I

wonder if you could direct me to best way to Bronx?"

"Sure! Just take the-" The man's directions were cut short when he noticed the pistol leveled at his stomach.

"I'm afraid I am needing your car señor."

Hesitating the middle-aged guy looked over the car's roof at his female companion who hadn't yet seen the gun.

"Sweetheart do you want to-" She asked as she came around behind the car. Petrified she froze, raised her hands and stared at Mathias who politely smiled at her.

"Buen dia señorita! Please keep your hands down." She dropped her gym bag and froze in place. "The keys, señor!" The man hesitated. "I will not ask a second time my friend!"

The man nervously handed them over.

Mathias perused the car as he unlocked the door and climbed in.

"Ahh! The M5 series BMW! Most impressive! How's the gas mileage?" Mathias asked as if they were old acquaintances.

Speechless the couple just stared at each other then back at their carjacker.

"It's okay . . . I guess." The man shrugged.

"No matter. Apologies for the inconvenience."

As they watched Mathias and their car disappear around the corner the woman firmly slapped her partner on the arm.

"What?!" He snapped.

"CALL THE FREAKIN' COPS!" She yelled.

"My phone's in the car!" He realized. She pulled hers from her pocket and handed it over.

The dumbfounded guy snapped out of it and dialed nine one one and reported the theft.

Within a minute or so a cruiser, which happened to be in the neighborhood, responded and from inside the park Mahone noticed the commotion out in the small parking lot and headed in that direction.

The two uniformed officers climbed out of the cruiser about the same time that Mahone and Morrissey jogged out through the side entrance to where the BMW used to be.

"What happened?" Mahone barked at the couple.

"We were carjacked! Some asshole with an accent!" The man explained as the two uniforms came around their car to the scene. The woman, not handling the situation as well as her partner, grunted, arms crossed and paced in small circles.

"I told you we shouldn't have come over to this friggin' neighborhood! Too many god damned Spanish!" She snorted.

Fuckin' Yuppies! Patrolmen Hernandez quietly mumbled to himself as he patiently sucked up the comment and stepped back for his partner to take the lead. Before his partner could speak Mahone jumped in.

"Hispanic accent, man bun, neck tattoo with a Glock nine?" Mahone rapidly questioned.

"Yes, yes! How did you know?" The guy asked as Mahone turned to the two uniforms. "But it wasn't a Glock. It was a Colt .45 1911." He explained. The woman stared blankly at her companion.

"I need your cruiser!" Mahone declared to the cops.

"Hold on a minute Lieutenant Mahone! This ain't no Uber!"

"How do you know my name?!"

"You kiddin' me?! Every cop in Manhattan knows who you are! Twelve major collars in one year including one'a the biggest drug kingpins in the country! Hey, is it true what they say about how many times you been shot in the-"

With a gentle nudge of the elbow, as the uniform continued speaking, Mahone ushered the cop back over to the still idling cruiser.

"How about right now we chase the bad guy and later we can have a beer and chat about my life's story? Deal?!"

"Deal!"

With Hernandez driving all four cops jumped in slinging gravel as they peeled out.

Still fuming, as for the second time they watched a car vanish around the corner, the woman vented on her man.

"Since when do you know about guns?!"

"*Grand Theft Auto!*" He proudly defended.

Based on the direction La Serpiente fled in, Mahone riding shotgun, directed the car up the FDR Drive.

"What's your call sign?" Frank asked the cops

then manned the radio, gave their position and put out an APB for the BMW along the FDR area as they drove.

"What about helicopters?" Morrissey asked.

"There's only four in the Department and right now one's in Staten Island and another is down for maintenance." The cop in the back seat answered.

Carefully keeping to the speed limit Mathias drove north on the FDR towards Harlem River Drive where he intended to turn left and head north then across the bridge into The Bronx. However the grey BMW was spotted by a patrolman on foot who radioed in the sighting and the car was quickly picked up by Mahone and his unit.

"It's gonna be a whole new ball game if this prick makes it out of The City and heads north out in the open and makes it onto the interstate."

Down in Lower Manhattan, at the 13th Precinct control desk several cops were gathered around the desk sergeant's radio listening in on the action when Wachowski happened by on his way to the sign in desk to check on a property record.

"What the hell's going on here?!"

"We got a high speed chase going on up in Spanish Harlem!"

"Where a'bouts in Harlem?!" Wachowski demanded.

"It started around Tito Puente Way but now they're screaming up the FDR."

"Fucking Mahone!" Wachowski hung his head, cursed and headed up to his office.

Units in from the 25th and down from the 40th in The Bronx had now become involved and closed off the exits east of the river over to The Bronx. La Serpiente realized they were closing in on him.

"Dispatch notify the MTA of the situation. Get descriptions of these guys out to the transit cops." Mahone radioed to dispatch.

All units, all units be advised: grey BMW, blond Hispanic male driver has just run the toll plaza onto the RFK. Repeat: grey BMW, blond male driver has just run the toll plaza onto the RFK.

"RFK, HRD, FDR, MTA. Is New York City's entire transport system built in code?" Morrissey challenged.

"The only part in secret code is which politician gets the graft!" The cop next to him in the back seat snipped.

Meanwhile, as the car chase was unfolding on the Upper East Side, Sebastian Coro, having watched from a coffee shop back on First Avenue, had correctly deduced by the platoon of squad cars screaming east towards the river, that the police believed his team had a water route lined up for their escape and saw his chance. He quickly crossed north up First Avenue then button hooked left and headed back west in the opposite direction.

Twenty minutes into the chase he had made it on foot over to Central Park North and found a bench just inside a side entrance to the park.

Violating a basic New York City tenant, Coro sat, pulled his E&E bag from his hip pocket and proceeded to count his escape money in the open.

In the flash of a New York City Second the small wad of cash was in the hands of a fleeing black teenager.

Sebastian Coro quickly realized the fact that there were two chances he was going to catch the apprentice thief, slim and none. His Hispanic temper temporarily rested control of his common sense mode and clouded his judgment. He gave chase out onto the street across Central Park North and over to the traffic circle where he drew his 9mm, assumed a two armed combat stance and took aim at the fleeing teen.

That's when the MTA inadvertently assisted in the chase when, in the last seconds of his life, Sebastian Coro was replaced by the forty-five mile per hour Uptown M22 bus.

Thirty minutes later the paramedics found what was left of Sebastian Coro's broken body over on the corner of West 111th Street where the hysterical bus driver sat on a curb, head in hands crying uncontrollably, passengers comforting her.

La Serpiente, maintaining his cool as only a trained combat veteran can, sped up the FDR and cut onto the 278 north. With the BMW now clearly in sight Patrolman Hernandez followed.

"You think he's heading towards Queens? Maybe a safe house over there?" Hernandez asked Mahone.

"Probably not. I think we upset the bastard's time table to the point he's not sure what he's doing!"

On a hunch La Serpiente flipped open the glove box and rifled through it. The gods of luck were with him as he found an envelope and discovered $375 in cash along with a gas & electric bill. He pocketed the cash and the utility bill found its way out the window.

"Now we got the bastard!" Frank, now only four or five cars behind declared as, speeding east along the RFK Bridge towards Randall's Island, they drew within firing range.

"What the hell you talking about? Got him for what?" The back seat cop asked.

"For littering! Mandatory fine in this city Buster!" Mahone joked. "$250 bucks and 10 days in jail!" Hernandez smiled and shook his head.

As La Serpiente led them south on the 278 along the island, without warning the BMW suddenly swerved right, jumped the median and headed back up the highway.

They chased him past the large, sign posted on a ten foot high chain link fence; 'NYC Environmental Protection' and into the sprawling wastewater treatment plant.

Thirty minutes later the island was crawling with cops, was cordoned off with road blocks and check points and nearly two hours later no sign of Erik Mathias aka La Serpiente had been found.

"Who the hell is this guy, Fucking Houdini?!" Officer Hernandez asked no one in particular.

Frank Mahone was less subtle as he slammed the

hood of the cruiser.

"IT'S A FUCKING ISLAND! HOW THE FUCK DO YOU DISAPEAR ON A FUCKING ONE ACRE ISLAND!"

Mahone's question had a logical answer: Mathias was no longer on the island.

While the hounds were occupied carefully and meticulously searching for the fox on the grounds of the water treatment plant Mathias had made it down to the water's edge and with $100 of the cash stash from the BMW had bribed a local in a Boston Whaler out for a day of fishing to take him down river to the Midtown piers where he disembarked to make his way across town and down to The Village. Unlike Sebastian Coro, Mathias would make the team's three o'clock rendezvous.

But first he decided on a short stop over.

****

Accepting the fact that Mathias once again gave them the slip Mahone & Morrissey got the two patrolmen to drop them back over in Spanish Harlem near the park in front of the Wilson Housing projects on First Avenue.

"Hernandez, thanks for your help, you guys did good."

"You two need a lift anywhere else Lieutenant?" The patrolman offered.

"No, we're okay but do me a favour and radio in to the 23rd and let the desk sergeant know we're in the area, okay? We'll be gone in an hour."

"Will do Lieutenant Mahone! It was a pleasure meeting you." The two patrolmen climbed back into their cruiser. "If you guys intend on hanging around this neighborhood, you might want a couple of uniforms with you, sir." Hernandez's partner advised through the open window.

"Thanks. We'll be okay."

Mahone fished through his pocket and came up with the piece of paper Wachowski gave him earlier.

"What are we looking for?" Morrissey asked.

"Address here says building three, apartment 106."

They crossed over into the barrio and found the office of the *Patriotas Cooperantes* on 665 East 110th Street, Tito Puente Way.

"Is it normal for Yanks to set up offices in apartment blocks?"

"Free market system brother! If there's money to be made, someone will do it!"

"What about the laws?"

"What laws?" Mahone sarcastically posed.

In the maze of fifteen story structures Frank stopped a local to ask directions.

"Si. It's in the Projects. The Housing Authority complex. Building three is on the left sir." The woman informed him.

"Thanks."

They made their way across the street and found the place and knocked. With no answer they entered the first floor apartment and saw it was feebly made up to look like an office.

A pair of grey, vintage metal filing cabinets occupied the corner on the right, two kitchen chairs sat against the wall to the front of the cabinet and a beat up aluminum tube table served as a desk. To the right, a former bedroom when it was an apartment, there was another door.

Mahone entered without knocking and went directly up to and addressed the attractive twenty-something chica at the desk.

"Hola."

"Hola, buen dia." A big smile signaled all the cooperation he probably wasn't going to get.

"Estamos buscando al director." Frank explained.

"El director no se encuentra en la Compañia, es su día libre."

"Es su día libre?" Frank repeated.

"Si señor, es su día libre." The shield of a smile she hid behind never wavered.

"Gracias chica."

"De nada, no es problema, estamos aquí para ayudarle señor officer." She smiled a little more broadly when she I.D.'d them as cops.

Outside on the street they headed over to 110th Street to catch the Downtown train to head back to the precinct.

"What'd she tell ya?" Morrissey asked.

"She said the director is not in today. It's his day off."

"What do you think?"

"I think anyone taking a weekday off isn't a very smart businessman, I think she's pretty and I think she's full of shit!"

"Rather shabby excuse for an office, even a charity!" Morrissey added.

"Two four drawer filing cabinets, no labels on the drawers! It's a front."

"For what do you suppose?"

"Probably one of a half dozen illegal South American political organizations also acting as fronts for terrorist organizations."

As soon as they were out the door the receptionist picked up her cell phone and dialed.

Si? A male voice answered.

"Two policemen were just here." She replied in perfect English.

Uniforms or detectives?

"Detectives Director. They asked to see you."

Thank you Rosario.

In a cross town office the Director hung up then, using a desk phone, placed another call.

"Operator, long distance to London please. Country code 0044 city code 345. The number is 724 2527." There was a brief pause.

"Yes hello. Banbury we need to talk." He demanded.

****

CHAPTER TWENTY

The Bald Hipster café
MacDougal & Bleeker Streets
Greenwich Village

In mountaineering it's called 'sewing machine leg', the rapid pumping of the leg with one foot half on the floor. It comes from extreme muscle fatigue.

The young couple at the table across from Raymundo Battesta were relatively certain he had not just returned from mountain climbing when he again drew their attention away from their conversation to stare over at his rapidly pumping right leg as he nervously waited for his collogues to reach the rendezvous.

He noticed the couple and, annoyed moved to a corner table in the back of the small, continental styled café and ordered his fifth cup of coffee.

It was nearly an hour later when a slightly less worse for wear Erik Mathias came through the door, spotted Battesta and made straight for his team leader.

Battesta leaned in close and struggled to control his anger.

"Where the hell have you two been?! It's after four!" He demanded. "Where is Coro?" By way of an answer Mathias tossed a copy of the early edition of *New York Post* on the table.

Battesta scanned the front page.

112th St. Raid!
Two Escape, Two Dead!

"It's on every fucking television station!" Mathias blurted out. "By six o'clock tonight our faces will be posted everywhere and entered into every facial recognition program in the city!"

"All over the country you mean!" Battesta corrected as he continued to read the article. "What's this?! *Two escape- two killed?!* The three o'clock T.V. news gave it less than a minute and reported there was a minor drug bust somewhere on 112th Street with three killed one escape!"

"What the hell news station did you hear that on?!"

"The only station they play in this fucking neighborhood, CNN!" Battesta swore.

"Raymundo! There's a reason CNN is free!"

"¡No es de extañar que Trump ganó!" Battesta swore under his breath. "¡Jesucristo! Hit by a bus!" Battesta swore aloud as he read of Coro's fate.

"This is all because you paid those incompetent imbeciles to launch the Caracas drone attack at Maduro before we were ready!" No longer able to retain his anger Mathias castigated Battesta.

"How were they to account for a maldito viento?!"

"They should have allowed for the fucking wind! The fucking coyote could have done better against the road runner!" Mathias snarled.

"And if your 'team' hadn't fucked up on the pre-strike intelligence report-" Raymundo immediately shot back.

"Si Maduro fuera bueno, no sería Maduro!"

"¡SI MI ABUELA TUVIERA RUEDAS, ELLA SERÍA UN COCHE!"

"¡Si mi abuela tuviera ruedas, ella sería un coche!"

"¡Estúpido! Lower your voice!" Battesta loudly whispered as he scanned the room. The couple over near Battesta's original table decided it was time to leave. "Besides, the American media reported it as a false flag operation by Maduro's supporters as an excuse to crack down on the opposition!" Battesta again defended. "No one knows the truth about our people being involved!"

"And since your failure he is still using it as an excuse to 'crack down' on people he suspects all over the country! Thousands have been arrested!" Mathias pressed the issue.

Having lost his wife and son to the SEBIN, Maduro's secret police, and now with his back-up plan falling apart, Raymundo Battesta struggled to focus on what was left of his mission. He suddenly became more conciliatory.

"Mathias, we've been over this ground already. With no reason to expect help from Washington or the rest of the free world, at least until we prove ourselves, we have to take out or replace Maduro any way we can! And the only way to do that now is to show the Americans we have the power and the guile! And that is to demonstrate our ability to disrupt their satellite communications to the point where they are compelled to negotiate with us!"

"Americans don't negotiate! They think they are above the rest of the world and listen to no one! They take what they want by force! What makes you so confident they will negotiate with two unknowns especially now that they've closed their embassy in Caracas?"

Raymundo leaned into the table, established eye contact and smirked.

"Mathias! The opposition party has a courier standing by to send a clandestine communiqué to the American embassy in Bogotá as soon as we send them the signal."

"What are you talking about?!" Mathias asked.

"A CIA operative posing as a Columbian coffee grower will get the message to the U.S. State Department."

Mathias, who by this time was on a completely different page suddenly became more serious and grew more attentive at this revelation.

"At the same time the Americans receive word we have struck, Juan Guaido's office will publically announce he has asked America to send troops to secure the capital! Maduro will be arrested and this hell will be finished!"

Mathias shifted in his seat and sat quietly staring for a long moment.

"And this was your plan all along?!" Mathias

challenged.

"Yes! Of course I didn't tell the team everything, you know the procedure as well as I!" Need-to-know basis. And . . . we never worked together before this, I had no idea who you were."

Erik Mathias sat forward and eyed Battesta.

"How do I know I can trust you now?!" Mathias challenged. By way of an answer Battesta produced a pen and yanked a napkin from the chrome dispenser on the table.

"Here is the code phrase we are to send to this phone number. It is in a Bogotá café." He slid the napkin across the table. Mathias picked it up and carefully read it.

"'*Arrogant people are the instruments of their own destruction.*'" Mathias read aloud. "A quote from Simon Bolivar. Very nice."

"Invasion, military aide, money or assassination. I don't give a shit how we do it! I just know I will die seeing that bastard is taken down!"

"We had our chance at assassination!" Erik to agitate.

"Let it go already! We are only two now, focus on what we need to accomplish to finish the last phase of the mission!" Battesta pleaded.

"All right then. Things stay as they are. We follow the plan." Mathias confirmed.

"I'll fly in on Friday the sixth. We'll meet and finalize everything with your new men." Raymundo closed.

But Erik Mathias had no intention of letting it go.

496

There was a reason the normally thirty to forty-five minute trip south to the Village from Uptown took Mathias several hours after escaping the police.

Following his getaway down the Hudson Erik Mathias had made his way ashore then to a Midtown internet cafe where he placed a long distance call. He reported to his South American contacts at the FARC splinter group headquarters in a non-descript bank office in Los Pozos, Columbia.

Exaggerating the mission's success to date, he was able to cajole a final payment and some backing from them. An hour after the call, through a secure account, he was emailed an account number at Chase Manhattan.

Even as he and Battesta were banging heads in the café, flight arrangements for one were being sorted for Mathias under an assumed name. His forged papers and passport would be available at Newark International by ten o'clock the next morning. For now he would stick to Battesta's original plan which was to meet him in Guiana as previously planned.

By the time they left the cafe separately agreeing to resume the mission, all was in motion.

***

13th Precinct
Lower Manhattan

"What's this?" Mahone asked as they made their

way down the long hall of the precinct house. He took the sheets of fax paper handed him from Morrissey.

"A report." Morrissey informed.

"On?"

"The spoofer gadget you illegally withheld from the most important investigation of my career." Mahone opened the folded over sheet and read. "Just before we left London I sent it by special courier to a tech friend who works at Siemens AG in Berlin."

Mahone assumed a visible expression of shock as he read the capabilities of the associated hardware and programmes of the most up-to-date spoofers.

"This on the level?" Frank asked without looking up from the five page report.

"If you're asking if the report is accurate, apparently you don't know anything about the German's penchant for technology."

"I know that during the Cold War the East Germans produced over 85% of all the technology used by the communist world! So yeah, I guess it is accurate." He handed back the sheaf. "You think these assholes have anything like this?"

"You're guess is as good as mine old boy. However, in truth, that sort of thing is smidge above my pay grade."

Just as they reached the end of the hall they were intercepted by Chief Wachowski's secretary.

"I got a surprise for you two studs! Chief

Wachowski says I'm to take you two upstairs." She announced as she led them up to the interrogation rooms two floors above.

"Is this good or bad?" Morrissey whispered as they stepped off the elevator on the fourth floor and made their way down the hall.

"Usually not good." Frank whispered back

"That's encouraging." Morrissey said without conviction.

The secretary led them down the corridor to Interrogation Room Two.

"Apparently they got one of the guys from the Harlem raid." She explained. The two cops exchanged glances.

"Where'd they nail him?!" Mahone asked.

"They didn't. Apparently he walked into the 25th Uptown and gave himself up. A Lieutenant Detective William O'Hara had him shipped down here less than a half an hour ago."

"Son-of-a-bitch! Irish do stick together!" Morrissey blurted out. The secretary turned to walk away when Mahone called after her. "Gina, send Detective O'Hara a bottle of Jameson's Irish whiskey. On Chief Wachowski."

Frank rang the buzzer and the two were allowed into the interrogation room.

The detectives stepped through the door and there, nursing a cup of coffee sat a haggard José Santiago who escaped the dragnet following the Harlem raid.

By the looks of the two interrogators, one

standing one seated across the table from him, it appeared he was spilling his guts into a tape recorder as he was being questioned by the pair of trained interrogators.

Santiago spoke with the voice of a broken man.

"With no expectation of help from Washington to take out or replace Maduro, Battesta intends to do it any way he can." Santiago paused intermittently to drag on his cigarette. "And the only way to do that he supposes, since the drone strike was such a miserable failure, is to show the Americans he has the power!"

"So this guy you keep mentioning, Battesta, he's the honcho?" The short one across the table asked

"Si."

Mahone and Morrissey exchanged glances.

"What about this other guy, Coro?" The interrogator quietly asked. Santiago sat and took a minute to compose himself before he spoke.

"Coro's participation was purely mercenary. He was in it for the money. Battesta was originally allowed in by the SEBIN because he could finance the whole operation. He has family money from the old oil days. Mathias was to lead us but when Battesta discovered he would not be running the mission he threatened to pull out so they gave him command. Mathias never got over it."

"Do you know how Battesta intends to show his power?" The tall interrogator probed.

"He intends to demonstrate he has the ability to disrupt satellite navigation communications." The two interrogators exchanged glances.

"World-wide?!" The tall interrogator asked.

"I don't know but at least everywhere there are Galileo satellites."

"Can you tell us his intended target? How he believes he can achieve this?"

"No. We were given no time table or target. We were briefed day at a time on a need to know. I overheard him on the phone mention Arecibo."

"Where's Arecibo?" The short cop asked.

"It's in Puerto Rico, outside San Juan." Mahone interrupted. "But that's just a ruse. A false flag to throw us off."

"How do you know?" The interrogator challenged.

"Arecibo's a radio telescope. Nothing to do with navigation or the Galileo system." Mahone informed the room.

"Who the hell are you two?!" The tall one asked.

Neither Morrissey nor Mahone answered.

"I repeat, who the hell are you two?!"

"Mahone and Morrissey. We were on the Harlem raid. Mahone shot back. "We're just here to observe. Be outta your hair in five."

"Why not GPS?" The short one pushed Santiago. "Why not attack the GPS if he wants to show us his power?"

Santiago slowly gazed at the two interrogators and shook his head.

"Either one of you play chess?" Santiago asked.

"Yeah, why?" The interrogator asked.

"What my colleague means is, to what end does Battesta want to attack the European satellites but not the American ones?" The tall one asked.

"Or the Russian ones?" The short one interjected. "Putin has troops in Venezuela protecting Maduro, why not attack the Russian sats?"

"Attack the Russian system? You people are out of the loop! Russians've been at it for nearly half a century now, devoted a third of their military budget and still are no closer to matching the GPS then they were decades ago! Attacking the Russian satellites would be useless, they're dysfunctional enough as it is! I'd of thought your CIA knew that!"

"José, you should know that our agents in Caracas have reported Maduro has imprisoned or executed up to 5,000 people since that attempted drone strike. What do you think he will do-"

"NO SHIT YOU STUPIDO GRINGO! WHY DO THINK I CAME TO . . ." Santiago now on his feet but still chained to the desk seethed but quickly made a concerted effort to slowly collect himself. "Why do you think I came to you people?! For more of your lousy freeze dried coffee?!" He slapped the half full paper cup across the room.

Having stood by quietly to this point, Frank could no longer restrain himself. He quickly stepped across the room and grabbed Santiago by the collar, pulled him up over the table and drew his face close in.

"HEY, ASSHOLE! We're fucking cops not fucking rocket scientists! Lives are at stake here and you said you wanna help! Now cut the shit and help or go back to your little jail cell and hope nobody else dies because of your little escapade in which case we can probably arrange judge O'Connor to get you the death penalty!"

The two interrogator cops grabbed Mahone but struggled to pull him off the prisoner.

"FRANK! Heel boy! Heel." Morrissey called over. Mahone pushed Santiago away and made his way back over to Morrissey.

"Detective Mahone, you and your guest can leave now!" The short one barked.

Frank looked down at the slightly pear shaped man and smiled.

"Gonna take a helluva lot more then you two to get us outta here. Now go back over and do your job."

A visibly shaken José Santiago unsuccessfully pretended to brush off the attack as one of the interrogators shuffled over to Mahone and Morrissey.

"Chief Wachowski's gonna get a formal complaint about this Mahone!" The tall one threatened.

"Yeah? Get in line Barney!"

Mahone and Morrissey stood fast and the two interrogators backed off.

"As I was about to say," Santiago continued. "The GLONASS K-2, their latest update has been postponed three times already and is nowhere near ready. Besides, Russia is in no position to help us.

More importantly what would America care if Battesta attacked the Russians? You think Trump would offer Putin any help then?"

If Raymundo's going to get help after he proves his point he believes he can get it through secret negotiations with someone in your government!" José Santiago spoke with conviction heavily laced with regret of having gotten involved in *Operation Galileo*.

"What's Mathias' story? Has he always been a mercenary?"

"He's no mercenary! He's a fucking terrorist! He's not right in the head. It was supposed to be Mathias who hijacked the school bus in England."

"Why didn't he?" Mahone asked.

"Battesta didn't trust him." Santiago snapped,

"Trust him to do the job?" The short interrogator asked.

Santiago slowly looked up and made eye contact as his face melted into a grave expression.

"Trust him not to kill all the school girls and burn the bus!"

A few minutes later, outside in the hall, Morrissey threw out a suggestion as they descended the stairs.

"Well, now that we know the target is GPS, we notify the Homeland Security, they call in the FBI and our part is done. I vote we find a nice restaurant, preferably with a well stocked bar, and enjoy the rest of the vacation we're not on!" Morrissey suggested.

"How do you figure our job is finished?" Frank challenged.

"All four bad guys, well three bad guys, have been nicked, the terrorist bomb plot is smashed and the world is once again safe for democracy, or whatever you want to call what's happening in Washington these days."

"Fair comment I suppose, seeing as how London has this Brexit thing so under control." Mahone fired back.

"Touché!"

"I'm not convinced our job is finished. I don't feel good not knowing exactly what Battesta's intended target is." Mahone added.

"INTERPOL and the trusty FBI, no doubt with the help of your Russian love doll, will take it from here. We've got enough paper work for two weeks, neither of us has had a proper vacation since the last time and we'll no doubt be testifying until St. Stephens' Day!"

At Morrissey's sarcastic reference about Irina, Mahone's lips involuntarily curled into a brief smile.

"So am I to take it that you're in with me until the end?"

"I thought I just made that clear?"

"No but. . . never mind. What the hell is St. Stephens' Day?"

"St. Stephens' Day is the day after Christmas in most civilized countries and you don't believe I'm about to let you tell all these exciting stories on your own do you?" Frank was genuinely flattered at the offer to share the paperwork. "Besides, I'm your partner, aren't I?" Morrissey added.

Mahone stopped in the middle of the stairs, cocked his head to the side and stared at Morrissey.

"Well, in that case, much appreciated!" In the first real sensation of camaraderie Mahone had experienced since April he extended a hand to Morrissey who smirked and shook it.

"By the way, I thought New York had a moratorium on the death penalty?" Morrissey suddenly threw out.

"They do."

"So who's this Judge O'Connor who's going to issue the him the death penalty?"

"No fucking idea. I made him up."

*** * ***

Wachowski's secretary knocked lightly and poked her head through the office doorway.

"Chief, Dr. P is here to see you."

"Any chance I'm not in?" He sheepishly begged.

"She saw you get on the elevator earlier."

"Shit!" He paused then answered. "Give me five minutes then send her in." He fumbled through his center drawer trying to find a convincing looking piece of paper and a minute later, without knocking, the precinct psychiatrist made her grand entrance.

"Good morning Doctor-"

"Chief Wachowski, I am yet to receive a reply

from the two messages I sent you regarding Lieutenant Frank Mahone!"

"Oh, sorry Doctor Crunt! I'll-"

"I've been here for over two years now, you know damn well what my name is! It's Doctor Prussé, Chief Wachowski! Prussé, Maria Prussé!"

"Oh , yes. . . . Doctor Prussé, sorry. Mahone's still on assignment in London.

"Don't bull dinky me Wachowski! I overheard two of your guys blabbering in the hallway not an hour ago. Mahone is back here in New York!"

"Oh! Well I haven't seen him but when I do . . . I'm actually filling out a FFDE A-20 right now . . ." He brandished the back of the typed form to the shrink so she couldn't see the printed side. "I'll hunt him down and send him to your office as soon as I see him."

"See that you do or my next move is a letter to the Commissioner!"

"I'll find him and send him right down to you Doctor." She stomped out without closing the door.

Crunt! One consonant too many! Wachowski mumbled to himself.

Mere minutes later Wachowski's office door opened and Mahone and Morrissey, just down from the interrogation area, entered.

"You must have read my mind!" Wachowski greeted.

"Why, were you thinking about shagging Megan Fox too?" Mahone cracked.

"You're hilarious Mahone. Afternoon Inspector."

"Greetings Chief."

"You need to make yourself scarce!" The Chief instructed Mahone.

"For how long?"

"For a while."

"Like for how long of a while?"

"Like long enough for me to think of some way to get this toxic femnazi shrink off your back!"

"Any suggestions on where I should disappear to?"

"Hey Bonehead, you're still on the exchange program remember? Go back to London! But where ever you wind up leave the department out of it will ya?!"

"Okay, just do me one favor?" Frank pushed.

"You know Mahone, at some point-"

"Yeah I know Ski, I'm gonna owe you a shit load of favors! I already do. Just do me this one last solid Chief! Don't let them send Santiago's statement over to the D.A. or the Bureau guys until I call you."

"You want me to sit on a felon confession indefinitely?!"

"No, no! That would be illegal! I promise you'll hear from me by tomorrow morning, day after the latest!"

"Dare I probe why, he asked with great trepidation?"

"Better you don't know now . . . but you will."

"Frank, when you finally trip over your dick and get caught, a day and time I chillingly feel is fast approaching, I'm gonna plead the Fifth! You savvy?!"

"I love you Chief!" Mahone called back after himself. Wachowski stood behind his desk and watched until Mahone and Morrissey disappeared from the office. The Chief shook his head and spouted a short monologue himself.

"I'm sorry Commissioner O'Neill, as far as I knew Patrolman Mahone, the former Lieutenant Detective, was on that exchange program he must have managed to somehow forge himself into! Other than that sir, I have no idea what happened!"

Out in the hall the two detectives went for the elevator.

"And I thought it was the U.K and the U.S had the special relationship!" Morrissey quipped. "You've got a real bromance going on there, you do mate!" Frank turned to Morrissey.

"First, fuck you. And secondly, looks like I'm on vacation too!"

As they passed through the office area the secretary scurried up to them.

"Detective Mahone you have a toll call from an Agent Kuksova. You can take it over at my desk"

"Thanks Gina!" He took a seat next to her desk and she passed him the receiver.

"Mahone here."

Frank, thank god! I've been trying to reach you! It was Agent Kuksova but Irina's voice was partially muffled by background noise.

"Why, what's wrong? You okay?!" Mahone was

distracted by the loud, steady whooshing noise surrounding Kuksova's voice.

We know their target! It's the Arecibo Radio Telescope in Puerto Rico!

"No, Arecibo is just a ruse! Their target is the ESA Galileo system in some Space Port somewhere!"

Guiana? The space port is in Kourou Guiana. How do you know that?

"Irina, what's that god awful noise I'm hearing?"

I'm on a BA flight to JFK. How the hell do you know they're going for The Space Port in Kourou?!

"We stormed the flat up in Harlem. Two escaped one killed. The other guy flipped. He spilled his guts! Why're you coming to New York and why are you flying commercial?"

I'll need all that info that guy gave you and don't let him go! She stressed.

"My Chief has everything under control. All the Intel will be sent up through the chain and a No Bail court order is being drafted. What's your itinerary?"

I'm coming in on BA117. We land at three, I've got a short layover then I've got a connect.

"Why didn't you just fly direct from London?"

I couldn't book direct without going through Madrid and that would have been an extra fourteen hours. But now it looks like I'm going to Kourou in Guiana!

"How long is that flight?"

It's along-assed flight! Probably about . . ." There was a pause. *Frank there's no time to meet up and fool around!*

"Typical woman! Always thinking with your crotch! I wasn't suggesting that."

What then? I know you're not thinking about coming with! There was no response. *Frank you're not coming to the Space Port! This case is now federal jurisdiction! You and Morrissey will be credited in all reports, you have my word! But under no circumstances will you . . .*

Five and a half hours later Detective Frank Mahone, seated next to Inspector Nigel Morrissey, was sipping drinks and relaxing in business class on Virgin flight 213 enroute to Cayenne - Félix Eboué Airport, Kourou, Guiana.

"This is not amusing Mahone!" Turning from her aisle seat Irina spoke over her left shoulder through the seat separation to where Frank and the Inspector sat directly behind her and a forty-something guy in a dark, three piece suit sat next to her. "You realize that if the Bureau makes any connection between you and me-"

"It's, **you** and **I**!" Nigel politely corrected.

"Stay out of this asshole!" She snapped. Morrissey threw up his hands and fell back into his seat. The suit next to her looked up from his *Wall Street Journal* and quietly smirked.

She again turned 180 degrees to scold them. "GOD DAMN IT FRANK!! This is not funny! It's my career if we're caught!"

"You said you wanted to get out of the lab and be a field agent! How's it feel living on the wild side Baby?" Mahone teased. The suit in the window seat next to Irina spoke up.

"Sir would you like to sit up here? We can exchange seats if you like, I don't mind."

"NO!" She barked "He doesn't like and I do mind! You two stay put!" She wagged a finger at the suit then at Frank.

"That would be lovely sir!" Frank complimented as he rose from his seat and stepped into the aisle. "Very kind of you!"

"You two stay put!" She snapped at the stranger. "Don't you dare! Don't you even think about- I forbid you two-"

As they exchanged seats a stewardess appeared in the aisle.

"Is there any difficulty sir?"

"Yes, thank you stewardess!" Mahone answered. "The lovely lady has just received some welcomed news-"

"Dire news more like! Border line fatal in fact!" Irina snapped slumped in her seat with folded arms.

"And we are in dire need of some more alcohol." Frank continued. "The lady would like a white wine. Straight wine or spritzer dear?" Irina sat board stiff, staring blankly at the seat back in front of her. "I think she'd like a straight wine to start. And bring me a Jameson Irish, neat please."

Suddenly the seat behind him bucked as Morrissey kicked Mahone's seat back. "Oh and two more Irish for my friends in the seats behind. Those are all on me."

"Yes sir." She retired up the aisle.

Realizing he hit a nerve, it was a short time later Frank decided to offer an olive branch.

"Come on, tell me about that clock tower stuff you mentioned."

"Don't suck up to me just because-"

"I'm not sucking up to you! I'm genuinely impressed that you know so much about this technology stuff. I don't! And I really want to catch up on it, in a professional capacity I mean." There was no immediate response. "C'mon! You're stuck with us anyway!"

Eyeing him with a healthy dose of suspicion she slowly launched into an explanation as requested.

"According to the DHS one of the system's most basic problems is that its signal strength is weak enough to be intercepted or blocked."

"What does that mean, exactly?"

"For one thing truckers with $29.95 jamming devices from any electronics store can evade their bosses or the police and have at times, accidently interfered with airport control systems."

"Of course you had to tell me that when we're in an airplane!"

"On a larger scale one of the things the administration is pushing North Korea on is to stop interfering and jamming radio and TV reception with their devices in South Korea."

"That's why jamming devices are illegal in the U.S.?"

"Yes, which is why they're all over the black

market in the U.S. Devices largely made and shipped in from China!" Irina added.

"Makes total sense!" Frank quipped. "So this fucking clown can control the entire system from his mother's basement using a collection of cheap Chinese junk he bought at Radio Shack?"

She leaned over to the side and stared at him.

"Exactly how old are you? Radio Shack went out of business over a decade ago."

"I knew that, I was just testing you. What else?"

"Whoever this guy is he can only interfere with certain pulses at a given wavelength from any four of the SV's at a time."

"SV's?"

"Satellite Vehicles."

"So Guidos looking to shift hot merc could probably use it too?" Frank inquired.

"If you mean Italian criminals dealing in stolen merchandise . . ."

"Yes."

"Just last year a group of bone heads were nailed in Bayonne, New Jersey when they accidently shut down the entire port of operations while they were on a heist job and trying to figure out how to use their new toy."

"Jesus! How'd you catch them?" Frank pushed.

"We didn't, the Port Authority did. Their security teams cordoned off the entire port and trapped them in a warehouse trying to lift 500 computers." She answered. "Making the atomic clocks smaller so that more of them could fit onto each satellite and thereby increase their stability could reduce errors to fractions of a meter. So with this new spoofer and its apparent capabilities . . ."

"Atomic clock? Must be pretty fucking accurate!"

"Well yeah but, it still has to be reset once in a while."

"Like how often?"

"About once every million years."

"Oh, a million years. But, do you get a written guarantee? You know, just in case it starts to go out around 999,000 years!"

"Your sophomoric attempts at humor aside, the clocks are regulated by a laser-cooled apparatus in Boulder, Colorado. It controls the primary time and frequency standard for the entire United States."

"The whole country?!"

"From Maine to sunny California!"

"Jesus! So any asshole with a grudge could. . ."

"Exactly."

"Why can't you just turn on a beacon finder and locate the missing spoofer unit?"

"The unit is designed to transmit to the earth to locate itself then coordinate with three other sats in orbit relative to where it is in space, not as if it was down here, on earth."

"A slight oversight."

"Additionally in accord with the theory of relativity, time in a strong gravitational field moves slower than in a weak field."

"You telling me that time in space is different

than here on earth?"

"As it is on any large planet with a significant density, yes. That's why there has to be a corrective on-board mechanism to keep earth time and space time in sync. Otherwise . . ."

"Otherwise the nav systems would be off and people would get lost!"

"Not just lost. Planes would crash-"

"Could we no talk about planes crashing? At least until we're on the ground."

"And trains would crash and burn killing all on board, ships would get lost at sea and most of the national truck haulage systems would fail. Little things like that."

"Okay so, we're not under any real pressure?! Stewardess, another round of drinks please." Several hours later the captain announced their final approach and the cabin attendants launched into their routine.

After landing the passengers disembarked into the sweltering heat without incident and made their way to the small terminal's baggage claim area to stand in line by the conveyer.

"We gonna have any trouble getting onto this space port?" Frank asked. "I mean since it's not U.S. territory?"

"We should be okay, parts of the base are an open tourist attraction. But I made some calls before I left London anyway. They're going through channels now."

"Channels? What channels?"

"The French military commander at the space port has to clear us through Paris."

"Couldn't we have landed at their airport?!"

"No, commercial traffic is not allowed. Even most of their workers use this airport."

"How do we get out there?"

"There's a nine o'clock shuttle from the hotel out to the base in the morning." She explained. "Incidentally Mahone, did you even think to call ahead for reservations before you so impulsively decided to scamper off on this little adventure?!" He stared at her blankly as the implications of her question dawned on him.

"Explain to me why you couldn't schedule an FBI air asset to use? Why you're flying commercial?"

"Under Obama the GAO discovered that the two Gulfstream jets the DOJ bought to fight terrorism were routinely being used by Comey and the big wigs as personal taxis. When the end-of year accounting was released and the 100 million dollar annual bill for aviation was made public the press pounced!"

"Then came Trump?!" Mahone smirked.

"Yeah, then came Trump! What's your point?!" She repeated with clear aggravation. Mahone couldn't resist pushing his point.

"Who not only restricted use of the jets, but paid for his own fuel when not flying on government business. I mean that's what I read in the papers, ya know. I'm just sayin'."

"Yeah, yeah. Can we talk about something else?" She snapped.

"I'm just always interested in learning more about how our government works. Or doesn't." He mocked.

"I think I see my luggage."

✱

CHAPTER TWENTY-ONE

**Hotel Atlantis
City of Kourou
French Guiana
Thursday, September 5TH**

Hotel Atlantis overlooks a pristine beach on the southern Atlantic shores of Guiana and although extremely modest by most western standards, it is considered by Guianese standards the premier holiday resort. The hotel grounds proper lie just over a mile south east of the *Centre Spatial Guiana* aka the European Space Port.

The four, three story, wood framed buildings which comprise The Atlantis proper, are located on the northern outskirts of the town of Kourou. With a current population of just under 30,000 it is the place where the famous prisoner Henri Charriere aka Papillion, is believed to have hid out after escaping.

The bright greens and tangerines which adorn the interiors of the modest yet clean Atlantis Hotel stand in stark contrast to the dreary wharfs of yesteryear which served as a last point of entry for French convicts destined for almost certain death on Devil's Island just fourteen kilometers off shore.

Having landed at just a little after ten that Thursday morning the first order of business for

Mahone and company was a shower, food and a viable plan. Although fitfully, the three were able to catch some sleep on the second leg of their flight in but, with the weight of the events of the last week catching up to them none were firing on all eight cylinders and it was obvious they would need a good lie-in in the near future.

It was half past ten that morning when the shuttle from the airport pulled into the car port at the hotel and disembarking the mini-bus it was Kuksova who kicked off the conversation as they moved to take their place in line to check in.

"I was thinking-" Irina said to Frank.

"Did it hurt?" Mahone asked.

"Not funny when I was ten years old, not funny now that I'm . . . not ten."

"Are you not tired?!" He asked.

"No, not really. I was thinking, if we're right and this is the time and place, that they're going to pull something then it has to be during a launch."

"And if we're wrong my dear girl?" Morrissey threw out.

"Then we get to watch whatever happens on the evening news!" Mahone interjected as they stepped up to the reception desk. Irina was able to check in without incident however he two cops with her presented their passports only to get a nasty surprise.

"What do you mean, full?!" Frank asked.

"I mean we are full, az in to zee top!" The middle-aged, effeminate desk clerk repeated. "At capacity. I am saying zat dare iz no mor room att ze inn."

"Jesus Dude! There must be a room somewhere in this one horse, podunk, ass end of the world town!"

"Probably all ze hotels are full monsieur."

"Good idea Mahone!" Morrissey whispered in Frank's ear. "Insult the one man who might help us as we're homeless in a foreign country and seeking help!"

"I am so sorry monsieurs, zer is a launch scheduled for Monday morning and when zer is a launch scheduled, zee tourists fuck here."

Frank and Morrissey exchanged glances.

"The tourists **flock** here!" Irina translated.

Though losing patience the clerk remained polite but firm.

Irina stepped back up to the desk and in fluent French spoke with the clerk. He listened then, smiling and eyeing Mahone, nodded and responded in English.

"Perhaps for zee mademoiselle we can come to some arrangement." He happily offered.

"By the way monsieur, what time is the launch on Monday?" Irina asked.

"Zee launch is scheduled for 12:10 from the Ariana launch pad. Also I mention zat if zere eez bad weather zey will delay zee launch for twenty-four hours. Also I might mention zat if you wish to see za launch, reservations are required."

"And where can I have some tour information?"

Irina asked.

He handed her a tri-fold brochure maintaining eyes on Frank and smiling. In obvious discomfort, Mahone nervously nodded back.

"Merci beau coup." Kuksova said.

A short time later all three were settling into room 307.

"Good thing the Concierge was so accommodating!" Morrissey noted

"And all for the low, low price of $100!" Frank commented as he and Morrissey were unfolding and setting up their military cots in the living room.

"Yeah, good thing!" An annoyed Irina called out from the single bedroom where she was dressing following her shower.

Like two naughty teen boys Mahone and Morrissey, feeling no pain after their two top off drinks from the hotel room's mini-bar while Irina showered, exchanged smirking glances as she emerged from the bathroom, her brain racing to formulate an attack plan.

"Well, the launch is Monday at one. So we've got about forty-eight hours to figure this out. I vote we do it over a light breakfast!" She offered.

"Sounds good to me!" Frank seconded.

"I third that motion! I could murder a good fry-up!" Morrissey threw in.

The all day breakfast in the thirty seat cantina, only half full at that hour, and located on the ground floor was a self-serve buffet styled affair.

"Frank, there's a problem!" Irina blurted out as

she stacked her tray with one of nearly everything on the buffet counter. The two guys stared without comment. Frank fixed a bowl of cereal and as it was French establishment there was no grill. Morrissey was compelled to settle for tea and a "Flippin' croissant".

"Talk to me." Frank replied to Irina.

"Today is the fifth. The POTUS leaves for Brussels tomorrow for the E.U.-U.S. Defense Summit on the ninth."

"Same day as the launch!" Frank observed.

"Exactly."

"Well that gives us a whole four whole days to find something." Morrissey suggested. "So what's the problem?"

"No it doesn't! He has to know the status of the spoofer device no later than Saturday!"

"That only gives us two whole days."

"We can't cut it too close. I only came down here to snoop around." Irina unexpectedly threw out. "Guiana is French territory, we have no assets here. I'm not technically authorized to be here and at this point can only assume-"

"Hold on, hold on! Not authorized?!" Mahone looked up in shock. Morrissey sipped his green tea nearly gagging at Kuksova's latest revelation.

"Not exactly. But . . ." She stuttered.

"So we're all three in violation of a shit load of international treaties and could wind up in some third world dungeon?!"

"That's probably not gonna happen. My point is-

"

"I'm not sure of your use of the pronoun 'we' Old Boy! I'm simply here on holiday!" Morrissey interjected before he threw back the tea he spiked with a mini-scotch from the honor bar.

"Tell me your boss knows you're here!" Mahone insisted.

"Yeah, yeah! He's the one volunteered me." She said through a mouthful of food.

"Your boss sent you here but you're not actually authorized? Could you be any more cryptic?!"

"I'll explain later. Look, if they intend to disrupt the holdover by altering the synchropahsers, all we have to do is . . ."

"There you go with that all that egg head shit again! It's me you're talkin' to now. Dumb it down will ya?"

"Okay, sorry." She lifted a croissant from her tray and mimed. "The little choo choo train has to go into the big train house on time or-"

"Not funny when I was ten!"

"You're still ten!" Irina shot. Morrissey spit his tea to the side in laughter.

"You two should definitely consider going undercover as husband and wife!" Morrissey quipped.

In between bites Irina continued.

"The typical cell tower clock has an oscillator similar to that of a wristwatch and can drift out of tolerance in minutes if it isn't fed a steady signal. How long a clock can maintain time on its own is called it's 'holdover'. Electrical grids which use clocks, also rely on GPS dependent devices called 'synchropahsers' which precisely regulate their current flow and also help locate faults in the flow."

"Yeah, you mentioned synchropahsers before."

"Lack of this kind of timing technology is why it took the Canadian tech folks months to locate the failure after the famous 2003 blackout."

"I remember that incident. So these ass hats are after the synchropahsers?"

"Probably."

"PROBABLY!? Come on-"

"Keep your voice down!" She demanded.

"You mean we came all this way, this far and we're not sure . . ."

"No, I'm sure. Kind of sure. I mean . . . as sure as we can be given the circumstances."

"Jesus, Mary and Joseph Kuksova! Do they train you guys before they give you a badge and a gun and cut you lose on the world?!"

"I told you I'm not a field agent!"

"And yet here you are, **in the field**!"

Ignoring Frank's rant she receded back into thought as she poured herself another cup of tea.

"They must have plans to plant something on the synchropahsers somehow. Either that or it could be some kind of holdover disrupter. You know, to spoof the-"

"Are you serious about all this?!"

"Serious as a congressional investigation!"

"So serious in a sort of half-assed, who-gives-a-shit sort of way?" Frank took the mini whiskey Morrissey handed him and used it to spike his orange juice. "Well at least we're sure they're probably planning on inserting something, somewhere, at sometime probably before, during or after the launch! Is that a safe bet?" Frank probed.

"Yeah. . . probably. Relatively speaking." She answered through a mouth full of toast.

"Okay! Good to know we're on solid ground." Frank quipped as he pushed away his bowl of mushy corn flakes.

Both men watched in astonishment as Kuksova went back and helped herself to two of everything again with the exception of the hot cinnamon buns. Of those she took three.

Frank stared in amazement.

"Fucking Bluto Blutarski!" He mumbled as he watched Irina delicately skate back to the table so as not to drop anything.

"What?" Morrissey asked.

"Nothing, John Belushi reference."

She set her newly loaded tray back down on their table by the window overlooking the vacant pool.

"When we had dinner I got the impression you ate like a bird!" Mahone commented.

Irina shrugged. "All girls eat like a bird on the first date! It's an unwritten rule."

"She does eat like a bird." Morrissey commented as he surreptitiously emptied the last mini bottle of scotch into his empty tea cup. "A bloody vulture!"

Paddy Kelly

****

Newark Liberty International
Newark New Jersey
Wednesday, 4 September

A day earlier, on the morning of the 4th, as Mahone, Kuksova and Morrissey were preparing to fly, Erik Mathias was heading to his gate in Newark Liberty International. First he stopped off at the information desk

"Can you direct me to the nearest land line please?"

"If you are to meet someone you are welcome to use this phone." She smiled at the well groomed Latino. "Or I could call for you."

"That's very gracious but it's a trunk call." He smiled back the young woman looked puzzled. "It is long distance."

"Oh, I see. The corridor on the left, half way down there's a bank of public phones."

"Thank you very much Miss."

"You're welcome. Have a nice day."

He located the phone and using coins he dialed the number direct. A man's voice picked up on the second ring.

¿Si quien?

"Good! I have the codes! The meet with the American contact is scheduled in a café in Bogotá as soon as the mission is complete. Are the crew ready?"

527

We meet tonight to distribute documents, weapons and a final review of our end plan. We can review all when you arrive.

"I land in the European space port at half past one tomorrow. Have someone meet me."

You think Battesta is suspicious?

"Raymundo suspicious? He's too stupid to be suspicious. His obsession with Maduro blinds him!"

¡Viva la revolución!

"Yeah, la revolución." Mathias unenthusiastically spewed.

****

Nearing the end of their breakfast Irina suggested they should check on a taxi or other public transport out to the base. Frank volunteered to go to the front desk and check.

In the lobby, in front of Mahone were two surly looking guys in their thirties asking about the shuttle. Frank's attention was captured when they spoke a dialect of Spanish to the girl at the desk but Frank's New York Puerto Rican kept him up on the conversation. Apparently they were there for tour information.

Both men were well built but not overly muscular, wore American ball caps and military styled khakis. Mahone couldn't help but notice they maintained a square-shouldered, military bearing as they left the desk and walked to the elevator, traits that seemed at odds with the fact that he heard them mention in passing to the receptionist that they were businessmen from Florida.

"May I help you sir?" The Carib native girl politely asked.

"Yes, I'd like to get information on the best way out to the space port. My friends and I would like to take a tour."

"Certainly sir."

Frank watched as the two men made for the elevator and observed as it stopped on the fourth floor.

Once there they entered room 409 where they joined three others.

Though not in uniform, two of the others were dressed similarly but the third man, just stepping out of the kitchenette with a large, black coffee in hand was obviously the honcho as he called them all over to the table.

One floor above Mahone and crew, in suite 409, Erik Mathias and his three man team were finishing off their breakfast. Wanting to maintain as low a profile as possible, they had ordered room service and were now preparing to finalize their plan.

As two of the gang cleared the table La Serpiente retrieved and spread out a 1:100,000 scale map of the *Centre Spatial Guyanais*. He spoke in Spanish with a Venezuelan dialect as he gave his brief.

"Prior to launch the ATV is housed here in this shed about a kilometer from the launch pad. The day before the launch they will move the vehicle components here so here is the ideal time and place for hiding the device on the ATV."

"Where on the ATV vehicle?"

"You have the plan I sent you?"

Ramirez brandished a single sheet with a detailed cross section of the Automated Transfer Vehicle, the module used to deliver the resupplies to the ISS. He laid the large technical plan of the ATV on top of a map of the base grounds

"Where did you get such detailed plans of this thing?" The tall one on his left asked.

"A special secret source. A man code named Deepthroat!" Mathias said quietly.

"He downloaded them from Wikipedia!" Ramirez answered. The other two cohorts laughed.

"Most of the base is restricted." Mathias continued and while he spoke he handed out forged employees' passes then pointed to the map with a butter knife. "This is the Visitor's Centre. The Soyuz Launch Pad, Ariana Launch Pad, Space Museum and school respectively. We are concerned with the ATV shed, here, and the Ariana Pad only. Paulo and Ramirez you two are outside maintenance contractors in for a few hours to trace an electrical problem in the school reported last Thursday. Here's the actual dispatch slip form Damien Electrical in the capital. Keep it with you in case you're stopped."

"That you didn't get from Wikipedia!"

"No. I rang the Damien company last week and told them I was from the school and that I would come by and verify. While I was there a twenty pound note bought me a blank dispatch slip on the premise I needed it to show base security. You can buy anything in this country if you have the money. A couple of hours later I called back and delayed the repair crew until next week."

"Serpiente, nice move!"

"Technically the launch window proper begins forty-eight hours prior to a launch but it's not until the setting of the upgraded security protocol, twenty-four hours later that full security measures are put in place."

"And those are?"

"Aerial surveillance, ground surveillance, strict pedestrian and vehicular traffic control through the main gate, the only one left open during the launch window, and significant overall CSG grounds security.

The two primary security forces are comprised of the 3rd Foreign Infantry Regiment – commanded by a Colonel LaParra and a detachment of Gendarmerie under a Captain Louis Renault."

The team's confidence steadily rose as Mathias continually impressed his crew with the details of his research.

"You have done your home work vato!"

"There is too much at stake here to approach this like amateurs! Why do you think I brought you three here?!"

"Where do you want the distraction?" Another asked.

"Leave that to me. But it will be away from the

front gate, outside the perimeter, near but not too close to the gate. When they are alerted they'll divert much of their security resources to that location giving you, Alpha Team, approximately ten to fifteen minutes clear to plant the device in the ATV and make it over to the north gate and get out. The gate will reopen after the launch."

"Are we confident about our security intel?" Ramirez questioned.

"The night before the 3rd Foreign Infantry regiment aided by the local Gendarmerie infiltrate the entire area and the place is locked down tighter than Angela Merkel with her legs crossed!"

"Anything else?"

"There will be some men from the Paris Fire Brigade as back up but they are under the command of the Legion and generally restricted to the launch pad area. They are not a factor."

"Which place is where they put it together?"

"The Launcher Integration Building is located 2.8 kilometers from the ELA launch zone, here." He pointed with the knife. "The company called Astrium assembles each Ariane launcher not sooner than two days before launch. This is where final assembly is done. The vehicle is then transferred to the Final Assembly Building for payload integration. This is done by a different contractor, the Arianespace company. It is here that you will have the only chance to plant the device on board."

"It's like a giant assembly line!"

"Three companies, one I.D.?" Torrente

questioned.

"Yes. Ramirez, Torrente remove and reverse your Damian Electrical I.D." They did as instructed. "Flip them. The reverse side is a valid Arianespace Company I.D."

"Impressive!" Torrente complimented.

"After that the vehicle travels the 2.8 kilometers to the ELA-3 launch zone where it is made ready for launch."

"So once on the launch pad it's inaccessible?"

"Completely."

"Where do you plan the secondary distraction?" Another asked.

"If needed, near the back gate is the best place. When they are alerted they'll divert security resources to that location giving you, Alpha, approximately five to ten minutes to clear the base any way you can."

"Security response times?" Rodolfo asked.

"That's one of the primary things Ramirez and Alpha Team are going to find out today, but we'll add one to two minutes either way once we see their response times just to have some breathing room."

"The diversion should draw most of the soldiers away from the ATV shed and give the Alpha team enough time to plant the package."

"What about the launch pad? Security I mean."

"The Ariana Launch Pad security contingent won't be at full compliment until twenty-four hours before launch. Prior to that there are only two sentries around the clock 48 hours prior to launch.

And remember it is crucial to stay six to ten meters inside the fence line, even if you risk being seen!"

"Why?"

"The entire ground perimeter is sown with motion sensors. The French bought them from the Americans after the U.S. evacuated Viet Nam!"

"How do we insure the device will launch itself once the ATV has reached altitude?"

"There's a pressure sensitive mechanism installed. Once the cargo bay pressure falls to less than one atmosphere the device will jettison its cocoon and activate homing in on the nearest Galileo satellite."

"¡Santa mierda! How they invent these Star Wars things?!" An amazed Torrente queried.

Mathias again referred to the cross section of the Automated Transfer Vehicle.

"The device will be planted on the port side, behind the aft bulkhead." Mathias continued.

One of the men brandished a small lump of grayish clay for all to see.

"This is NP10. The partition here, is designed to withstand an explosive force of 0.8 to 1.2 to enable possible survival of any crew members in the aft compartment in the event the ATV is used for crew transport. This charge, at 1.5 is one and a half times stronger than half a kilo of TNT."

"A **little** stronger then dynamite! That's like a block of C4!" Torrente blurted out.

"Yes but this NP10 is diluted with PIB and mineral oil to soften the explosive force."

"How much?" Torrente questioned.

"Just enough. The wall can block the blast but it's still enough to rupture the exterior walls, destroy the ship and release the device into space."

"Serpiente you said nothing about killing!" Torrente protested.

"You have a particular love of astronauts?!" Mathias challenged.

"Torrente! He's being an asshole. The ship is fully automated. There is no crew on board." Ramirez clarified.

"With over 800kg of propellant on board along with all the flammable stores it is assured everything will be destroyed after the device is blown clear!" Mathias assured. "You two have all you need for the tour?" He asked The man sitting next to Ramirez.

"Si Serpiente."

"Rodolfo, while Torrente and Ramirez are on the tour you stay here and guard the weapons and the device. I'll be back just after lunch."

"Where are you going?" Rodolfo challenged.

"I have some unfinished business to attend to." He answered as he rose to take his jacket. "You have your tourist camera?" Mathias asked.

"Packed with a new and a back-up disc."

"And the laser range finder?" He directed towards Ramirez.

"OY, Pendajo! This is not my first mission!"

Without comment Mathias grabbed his phone and jacket and left the room.

The Galileo Project

****

There was a moderate line at the reception centre when, along with eighteen tourists Ramirez and Torrente handed in their tickets and boarded the two car Disney-like tram in front of the Space Port reception centre. They were careful to sit in opposite cars and opposing sides of the vehicle.

Both carried standard hand held cameras but Ramirez was also equipped with a somewhat obtrusive, older model, laser range finder. Only slightly smaller than a small toaster it was an essential piece of gear for the saboteurs as most of their plan was developed from maps yet dependant on having accurate distances from one objective to the next.

The young female tour guide, manned the over-sized steering wheel, adjusted her Madonna mike headset and cordially greeted her tourists, pulled away from the reception centre and launched into her tour spiel.

"Back in the Nineties, with the establishment of a 97% launch success rate and after petitioning and securing several contracts to launch satellites for the international community, the European Parliament decided to increase its investment in space launches." The twenty-something, French tour guide spoke clearly in well articulated English as she shepherded her small group of tourists through the grounds.

536

Paddy Kelly

"The Guiana Space Centre or the Centre Spatial Guyanais, became the world's first space port. While officially a territory of the French Republic it operates in cooperation with all twenty-seven E.U. members."

"SOON TO BE TWENTY-SIX Love!" A tipsy Englishman yelled from the front of the second car.

The driver made no response aloud but her internal dialog immediately sprang to life:

Oh good! A drunk Roast Beef on my tour car! Thank God for Brexit!

Glancing in her left wing mirror the young guide maintained her smile along with her tour spiel until she gradually became suspicious as, for the second time, she spotted Ramirez two seats behind her acting strangely with the small binoculars-like device to his eye scanning the open field.

"Sir, as mentioned in your pre-tour brief, we ask you to please not film the launch pads as we pass by. Thank you." In the rear view mirror she watched as he seemed to ignore her, hesitated then finally lowered the range finder.

By this time Mahone et al had caught a taxi and were riding out to the space port with the intention of also taking the tour to get oriented to the whole layout of the base and better formulate a plan of action.

"Why have it out here in such a desolate place? Why not use Florida or Houston?" Mahone asked from the back seat of the taxi where he sat with Irina. Morrissey rode shotgun.

537

The Galileo Project

The Rastafarian cab driver's eyes shot to the rear view mirror before he launched into his glassy-eyed, marijuana laced astrophysics lecture.

"Here brudder we is closer to the equator, so da angular plane of da eartf require less energy to reach a geostationary orbit man! Also fallin' day-bree from da second and third stages of da rockets be havin' less of a chance of impacting human habitations, don't you know man?"

"So the rockets are launched with the earth's rotation?" Frank clarified.

"Ya man! Like a giant sling shot!" The taxi driver explained. "Also da anti-clockwise rotation of da eartf help to boost da launch. Just like when David slew the giant man! Don't you read your bible brudder?"

Morrissey turned and addressed the back seat.

"Any other questions Detective?"

"What'a you think?" Frank whispered to Irina. She bobbed her head.

"Grammar notwithstanding . . . yeah, he's right." She agreed.

Meanwhile Mathias' two thugs, aboard the tour tram did their best to act touristy but had to focus on their assigned mission. None on their team had actually ever seen the space port so the Intel Ramirez and Torrente would bring back was vital. In reality, La Serpiente and gang were under the same time and security restraints as Mahone, Kuksova and Morrissey.

Just past the halfway point of the tour the guide

tried to focus on her job as she again spied Ramirez fumbling with the suspicious binocular-like gadget only this time he was also taking notes.

"The Space Centre also includes the *Îl du Salut*, the island you may know as the infamous *Devil's Island*, which is actually two islands. These islands are under the launch trajectory for the geostationary orbits of the Ariane rockets and for safety, must be evacuated during launches."

The port has been active in launches since 1996 and covers an area of approximately twenty-one square kilometers."

"Uh, 'scuse me Dahrlin'." A large over weight American in a pristine, white cowboy hat called from two seats back. "Twenty one kill-o-meters, what's that in real distance?"

"I'm sorry I'm afraid I don't understand sir?"

"Americans! Still in the Eighteenth century!" A Canadian man whispered to the woman next to him. "It's about eight square miles!" He called up the aisle.

"Eight point one!" The woman with him quietly corrected.

The tour finished, the tram slowed as it turned back into the reception area.

"Now ladies and gentlemen we end our tour of the European Space Centre here next to the Space Centre Museum. The museum is open until six o'clock this evening and admission is seven euro for adults and four euro for children. Thank you for coming to the GSP and please enjoy the rest of your time in Guiana."

The passengers disembarked and as the tour guide parked the empty tram a female colleague approached.

"Janine can you possibly take my-"

"Sorry Beth, one minute." She brushed past her colleague and made for the two security guards sitting at the coffee bar.

"Jacob, there was two guys on my tour and they were acting kind of strange."

"Probably Americans!" The native Guaianian quipped.

"No! Listen. I had to ask him three times to stop taking pictures when we passed through the restricted zones."

"Janine! How long you been doing this?! You know some of these tourists is just ignorant peasants out of the house for the first time!" He argued. The other guard chipped in his two cents as well.

"Yeah, half of them think the moon landings were a hoax and the earth is flat!"

"Maybe they were peasants but I have never seen a peasant with a camera that looked like a bloody small toaster!"

"Janine-"

"Or a pair of binoculars with what looked like an LED on top!" She insisted. The two guards exchanged glances.

"Okay show us these two suspicious characters!" She led them off to where she last saw Ramirez and Torrente but they were gone.

****

Two hours later Mahone and company were also back from their tour, which launched just after Ramirez's and so decided to sit back at a small café next to the hotel to plan.

"Barring some unforeseen event like weather or something I don't see them cancelling the launch." Irina proposed as they sat at an outside table. "That said, whether we approach the Director or not, it's not going to affect the launch. If we're wrong no harm done but if we are right and they have some devious thing planned during the launch . . ."

"I hate to say it Frank old boy, but I agree with Anna Karenina." Morrissey said into his cup of tea. "I still say we have to alert him, even if it is surreptitiously. He's the only man with the authority to call all the shots on the facility."

"I'd still like to have something more concrete." Frank added. "Let's think this through." He argued. "We go to the Director now, tell him we may have information which might mean there's some bad guys, who we know nothing about, who are here to do something, possibly to the launch. Without details . . ."

"He has a point." Morrissey suddenly jumped ship on Irina.

"How's he gonna take that? Besides possibly having us locked up, contacting our embassies, and confiscating everything we brought with us. All of which will last until well after the launch."

"If we don't alert him and something happens we're all in the shits! Permanently!" Irina countered.

"What do you mean by 'WE'? I'm on holiday!" Morrissey jovially announced.

"Yeah! The head of an elite unit of the Metropolitan Police in Scotland Yard who just happened to be on vacation, where one of the most dangerous gangs just happened to be operating thousands of miles away. Nobody would put that together!" Irina fired back.

"Okay, so we tell him?" Mahone asked to clarify. The two others nodded weakly. "Okay, who gets to go?"

"What'a ya mean who goes?" Kuksova challenged.

"I mean do we draw straws, loser goes or do we-"

"We all go! We're all gonna take a bite of this shit sandwich! We're a team aren't we?!"

"Agent Kuksova, please explain to me how it is that you forbid me to come down here, then-" Frank started.

"It's 'forbade'." Morrissey interjected.

"What?!"

"Forbade, past perfect."

"Thank you Noah Webster." Frank nodded then turned back to Irina. "You fucking **forbade** me to come down here but now we're a team?"

"Are we not?" She smiled coyly as they made

eye contact.

"Detective Mahone, were you not married at one point in your life?"

"Shut up Nigel!"

"Just pointing out the futility of arguing with a woman."

"Okay, we all go." Mahone relented. "But-"

"I knew it, there's a 'but'." Irina complained.

"What's his name? This Grand Poobah of astrospace?" Frank pushed. Irina flipped through her phone screen.

"Didier Faivre, Dr. Didier Faivre." She announced. "What's the 'but'?" She pushed.

"But you give me until morning, I come up empty handed and first thing in the morning we get over to the base and tell the Director everything we know."

"Or, as the case may be, everything we don't know." Morrissey added.

"You're an antagonistic little shit, you know that?" Irina quipped. "Alright. FIRST THING tomorrow morning!" She conceded. "Might as well wait I suppose. He's gone for the day anyway."

Both guys were surprised by the tag to Irina's statement.

"How exactly do you know that he's gone for the day?" Mahone challenged. Irina averted her eyes as she responded.

"I . . . might have called over to his office. Before. At the hotel . . . when I went to the toilet."

"You were gonna alert them! With zero evidence

you were gonna start a panic the day before a launch! What happened too all the 'We're a team aren't we?' stuff?"

"I'm doing just doing my job!"

"I vas only do-ink my job, mein Kapitan!" Morrissey snickered.

"Shut it you!" She admonished.

"Do you have any idea what kind of money we're talking about to cancel an operation of this size on such short notice? $600 million plus! Not to mention that before another one can launch the ISS crew would have to rearrange their work schedules, interrupt important experiments and depending on how soon another ATV could be made ready for launch possibly dig into their reserve supplies?"

"Okay Dick Tracey! With less than thirty-six hours left what are you proposing?"

"First off I suggest we start acting like detectives!" She and Morrissey exchanged glances. "As I've said, we need more info, more evidence. Something that no one can argue with." Mahone argued.

"Like what?"

"We start by searching the hotels. If one of these ass clowns is down here then we know we're on the right track." Frank explained.

"I'll call the Met and get some handwriting samples from Battesta's car rental form in London to check against the registers." Morrissey offered.

"Good idea. I'll get a hold of the precinct to see if the Chief can get us on an update on the New

York raid info."

"I've got some INTERPOL photos. I'll make copies we can show around." Kuksova added. "And I owe my boss an update on the situation."

Morrissey stepped away from the table to make his call as they all manned their phones.

Irina got through immediately to her supervisor in D.C.

Kuksova talk to me. He tersely growled.

"Sir, we think we've traced the last two from the New York raid and we think they're held up in Kourou, Guiana."

French Guiana?

"Yes sir. We're fairly certain it has to do with the international space port. There's a launch scheduled for Monday morning."

Kuksova, whatever you do don't alert the space port Director unless you have absolute certain evidence! First thing they'll do is cancel that launch! You have any idea how much it costs to cancel one of those launches?

"About $600 million plus. I suppose."

Wow! I'm impressed that you know that Kuksova!

"Well sir when you're working in the field you have to know these things."

Well done. The Big Guy's meeting in Brussels is scheduled for Monday at eleven. I need to hear from you no later than Saturday morning, irregrardless of your status, you got that?!

"Sir, I don't think irregrardless is a word."

What are you a god damned grammatician? Don't get cocky! He hung up.

Morrissey returned to the table with some news.

"Gunga Din texted us the info we found at the car rental agency." He read from his phone as he spoke. "Battesta used the pseudonym George Menendez, Dr. Gorge Menendez in on business from Santiago."

"So we're looking for a guy, probably flying solo, under the name Battesta, or an alias possibly Menendez, although he probably wouldn't be using either of those but he just might be tied to the 'doctor' thing." Frank confirmed.

At barley a kilometer east to west and two kilometers north to south a relatively fit elderly person could cover the town of Kourou in half an hour end to end so they agreed to search the hotels for any sign of a clue.

"According to the online *Lonely Planet*, not counting small private accommodations, there's ten hotels all together." Irina read from her phone as she scanned.

"Okay, good start! Text us three hotels each and we'll split up. Rule out B&B's and hostels for now we should be able to make the rounds in two or three hours tops. So meet back here in two?" Frank proposed.

"Make it three." Irina suggested.

"Okay, three hours. Look, we hurt these dick wads back in Manhattan now they're down two players, so it's a pretty safe bet they've scraped up some more assholes to join in all their little reindeer games!" Frank advised. "If either you get a hit before three o'clock contact the others. DO NOT be a hero and go it alone! We Green?"

"I assume that 'green' means to agree?" Morrissey questioned. Irina nodded yes.

"Okay," Frank continued. "Internet, Google maps, the strongest black coffee I have ever had in my life and the Space Cops are ready to take on the case of the missing spaced-out assholes and the Space Port!"

Kuksova turned to Morrissey and spoke.

"That guy has a **really** perverse sense of humor!" Irina mumbled as she watched Frank walk away. Standing beside her Morrissey shrugged.

"I suppose after you've been shot three or four times and almost die two or three of those times, it has a tendency to alter your perspective on life." Morrissey opined. "Ciao Bella!"

"FOUR TIMES?!" She blurted. "Really?!"

Morrissey nodded as he walked away.

"See you later." He said.

"Later." She mumbled. Still partially in shock she scurried down the small hill to catch up with Frank.

"Hey." To mask her enthusiasm she slowed when she was just behind him then walked to catch up.

"Hey yourself." He greeted.

"I just wanted to say that-" Unsure of exactly how to express what she wanted to say she stuttered. "I just wanted you to know that-"

"How much of a pleasure it is for you to be working with me and that I'm the most professional, talented, dedicated cop you've ever worked with in addition to the fact that the night in London we spent together was-"

"Aside from catching bad guys do you **ever** take **anything** seriously?"

"Sorry! Look, I know what you want to say to me and . . . thank you." He made eye contact. "No, really, thank you. And don't get me wrong, I like Dick Tracey, but you couldn't have called me Sherlock Holmes or John McClane instead?"

"Who's John McClane?" She asked.

Mahone stopped and stared at her blankly.

"You have got to be shitting me!" He spat.

"Gotcha!" She giggled.

Irina kissed him on the cheek and made her way back up to hotel reception.

*** * ***

"Hi."

"Bon jour Madame. What may I do for you?" The female receptionist asked.

"I'm a little worried." Irina put on her concerned mask.

"How may I help?"

"My brother was due in last night and he didn't show up. He was supposed to book in here as well."

"What is the   name of your brother Madame?"

The desk clerk manned the keyboard and typed as Irina spelled out Battesta, Raymundo Battesta.

"I'm sorry Madame. There is no one by that name registered now or for the next week."

"Oh! I just remembered!" She declared before she pulled a copy of the INTERPOL photo of Battesta from her shoulder bag. She folded over and concealed the police info along the bottom of the head shot before showing it.

"He's rather distinct looking." Kuksova added as she held the photo up to the receptionist.

"No, sorry Madame. I don't recognize him. But if you would like I can copy the photo and have it here in case he appears."

"Thank you very much but, that won't be necessary."

Morrissey's first draw was a low budget place christened the *Lodge Tikini-4* which was not much more than a series of refurbished bungalows. He also drew a blank.

At the *Hôtel Le Gros Bec* Kuksova came up with another goose egg while Frank walked to his next hotel, not only the furthest point on their search but the furthest from town at just over three kilometers away.

It was while puffing his way down the incline to the beach front resort that Mahone was reminded of his still healing lung.

The *Hôtel Mercure Kourou*, on the other side of town, Morrissey's second target, had no new check-ins in the last two days and so he moved on.

Mahone felt compelled to pull himself together as he pushed through the revolving glass door and came out into the luxurious lobby of the *Les Roche Resort*.

Observing the well-dressed guests littering the foyer he immediately caught the attention of the smartly uniformed folks behind the massive, semi-lunar, glass and mahogany reception desk across the wide lobby floor.

As he made his way to the desk a large black man behind it smiled and nodded as if to offer help but was suddenly headed off by a small native girl who wedged herself in between the big clerk and the desk.

Dragging a step stool from behind the counter she mounted it, folded her hands on the desk, smiled broadly and greeted Mahone in a very strong Nigerian accent.

"How may I be of some service to you this day dear sir?!" She assertively spouted. Frank smiled.

"I am traveling with some friends from Miami and last night in the Bahamas things got well . . .a little crazy."

"Are you being injured in some way good sir? Shall I ring for some medical help if needed?" She reached for the desk phone.

"No, no! Nothing like that. It's just that we seemed to have misplaced one of our group. I called his wife in Florida and she said he was booked in here. I wonder if I could trouble you to see if he made it in yesterday?"

"We are not supposed to give names-"

"I have his name. Doctor Battesta, possibly just Battesta or perhaps under R. Battesta?" He added. "He was travelling with our family physician, Dr. Gorge Menendez."

She manned her keyboard.

"I am most terribly sorry Mr.?"

"James, James Eisiku. You can call me James."

"EISIKU! You are Nigerian!" She became ecstatic. "That is a fantastically coincidental thing!"

"Well I was adopted so I never really knew my actual parents. But Joshua and Delilah were fantastic to me growing up!" He explained with enough sincerity to make the Pope queasy.

"You have a most beautiful story James!" She smiled with deep sincerity. "I am most terribly sorry that I cannot be helping you!" She sincerely apologized.

"Thank you anyway for trying." Mahone turned to walk away.

"Oh, sir, sir! We do have a Doctor Raymundo registered, but it appears he's late to check in."

"Late? How late, exactly?"

"He should have been in this hotel this very morning."

"May I ask where he was coming in from?" He pushed. She looked around, leaned in close and whispered.

"We are not supposed to divulge dee details of dee guests in dee hotel! It is strictly forbidden!"

"I just need to know his point of departure."

"It is against policy. I could be sacked!"

Mahone surreptitiously fished a €50 note from his pocket and slid it across the desk. It vanished immediately.

Cautiously glancing around, she once again consulted her computer screen she spoke softly.

"He apparently flew into Miami from JFK yesterday and was due to land here this morning but, I have no idea why, after such a long flight, he would not come here to shower and rest. It seems he had more pressing business James."

"Thank you!" Leaning in to read her name tag Mahone smiled. "Thank you Regina!" He hesitated before he walked away. "You don't happen to have a brother who's a prince do you?" He quipped.

"No, why do you ask?" She was puzzled.

****

Earlier that afternoon as Mahone's folks were sipping tea, debating about hotels and realizing that maybe they hadn't thought things through all the way before leaving New York, Erik Mathias arrived at the Cayenne - Félix Eboué Airport in a rental car to meet Raymundo Battesta.

"Is all ready?" Climbing into the car without formality Battesta pushed.

"Yes. I've contacted the two men I mentioned to you on the phone and they are due in this evening. I'm to collect them at six tonight."

"And you trust them?" Raymundo pushed.

"They are dedicated and professional. I've worked with both before. You can assess them yourself when they come in. I have a room ready for you at the *Les Roches Hotel*. It's a three star right on the beach. Room service, pool all the amenities."

"I'm not here to see the sights! We have a mission!"

"Si Jefe! I just thought it better for cover if you looked like the successful businessman from Florida you are supposed to be! Also, it is not a good idea for all of us to stay in the same hotel. Besides, you wouldn't like the place I'm staying, it's a very second rate establishment."

"Take me to the hotel, I need to clean up."

"Jefe, I have something very important I need to show you first."

"I NEED TO CLEAN UP AND EAT! I'VE BEEN ON A GOD DAMN PLANE FOR HOURS!"

At being chastised like a child bile rose to Erik's throat. He fought back the anger. "The food was worse than that slop they fed us in the SEBIN prison!"

"Raymundo, fifteen twenty minutes, please! The guard postings are time sensitive and there is something I need you to be aware of. It may affect your plans."

A frustrated Battesta suppressed his unprovoked anger, sighed and agreed.

"If you think it will affect the plans. Show me."

"I'm nearly certain of it." Mathias commented as

they drove in the rental car to the wooded outskirts of the forest just out of sight of the south west perimeter of the Space Port.

It was approaching five o'clock that afternoon when Mathias returned to the Atlantis Hotel and received the report and photos Alpha Team had assembled during the tour earlier in the day.

CHAPTER TWENTY-TWO

**Hotel Atlantis
Room 409
Friday, September 6th**

Back at the Atlantis Hotel, seated around the table in their fourth floor room, La Serpiente's gang were once again consulting the technical drawing of the Automated Transfer Vehicle along with Alpha Team's intel, hand sketched maps and cell phone surveillance photos along with notes spread across the table.

"The ATV is four and a half meters by ten meters long." Mathias reviewed. "The main bulkhead is about a third of the way back and there's an access hatch to the cargo bay here on the port side."

"Won't it be locked?" Ramirez inquired.

"Yes. And here is the key!" Mathias brandished a standard long stem, hex head and passed it to Ramirez.

"That's it?! An ordinary, everyday hex key?"

"As of yet no one has broken into a supply ship in space. Hex bolts are all that is required" Mathias quipped. As he began again he noticed Torrente fiddling with his phone.

"Torrente, pay attention! If something happens to Ramirez it will be you who will have to complete the mission!"

"Si Jefe!" He tucked his phone away.

"Once inside you will see shelves along both walls of the cargo bay. Hide the device pressed up against the bulkhead as firmly as possible, in amongst the food parcels." He passed the shoe box-sized device to his colleague. It was wrapped in a fast food box. "The spoofer device is purposely designed to be about the size of a standard ESA food packet. It's not uncommon for friends to send commercial food to astronaut friends so this should be okay.

Once inside the capsule tuck it into one of the food shelves. The packets are held fast by black cargo straps but they are adjustable if you need to loosen one to hide the device."

"Very good." Assessing its weight Ramirez hefted the device in his hands.

"Brother, it is imperative you plant the charge and the spoofer on opposite sides of the bulkhead! Set the charge on the aft side, just under the emergency oxygen supply tank. The spoofer device goes in the main cargo compartment."

"So you've already told us!" A clearly annoyed Ramirez shot back. Mathias presented the pre-rigged explosive charge. It was less than half the size of the spoofer device.

"To set the timer on charge press the 'set' button on the Casio watch." He pointed and demonstrated as he spoke. "Set the time, and press 'set' a second time. Got it?"

"Like taking satellites from a baby!" Torrente

commented.

"You should be no longer than one to two minutes inside the vehicle. Three minutes from the time you enter to the time you are relocking the cargo bay hatch! Entendes?"

"I've got this!" Ramirez indignantly insisted.

Mathias momentarily considered reassigning Ramirez and executing this phase of the mission himself, but instead maintained his focus and patience.

"Rodolfo will be waiting with a car at the rear gate to meet you after the launch when the gate is open again."

"Where will he take us? It is certain they will close the N1 road in all directions."

"There's an old logging path through the forest. It by-passes the N1 road then cuts a bit west. You should be in Suriname by that afternoon where you'll lie low in a safe house until we can get you transport back to Caracas."

"The alarms and sensors when we breach the rear gate?" Ramirez pushed while he carefully stowed the items in a DeWalt electrical tool bag.

"If the distraction is needed, the base's system will have already been triggered. Once set off the system stays active until shut down at the main control center. You will have enough time to reach the perimeter and get out."

"And if Rodolfo isn't there?" Torrente challenged.

"You see to your part of the job and I'll see to

mine!" Rodolfo snapped.

"If something goes wrong make your way straight west one kilometer. There's a monument to the Holy Virgin Madonna at a dirt crossroads about here." He pointed to the map. "That's your secondary meeting point. Any other questions?"

"And you?" Ramirez questioned Mathias.

"After they respond to the distraction I'll be heading south via the river into Amapa."

"Why Brazil?"

"I have friends in Macapá."

"Torrente, what are you doing?!" Mathias snapped.

"Calling room service to leave a wake up!"

"There are four cell phones in the room for god's sake! Torrente put down the phone!"

"Okay! Then when do we meet after?"

"We meet all together back in-" Rodolfo began.

"NO! They'll be no meeting as previously discussed!"

"Why no?"

"Because we aren't fucking Bonnie and Clyde and this isn't a bank robbery! After this operation the security services of the entire world will be looking for us! We split up and stay apart! If one of us is caught. . ."

****

CSG Mission Control Centre
Launch Coordinator's Office:
19:47, Saturday 7th

"How certain is this data?" The grey-haired, distinguished looking man seated behind the desk, his jacket off and tie open at the collar, asked with the lethargy of a man who had worked the last twelve hours straight.

Despite the late hour The Mission Control Officer sat side-by-side with the Flight Director in front of the desk of Dr. Didier Favire, overall Director of the Centre Spatial Guyanais.

"How certain are we?" Favire asked.

An unpredicted weather front had suddenly developed in the Pacific and was presently moving east at nearly 160 kilometers per hour. Picked up only an hour ago it was now approaching the western edge of the Peruvian coast with a predicted path that would take it just south of French Guiana.

"Meteorology doesn't think it will dissipate once over land?" The Doctor asked.

"To some extent, possibly. But there's no way to predict how much." The MCO explained.

"In addition the weather guessers predict that if a second warm front moves up from the Amazon it could intensify the storm." The Flight Director informed.

"As of eight tonight we're officially clear of the Atlantic front formation but given the speed at which the Pacific front is moving, it is due over the Brazilian rain forest not later than midnight tonight, predicted to reach the east of Brazil, south of us by zero seven hundred hours Monday morning."

"That's the predicted course. If she deviates . . . even a few degrees she could be directly over us by breakfast Monday."

"Jean Luc?" The Director sought a final opinion from his Mission Control Officer

"Waiting out the storm, then having hit here would mean waiting for the next available launch window."

"When would that be?" The Director turned to the MCO.

"The nineteenth!" Jean Luc responded.

"Ten days. That's long. Claude?"

"Food and water supplies on the ISS are not an immediate consideration but there are several time sensitive scientific items on board the Ariana that would be lost thus cancelling several private contracts."

"Is an early launch feasible?" Dr. Favire inquired.

"The ATV can be ready to go with payload in a few hours and the Ariana can be on the gantry and fueled by five in the morning." He consulted his watch. "All we need do is fuel the Ariana."

"How long?" The Director asked.

"Ten to twelve hours if all goes well."

"Sir, with a launch time of noon tomorrow, if you give the order, we could easily beat the storm by twelve hours or more ." He explained.

Dr, Faivre momentarily considered the situation.

"Claude, notify everyone. We are going early!" Faivre ordered.

"Yes Director!"

"I'll meet you in the control room as soon as I call my wife." Doctor Faivre explained as he reached for his Smartphone.

"Very good sir. I'll notify Toulouse and ESOC tracking!" The FD announced as he left.

*** * ***

Atlantis Hotel
Room 409

At precisely 04:00 that Sunday morning Rodolfo along with Torrente & Ramirez, the Alpha Team, rose, dressed and quietly slipped out of the hotel through the back door.

Driving a rental car obtained with false I.D., Rodolfo dropped them off in the early morning dark on the road in a culvert about 150 meters from the front gate.

The work order along with their reversible identity badges gained them passage through the front gate where they were warned by the gendarmes on duty that they were restricted to the small school grounds and forbidden to trespass to the northern areas of the base where all the rocket assembly and launch sectors were located.

They of course knew the launch pads were eight kilometers north from the gate but they only needed to travel just under two and a half miles from the school, about four kilometers, to reach the Launch Integration Building where the ATV currently awaited transport to the Final Assembly point.

Meanwhile, not wanting to leave the hotel before normal working hours so as not to arouse suspicions, Mathias with Rodolfo who slipped back into the Atlantis, were packing up and sweeping the room before moving to their assigned positions to set up distractions, if required, to cover Alpha's escape.

Not realizing that soon they would essentially be 'locked in' the base, Ramirez and Torrente slipped from around back of the school where they were supposed to be working on the electrical systems and made their way along the dirt service road until reaching their permitted outer limit when they moved into the thick foliage lining the eastern plain of the base. This they followed until reaching the rear of the cluster of secondary buildings they sought.

Remaining as unobtrusive as possible in their Damien Electrical contractor's uniforms, a known contracting firm at the Space Port, half four when they entered the Launcher Integration Building.

Unbeknownst to the Alpha Team the ground crew's payload integration duties, having been completed overnight to facilitate the new launch time of the ATV, had been granted permission to sleep late that morning and so had not yet arrived.

They moved to the back of the hanger where the ten meter long, four meter wide white cylinder that was the ATV capsule sat on a custom made stand on its side just off the floor.

"It looks a lot smaller on the T.V.!" Torrente exclaimed.

Ramirez got straight to it as he rolled a nearby tool cart over next to him, produced the hex key and looked down onto the tool cart.

"Naturally!" He mumbled. Hanging from the side bar of the cart was a complete set of two dozen hex keys of all sizes.

He set the tool bag down, carefully stepped to the side then got to work on the hatch.

"¡Mierde!" Shocked to see there were nearly two dozen hex bolts to be undone to gain access he quickly got to work. "Torrente, take this and start on the other side of the hatch!" He commanded handing his partner another hex spanner from the tool rack.

Removing the bolts they set them one at a time on the tool rack.

Just as Ramirez managed to remove the final bolt and lift the man-sized hatch off the capsule they heard footsteps come into the hanger.

He quickly and quietly set the hatch aside as both their brains, racing at 100 miles an hour, instinctively told them to duck down behind some crates. Heart pounding, hoping the intruders would leave as quickly as they had arrived, the two waited.

"If they come around over here I'll distract them!" Ramirez whispered.

"What?"

"If need be I'll distract them!" He quietly spat.

The two voices, vigorously joking in French, at first seemed to veer off and away but at the last minute again altered path and headed right over to where the ATV sat by the stack of crates and piles of packing material.

Ramirez made an instant decision. He placed a hand on the shoulder of Torrente and whispered.

"The mission is in your hands brother!" Sliding the tool bag with the spoofer and demo charge in it, he said, "Go now!" nodding towards the open hatch.

He waited until Torrente grabbed the tool bag and had scurrued over to and ducked inside the ATV before he began singing loudly in Spanish while slowly pushing the tool cart as if he were shopping in a supermarket.

"Para bailar La bamba, Para bailar La bamba! Se neccassita una poca de gracia!"

He caught their attention drawing them away from the capsule and they angrily yelled at him in French.

"Hey you! What are you doing here?" They moved towards him but he maneuvered to head them off before they got too close and lead them away from the ATV.

"Para bailar La bamba, Para bailar La bamba! Buen dia mi amigo! ¿Cómo estás?" He cheerily greeted.

"What the hell are you doing here?!"

"¿Cómo?"

"I said, what **the hell** are you **doing here**?!"

"No hablo Ingles!"

"We're not English you ass!"

"Ohhh! Francés?!"

"Oui! Francés!"

"No hablo Francés!"

Inside the ATV Torrente used the opportunity and working quickly, jammed the spoofer device behind a row of boxed food packets on the upper shelf then moved back aft beyond the interior bulkhead to attach the NP10 charge low against the bulkhead behind the partition.

But as he was searching around for something to tamp the charge more firmly against the bulkhead one of the French techs walked over to and poked his head into the ATV and scanned inside the capsule.

A terrified Torrente, frozen in time, willed himself to become one with the shadowed, far aft corner of the capsule and held his breath. It worked.

Seeing nothing the tech retreated.

A third tech, apparently a section supervisor, wandered in, saw his man with Ramirez and came over to question him. Ramirez stood pulling a stupid face as the two spoke rapidly in French and finally appeared to come to a decision.

The two took Ramirez forcibly by the elbow escorting him out of the hanger while dialing security on one of their cell phones.

Meanwhile Ramirez, continually pointing at his I.D. badge while babbling in unintelligible Spanish was buying time by occupying the two techs.

"No hablo Francés!! No hablo Francés!"

As they left the supervisor called back over his shoulder.

"Phillip, do a last good look around before you lock her up. If those idiots last night forgot to secure the hatch they may have forgotten something else!"

"Oui Marco!"

******

Paddy Kelly

CHAPTER TWENTY-THREE

The Centre Spatial
Main Administration Building
07:10, Sunday

For the third time in ten minutes Dr. Favire glanced up from his desk and perused the three badges. One FBI, one NYPD and one London Metropolitan Police.

"So there are terrorists on my base looking to sabotage something?" Dr. Favire sought to clarify.

Like three school children in front of the Headmaster's desk, Kuksova, Mahone and Morrissey stood between him and a pair of armed Gendarmes.

"Yes sir." Irina confirmed.

"And who exactly are these terrorists?"

"Well sir, we don't know. Exactly."

"What precisely are they here to terrorize?" The Director pushed.

"Monsieur Directeur, we're not sure sir." Irina sheepishly demurred.

"Maybe, possibly tomorrow's launch Doctor." Mahone attempted to salvage their story.

"Well if what you are telling me is true about these mythical terrorists they are in for something of a surprise. The launch has been moved up to today at noon due to weather."

Frank glanced at his watch.

"SHIT!" He blurted.

"The base is now sealed off and we will launch in less than five hours."

"That doesn't give us much time sir!"

"Detective, we have the finest most stringent security of any base on the planet, to include your Cape Canaveral!" He insisted before turning to the older Gendarme. "Capitaine Renault, have your men had any reports of unusual activity anywhere in or around the port in the last twenty-four hours?"

"No Monsieur Directeur. There have been no disturbances reported."

Just then Capitaine Renault's shoulder radio crackled to life. He pressed his finger to his ear piece and listened intently.

"Oui! Je suis sur le chemin!" He spoke into his radio. "Director, there has been a disturbance! I must go!"

"Capitaine, what is it?!"

"Monsieur Directeur an intruder has been discovered in the Launcher Integration Building. A pair of techs are holding him in the cargo bay. My men are responding. I will keep you informed." He signaled his armed guard for them to leave. The two policemen dashed out and Kuksova turned to back the Director.

"Sir there are certainly more! The least you can do is-"

"Agent Kuksova, let us wait and see who this intruder is. If we have him in custody we will certainly get more information." His desk phone rang. "Yes?!" His face melted into extreme concern while he listened for a short time longer then hung up. "A roving patrol from the 3rd Regiment has found a body."

"Where?!" Mahone demanded.

"Detective, I-"

"Where damn it?! I'm a homicide detective! Get me a ride out to that body and tell your people not to touch anything!"

"We have Gendarmes who are fully prepared to handle this!"

"BE SERIOUS!" Frank shouted as he threw his arms in the air and turned away.

At that point Irina stepped in and, speaking French confronted Dr. Favire.

"Monsieur Doctor Favire, how many of your Gendarmes are qualified homicide investigators with more than fifteen years experience with more than three hundred murders in a metropolis like New York City?"

"Admittedly none." Faivre relented and rang down for a car while Frank issued a series of orders.

"Morrissey stay here in case any of the others suddenly appear. I'll contact you from the scene, let you know what we found and we can plan from there, agreed?"

"We are Green Detective Mahone!" He answered. Kuksova became indignant at being left out

"Well, since you're suddenly in charge, what about me Herr General?!" She jumped in. Frank turned to her and smiled.

"Well, you do have special training, a very specific skill set and you are a qualified FBI agent with some training in forensics. And it's gonna be a long day!" Kuksova nodded with approval. "You can make some coffee!" Frank cracked as he turned to leave. Kuksova was not amused. He popped back through the door. "Well? You comin' or what?!" He signaled. She followed. "Besides, your French might come in handy."

"You know there's a time for jokes!"

"Lighten up beautiful."

A jeep met them downstairs and they climbed in.

"Just out of curiosity, where did you get three hundred homicides?" Frank asked as they headed across the base.

"Just a wild assed guess. Murder rate in New York last year was about two hundred and ninety, I didn't know how many you were involved in, so I took a wild assed guess!"

"You SWAG'ed I was there for nearly 300 murders?"

"Why not? You always seem to be where there's trouble and if there's not any trouble you usually manage to bring some!"

"Good job girl! Now you're getting' the rhythm!" He nodded.

Ten minutes later Mahone and Kuksova arrived at the eastern most sector of the outer perimeter where several soldiers and the two Gendarmes from the director's office were waiting.

"Your men haven't touched anything?!" Frank asked as they made their way down a small embankment and over to the wood line where a squad of soldiers from the 3rd Regiment had temporarily cordoned off the scene.

"There is not much to touch monsieur!" The Capitaine informed.

Mahone and Kuksova seemed to work as an experienced team as, without discussion they split up and Frank went to the body and Irina slowly circled the perimeter three feet or so out from the corpse looking for clues then questioned the soldier who was the first to stumble on the scene.

Frank crouched and scanned the body. It was a middle-aged male, which lie on its left side facing away from him into the base of a large tree.

Rolling it over it was immediately obvious the body had been mutilated. The right calf, thigh and most of the upper arm were missing however the face and neck were intact.

"What do you think detective? Animal attack?" The French Capitaine inquired. Frank saw the face.

"Son-of-a-bitch!" Mahone cursed as he sat back on one knee.

"You know this man?!" The Capitaine asked.

"Irina!" He called her over.

Mahone produced a copy of the INTERPOL report from his pocket and handed it to the Capitaine.

"Raymundo Cancalo Jordão Battesta." The gendarme read. "Is he known to the FBI?"

"Yes through INTERPOL." Irina answered.

"Find anything else?" Frank asked her.

"Drag marks. He was either killed or perhaps just dumped up there then dragged down here for some reason." She declared.

"Animals." Frank said. "Bite marks in what's left of the thigh and arm." He pointed with a stick to the dried over, ripped open flesh and gauges in the exposed femur bone.

"Why would animals kill a random human?" Irina asked.

"It wasn't random and it wasn't animals killed him." Frank carefully pulled back the corpse's shirt collar to expose a deep wire cut circling the entire neck.

"A garrote!" The Capitaine declared.

"There must have been a little spat over leadership following the Harlem raid!" Mahone observed. "We raided a safe house in New York a few days ago." Mahone explained to the others standing around. "This guy and one or two others got away."

"Although one of them might have had their suspicions about him." Irina added.

"Probably Erik Mathias!" Frank said.

"That would be my bet." Irina agreed.

"Either that or Matthias was playing for another team all along!"

"Whoever it was he couldn't be sure what Battesta would do after they parted company in New York so probably thought it better to take care of him here in Guiana then in New York for what he had planned."

"So what do you think he has planned?" She probed.

"Based on all that scientific mumbo jumbo you been filling my head with I'd guess something to do with launching a spoofer! Probably hitching a ride with the rocket."

"Jesus! Frank, we have to find out!"

"Only way to do that is to find the others!"

"So there are likely more?" The French cop asked.

"You can bet on it Capitaine." Irina added.

A young Gendarme made his way down the short embankment to the group.

"Excusez-moi Capitaine, un message!"

"Merci. I have to take a message." He climbed back up to the jeep.

"Is there any advantage in having them preserve this scene?" Irina asked Frank.

"Not unless you think there's a federal interest in it. We know the who, what, when and where. At this point we need to focus on finding anyone else who's out there and if there really is a spoofer device involved."

Irina and Frank compared notes until they saw the Capitaine waving at them to come back up the hill to the road. Halfway up the small hill Frank stopped, turned to Irina, and with piercing eye contact spoke to her.

"I . . . we are gonna catch these bastards!" He

unequivocally declared.

"I know!" She smiled broadly. At the top of the embankment the Capitaine appeared noticeably distressed.

"The other one we had in custody has escaped and is loose on the base!" He informed the others. "And . . ."

"And what?!"

"And the tech he attacked when he escaped says there were two of them in the Integration Building."

"Capitaine, we have to find those men!" Irina emphasized.

"If the space port is sealed off they should still be on the grounds." He reassured. "I've ordered an APB with descriptions be issued to all units. We will find them!"

"This just keeps getting better and better!" Mahone declared.

****

The Gendarme captain manned his shoulder mike as another message came in. He listened then turned to the Americans.

"I'm sorry Madame, Monsieurs, we are already in the red time zone. Whatever this is it will have to wait. We are ninety minutes from launch time. No one is allowed out on the grounds until after liftoff."

However Mahone was in no humor to run and hide.

"Captain Renault, once those two are off the

base, safe and sound and back under which ever rock they crawled out from under, in a year maybe two they'll regroup, come back and try again."

"Try what again?"

"Whatever it is I intend to fuck up on them! I want them, both of them!"

"I am sorry monsieur detective, but-"

"More importantly we need to know for sure whether or not these assholes are part of a bigger, wider effort, so if you want to arrest me you can arrest me, but I'm going after them!"

"If that is how you feel monsieur Detective Mahone, I won't arrest you. I admire your perseverance if not your judgment. But my men are on high alert, I can guarantee nothing for your safety!"

"That's all I can ask for."

Renault set a frequency on a hand held radio he took from the jeep and offered it to Mahone.

"Take this, when you locate them call me I will send backup. I will tell my men there is a crazy American policeman chasing the saboteurs, please try not to shoot him!" Frank turned to leave but was stayed by the officer's hand on his arm.

"Monsieur Mahone, regarde! If he is thinking to get off the base we have the southern sectors sealed off. Your best chance is to head to the north east perimeter."

"What's up there?"

"The Russians! It is the Soyuz area. It is the only other exit aside from the main gate in the south,"

"Don't you already have men up at that location?"

"By now the Russians will have everyone clear of that area until after the Ariana 5 clears the pad and is out over the Atlantic in about one and a half hour's time from now"

"Renault, I have to tell you, many people in my country distrust the French, but-"

"That is because Americans, like the English, write their own history! Your people conveniently forget it was not Mel Gibson who defeated the British in your revolution. It was the French navy!"

"Trust me when we get through this and are back home, I'll remind them!"

"Monsieur Mahone, bon chance." He offered his hand and they shook.

Mahone nodded.

"Frank look, I-" Kuksova started.

"Irina, we've got conflicting reports of how many of these ass hats are actually out here. When I was at the front desk I spotted some dodgy characters. I think it was probably bad guys. When you get to the Control Centre phone the hotel, I.D. yourself and see if you can find out how many were checked in and if they've checked out. When you get that radio it to me so I know how many I'm looking for."

"Mahone listen . . ." She started. He cut her off.

"Is this the part where it's appropriate to kiss you?" He teased.

"NO! It's not appropriate to kiss me! This is

576

2019 and we're professional law enforcement officials on the job!"

"Oh, sorry!" He raised his hands and backed away. She followed.

"It's 2019." Irina continued. "So it's appropriate for the woman to kiss the guy." She kissed him with more passion than either expected. The Captain, standing off to the side, only partially averted his eyes but smiled and nodded his approval.

"People, people vite, vite!" Renault called from the jeep.

"There are at least two of them out there, maybe more! Be careful!" She warned.

"I like the odds! Besides I'm not gonna tackle them without a gun. As soon as I find them I'll give Renault a shout on this thing."

Renault along with the guard who had been waiting aside and Kuksova rushed to the jeep and drove south to the Mission Control Centre. Mahone headed north up the N1 main road.

At the same time, on the north end of the base, in a small side hanger behind the Integration Building Ramirez was dragging a dead soldier of the 3rd Regiment into a work room where he quickly stripped him of his uniform, I.D. and FAMAS F1 5.56 automatic rifle along with the three magazines of ammo the soldier had been issued that morning.

After donning the uniform and performing a functions check on the weapon, Ramirez quickly plotted a course to slip out of the base posing as a guard.

****

Upon entering the Mission Control Centre Renault had arranged for a young tech to babysit Kuksova and Morrissey.

Both were taken with what greeted them inside.

A spacious, vaulted ceiling control room dominated by four rows of long work tables with work stations for forty to fifty engineers. With about half of the full complement of engineers and techs present today, each was seated in front of their own monitor. Four giant flat screens which dominated the front space of the chamber hung high on the front wall. Three were end to end while the largest sat below the the other three.

The tech assigned to escort them led the two into the observation theatre, which was the size of a small cinema, sat them down in front of the viewing area with front row seats to the control suite below and from his lab coat pocket he produced a Madonna mike headset and plugged it into one of several jacks along the chair rail under the large observation window.

"VIP seats! Normally reserved for dignitaries." He proudly explained. "I'm Leon! So youse two are coppers eh?!"

They both nodded and smiled.

"We have an in-house translation program hooked into the com system for the forty or so countries we deal with. I'll keep youse up to date as we go."

Nearly the entire front wall of the control room was taken up with a ten by four meter high plasma screen hanging below the three faceted protrusion currently showing a live shot of the Ariana launch pad.

The live feed displayed on the large plasma screen displayed a split picture in three sections. Half the screen showed the ready to launch Ariana 5 standing next to the gantry while the other half of the screen, split in two, showed a graphic with weather, altitude, speed and distance readings, all at zero for now while the final section showed the projected flight path data over a selected arc of the earth.

"The control area, it's so small!" Morrissey commented "Two dozen people at three or four rows of desks!"

"It's all that is required for this launch. It's only a resupply mission to the ISS. Although we are testing some new features on the Automated Transfer Vehicle."

"I remember watching the Apollo launches on TV as a kid." Morrissey commented. "There were two hundred blokes in the room!"

"Two hundred and twenty-five to be exact. With nearly 2,500 backing them up!" Leon the tech commented. "Your telephone is not the only area where advancements in size have been made Mr. Morrissey."

"That rocket seems pretty big!"

"The Ariana 5, not the largest commercial rocket, she's only fifty-one meters tall, about half that of NASA's Saturn 5. Her total payload is only 21,000 kilos or 46,000 pounds compared to Saturn's 48,600 kilos or just over 107,000 pounds."

"So half as big half the lift! Where's the advancement after half a century?" Morrissey challenged.

"The Saturn 5, a marvelous feat of engineering to be sure, cost the Yanks just short of six and one half billion dollars. We built the Ariana 5 for a total of 137 million Dollars U.S. that is."

"Saved a few pennies there, eh?!" Morrissey added.

"With that budget we could build more than forty Ariana 5's and equip them with Space X's nine Merlin engines each, you know like the Falcon 9 from Space X?"

"Yeah, Space X. Falcon nine. Got it." Morrissey pretended to be paying attention. He didn't get it,

"As it is we can now produce the Ariana at a rate of about one every ninety days."

"Okay, you've made your point Zevon!" Morrissey growled.

"It's Leon sir, with an 'L'"

"Is this being televised?" Irina purposely interrupted.

"Yes, online." The tech responded. "But since it's only an ISS resupply mission probably not to many viewers."

"How many?" She asked.

"Perhaps one or two million." The tech shrugged,

"Pishaw! Only one or two million. Hardly worth bothering." Morrissey quipped earning him an elbow to the ribs from Kuksova.

"Behave! We're guests!" She quietly chastised.

ALL STATIONS PLEASE STAND-BY FOR COUNTDOWN. The Directeur des Operations' voice announced in French over the P.A.'s open channel.

Down on the floor messages criss-crossed the in-house radio channels as radio traffic between stations increased.

"Operations reports upper and lower stages sealed." An engineer reported.

"Thank you. All systems report." The DDO directed into his head set.

"All systems report green for launch." Leon relayed as he listened.

All sections we are go for launch. The DDO announced over the P.A. a minute later.

LCOM, notify ESTRACK that CSG is ready, confirm they have us on their boards.

Yes sir! The LCOM engineer placed the call.

Sir, ESTRACK control reports they have us and are standing by.

Indicating the readouts now appearing on the giant flat screen, Leon the tech leaned in to Irina and Morrissey.

"The vehicle's trajectory, which you can see on the bottom right of the screen, is actually tracked from several positions across the globe but is being supervised and commanded by CST, in Toulouse Space Centre in France." He informed them.

"And Vodophone can't get me decent reception past Croydon!" Morrissey quietly quipped.

"So, actual ignition occurs seven seconds after the engines are ignited and just over two minutes later the SRB's will be released and the core rocket engine will take over."

"What's SRB's?" Irina asked.

"The two Solid Rocket Boosters attached to the sides of the launch vehicle."

"At three minutes and twenty seconds or about 107 km mean altitude, the fairing separation takes place. That's the enclosures on the tip of the rocket which hold the cargo."

"Uh huh." Morrissey grunted trying not to nod off.

"The fairing covering the nose cone will fall away before the upper stage separates and it will take approximately forty-two minutes to reach LEO if this were a normal satellite launch but on this mission, following its jettison, the ATV will launch and head straight for the ISS."

"Dare I ask?" Morrissey, arms folded and slumped down in his seat asked.

Irina, nervous enough about possibly having blown her mission to uncover the details of what she was sent by her boss to do and now preoccupied with Frank's well being, was swiftly losing patience with Morrissey.

"Low Earth Orbit! Automated Transfer Vehicle! International Space Station! Try and keep up will ya!" She snapped just before she leaned over and sniffed the air around the Inspector. "You been drinking?!" She accused.

"Not since breakfast." The Inspector weakly defended with a shrug. "Why?"

"Leon, please continue. I find this interesting, even if some people don't." In reality she needed the monotone of Leon's droning to take her mind off the possibility that she wondered if the rocket might explode at any moment.

"Thank you Agent Kuksova." Leon spouted. "Most people think a launch is three, two, one push the button. It's not like that at all! The main stage and the boosters actually ignite together, but it takes seven seconds of initial burn before lift-off, a full seven seconds after the button is pushed. Then once airborne the boosters burn for two minutes and twenty-seven seconds then are released from the main stage. About seventy kilometers mean altitude, ninety-five kilometers downrange."

"Impressive system Leon!"

"Quit kissing up Morrissey!" Irina attacked.

"I am being completely serious! I'm impressed!" Kuksova wasn't impressed. Leon the tech was.

The tech sat up and adjusted his headset as he picked up an interesting development which he relayed to Kuksova and Morrissey.

"What is it Leon?" Irina asked with noticeable concern.

"Some of the engineers reported they're getting an erroneous weight reading. Apparently coming from the ATV."

"Is that dangerous?" Irina asked with noticeable concern.

"Probably not. The on board sensors are registering just over 100 kilos extra. Somebody likely tried to sneak some extra food or something up to the ISS. Maybe a friend of one of the crew. It happens, but shouldn't affect the mission." He dismissed.

STAND-BY FOR FINAL COUNTDOWN! Came the order over the open P.A.

"Grab some popcorn ladies! The show's about to start!" Morrissey declared with childlike glee as he settled into his seat.

They all peered up to the over-sized plasma screens as the blast cones beneath the boosters began to dance and the powerful engines slowly came to life.

"Is there nothing we can do to delay the launch?!" She knowingly asked. "At least until we find these guys?!"

"Sure! Just wait here and I'll run and fetch a giant fire extinguisher!" Morrissey casually asked.

"You're on thin ice! Nigel!"

At mention of his first name Morrissey pursed his lips and crossed his arms in anger.

The giant sound dampers created huge clouds of vapor as they spat tens of thousands of liters of water across the pad to lessen the noise and help prevent structural damage to the surrounding buildings and roads due to sonic vibrations.

The main stage spewed its tiny, centre, blue flame and the gantry cables fell away from the rocket.

We have ignition of all engines. The house P.A. Announced

****

Earlier, while things were gearing up in the Mission Control Centre and Leon was getting his two guests settled in, Mahone, having correctly deduced that in the short fifteen to twenty minutes his adversary had to flee the Integration Building where he was being held in, and with the guard perimeter patrolling a mere kilometer to the south, the would-be saboteur probably headed north, north east to the vicinity of the Soyuz area of operations as Captain Renault had suggested.

Making his way to the Integration Building Mahone carefully entered and spotted someone slumped on the floor dressed only in underwear and combat boots. He dashed across the work space and quickly felt the man's neck for a pulse.

His fingers came away with fresh blood on them. The dead soldier's throat was scarred with a vicious garrote laceration circling nearly his entire neck. The blood not yet fully coagulated told Frank he was closer than he thought.

The trooper's uniform and rifle were gone but for

reasons of carelessness or just plain haste the soldier's Glock 17 pistol was still in its holster. Ramirez had only taken the more powerful FAMAS assault rifle and its magazines.

Taking the Glock and briefly searching for more ammo but finding none, Frank went to the rear of the building where he spotted tracks leading out the back door and into the soft sod, the depth and width of which clearly indicated a man running,

Mahone's confidence grew.

Banking on a guess that Mahone, as a cop, likely only had a handgun and the fact that he himself was carrying a fully automatic FAMAS 5.56mm, Ramirez was flushed with confidence as he took refuge at the far end of a still under construction, 100 meter long, concrete storage building. However not knowing how many were after him, he balanced his confidence with caution.

It wasn't long before Mahone's instinct of moving north paid off and he tracked Ramirez to the only available cover in the vicinity, a small cluster of block houses about half a kilometer from the Ariana launch pad. Having no windows, doors or inner walls yet installed Ramirez was able to spy all the way through the shell of a structure out into the open field without himself being seen.

Anticipating this possibility Mahone carefully and silently approached the other end of the building, paused and scanned for his target.

Suddenly the loud rasp of Mahone's radio squelch startled him but worse yet alerted Ramirez to Mahone's exact location at the other end of the building which caused Ramirez to fire several rounds in Mahone's direction then break and run.

Steadying himself against the building Mahone fired two shots at the fleeing fugitive but immediately realized he was clearly out of range.

"SHIT, SHIT, SHIT!" He cursed as he fumbled for the walkie talkie.

"WHAT?!"

Mahone you copy? Irina's voice came over the air.

"Yeah, talk to me!"

Frank the hotel's reception says four Hispanic males checked in three days ago. The room was paid by electronic transfer from Caracas. I've got the Bureau running checks on the names used.

"Venezuela, four of them?! So, there're two spotted here on the base, the other two must be standing by someplace for the getaway. Get the Frogs on the alert in town and-"

Frogs?

"Excuse me your Most High P.C.'ness. I mean our most esteemed, French Police Officials and Allies!"

Where the hell could these guys intend to go? This place is surrounded by swampy jungle on one side and open ocean on the other?! She postulated.

Irina, there's two minds I never delve too deeply into: The mind of an avowed, crazed terrorist and the mind of a woman! I've got one asshole cornered here, I gotta go, call ya later."

Hey Mahone?
"What?!"
Don't come back with any extra holes!
"Thanks! Where were you a year ago?"

A burst of automatic weapons fire chewed at the cinder blocks just above Mahone's head as he ducked behind a small stack of crates. With no idea of the direction the shots came from he decided to stay frozen and listen. They were soon followed by a second burst lower and to the left.

The second, shorter burst, skipped along the blacktop five meters out signaling that Ramirez didn't really have Mahone zeroed in he just wanted to keep Frank's head down while he put some distance between them.

"Well, here we are again, bullets flying in the wrong direction!" Mahone whispered to himself. "At least I know I found the asshole." Frank consoled himself. He ejected the magazine on the 9mm and found only nine rounds in the fifteen round mag. "Fucking NATO cutbacks!"

Carefully peering around the crates he saw no sign of Ramirez but figured there were only two directions he could have gone and disappeared so fast. Wanting to avoid the Ariana pad he figured Ramirez would do the same so worked his way a little further north by north east from cover to cover.

Now two or three hundred meters west of the Soyuz pad area, Frank decided to maintain cover and concealment and try to stay between his prey and the only feasible exit from the base on the north side by circling the building and sweeping across the open area between the two launch pads.

Ramirez, also being a combat veteran, predicted Mahone's strategy and so scanned for an elevated vantage point.

He slung his weapon and climbed the ladder of a water tower used to feed the sound dampers of the engine blasts of the rockets just before lift-off. He calculated that Mahone's weapon, which he now knew to be a handgun, would be well out of range.

Mahone realized Ramirez couldn't chance moving south because the 3rd Regiment had it cordoned off and so staked out an obvious crossroads he thought Ramirez would have to traverse to get back to the east side of the base and access the north perimeter fence while avoiding the ground sensors.

Knowing that his adversary had a NATO caliber weapon and so had the advantage of range, Mahone decided that what he would do if rolls were switched would be to seek high ground to use as a vantage point.

Other than the launch pads, the water tower in the vicinity of the Ariana pad was the highest point available.

It was then that Mahone happened to spot his prey slowly mounted on the ladder, but well out of range.

Ten or fifteen meters out from the base of the ladder he also spotted something he could use.

Standing next to a work hut near the base of water tower, were three one hundred and fifty-nine liter, or 45 gallon drums of petrol next to some building materials.

Mahone ran around the back of the long structure as fast as he could then up the long side of the building all the time knowing at some point Ramirez would have to come down, but hopefully not before he got within firing range.

Mahone scurried around some heavy machinery to get closer, took careful aim and fired off one round for accuracy. The round hit the dirt twenty meters short of the work hut.

On hearing the shot Ramirez's head snapped up and he carefully scanned the perimeter.

A second shot hit the hut's window just above the fuel drums.

Now carefully coming down the ladder Ramirez could hear Mahone's shots were more than fifteen to twenty seconds apart and wide of the ladder by ten meters.

"Pinche gringo pendajo! Can't shoot straight!" He laughed. As another shot rang out he spotted the petrol barrels. "And stupido doesn't even know you can't light diesel without a spark!"

Another shot near the base of the ladder from an unseen location and Ramirez began to worry. He double timed down the ladder and Mahone's fourth shot hit a petrol drum causing it to steadily spew diesel fuel.

But Mahone wasn't concerned at the moment

with shooting Ramirez. He was shooting at some ten foot long iron plates leaning against the water tower which were stacked next to the three drums of fuel.

On the fifth and sixth shots Frank achieved his goal and the rounds sparked off the iron plate igniting the leaking fuel drum and blowing Ramirez back off the ladder onto the roof of the block house where, stunned he rolled off and slammed hard into the ground.

Mahone, still catching his breath form the dash around the long building, ran towards the flames with all he had left.

A minute later, wheezing heavily, Mahone cautiously jogged up to the burning fuel which was splashed about but could find no trace of Ramirez.

The left side of his chest hurting even more by now, Frank had little choice but to stop, rest and watch helplessly when, three hundred meters across the field he suddenly saw Ramirez duck into a concrete alcove out about 100 meters from and below the Ariana pad.

Propped against the corner of the blockhouse Frank watched helplessly as Ramirez turned, looked out across the open space and waved at Mahone just before he ducked into the big tunnel.

Frank's mind raced to reformulate a strategy. There was no chance he could run after the Ramirez, at least not for the next minute or so, much less chase him down a dark tunnel with only three shots left.

In the shadows of the tunnel Ramirez also took a breather and checked his ammo and decided to change magazines.

Without warning a great gush of rain suddenly showered outside the enclosure. He looked out of the tunnel and up to the clear blue sky and was surprised at the sudden onset of the downpour.

Unfortunately for Mrs. Ramirez's little boy, the one who at the age of five said he wanted to be a veterinarian, aside from not knowing the launch had been moved up, what he thought was rain was actually the industrial sound damper system just above the concrete alcove he was hiding in.

Ramirez was seconds away from discovering exactly what a 'flame trench' is.

He was in one of the three exhaust portals connected directly to Flame Trench #2 of the Ariana launch pad.

The roar of the boosters igniting seven seconds before liftoff allowed him time only to turn and suck in one last breath of scalding hot air before he actually saw the ball of red-orange flame rolling down the tunnel at him a split second before he was reduced to a lump of charcoal.

Mahone, although some four hundred meters away behind a cinder block storage building, instinctively ducked when he felt a blast of hot air as the launch sequence had begun.

Almost a full thirty seconds later, as the roar of the powerful Vulcain 2 engines faded into the sky, the sound dampers stopped spraying their tens of thousands liters of water and once the vehicle was free of the pad Frank tentatively peeked out around the corner following the exhaust trail, up into the air to see the Ariana 5 slowly climbing into the afternoon sky.

His mind involuntarily drifted back to the Seventies and the first time he watched the broadcasts of the NASA missions.

Snapping out of his stupor he realized there was still one renegade out there somewhere but thought it strange he had not encountered the second saboteur. Then it dawned on him he was nearly a half mile back from the main road. Reasoning that the 700 men of the French 3rd Regiment backed by the Gendarmes could track down the second guy he started walking.

As he made his way out to the road he glanced back across the distance at the darkened flame trench.

"Gives 'hot on his trail' a whole new meaning." Mahone mumbled as he walked.

Again the loud scratch of the squelch signalled his radio had sparked to life.

"Mahone here."

Frank, you okay? It was Irina.

"Yeah! I'm good. What's up?"

The gendarmes here have notified police headquarters in Kourou. They've contacted the airport and have directed the tower to hold all out-going flights until they can get positive I.D. all on all passengers. Additionally the French Coastguard

*has redirected the few boats they have to search the
area around the north beach.*

"Good job Kuksova! I knew there was a reason I
kept you around!"

*Still not funny Mahone! And just a friendly
reminder, this is still a federal case!*

"Yes your Captainship! I'm coming in on the
main road. It's only a few kilometers so I should be
back at the MCC by next month."

I'll try and find a ride and meet you out there!

"Good. Meanwhile find out if there's any other
way out the last three might be able to take to get
out of here besides the airport.

*Okay, make your way out to the main road. I'll
ask Captain Renault to meet you there with the jeep.*

"I'll be there in ten . . . make that twenty
minutes."

*What happened with the infiltrator? Did you
catch him?*

"No."

WHY FOR GOD'S SAKE?! She yelled into the
radio.

"I stopped chasing him when he stopped
running."

"Why'd he stop running?!"

"He got burned out."

***

CHAPTER TWENTY-FOUR

Mission Control Centre

When the jeep and driver arrived back at the MCC Captain Renault perused Frank's dishevelled body drenched in sweat, his torn clothes, multiple scrapes and that he was in obvious pain from his damaged lung. Mahone was compelled to lean on the wall to remain upright.

"Monsieur Mahone, if I may say so, you look like shit!"

"Just another day at the office Captain."

"You wish to go the station and have a shower, perhaps rest?"

"No, no thanks." He scanned the lobby. "Where's Agent Kuksova?"

"In the observation suite. I will take you to her." Renault led the way.

Once in the observation theater Irina spotted Frank and ran to hug him but was quickly repulsed by his sweat-drenched, ragged state.

"Jesus Frank, not exactly smelling too good! Also, you look like shit!" She exclaimed.

"What'd I miss a fucking meeting or something?!" He shot back. "It's like the surface of the sun out there, I'm wearing two hundred and fifty dollar Florsheims and I been chasing assholes for the last week and a half across two hemispheres!"

"Sorry, I was just . . . I was a little worried." She

flushed as she spoke.

"I know . . . and thank you." He kissed her on the forehead. "Now, we got any skinny on these other dick wads?"

"Is there an NYPD police code book? I'd like to teach some of these Mahone-isms to my crew back in London!" Morrissey joked.

"Frank this is Leon, Leon Detective Mahone. Leon is an engineering tech here and has been briefing us on the launch proceedings as they occur."

"So where're we at Leon?" Mahone asked. "On the launch I mean."

Leon continued the running narrative to his guests.

"Actually we are now at a very critical point! The vehicle is about to pass through Max Q." Leon explained.

"What's max Q?" Frank asked as he fell into a seat.

"The point with the greatest degree of stress on the rocket," He explained. "The air reaches a point where it can no longer move out of the way fast enough and the vehicle must make one last punch through to escape earth's atmosphere. From here on up the atmosphere only gets thinner. If anything was going to happen, structural disintegration, explosion anything, it will probably happen in the next minute or so." Frank and Irina exchanged glances. Leon continued . "Aside from the lift off, the Max Q phase is the most dangerous phase of the mission."

Leon added.

All eyes stayed glued to the giant plasma screen they watched as the on board cameras showed the Ariana cleared the last of earth's heavy atmosphere and began to climb into space.

"Fingers crossed then!" Irina elbowed Morrissey who was falling asleep in his seat. He grunted and crossed his fingers.

In all the excitement it hadn't occurred to Frank or Irina that something could happen after take-off and so the stress was once again renewed.

Two sets of hands involuntarily gripped chair handles tighter then need be.

Irina's hand unconsciously found Frank's.

All eyes stayed fixed to the plasma screen.

"Annnddddd . . . we're through it!" Leon gleefully announced.

Everyone breathed a sigh of relief and there was a short round of applause down on the control deck. "That's the worst of it." He shrugged.

"So we're pretty much on schedule and running smoothly now?" Mahone sought to confirm from Leon.

"There was a minor anomaly with weight but they should be releasing the ATV right on schedule."

"So! Looks like the good guys won this round! Our job is done here." Mahone glanced over at Irina and brandished a triumphant smile. She nodded and smiled back.

"Next we'll lose the two strap-on boosters and

the main rocket frame will take over." Leon informed.

Irina pursed her lips and glared at Morrissey, slumped in his seat.

"WHAT?!" He challenged.

"You make a strap-on joke and I'll punch you!" She whispered to him

"Soon the computer will tell the Vulcain 2 engine to commence its shut down sequence."

"Then it's officially in space?" Mahone asked.

"Yes, then technically it's in space." Leon confirmed. "At that point the ATV and final stage are all that will be left of the vehicle and then there will be a series of short boost phases by the final stage to get the ATV on course to the ISS." Leon explained.

"Sounds simple enough!" Frank commented.

Meanwhile, many miles above the surface of the earth, living on what little air was trapped in the ATV capsule, it was like a life-sized rag doll that an increasingly anoxic Torrente was thrown about the interior of the bus-sized, cylindrical capsule.

"Sir, be advised, we're getting an unusually high CO_2 reading in the ATV." The systems engineer reported.

Then engineer next to him chimed in.

"Perhaps ambient gas from before the launch?"

"There shouldn't be any CO_2 in the ATV!" The DDO responded.

"Sir, CO_2 level is climbing!"

"Maybe there's a leak somewhere?" One of the

structural engineers suggested.

"Communications, notify ESTRACK, see if they've still got us on their boards." The DDO instructed.

"Yes sir."

"Sir, ESTRACK control reports roll normal at eighty-seven kilometers down range, attitude and trajectory on track."

"Communications?"

"Yes sir?"

"Can you confirm we have downstream signals of all tracking stations continuous with ESOC?" The DDO requested.

"Affirmative sir. All stations report no anomalies."

"Flight Dynamics report." The DDO requested.

"FD reads no anomalies at this time Director. Course, orientation and trajectory all nominal."

"Alright, continue to monitor and keep me posted."

"Will do sir."

Up in the observation area Leon kept the others abreast of events.

"If the ATV were crewed at this point the astronauts would be experiencing up to 2G's." Leon spouted.

Inside the ATV, Torrente was picking himself up off the rear bulkhead and recovering from the few seconds of 2G force he had endured when the ship began to climb through the thermosphere into the Kármán Line at 100 kilometers.

Seconds later, nearly unconscious, he screamed when his feet slowly lifted from the floor as he began to experience the first throes of weightlessness. Helplessly floating about the capsule he desperately attempted to clear his mind.

Never having a firm grip on technology, he reasoned that now, being so much closer to the satellites, his cell phone should have an increased chance of working. With considerable effort he dug his phone from his pocket and frantically dialed. Predictably, there was no signal.

The residual oxygen in the large capsule was getting thinner with each breath and finally he was compelled to stop frantically punching buttons on his I-phone and scrambled to try and find something to breath with.

Back down in the observation theatre Leon the tech carefully explained to his three guests; "This particular model of the Automated Transport Vehicle is the first experimental model fully equipped to support a crew."

"So they'll be astronauts in that thing?" Irina inquired.

"As early as next year!" Leon proudly informed. "Like a giant space taxi, a crew will actually be able to steer the vehicle with supplies to the ISS and bring back crew who are due for rotation!"

Now gasping for air, having barley survived the first phases of the launch, a dishevelled and heavily panting Torrente silently thanked God when, using the flashlight on his phone, he was able to claw his way through the pitch dark to spot a wall placard on the forward bulkhead of how to activate the onboard emergency oxygen system intended for use when the ATV would be crewed.

He frantically ripped the full face mask from the wall case and strapped it to his head tightening the straps to ensure a good seal.

A minute later, just as he began to relax a little, Torrente was startled and began to breath twice as fast through his mask when he heard the fairing at the tip of the last stage released and drop away.

Still mounted on the last stage, the ATV was now exposed to open space.

"With fairing away, in the next few minutes the payload. . ." Down in the observation theatre Leon continued, ". . . at this stage the ATV, will be released." Leon elaborated.

Stand by for extinction of upper stage and ATV launch. Came the announcement over the house P.A.

"Following that the upper stage fires and launches the ATV into space to head off to the ISS for docking!" Leon announced.

Torrente screamed through his mask as the booster rockets on the last stage fired the ATV deeper into space.

Final separation complete. The DDO announced. *The Ariana is returning to the upper atmosphere and the Automated Transfer Vehicle is on course to the ISS!* The DDO put out over the open P.A.

An uproarious cheer followed by an extended applause and filled the MCC suite and brought with it a collective sigh of relief.

Having gradually slid forward to the edge of her seat until she nearly fell off, Kuksova finally dropped her shoulders, pushed herself back upright and breathed a deep sigh of relief.

"Thank God that's over!" She said aloud.

"Amen to that sister!" Morrissey threw in.

"Wow! Thanks guys!" Leon was pleasantly impressed with the unexpected level of personal investment the others appeared to have in the mission. "That's really cool you guys are so into our launches!" He naively thanked.

"We just wanted it all to go well." Morrissey nodded as he patted Leon on the back. "We're big fans of the program, that's all, Miss Kuksova and I. Isn't that right Irina?"

"Are you Miss Kuksova? Really?" Leon coaxed.

"Yes, REALLY, REALLY HAPPY it all went well!" She reinforced.

However, up in the ATV not only did Torrente's unrealistic fantasies of having enough oxygen until being rescued after docking with the ISS suddenly come to a screeching halt, but now almost thirty minutes into his misadventure, he suddenly remembered the NP10 explosive device.

With no idea of how long it would be until the ATV docked with the ISS and under the mistaken impression he might last until then, he scrambled through the floating debris to find and disarm the small NP10 charge.

His mind's naturally slow state being aggravated by the creeping anoxia, he struggled to float himself over to the port side of the capsule to rummage through the mess the disheveled cargo had become during his panic stricken struggles.

With a clear sense of joy Leon addressed the group. "Now we've got over an hour until the ATV starts its long journey to the ISS." Leon informed the group. "I'm going for some coffee. Can I bring something back for anyone?" He politely offered. They all declined.

A minute later, swimming through the dozens of gently floating parcels strewn through the cluttered air of the ATV, Torrente was ecstatic when he finally plucked the bomb from the air.

He immediately removed it from the food box Ramirez had disguised it in and smiled as he spotted the cheap Casio watch and remembered the arming and disarming sequence Mathias had related to Ramirez.

At least he thought he remembered it.

Without warning there was an intense white flash and along with three brave Russian cosmonauts from the Nineteen Sixties Torrente, the ATV and a couple of tons of supplies became space debris as the ATV exploded in a sudden and silent flash.

Down at the MCC all the craft's radar signatures and tracking images suddenly vanished along with the tiny blimp on the giant over head plasma screen on the front wall.

With close attention to the disturbance rippling through the command area down on the floor, Leon scurried back to his seat, plugged his head set back in and turned to the others.

"Control has lost tracking!" Leon relayed what he could hear. "They confirmed radar image is no longer visible and the on board cameras are no longer transmitting visuals!"

Radio communications on the floor confirmed what Leon had just observed.

"Sir, we've lost contact with the ATV!"

"What do you mean?"

"Sir, we've just experienced a two second anomaly followed by a sudden loss of all image and telemetry with the vehicle!"

"All stations report. I need to know what's happening. Have we just suffered a catastrophic event or is this a transmission problem?!" The DDO put out over the open com line.

As directed, one after another, all stations reported in and all reported complete loss of the vehicle. The DDO followed on with the announcement no ground crew member ever wants to hear.

All right, communications note the time, all stations preserve your data!

Captain Renault approached Mahone and the others.

"I am sorry but I must ask you to leave!" He requested.

"Why?!" Irina's question was answered by the P.A. system.

May I have your attention please. This is the DDO. Attention in the facility. As of now we are in lock-down. Assistant DDO notify the DEC. Institute all MEMT procedures. All stations ensure that all your data is preserved!

"I must take charge of security procedures." Renault quietly explained to the group before the stepped away.

"Well! We didn't get to watch it on the evening news. We had a bloody ring-side seat!" Morrissey cracked.

"I can't believe we failed!" Overcome with despondency Irina fell into the nearest seat. "All that time and effort. The resources! We had them at every turn!" Irina slumped down in her seat.

Down on the floor events were moving rapidly.

"Sir we have incoming from the ISS!" The commo engineer reported to the DDO.

"Put it on the open com channel."

CSG Kourou, CSG Kourou ISS here. Be advised we observed what appeared to be a small explosion and have lost radar contact with the ATV. Can you confirm?

"ISS, we can confirm there was an anomaly detected. As to the cause and extent, we are efforting that event as we speak." The DDO responded.

CSG, ISS. Will stand-by. Out. Astronaut Drew Morgan affirmed.

Up on board the ISS, in the command center, Mission Specialist Christina Koch floated over to Morgan.

"What'd the CSG say?" She enquired.

"They requested us to stand by."

"What do you think happened?"

"Not sure but . . . I think we just lost our Sandra Bullock movie for tonight." Morgan joked.

They were interrupted when the radio sparked up again.

ISS, CSG here. ISS come in.

CSG go for ISS. Morgan responded.

ISS, ATV's last known pos was well west and below your current position however try and keep someone in the cupola on the off chance there might be debris. How copy?"

Understand ISS. Attempt to site debris if possible. Will comply CSG. ISS standing by, out.

"Chris, see if you can locate Aleksey and let him know what CSG has requested. Tell him I'll be down in the cupola."

"Will do Drew. I'll meet you down there."

Back down in the Mission Command Centre the ground crew were hard at it.

"Sir we've confirmed all locations have lost tracking and telemetry! The ATV is no longer visible on any radar!"

After making their way down the aisle of the observation theatre and up to the large window looking down to the Mission Control floor, Frank, Irina and Morrissey stood off to the side with sporadic reports from Leon, who also sought to hear what he could of what went wrong.

"Jesus, I can't believe I blew it! My first field assignment." Irina sighed.

"What'a you talkin' about?" Frank asked.

"The real mission wasn't to sabotage the Ariana 5 at all."

"What are you on about girl?!" Morrissey challenged. She looked up and stared.

"Bastards were after the ATV all along!"

"What in God's name for?!" Morrissey challenged. "It's a bloody delivery vehicle! There's no strategic value in it, no weapons!" Morrissey probed. "They'll have another one built inside of six weeks!" He encouraged.

"I have no idea why, but this is the sixth time these guys have launched an ATV and the next one's even on track to carry astronauts! They've got a 95% success rate, so-"

"96% Miss Kuksova!" Leon interjected.

"Thank you for your timely help Leon!" Her sarcasm was lost on no one.

"So what are you saying?!" Morrissey pushed.

"This was no malfunction! I'm saying it's not exactly *Amateur Hour* around here! These guys have got more degrees than a Kelvin thermometer! These things don't just blow up!"

"You think . . . .you think they wanted to use the ATV to launch their own spoofer device?" Mahone realized even as he asked the question.

"Bloody hell! If those knackers got that thing

launched we're-" Morrissey started.

"Royally fucked!" She sank further down in her seat. Frank back handed Morrissey's arm to signal him to ease off.

"My first field mission and I not only fail, I destroy the earth's entire GPS system!" She moaned.

Frank walked over and stood next to her.

"Hey Kuksova!" He kicked her in the foot then took her by the chin. "What'a you twelve years old! This ain't over till it's over!"

"OF COURSE IT'S OVER MAHONE! WHAT THE HELL DO YOU THINK THIS IS?!! TUESDAY NIGHT FOOTBALL?!"

"It's *Monday Night Football* and no show is over until the fat lady sings god-damn-it!"

Unnoticed by anyone in the middle of the controlled chaos the MCC had become, one of the techs from the Integration Building had just won his argument with the front door security guard and entered the MCC floor carrying something.

He made his way across the floor and located the DDO.

"Monsieur DDO, you might want to see this." The tech showed the Director a family-sized box of McDonald's Chicken McNuggets. The DDO stared down at it and turned red.

"What the hell IS WRONG WITH YOU?! Does your watch indicate it is one o'clock?! Is it lunch time for you?!"

"Director look inside!" The tech reiterated.

The annoyed director relented and did as requested. From the observation deck Irina stood and stared down through the wall of glass at the tech and the DDO as he removed the gizmo in the box.

"Son-of-a-bitch!" She declared as she ran past Frank and broke the land speed record for the 40 meter dash suddenly appearing down on the floor of the MCC next to the DDO.

Frank looked at Morrissey who shrugged. "Poor girl's lost her mind."

They followed her downstairs.

Without speaking she reached over and took the device from the DDO then threw open a latch. They all watched as, like a pair of wings, two small solar panels sprang forth and a pinpoint-sized, red LED slowly began to blink.

It was what she recognized as the Super Spoofer device.

"Took me a while to get up here!" The tech said apologetically. "Security wouldn't let me through. Must be something going on."

"Where did you find this?!" Irina demanded.

"Excuse me, who exactly are you?!" The DDO demanded.

"Agent Irina Kuksova, FBI!"

"Well Agent Kuksova of the FBI, what exactly are you doing here and what is his contraption?!" The DDO demanded. "And who are you?" He demanded of Mahone who came up behind them.

"Lieutenant Detective Frank Mahone, NYPD."

"Don't tell me! You are the crazies Dr. Favire denied entry to earlier this morning!"

"Look at me! Where did you find this?" Irina demanded of the tech.

"I found this on board the ATV in the Integration Building before we sealed it up." He explained. "At first we just thought somebody accidently left it when they forgot to seal the hatch last night. My boss told me to have a look around before I secured the hatch on to the ATV. So I did and I found this on a food shelf and thought it might be important. It's definitely not a food packet. I've never seen anything looks like this! Then, after we caught that Spanish guy, I heard there was some secret spy stuff going on around the station so I brought it here."

"Well you did the right thing!" Irina declared.

"So what is it?" The tech again asked.

"It's a spoofer device! It's **the** spoofer device!" With open arms she started over to where Frank was standing next the tech. Mahone opened his arms. When she reached them she wrapped her arms around the tech, kissed him then walked back over to the DDO. Mahone stood staring with his arms still out.

"Sir, this is a spoofer device we believe the saboteurs were supposed to stow away on the ATV and then somehow release into orbit to disrupt the Galileo satellite constellation!" Irina explained.

"To what end?" The dumbfounded Director demanded.

"We're not sure yet sir, but the Bureau in

conjunction with the NYPD are attempting to find out.

"AAAHHHEMM!" Morrissey loudly coughed.

"Oh yes, and with help from the London Met through Inspector Morrissey here and Scotland Yard!"

"Well?" Leon the tech showed up.

"Well what?" She asked,

"What is that weird looking thing?! It's blinking! Is it gonna explode all over the place?"

"No. It's inert." Mahone assured. "It is isn't it?" He asked Irina.

"Yes." She reboxed it and offered it to the DDO. "Monsieur Director, do you have a safe on the base?"

"Yes of course, in the office of the Gendarmes."

"Leon, go and find Captain Renault, tell him to come here please."

Leon looked over at the DDO who nodded his consent and Leon complied.

"We must keep this locked in the station's safe for now. Please allow no one near it!"

"NOW! Don't you feel a bit silly?" Morrissey's crude attempt at levity was lost on Irina as Mahone brought another realization to the fore.

"Let's not go pattin' ourselves on the back just yet! We still have an unknown number of wackos running around out there!"

"Monsieur Director, I need to use your phone it's an emergency!" Irina requested of the DDO. "Is this phone connected to an outside line?"

"Yes, use line three." He instructed. She dialled.

Mahone swooped in to occupy the DDO as Irina used the phone.

"Operator this is Agent Irina Kuksova of the FBI. I need an emergency outside line to the J. Edgar Hoover Building in Washington D.C.!"

Frank overheard and reached over and cut her off.

"What are you doing?! I have to get this to my boss!"

"Not yet!"

"Why? Explain why not yet damn it!"

"The fat lady ain't sung yet, that's why." Kuksova was stumped. "We've got to find Renault and get to the airport!" His line of thought dawned on her.

Frank and Irina hurried out to find Renault.

"So, is this gadget thingy important?" The tech form the Integration Building innocently asked Morrissey.

The Inspector took the young man by the arm and led him towards the exit.

"Tell you what lad! I'm on holiday so let's you and I let the DDO hand that over to the gendarmes then go down to the canteen." Morrissey coaxed. "I'll buy you a whiskey and tell you all about it."

"We don't have spirits in the canteen sir. Only beer."

"Not to worry laddie!" He pulled back the flap of his jacket to reveal his flask. "'Always prepared!' That's our motto at Scotland Yard!"

"Sir I think that's the motto of the American Boy Scouts."

"Bloody Yanks! Think they own everything! So we'll have a drink anyways!"

"But sir, it's the middle of the afternoon!"

"Yes, in Guiana. But its well past six o'clock in London!"

****

Minutes later Mahone and Kuksova along with Renault in full escort raced the short distance to the airport.

"Captain, can we kill the sirens?! I don't exactly want to make a grand entrance." Mahone requested.

"Of course! Pilote, éteignez votre sirène!" He ordered.

"Oui mon Capitaine!"

He directed the driver to turn off his siren then radioed the other two vehicles to follow suit.

At the spacious airport, more akin to a military airfield and disproportionately large in contrast to the small town of Kourou, they found the one terminal surrounded by gendarmes reinforced by 3rd Foreign Infantry Regiment troops some of which were still arriving.

Captain Renault immediately sought out their commander, Colonel Laparra. Following a short conversation the Captain escorted the Colonel over to Frank and Irina.

"Lieutenant Detective Mahone, Agent Kuksova

may I introduce Colonel Antoine Laparra, commanding officer of the French 3rd Regiment etranger d'infanterie of the French Foreign Legion." They shook hands and greeted.

"Colonel Laparra, now that we know Battesta is dead it's my guess this guy took over." She flicked through her phone and found a photo. "This is a photo from the FBI's Terrorist Screening Base. He is probably at least one of the ones we're looking for here. He was arrested three years ago for a firebomb attack on the admin office at Berkley."

"What was he doing at Bezerkly?" Frank asked.

"Student believe it not."

"They still have students at Berkley?"

Renault returned with Irina's phone after speaking with the reservations manager at the check-in desk who accessed the manifest records for the last forty-eight hours.

"There were no flights this morning because of the launch and there were only two flights north yesterday. One to JFK the other to Heathrow."

"He's on the flight to London!" Frank declared.

"How do you know that?!" Irina challenged.

"Where else is he gonna go? He failed his mission costing his handlers thousands of dollars, he can't go back to Caracas. He'll be hunted all over South America. He knows the CIA, FBI and DHS along with Border Patrol are looking for him so he can't land in New York. He's on his way to London!"

"That sounds like a helluva long shot to me

Frank! There's no way you could possibly know he's heading to London! He might not even be on either plane!" Irina challenged.

"Email that FBI photo to the Captain's phone." He instructed and Irina complied. "Captain, four men checked in at the Atlantis hotel in the last two days. Please have someone ring the hotel and ask for their names."

"Oui Monsieur Mahone." Renault issued the orders to the gendarme standing next to him.

"Now what?" Irina asked.

"I lost my phone up near the launch pads so use yours. Ring Morrissey back at Mission Control. Put me on when you get him."

Inspector Morrissey here.

"Nigel its Irina, hold for Frank."

"Morrissey, Hamlet Security! What was the name of that executive your guys were questioning?"

Banbury, he's the CEO. Anakin Banbury. Why?

"It was never about the money, although if you do a recount I'd be willing to bet you'll find at least some missing. Probably used it to finance their operation for a while."

Well if not the dosh what was it about then?

"Remember the hole in the dashboard of the armored van?"

I do.

"The proto type device that the ESA scientist told Maureen and Enfield about when they interviewed him? The one that mysteriously went missing during the chaos of the early days of the ESA? That was the prototype spoofer that was in the stolen armored car. Banbury somehow got mixed up with the South American gang and was probably paid a good bundle to agree to test it. What better time to test it than when the press had the world worked up into a frenzy and distracted while going paranoid over a mythical computer virus?!"

Jesus Yank! You should'a been a bloody Peeler!

"I'll take Peeler as a compliment, whatever the hell that is. Meanwhile get on the horn and get your SHIT Squad to get a stake out team posted at Banbury's office and residence."

What are we looking for?

"Irina's gonna send you an FBI Wanted photo and some background data. Send it to your people and tell them this man is expected to arrive in the next twenty-four to forty-eight hours. Hold him. Hold him at all costs!"

You think he's our man?

"Yes, yes we do. Kuksova figured it all out just now."

Well! Kudos to her! Tell the old girl I said so!

"I will." He hung up and handed her the phone back. "Nigel says 'well done'."

"That was completely unnecessary Detective!"

"I know. Now contact your boss and fill him in."

Irina sent off a quick text announcing the mission was complete and that she would give a complete debrief on return.

"Well. I guess that wraps that up!" Frank

concluded. "What say you and I go back to the Atlantis, take a very long, very hot steamy shower, and I help you celebrate the success of your first field assignment by treating you to a steak and lobster dinner?!"

"Sorry Lieutenant Detective. You have a flight to catch."

"I know! And don't think for a New York City second that I can't wait to get home, after our dinner of course, put my feet up and crack open a nice fresh bottle of Jameson's and-"

"What I mean is you have a flight to catch . . . to Brussels!"

"Why in God's name would I want to go all the way to Brussels when I can have bad French food right here in-"

"You are, we are, going to Brussels to brief the President's staff. My boss wants me there when he debriefs Secretary Pompeo." She smirked.

"Let's get this clear! I'm not going with you just because you want me too!"

"Oh yeah tough guy?! If not because I want you to then why are you going?"

"Because I'll give a year's pay just to see you shake Trump's hand and say, 'thank you Mr. President'!"

"Don't hold your breath!" She snipped as they headed out of the terminal.

****

Sometime during that night it began to rain. At sunrise, after nearly an hour of mounting gusts, the wind blowing across the old, dirt logging road had gathered enough force to topple the four foot tall concrete statue of the Virgin Mary.

Rodolpho, having waited in the car with his luggage, the long afternoon and through the cold, windy night, decided that the fallen statue was a bad sign, an omen sent from God.

He cranked up the car and drove north through the forest towards the Suriname border.

Less than twenty-four hours later Gunga Din, Ali and FNG served arrest warrants on Anakin Banbury and Erik Mathias, aka La Serpiente at Hamlet Security's downtown headquarters.

Mathias was taken when he tried to flee down the fire exit stairwell. Banbury however was not taken.

As the Bobbies were leading Mathias away Ali and Gunga entered Banbury's office to find him sitting behind his ornate, Louis the XIVth desk slumped in his high back chair.

"Looks like somebody beat us to it." Ali declared as he spun the chair to face the door. Banbury had been strangled to death. With a garrotte.

In a nationally televised event Morrissey and the SHIT Squad members were all awarded the *Queen's Police Medal for Gallantry and Distinguished Service* by Met Police Commissioner Cressida Dick as a disgruntled Sadiq Khan sat off to the side. Morrissey informed his boss the Squad strongly preferred to not receive their awards from the controversial mayor.

An additional medal was presented to Inspector Morrissey and later draped across Maureen Dunn's picture in the squad room until it could be given to her husband.

****

CHAPTER TWENTY-FIVE

The Plaza Hotel
Central Park South
NYC, N.Y.

A cool but gentle autumn breeze wound its way down Central Park West and across 59th Street to the Pulitzer Fountain on Grand Army Plaza that morning as the horse drawn Hanson cabs gathered along the park fishing for the first of the morning's tourists.

Up in suite 707 now Special Agent Irina Kuksova rolled over in bed to hear the television on low and spot Frank Mahone standing in front of the bathroom mirror shaving.

On the T.V. screen at the foot of the bed Don Lemon prepared to announce the fifth 'Breaking News' story of the morning. Despite the fact it was only the first hour of his broadcast.

Breaking news in from South America: Venezuelan secret police stopped some FBI agents from interfering with a satellite launch in Guiana at the European Space station in Guiana.

Anderson Cooper who, was seated next to Lemon in the studio chimed in.

According to our sources Don it was a close call!

Yes Anderson and this of course begs the

question: would such people attempt these kinds of terroristic acts if not for Trump?

"Wow! I finally get what you mean about those people!" Irina commented.

"Ya can't fix stupid! Turn those Bozos off will ya?!" Mahone grumbled as he finished up and began to dress.

"What, you don't you like the Clown News Network?" She teased.

"Ya know there's reason he was voted 'Worst Journalist of the Year' by the *Columbia Journalism Review*!"

"Come back to bed! It's only eight o'clock!"

"Sweetheart, not that the last four nights haven't been the greatest nights of my life, not counting getting to meet the President! But . . ."

"But you've got to go to work and keep the streets safe for democracy! Is that it?"

"I'm due down at the Police Plaza at nine."

"'Special Investigations, Office of Anti-Terrorist Planning & Prevention'. You'll need an extra desk just for your name plaque!"

"As former NYPD I actually get two desks."

"It was a nice ceremony, in Brussels don't you think?"

"Yeah and you know my favorite part?" He asked.

"The part where Secretary Pompeo personally promoted you?"

"No, the part where you shook Trump's hand

and said, 'Thank you Mr. President'!"

"I was being polite! 'Respect the office', right?!"
She finally climbed out of bed and headed into the
bathroom continuing the conversation through the
door. "What ever happened with your police
psychologist friend?" She asked.

"Talked to Chief Wachowski last week when we
got back."

"And?"

Frank cracked open the door and held up two
neckties so she could see them, one bright red one
navy blue.

"The red." She said.

He smiled and chose the blue. He stepped to the
mirror to put it on and answered her query as he tied
his tie.

"It seems a certain forty-five year old, unmarried
Dr. Prussy had a nervous breakdown and got herself
put on permanent holiday!"

"A psychiatrist cracking up! That's a good one!"

"Apparently she got too stressed out talking
about the reality of life on the street for cops all the
time and so took a job as a child psychiatrist in a
private academy out in Long Island. Poor kids."

"Maybe it suites her."

"At least the patients will be on her level."

"Frank?" Irina asked as she stepped out of the
bathroom.

"Yeah?"

"Space Port Security initially reported there were
two perps skulking around the Integration Building.

We only found one. I wonder what happened to the other one?" Irina postulated.

"I wouldn't be too concerned. We foiled their mission, that's all that's important."

"Yeah, you're right we stopped them, at least for now."

"That other guy's probably floating around somewhere." Frank commented.

*

Back at the MCC in Guiana technicians, engineers and supervisors were settling in for the last of week-long meetings of data review and report writing in an attempt to find out what exactly happened to the Automated Transfer Vehicle and how the facility had been infiltrated when the radio sparked to life.

CSG this is Lieutenant Colonel Parmitano on board ISS come in please. CSG ISS, come in please.

"Go for the CSG ISS."

Can *you possibly relay if there was any contraband or a . . . possible . . . ah passengers onboard the ATV at the time of catastrophic failure? Over.*

"Not to our knowledge Colonel. But we are looking into all aspects. In fact the investigative board are convening the last of their meetings as we speak. We'll keep you informed. Over."

Ahh . . . much obliged CSG! ISS out.

Parmitano signed off and floated back down to

the multi-faceted windows of the cupola of the Tranquillity module where Mission Commander Alexsey Ovchinin was relaxing and taking in the panorama of the earth.

"What did they say?" Alexsey asked.

"They'll keep us informed."

"Good to know."

"Perhaps we should take a picture to show them later?"

"Good idea." Alexsey concurred.

From his cargo pocket Parmitano produced his mobile phone and snapped several shots of the outside of the cupola.

"Commander, I have seen many strange things up here on my four journeys but . . ."

"I know what you mean Luca. I know what you mean."

They returned to staring out the port side of the cupola to observe the human arm and hand tightly gripping a tattered Chicken McNuggets box as it gently floated outside the ISS.

THE END

Paddy Kelly

Also by Paddy Kelly

Operation Underworld

The American Way

There's an App For That!

There's an App For That Too!

Kelly's Full House

Politically Erect

American Rhetoric

The Wolves of Calabria

The Galileo Project

Children of the Nuclear Gods

Ghost Story
(A play)

Synopsis and option information available on line at:
www.paddykellywriter.com
or by contacting

www.paddykellywriter.com

The Galileo Project

Lightning Source UK Ltd.
Milton Keynes UK
UKHW021957080819
347643UK00010B/372/P

9 781786 952073